NO
SAINT

Love in London

To Have and Hate

(Not) The One

The Stand Out

Phillips Brothers

In Like Flynn

Down Under

Rafferty's Rules

Great Scots

Hard

Easy

Hardly Easy

Hot Scots

One Hot Scot

One Wicked Scot

NO SAINT

·MY KIND OF HERO·

DONNA ALAM

Montlake

Text copyright © 2025 by Donna Alam
All rights reserved.

Published by Montlake, Seattle

www.apub.com

Amazon, the Amazon logo, and Montlake are trademarks of Amazon.com, Inc., or its affiliates.

ISBN-13: 9781662521041
eISBN-13: 9781662521058

Cover design by @blacksheep-uk.com
Cover photography by Michelle Lancaster

Printed in the United States of America

Love makes your soul crawl out from its hiding
place.
—Zora Neale Hurston

Prologue
MILA

"Don't hold out for the hotties over six feet tall. Avoid those tall kings blessed in the underwear department. Shorter men lack attitude, show gratitude, and they've learned what their tongue is for." Ronny's dating advice floats into my head.

My next-door neighbor has the strangest life philosophies.

Oh, Ronny, you've got it all wrong, I think as the stranger's lips slide down my neck, drawing a tiny moan from me. With a shorter man, I would've missed the delicious stretch of my body as I reach for his shoulders. How his large hands make me feel so dainty as they fold around my hips. You can keep your average-size kings with their average-size peens because if I'm going to rebound, I want this man right here.

But this is . . . not me. Not usual-programming Mila.

This version of Mila is living an existence that's spinning out of control. It's why I was hiding out in the coat closet with just a bottle of champagne for company until a little while ago. A paper bag might've been better for my spiraling anxiety, but the vintage bottle of Bollinger was the next best thing.

But they do say bad decisions make for good stories, so maybe I shouldn't be too angry with myself for hurling the bottle at the door. As my hideout was discovered and the door crept open, I muttered some excuse and crouched to pick up the bottle. I didn't feel like apologizing—I wanted to curse and yell in the handsome stranger's face. Tall men. Short men. Round men. Muscled men. Cheating men. All of them.

But as our fingers reached for the champagne bottle at the same time, our eyes connected. The curiosity and kindness shining in his made me pause. And I wasn't alarmed when he stepped inside and closed the door behind him. *More like intrigued.* We exchanged a few words in the dim light, and he made me laugh. I'm not entirely sure how that led to us making out like a couple of horny teenagers during a game of spin the bottle.

Only, I've never been kissed like this before, as a teenager or not. Hot breath and hotter lips, my eyes fluttering closed under the weight of a pleasured groan. Need thrumming under my skin and heat swirling and pooling between my hips.

No, I've never felt like this. Not even with . . .

"It's not you, Mila. You've done nothing wrong." I frown at the sudden echo of Adam's voice. Penis!

The stranger stills, his lips slowly retracting from my throat.

"You or me, beautiful?" His finger hooks under my chin, angling my gaze to his.

That voice, so deep and sort of dreamy. And that accent . . .

This isn't your average-size king. He's more like a California king, though I think he said he was from New England. But he's movie-star perfect. Tall, broad shouldered, and sort of tawny. *Like a lion.* Come to think of it, that's a much better description for him. I'm pretty sure a California king is a mattress size.

"I'm sorry." I give my head a tiny shake, realizing he's watching me. Intently. *Like he's absorbing everything.* "What did you just say?"

"You said *penis*. Are we talking about yours or mine?" In the low light, the corner of his mouth curls, flashing an honest-to-goodness dimple. "I'm not a fan of surprises. Especially that kind."

"Oh." I roll my lips inward, trying not to giggle. I might be tipsy. Or maybe I fell and hit my head and all this is just some kind of sexy imagining. "That wouldn't be me," I reply. "I don't have a penis, I mean."

I used to be engaged to one. But not anymore.

"I'm glad." He draws closer before he stills, his eyes lingering on my lips. "Just so you know, I'm at the other end of the scale."

"You have a penis?"

"Right now, I have a lot of penis."

"As in multiples or . . ."

His laughter sounds like the punch line to a dirty joke.

"Th-that's actually a thing," I begin, all awkward and stuttery. "I saw it on TV. Not actually *saw it*. I wasn't surfing porn or anything. It was an interview."

He presses a kiss to the corner of my mouth, and I feel the smile in it. "You don't say."

"It was on m-morning TV." My hand slips from his shoulder, drawn by the silky lapel of a midnight-colored dinner jacket that fits his broad frame like it was made for him.

"God, your mouth is so pretty."

"Thank you." I suck in a tight gasp as his thumb strokes my bottom lip.

"Can I kiss you again?"

But he's not really asking for permission as his lips chart my jawline and his touch brushes down my throat. *Pop* goes the top button of my sensible work shirt.

3

"Anyone might walk in." But I'm not really denying him as my grip tightens. Beyond the closed door, London's elite quaff champagne and dance drunkenly to the band as it crucifies another Oasis cover. Another wedding reception spilling into the late hours.

"Only if you have another bottle to throw" comes his husky reply.

"I'm all out."

"Do something for me?"

"Depends," I whisper as he loosens another button. His lips press the swell of my breast.

"Say *penis* for me again."

My lips fight a smile as I angle my gaze his way. "Why?"

"Science" comes the hot sibilant burst.

I give my head a tiny shake—amused acceptance or maybe delight. But as I purse my lips in preparation, his mouth—petal soft—brushes mine. I make a noise, a tiny sound of pleasure, almost anticipating the next sultry slide. My insides shimmer as his hand grazes my hip, pinning me against the wall, the scent of his soap and expensive cologne invading my senses.

"Tastes like I thought it would," his low voice rumbles.

"Penis on my lips?" How ridiculous.

"If you're offering."

"You wish."

"Gorgeous, and a mind reader too."

His words make me feel all tingly. I forgot there was such a thing as flattery.

"What's your name, beautiful?"

"Mila. Yours?"

"Fin." He takes my hand in his, bringing my palm to his lips. His eyes fire bright as he presses it to his chest.

An invitation, I think, as I trail my fingers down, down, and over his belt. My insides turning molten at his raw, needy sound.

"You weren't lying," I whisper, gripping him. He's so thick under the fine fabric.

"No, I was not." His reply is so sweetly agonized. "Beautiful Mila, champagne thrower, closet dweller. Not all men are liars."

"Jury is still out on that one."

"I have a truth for you." His finger toys with the hem of my skirt, his eyes seeking permission.

"What's that?" My gaze drops as he does, my heart beating frantically with anticipation.

"I can't wait any longer to get my mouth on you."

Chapter 1
MILA

Just think of the sunshine.

There's something about it that just puts a positive spin on the glummest of days. Not that I'm glum. I can't be glum. I'm on an all-expenses-paid trip to an exclusive island resort—and I'm getting paid for being here!

It would be rude to be anything other than grateful, I remind myself as I pick up my iPad and check off another few items from my checklist. Then drop the pen because I'm not used to these gel nails.

"Slippery little . . ." Got it. Beauty is pain, so they say, and chewed nails are just icky.

Where was I? Ah.

Chairs ✓ **12** Perfectly aligned and suitably swathed.

Dais ✓ Appropriately dressed.

Not that I expected anything less. This resort has more stars than I have fingers on one hand. *Nope. Not doing it,* I think, firmly ignoring the reflex to glance at the band of pale skin where my engagement ring once sat. I'm not thinking about today's date either. So what if this is the day I was supposed to get married myself. Who cares? Not me.

Back to my iPad and list.

Lanterns ✓ Two per pew. Evenly spaced.

Carpet aisle of rose petals & floral displays. These are yet to be positioned, thanks to the potential for wilting.

I pause and tap the pen to my lip. Maybe the heat is why I feel a little off. The almost oppressive humidity. But the sun is shining, so I *will* be happy, even if I need to staple my smile in place!

Though it has rained every afternoon since I got here.

That's it! I'm worried about the rain. I breathe an actual sigh of relief. I'm a wedding planner, not a miracle worker. There isn't one place in my current contract that suggests otherwise. And Evie, my bride for today, chose this venue. I have to assume she's prepared for the hem of her Valentino wedding gown to be a ruined, her hair to frizz, and her makeup to run. *Rather her than me.*

The weather might be out of the realms of my control, but I'll do my darndest to make sure everything else goes off without a hitch. Which it should, considering the money the couple has thrown at this and the hours I've spent planning this wedding down to the finest detail.

But sometimes things just go wrong. Like relationships. People break promises, and penises fall into . . . well, places you never thought they'd ever fall. And before you know it, your business is in tatters and you're sleeping on your grandmother's ancient and lumpy sofa, wondering where it all went wrong.

But enough about my life, because today is about love and a union that's about to help me get everything back on track.

"Hey, bestie!" Sarai, my assistant, ambles into the open-air pavilion, with its traditional alang-alang roof. "The bridal party's helicopter just landed."

"Oh, good!" Relief floods my veins as I pull on the neckline of my linen dress, hoping to stimulate a little cross breeze along with that sudden ease. They were supposed to be here yesterday, but the lives of the rich and fabulous are a mystery to us mere mortals.

Sarai gives an impressed nod as she takes in the decor. "Bougie. I love it."

Sarai isn't technically my assistant; rather, she's employed by the hotel. As well as signing a watertight NDA, I agreed to manage the wedding without the involvement of my staff. In fact, the bride and groom, Oliver and Evie, insisted on it. I thought it best not to mention that I don't actually have a staff, thanks to a recent . . . restructure. *Yes, let's go with that.*

"We're just waiting for the florist." I gesture to the wedding dais as I pull the silver chain away from my neck and stealthily use my thumb to wipe away a trickle of perspiration.

"The flowers arrived ages ago. They're in one of the kitchen's cold rooms."

"Oh. Why didn't you say?"

"I did." Sarai frowns and points to her face. "Didn't you just hear the words come out of my mouth?"

Not for the first time since I arrived, I find myself thinking Sarai and Ronny, my next-door neighbor, would get along like a house on fire. They'd probably run rings around me.

"Why didn't you tell me *when* they arrived?"

She shrugs. "You weren't around."

Sarai definitely isn't cut out for the service industry.

"Well, I might go and take a look." Because a few minutes in a large, cold box sounds so tempting right now.

"But you can't leave. The bride and groom are on their way here."

"Already?" As I pivot to face her, the heady scent of frangipani travels on a passing breeze. "They're not enjoying the resort's welcoming signature cocktail?"

"They don't look like they're in the cocktail kind of mood."

"What do you mean?"

"That they don't look like I thought they would."

I frown. Evie and Oliver are *such* a good-looking couple. They're exactly the kind of people you expect to find sipping cocktails in a six-star hotel. And this is such a perfect place to get married. The resort is so achingly stylish—think dramatic hues and dark volcanic stone, private pools and terraces with endless views of azure sea and sky. It has every amenity a wealthy guest could expect, but what makes it ideal for *this* wedding is the level of privacy offered. Not only because we're on an island with very limited access but because the resort also sits high on a cliff.

I get their need for privacy because their wedding plans have been the talk of London for months. The press made its desperation to discover the details so obvious.

"What I mean is they don't look happy," Sarai adds.

My stomach sinks. The couple seemed so in love. But then, I thought the same about the Myers-Smith wedding until I—and the bridesmaids—stumbled in on the bride and the best man in a compromising position.

But this couple is different. There's no need to fret about their wedding not going ahead.

Is there?

"Maybe they're just hangry—I mean, hungry," I say. "It's a long flight from the UK, and in-flight meals aren't great." Though I suppose they weren't flying economy.

"The food served on a private jet is bussin'."

"Is it?" I suppose that means good. And of course they'd fly private.

"Five stars and personal chefs all the way."

"Yes, you're probably right."

"No *probably* about it. *I* flew back to the States with F—with Mr. DeWitt after the holidays. Like I said, the food was bussin'."

I give her an uncool thumbs-up, not sure what else to say. The resort is part of the DeWitt chain of hotels. But Sarai can't be more than twenty. So Mr. DeWitt must be . . . the grandson, maybe?

"They've been here before, you know? The bride and groom."

"Yes, Evie said."

"That's why I said they don't look happy like they usually do."

"Getting married can be stressful," I reply. "And who knows—maybe their flight was turbulent. Or their helicopter connection unpleasant."

"Or maybe they've changed their minds."

Under my iPad, I cross my fingers and send a silent plea to the heavens. *This wedding* must *go ahead.*

"Mr. DeWitt did mention they're under a lot of pressure, that they're living in a hotel because they're having the private apartments of their country home refurbished."

"He said that, did he?"

"Yeah. Do you know they own a safari park?" she adds, clearly enjoying her insider knowledge.

"Yes, I did know that." Thanks to an online article I read before I got to meet them. It detailed how they met, and then I watched the viral Pulse Tok video of Evie hightailing it out of her first wedding ceremony. Poor love, she's so sweet and kind, I felt awful for watching it. But I was scoping them out, I suppose, while hoping they wouldn't do the same. And they mustn't have, or else I wouldn't be standing here today. "How old is Mr. DeWitt, Sarai?"

"I don't know." She gives a flick of her shoulder. "Younger than my dad. But I'll tell you something," she says, pressing her forefinger and thumb together. "The man is *fire*."

Sarai's dad is the general manager of the resort. It's probably a good thing she's only on the island during her university breaks.

"Look. Here they come now."

My gaze glides past her to the trio emerging from the canopy of lush greenery. Oliver Deubel's unmistakable broad-shouldered silhouette, and Evie walking next to him, her hand in his hand. Their third—Mr. DeWitt, I assume—strolls alongside, the sun glinting from a head of dark-gold hair.

"Do I look okay?"

My attention snaps back as Sarai pulls on her blouse. The hospitality staff wear a corporate version of the traditional *kebaya* outfit, though in much more subdued tones: a wrap blouse, an ankle-grazing sarong, and a cotton cummerbund. With her clear skin and luminous dark eyes and hair, she looks like a picture from a glossy travel advertisement, right down to the pink lotus flower pinned to the back of her head.

"Mila?"

"Sorry. You look lovely." I pull my attention away as a niggling sense of unease pokes at me. I slide my hand over my hip, cursing my choice of dress. Linen might be good for the climate, but it currently resembles a dish towel. "Do I look okay?"

"You've got satay sauce here." Sarai taps her sternum.

"What?" My stomach dips, my eyes along with it. "Ah, hell." I put my iPad down, lick my finger, and frantically rub the non-budging stain. "Why didn't you say so earlier?"

She shrugs, but I only see it in the periphery of my vision as the happy couple steps into the shade of the pavilion, leaving their friend just beyond.

"Mila." A smiling Evie slides her sunglasses to the top of her head as Sarai dashes out the other way, pausing only to greet the pair with a traditional but hurried prayerlike *sembah* greeting. A bit like a namaste. "How are you?" Evie's tone is warm as she offers me her hand.

"Wonderful, thank you." I keep one hand over the stain as we shake hands. "How was your flight? Flights?" My attention briefly follows Sarai, taking in her animation and her gesticulating hands as she advances on the other man. Tall and fair, he's dressed for the office, not the climate. He slips off an expensive-looking suit jacket and throws it over his shoulder, using his finger like a hook, all ease and supreme confidence.

Just imagine the penis on that, a little voice whispers in my head. *The weight—the girth!* For some reason, the voice sounds suspiciously like Ronny's. It's the kind of observation she'd make, anyway. But I know what she—*I*—mean, because he has big dick energy written all over him.

"There was a little weather." Evie's voice pulls my attention back, and I fix on my go-to professional smile. "But we're glad to be here. Right, Oliver?"

Her fiancé makes a noise of agreement, though he barely looks up from his phone as he thrusts out his hand.

"Mr. Deubel, it's good to see you again."

"Oliver," he corrects, not for the first time.

He's just so intimidating, it's what my brain seems to reach for every time he's near. But as Sarai's laughter carries, his attention shifts.

"What *is* he doing?" he murmurs as he slides his phone away.

"What he does best." Evie's eyebrows seem tellingly raised. "Charming the female population."

Someone *definitely* needs to have a word with Sarai's dad.

"Mr. DeWitt is the owner here. Do I have that right?" I keep my tone mild. My job isn't just about bringing the bride and groom's dream wedding to reality. It's also to be a friend. A paid friend, yes, but a friend nonetheless. And friends care. And wedding friends care about the tiniest details, the things that only the couple (the people paying my fee) give a stuff about. Like, are the aisle markers uniform? Are the decor accents in line with their vision and color scheme? I also care enough to keep any eye on potentially troublesome characters. Those who might impact the couple's big day, because no one gets in the way when I plan a wedding day.

"Major shareholder," Evie says with a vague wave. "I think it's a family thing."

"Fantastic." Rich and entitled and abusing his position. *I'll be watching you like a hawk, Mr. DeWitt.*

"He and Oliver are partners in Maven Inc. He's also Oliver's best man."

"Some might take issue with the title," Oliver grumps, eyeing the rows of tastefully festooned chairs.

It's my experience the title *best man* often brings out the *worst* in the male of the species. Not every man and his inner dog, but enough of them.

"It's not his fault women adore him," Evie says.

Like he doesn't even encourage it, I think cynically. But I say nothing. Which is sometimes the best thing a wedding friend can say.

"When are the rest of your party getting here?" *Because you're cutting things a little fine.*

Evie pulls a face: all scrunched nose and discomfort. "I'm afraid that's another story."

"Oh?" I inquire airily. Meanwhile, something inside my head screams *Aaaaa-rgh!* They can't be calling this off. They just can't!

"There's been a slight change of plan," Oliver intones, all brusque business and no-fucks attitude as his fiancée's expression softens with something that looks worryingly like an apology.

"Wait till Fin gets here, honey. We can explain then."

Fin? The name pokes at me like a sharp pin. I glance Sarai's way to find Mr. DeWitt's long, confident strides carrying him toward us. He has a fluid kind of grace, and poor Sarai can't take her eyes off him.

Stepping into the shade, he slides off his sunglasses and pushes his hand through a tawny mane. By my sides, my fingers rub together as though experiencing some kind of tactile memory. Everything inside me seems to tighten in anticipation as my brain seeks to make sense of what I'm seeing.

Or maybe that should be *who*.

"Oh, fuck!" My heart slams so hard against my rib cage, I'm surprised I don't topple over with the violence of it, my hand flying to my mouth a split second too late.

Fin. Gorgeous, kind, hot-as-hell Fin. The man who found me in the coat closet and wiped away my tears. *The man who made me feel things I hadn't felt in forever.* He shouldn't be here and shouldn't be smiling at me like that!

Like the cat who licked the cream and is thinking, *Hello, second helpings.*

Also, double fuck, because I cursed in front of clients. That's like breaking one of the wedding planners' ten commandments!

Best wedding friends are supposed to be the calm voice of reason, not the ones losing their shit. They're categorically *not* allowed to get caught up in their own dramas, even if their dramas follow them to the other side of the world!

"I am so sorry," I begin, as professional Mila is sucked back into my body. I'm a problem solver, not a problem causer. I am calm, collected—a master of restraint!

"It's a reaction Fin often elicits," Oliver murmurs, unbothered.

"It wasn't at all appropriate, not to mention uncharacteristic, because I never, ever swear." *On the job,* I mentally amend.

"Never?"

That voice. So smooth and deep. *And usually reserved for my special alone times.* My stomach flips as, against my better judgment, I glance Fin's way.

His expression flickers, like a lion twitches its tail just before pouncing. "Because I seem to remember otherwise."

Chapter 2
MILA

Am I having a stroke?

But if I were having a stroke, we wouldn't all be in a catatonic state. It feels like the universe has hit the Pause button, because no one seems to be moving as the suggestion in Fin's drawling tone echoes through the air.

Fin from all those months ago. Four, to be exact.

You're such a good girl for me.

I push away the sudden echo of his velvety words. If they were made of actual velvet, the pile would be threadbare through overuse. *Again, during my special alone times.*

That night, my own words were much less smooth than his, though he seemed to enjoy the litany of expletives that accompanied my climax. *Like I said, there's a time and a place.* And not only did he call me a good girl, but I liked it. *Inexplicably.* But what I don't appreciate is the possibility of being outed.

I am a professional. I do not get caught in closets with members of the bridal party.

Except I did. And now I'm looking at the man who has been the basis of my fantasies since. Well, not all my fantasies. He doesn't appear in the ones where Adam loses all his hair and gets adult acne. But he does star in the one where we run into that cheating piece of shit in Chinatown. In my mind, it's usually a crisp autumn evening, and Fin is all adoring looks and stolen kisses, when we just happen to bump into my ex. After a few exchanged words (where a fierce Fin scowls and doesn't let go of my hand), Adam watches us leave, all sad looks and pining as he collects his sesame chicken for one. Meanwhile, Fin and I walk off into a sunset of bursting love hearts.

So I might have thought about him in several contexts. Hot and demanding. Loving and protective. But more than that, imaginary Fin has worshipped at the altar of Mila way more times than I'd like to admit. And now he's here, looking all sexy in the daylight.

What on earth . . . Is the universe bored? Did she decide I haven't suffered enough this year? She has no business sending him—

Oh, God, I think with a lurch. *Maybe I've manifested him.*

Ronny is always yammering about manifestation. She says the key is to visualize your goals, and *visualization* sounds like another word for *fantasizing* to me. Maybe my daily (nightly) imaginings—while using the memory of his touch and his voice, and his . . . other things to get myself off—have brought him here.

Am I to blame for this?

As if I don't have enough to worry about. A bride and groom who turn up late, telling me their lack of guests is "another story." Well, I don't want a story. I can't afford for this wedding not to go ahead. I need it to be a success, and I need Trousseau, my company, to be responsible for that success. After watching my business inexplicably circle the drain of failure for months, this wedding is my final chance to save the thing I've put my heart and soul into.

I've had hundreds of satisfied clients over the years, and such joy and satisfaction knowing I played my part in their love stories. It's been hard to understand how I went from a calendar booked out years in advance to clients suddenly unwilling to take my calls.

But this wedding is my chance to put it all behind me. There's just too much at stake for them to cancel!

My livelihood, my home, the means to improve my grandmother's health.

Then, just like that, the universe presses Play, animation and action flooding the space.

"So you two have met?" Evie's attention flicks between Fin and me.

"No." I shake my head vigorously. This is the stuff of nightmares. Despite my denials, Fin answers otherwise.

"Yeah." His gray eyes sparkle almost silver with amusement. "It's Mila, right?"

My name on his lips sounds the way my orgasm felt.

No. No. *Stop that, brain! And stop looking at him as though he still has his hand in your underwear.*

Making a grasp for my necklace, I scissor the blue pendant back and forth. "I'm sorry, I don't remember." I drop the pendant like it's hot because that sounds as though I make out with strangers in cupboards all the time!

"Huh." His mouth curls provocatively, and I swear his taunting tone reverberates right through to the marrow of my bones. "Not even a little?"

There is nothing little about this man. Not even his pinkie fingers qualify. And he's clearly not buying my response as my embarrassment suffers a case of secondhand cringe. Maybe I should just say I suffer from face blindness.

"I suppose you do look a bit familiar," I admit, my shoulders hovering just under my ears.

"Could she mean *generic*?" Oliver unhelpfully puts in as he gestures Evie closer to show her something on his phone.

"Which part?" Fin asks, his voice pitched low.

"Pardon?"

"Which *part* of me is familiar?"

Seeing your fantasy in the flesh again is so disconcerting. Hearing him use that low and gravelly closet tone of his, even more so. As for which part of him I remember most, I'm not going to say, even if months later I'm still obsessed with his mouth. His pillowy, kissable mouth and the dirty things he whispered that lit up my insides like Christmas lights.

Except, I realize his mouth doesn't look exactly the same.

"Were you, by any chance, at the Singh-Arthur wedding?" I ask overly loud. This is a red herring. I have no desire to evoke the actual event.

"Were you?"

"My eyes are up here," I hiss, making a V with my fingers and pointing them at my face.

"Yeah, but you have a stain," he says as his eyes dip again.

I die a little inside, then slap my hand to my chest like I'm about to swear allegiance to my own mortification. How awkward! How embarrassing! How about a sudden sinkhole swallow me!

"Sorry," I say loudly again. "I just didn't recognize you because of your . . ." I tap the side of my mouth as though I can't find the word before spitting it out as though it tastes bad. "Mustache."

"Some would call it a *mustache* and others an *affront to womankind*," Evie says.

What she said.

If he'd had a mustache when he stepped into the coat closet four months ago, things might've ended very differently. *But they would've begun the same way,* my mind whispers. With his comfort and his kind words at a time I really needed them.

"You don't like it?" He gives an easy smile, the kind that brings out the hint of a dimple. "I've grown quite attached to it myself."

"Much like a parasite clings to a host," Oliver mutters.

"It's awful," Evie adds. "And stop flirting with Mila. She's onto you."

"I'm not flirting. I'm reestablishing a connection."

Oh, I don't think so.

"She's far too sensible for you," Evie retorts, turning my way. "I expect you've crossed paths with Fin more than once in your professional life. I sometimes think he's London's most popular groomsman."

"Always a groomsman, never a groom," he says in a low, purring tone.

A hot shiver pulses through me.

"He's popular, all right," Oliver adds with a meaningful glance.

"What's that supposed to mean?" Fin frowns. Something tells me he doesn't do that often.

"Just that we were going to ask Mila to make sure all the coat closets were locked, given we know how fond you are of those kinds of spaces," Evie puts in.

Panic blooms like an inkblot in my chest. Does that mean they know about—

"But then I remembered how hot it is here. No need for coats. Or coat closets. You'll have to take your trysts elsewhere."

The feeling in my chest takes on a different tone. From panic to . . . *oh.*

Fin DeWitt is one of those. A wedding fuckboy? One I got off with. *One who got me off?*

"And could you just *try* to stop making women fall in love with you?" Evie folds her arms. "Turn off the charm. Just for five minutes."

"It's not necessary on my account," I put in pertly.

"Oh, no, Mila. I was talking about the young girl."

I'm not sure whether that makes me feel better or worse.

"Sarai?" Fin's expression twists as he dumps his jacket over the back of one of the chairs. "She's just a kid."

Feeling a little better.

Evie glances my way and gives her head a tiny admonishing shake. "Women eight to eighty just can't help themselves around him."

And . . . worse again.

"Not all women," Oliver corrects, his hand sliding around his fiancée's waist.

"That's because I like my men growly and grumpy. I wonder why that is?"

"You must be perverse." Oliver pulls his fiancée closer.

Evie tips onto her toes, pressing a kiss to her groom's cheek. The pair begins to whisper and laugh in a sweet-looking PDA.

"Not in front of the kids," Fin says, but he's smiling—a full-out dimple smile—like he's truly happy for his friends. "Love," he says with a shrug.

"Yes," I answer simply. Life has been such a roller coaster lately, and it's been hard to remember why I do what I do while trying to keep my head above water. But seeing Evie and Oliver so obviously in love is a reminder that I have one of the best jobs in the world.

I just need to get it to a place where it pays my bills again.

"What about you? Mila." Fin seems to almost taste my name. "How do you like your men?" Slipping his hands into his pockets, he saunters closer.

I like my men the same way I like my coffee. Ground to dust and kept in my freezer.

"Marrying other women," I say instead. "And in fabulous locations like this!" I tack on, sounding more like an old-fashioned game show hostess and less like a woman scorned. I mean, I'm not a woman scorned. Just a woman disappointed. I suppose I imagined our closet encounter as something special for him too.

"It's good that you've met," Evie says as she untangles herself from Oliver's embrace. "Especially as Oliver and I have a favor to ask you both."

"Both?" I glance Fin's way. He seems just as bemused as me.

"Yeah, you see, the thing is, we're not getting married."

"Oh . . . dear." *Oh, fuck*, more like. I reach for the back of the nearest chair, feeling like I've been punched in the gut. This is a catastrophe. I'm going to end up homeless—sleeping rough on a bench in Victoria Station!

"I'm so sorry. Especially after all the wonderful work you've put in."

"This isn't about me," I answer, lying through my teeth. "I'm just so sad to hear you're not getting married."

At least I've been paid, though the money is long gone. But this wedding was meant to be Trousseau's relaunch. Also . . . how come they don't look like a couple on the verge of a breakup?

"Today." Evie gives her head a tiny shake. "We're not getting married today. I should've said," she adds, painting on a bright smile. "Things really aren't as dire as all that."

Maybe not for you, I think as she reaches for Oliver's hand.

"We're not staying on the island," he says. "We're moving the wedding elsewhere thanks to a breach of confidentiality and the press learning of our plans."

"It wasn't me," I answer reflexively, which probably makes it sound like it was. But I signed the NDA and I had plans, dammit!

"No, of course," Evie says with a frown. "It was probably my stepsister. It seems she's recently given up on finding a husband and become an influencer. She's super pissed she didn't get an invite."

"As we understand it, the *City Chronicle* already have boots on the ground."

Oliver makes it sound like a military campaign. Maybe it is to him.

21

"When did you hear that?" Fin asks.

"Before we left."

"And you didn't think to say anything?" he demands, his expression hardening.

"I'm doing so now," Oliver deadpans. "You were already in Jakarta."

"I could've stayed there." Fin opens his hands, clearly confused as to why he's here.

"They've chartered a boat, Fin," Evie entreats. "They're probably already out there, sitting in the bay. They might even be filming us right now! All I want to do is marry the man I love without those vultures watching on, just waiting for me to run again."

The viral Pulse Tok. Seeing her distress makes me feel dirty once more for watching it.

"I'm so sorry this has happened to you both," I offer, meaning every word. "It's so awful." Awful that they're being forced to run. Awful that, on the board game of my life, I'm about to be sent back to square one.

"There must be something we can do," Fin says, his gaze seeking mine. "Privacy screens or something?"

"Perhaps we could—"

"You know how they are, Fin." Evie pivots my way. "There's this awful gossip column that hounds me. It's called A Little Bird Told Us, and since that stupid Pulse Tok video, they've barely left me alone. They seem to know where I'm going to be and when, hiding in bushes and climbing lampposts. I can't even catch the Tube anymore! It's like living in a fishbowl, people staring at me and wondering *Is that her—is that the girl from Pulse Tok? The one who had a mental breakdown in the church.* I've become notorious—I just can't be all over the internet in my wedding dress again!"

"It's all right, darling." Oliver pulls her to his chest. "It's decided," he adds, his tone determined.

"We have to leave," Evie says, struggling to maintain her composure. "But we can't do it without your help."

"Whatever you need," Fin answers, her distress pulling at both our heartstrings.

"You're a good friend." Still in Oliver's embrace, Evie reaches out to squeeze Fin's hand. "We need you two to get married in our place."

Chapter 3
MILA

I consider sticking a finger in my ear and giving it an unladylike wiggle, because surely I misheard. Maybe she said they were getting married *in space*, which would be no less crazy than what I thought I heard.

I jolt suddenly as, next to me, laughter bursts from Fin's chest. Loud and unapologetic, it's like someone just told him *the* best joke.

"Evie, you crack me up." He gives his head a slow shake; the kind that makes me think there's some previous conversation behind it.

"I'm not joking." But she is smiling, so maybe this is the kind of relationship they have. Maybe their friendship group is all about terrible jokes and winding each other up. Or maybe it's a wedding tradition, sort of like the way a Cuban bride charges men to dance with her on her wedding day, the bills pinned to her dress much like they're shoved into a stripper's thong.

"In which case, you're out of your fucking mind."

So neither a joke nor a tradition. And the fact she still has her hand on his forearm seems less a sign of friendship and more an attempt to stop him running away.

"We don't mean get married for real, obviously." She gives what sounds like a pressure-filled titter. "Just pretend. You'd pretend to be the groom." She turns to me. "And Mila would pretend to be me."

"Me?" I squeak as a heavy stone plummets through my insides.

"Can't have a wedding without a bride." She smiles again, though this one looks more like a grimace.

"I can't marry him!" I explode, my head swinging his way like a turret on a tank.

"Surely we haven't found the one woman on the planet immune to your charms?" Oliver drawls.

"Pretty sure she's aware of my charms," Fin murmurs, sliding me a look that's pure provocation.

My face bursts into flames—at least, that's what it feels like—as I do a very solid impersonation of a guppy now. "B . . . b . . . but you have a mustache!"

"I know it's a lot to ask," Evie puts in, "and I know that thing is a little off putting—"

"Leave the 'stache out of this," Fin retorts.

"Are we hurting its feelings?" Oliver asks. "I wasn't aware it was sentient."

"If you really don't want to do it," Evie continues, ignoring the ridiculous conversation both men seem to insist on, "I understand. It's just—"

"That this will likely be the last wedding you ever book after I blacken your name in the industry."

"Oliver!" Evie whips around and slaps his arm. "Don't be an asshole."

"Yeah, Oliver. Take a day off," Fin puts in with a grin.

"Honey, you can't always make people do what you want," she adds.

"I seem to have managed so far."

"Not even," she says, pressing her hand to her hip. "And not right now. Not with that attitude."

"Eve, be reasonable." Oliver lifts his hands to her shoulders. "We need decoys, and the clock is ticking. And just a tiny reminder, darling. This was your idea."

"Of *course* it was!" Fin's second outburst of laughter sounds incredulous.

"But I'm not gonna force her," she maintains, as though there isn't anyone else present. Let alone the person they're trying to persuade. *Desperately persuade*, even?

"No one's going to force me to do anything," I put in, holding my hand up like a stop sign. "And also, Mr. Deubel, I don't appreciate your threats." I don't have to listen to them either—not given the state my business is in.

"It's not like she really has to marry him," the grump grumps, still sparing no attention for anyone not Evie. "We're offering the woman a week in paradise and fifty thousand pounds to exchange a few meaningless words with Fin and his furry friend."

"Wedding vows aren't meaningless!" Evie splutters.

"They are when you don't mean them."

"Excuse me." I raise my hand again. This time like I'm in school. And a self-designated teacher's pet. "Did you just say fifty thousand pounds?" Unless hearing things is a sign of true desperation.

Oliver's icy-blue gaze cuts my way. "Oh, we don't have to force anyone. Do we, Mila?"

"I didn't say I was accepting your offer," I retort, using the same tone. My heart thumps, and my mind begins to whir with the possibilities. If he's serious, it would be fifty thousand reasons to take him up on his offer. While it's not quite the style of success

26

I was aiming for, it would help. *Like a lifeline.* I could improve my grandmother's standard of living. Invest in my business, advertise, maybe. Could I be Fin's fake bride for a few hours? It would be awkward, and I'm not much of an actress, but I could pretend to be into him for the right price.

Like you pretended in the coat closet?

Once more, the disdaining voice in my head sounds suspiciously like Ronny. That night was a one-off. But I can be professional. I'm not a slave to my impulses.

You're so gonna need a chastity belt.

Evie pivots suddenly to face me, pressing her hand absently to her forehead. "I'm so sorry, Mila. I've gone about this all wrong. It sounds like we're offering you a bribe, but that's not right. Please accept my apology. I'm just a little overwhelmed."

"I understand." I understand rich people exist on another plane—another dimension. Who has fifty thousand to spend on this ridiculousness, bribe or not?

"You see, what Oliver meant to say is we'd be willing to pay you for your time. A *bonus*, I suppose you'd call it."

"We would be so very grateful if you could help us out." Oliver's reiteration is almost toneless.

"I can't tell you how disappointed we are not to be experiencing the day you've planned for us. And again, I'm so sorry to put you in this position."

"Well, this is all fine." Fin pulls a chair out from the carefully arranged rows and sits. "But isn't anyone gonna try to persuade me?"

"No," Oliver asserts flatly.

"I can't believe you didn't think to tell me about this hare-brained scheme." Fin folds his arms across his chest, crossing his long legs at the ankles. While the actions aren't for my titillation, I can't help but notice the way his shirt stretches taut over his biceps and the fine fabric of his pants molds to his thick thighs.

27

"We just want to get married without drama and drones flying around, taking our pictures and tainting our love." Evie's expression makes my heart ache.

"Yeah, yeah, I know," Fin agrees begrudgingly.

"Please don't blame Oliver. This was my idea, but it wasn't really a plan. It was more like a wild stretch of the imagination. All this way, I kept hoping and praying the news we had before we left was wrong. Because this"—her hand indicates the space, the dais, and the endless azure view—"this was my dream wedding. Just us and the people we love, on the island we've come to adore. The piece of your heart you loaned us, for which we'll be ever thankful for."

Fin makes a noise—it sounds like capitulation—as he sits forward, dropping his elbows to his knees. "You're an asshole," he asserts, his gaze narrowed Oliver's way. "You knew I wouldn't be able to say no to her."

"No one can." Oliver doesn't exactly sound happy about that fact. "When was the last time you had a vacation? Wouldn't you like some time alone with your little friend?"

Fin slides his thumb and forefinger across his top-lip parasite. "You make me sound like a deviant," he says, repeating the action, actively stroking the thing.

Why do I find the action mildly erotic?

Stop that, brain!

"You manage that all by yourself." The corners of Oliver's mouth tip, deep grooves suddenly bracketing it. *Surely not laugh lines?*

"I guess the business can cope without me for a few days." Like an auctioneer bringing down his gavel, Fin slaps his hand on his thick thigh.

"I doubt the business will even notice," Oliver murmurs in response.

"Could you enjoy this vacation in reasonably close proximity to Mila, do you think?" Evie's tone turns tentative.

"What?" I ask, my attention whipping her way.

"Just a few days?" Evie holds up her hand, her thumb and forefinger an inch apart, her delivery tilting her statement into a question.

"My flight back to London is booked for Monday. I'm really not sure I can . . ."

"But if they're watching you," Evie implores, "we might *actually* have a honeymoon. A few blissful days of peace."

"You're pushing your luck," Fin grumbles, leaning into a hot reprimanding tone that doesn't turn me on. *If you discount the way my stomach flips, I suppose.*

"I know," Evie replies, all hope and big, pleading eyes.

"Fine." Fin rolls his eyes dramatically, but it doesn't hide his amusement.

"Oh, thank you!"

"Wait!" It has felt like watching the friends play table tennis; backhand one way, a volley return. But now it feels like I've swallowed the ball. "They'll realize we aren't you," I splutter, as my panic spikes. I can't stay here, and I can't spend days hanging out with *him*. Lying around the pool in my swimsuit, eating dinner together and pretending to be in love. I've already thought way too much about him since our closet encounter—and he'll guess! I mean *obviously* we won't need to sleep together, because the resort has villas. Some of them have four bedrooms—two each! But close proximity might mean a slipup. Just look at what happened in that closet!

"No, I don't think so," Evie says equably.

"I don't look a thing like you, and he doesn't look at all like Mr. Deubel."

"You say that like it's a bad thing," Fin drawls.

"I'm just saying you're fair and . . ." *so very hot* ". . . and he's not." My cheeks begin to burn as I swing to face Evie. "I could never pass for you."

"But we're roughly the same build."

"What?" My eyes dip, then dart to her. Evie is lithe, built on athletic lines, and I'm . . . fluffy. *I prefer fluffy.* Like a penguin right before their seasonal molt. But as no woman likes to point out her flaws to an audience, I go with "I've got to be four inches shorter." Never mind several inches wider. And then there are my boobs. I have enough boobs for two women. Not four of them or anything, just a lot.

"You could wear heels."

"And this?" I pull at a lock of hair that has fallen from my no-nonsense bun.

"I have a cathedral-length veil. Besides, women change their hair color all the time."

"There's no way I'd be able to squeeze into your dress."

"Of course you could."

Does this woman need glasses? But this is all beside the point. The real problem is I can't be expected to spend days with Fin. Talk about awkward! I glance his way, expecting to find a little support or solidarity, not to find his gaze skating over my curves. *The brush of it feels like a seductive caress.*

"And even if I can fit into your dress," I add, though some might call it clutching at straws, "what will you wear for your wedding?"

"I don't care how I'm dressed. I just want to marry Oliver."

"She's got two," Fin puts in flatly.

"What?" My attention bounces between the pair.

"She's got two dresses." He shoots Evie a pointed look. "Couldn't make your mind up, could you?"

She bends forward with a cackle that she tries to smother with her hands. "It's extravagant, I know," she admits, pink cheeked. "But I only intend on doing this once."

"It's not too awful," I find myself offering as I slip into professional-planner mode. "Chinese brides wear up to four dresses over the course of one day."

"Well, now I don't feel so wasteful."

"Could we get back to the matter in hand?" Oliver practically shimmers with frustration.

"Oliver!" Evie chastises, sending me an apologetic glance. "Be nice to Mila before she jumps on the first boat out."

But could I? Really? Because the more I think about it, the less likely that seems. The idea is crazy, and the experience will be awkward, and spending time with Fin will definitely hit some of my more tender spots. But compared to what I could gain—what that money would do to my life—those fears seem insignificant.

I could think of it as a holiday—a few days lying around the pool, brainstorming a new business plan. *Given the collapse of my previous plan and this wedding catastrophe.* And they want this. In fact, they're desperate for my help.

"How long?" I glance up. "Exactly how long do you need me to stay on the island?"

My would-be bride and groom exchange a look, before Evie answers. "Until Friday."

"Well, I'll be missed at the office," I begin. The office also known as my grandmother's kitchen table. "And this is a busy period for me. Very busy."

"Of course," Evie says.

"Which is why we'd pay you fifty thousand—"

This is as far as Oliver gets, as, in a flash of daring, I cut him off.

"A hundred thousand." I force my chin higher as Fin chuckles and Oliver quirks a haughty brow. "I'll do it for a hundred

31

thousand. I have appointments that I'll need to reschedule," I say, spinning my audacious tale out of thin air. "Potential clients who might not take kindly to such short notice." I fold my arm across my front, cupping my elbow tight as I press a pondering finger to my lips. The truth is, the instinct to backtrack, to say I'll take Oliver's initial offer, is great. "Which, in turn, could ruin their trust in me. And, ultimately, their bookings. That's potentially a loss of revenue for me."

"And a hundred thousand pounds would remedy that?"

Oliver's tone makes my heart thump in my throat.

"No." This comes from Fin.

I pivot, ready to argue with him, anger a hot flare inside me. How dare he?

"It might cover your loss of man hours and revenue, but what about the damage to your reputation? Not to mention the potential for other unforeseen repercussions."

My God. He's on my side. But why?

"Yes, you're right," I say spikily. "I suppose I just didn't want to look greedy."

"It's not greed. It's just business," he says easily. *And the fact that he's obviously quicker on his feet than me.* "I'd say a quarter of a mil is nearer the number." He gives a considering nod, like we're talking about Tic Tacs and not a quarter of a million pounds.

A quarter of a million pounds! I almost do a happy dance. I could move my grandmother to a facility *with* facilities instead of overworked staff and run-down services—I could secure her a room in the place the nurse told me about! Oh, my days. I could rent a flat *and* an office! Maybe even hire an assistant. But I'm getting ahead of myself.

"I hate to say it, but you could be right," I reply evenly and not at all as though I'm about to pee my pants in excitement.

"What do you think, Evie?" Fin directs a pensive look his friend's way.

"Well . . ."

"Two hundred thousand," Oliver bites out, cutting his fiancée off as he reaches for her hand, as though to say *Don't.*

"That sounds fair," she says with a soft smile. "What do you say, Mila? Does that sound like fair compensation?"

Two hundred thousand ways to get my life back on track. I can hardly believe it as I manage to croak out, "Done."

"Apparently, I have been," Oliver mutters.

"Not quite," I murmur, thanks to this audacious streak. I may own a failing business, but that does not make me a failure. God, where is a pen and paper when you need them. I should write that shit down and make it my mantra.

Oliver gives an arctic twist of his lips, but his disapproval won't put me off now.

Evie and Oliver's wedding was supposed to be a turning point for Trousseau. It occurs to me it might still be.

I am the architect of my own life, I silently intone. And as the pair are still getting married, in part thanks to me, I should . . .

"I want Trousseau, my company, named as the creative force behind your wedding. Your actual wedding. And I want to be credited in any statements or images you release."

"Who says we'll be releasing any?" Oliver murmurs as he straightens his cuffs.

"You will because you want to control the narrative," I reply. "While also appeasing the press."

"Of course we'll do that," Evie puts in, sending daggers her fiancé's way. "Because it's true."

"Fine." I swear her groom almost rolls his eyes. "We can attribute the success of our wedding as being down to you and your company. Any publicity will be carefully curated, painting your business in a favorable light."

"Thank you."

"As opposed to the negative kind of attention that will befall it should any of this get out."

"I already signed an NDA," I remind him. As if I'd ever admit to any of this.

"Thank you, Mila," Evie says, reaching for my hand. "You can't know what this means to us. To me."

"Fin?" Oliver angles his gaze my pretend groom-to-be's way. "What are friends for?"

"Stitching you up and shit talking your facial hair?" Fin replies, unfolding his large frame to stand. He glances my way, his expression inscrutable.

Finding me here must've been as much a shock to him as it was to me, though he's certainly adept at rolling with the punches. But he didn't have to do that, talk the price up. So why did he?

This all feels so bizarre. Unreal. Like any moment, one of them will yell *Psych!* and I'll find out it's all a joke. And I'll probably cry as the pee-my-pants excitement turns to crushing disappointment.

But then, Fin reaches for my hand. My skin totally isn't tingling at his touch, and his smile absolutely isn't warming me from the inside out. Or so I tell myself.

It's just a few extra days. I can cope with that.

My mind jumps from *days* to *date*, and I find myself biting back a silly grin. *Baba would be so smug.* But the date—today's date—is just a coincidence. It's not like she was right about the name of my supposed groom. *What did she say it was, again? Not Fin, that's for sure.*

Baba, my very lovely but very strange grandmother, likes to think she has "the sight." And about 50 percent of the time, it appears she has. But even a stopped clock is right twice a day.

When the old dear told me she had a vision, I didn't pay much attention. Not even when she said she saw me in a white dress and insisted I'd still be getting married on the day Adam and I originally planned. *Even though he'd already dumped me.* I knew she wasn't being cruel. It's just her age and her recent diagnosis that makes her believe she read the same news in my coffee grounds.

But I don't believe in any of that old-country stuff. Like how malicious fairies come out after midnight or how howling dogs are indicative of a death. I don't have any beef with black cats and don't believe a broken mirror brings bad luck, unless you count clearing up the mess.

I do wear the blue pendant she gave me when my parents passed, but that's because it has sentimental value, not because I think it protects me from evil. It didn't stop me from suffering a broken heart.

Still, if I ever *did* tell Baba about this, she would be smug. But then, she has dementia and recently moved in to a residential care home.

I'd better call them and explain I won't be around for a few more days.

"If you need a hand getting into that dress . . ."

Fin's taunting tone pulls me from my introspection, back to the moment and the magnitude of what we're about to do.

"That won't be necessary," I reply in a businesslike tone. Taunting and teasing aren't part of this deal, and there will be no repeat of our closet encounter. Even if he did help increase my fee.

"It's the least I can offer, given we're about to get married."

"Pretend married," I retort. Realizing my hand is still in his, I pull it away, ignoring how the motion feels like a caress.

Clairvoyance, my backside. Unless Baba just forgot to mention my wedding day was fake.

"Pretend marriage," he agrees, a smile leaking through his words. "Real kiss, though."

Chapter 4
MILA

Poor Evie. She wasn't joking.

As I sit at the dressing table in the resort's bridal suite, I feel a little skeevy as I search for the gossip column she mentioned. I know her distress was genuine, but I'd be an idiot to take it all at face value, wouldn't I?

An idiot already wearing her *wedding dress,* a little voice offers as I pull up the latest in a very long line of posts about the couple.

A Little Bird Told Us . . .

we're looking for a man in finance . . .

More specifically, we're looking for Oliver Deubel, because what could he and his gorgeous doggy-doctor fiancée, Evie Fairfax, be doing leaving the private terminal at City Airport last night? Where, oh where could they be going? Has Evie packed her bikini, or did she have something else in mind to wear? And might that garment be white or come with a veil? She *was* spotted in an exclusive wedding boutique recently trying on a host of designer gowns.

Might she have packed something old, something new, something borrowed, and something blue?

Could that have been the sound of wedding bells we heard over the roar of Maven Inc.'s private jet's engines?

And where, oh where could the rest of his crew be?

We know the ladies' favorite, gorgeous Fin DeWitt, is in Jakarta on "business" right now, and we have it on good authority that the mysterious Matías Romero has dusted off his tux and is likewise Far East bound.

Messrs. DeWitt and Romero, if you're reading this, *this* Little Bird would be your plus one any day of the week. Especially to, say, an exclusive (elusive?) wedding.

So much mystery. But watch this space, my little tweeters, because we'll be back with juicy news *very* soon . . .

Notorious. That was the word Evie used. If she's notorious, these newshounds are scum.

"Did you really say that to him?"

I drag my attention away from the truth of Evie's life and back to the reality of mine, lifting my gaze to the dresser mirror. Sarai stands behind me, her head canted quizzically, her eyes sparkling with humor.

Did I really say . . . oh, *that.*

"I didn't mean to," I begin, still distracted. "It just fell out of my mouth." I pluck a tissue from the box and blot my lipstick. But it didn't so much fall out of my mouth as it was propelled, missile style.

"Man, that sends me!" she howls, her body a sudden explosion of energy. "I wish I'd been there to see his face."

It is a very pretty face, even if his mouth spoils it. Not the shape of his mouth, because that's quite lovely. It's not even the feel and press of it, because that was also very nice, as I recall. It's the stuff he says that ruins the effect.

Except, he did help me get more money from Oliver.

But I don't remember him as being annoying. Then again, he's also hotter than I remember. Bigger. Better looking. And way more maddening.

All in all, Fin DeWitt is a bit of a mixed bag.

Like he's not pressing every single one of your hot buttons, whispers a voice in my head. Once more, the voice sounds like Ronny's. I imagine picking it up by the collar and booting it away. Boof! *Be gone.*

But what's done is done, and what's about to happen I can deal with. I need to keep the potential consequences in the front of my mind, because no man, hot and annoying or otherwise, is going to ruin this for me. I'm holding tight to this opportunity, this chance to get back on my feet.

"It's seriously classic, Meels!"

"What?" *Meels.* Oh, that must be me. "It was rude of me." Even if Fin laughed and I felt his laughter in the center of my chest. "I don't know where it came from," I say, sliding my pendant back and forth on its thin chain.

"*'I'm not kissing you and that half-grown Chia Pet'* is a modern classic," Sarai says. "Someone needs to put that shit in a book—it'd go down in history along with Mr. Darcy's *She is tolerable, but not handsome enough to tempt me,*" she adds in a tone that's all Oliver Deubel. Or Mr. Darcy, I suppose.

Dammit. It did sound a bit like that.

As though *I* could be the Mr. Darcy in this scenario! I suppose we do seem to share moments of monumental social awkwardness.

"I just panicked." It wasn't bravery or banter, and there's nothing half-grown about it! It was just word vomit. Like now—I'm not really sure why I told her, apart from the fact my nerves are rattling like a ring full of keys.

"Real kiss." Every time Fin's words float across my frontal lobe, my stomach flips and I get a little flutter somewhere farther south. And then I have to have a stern word with myself, because that is *not* happening. A quick peck at the end of the ceremony is fine, but anything beyond that is off limits. I won't ruin this opportunity.

"You're sure about that?" Sarai flops to the huge bed like a landed fish. Bending her elbow, she rests her cheek on her palm.

"Yes, I'm sure." Deadly sure.

"Because it sounds like angry flirting to me."

"What? No!"

"Come on, what man wouldn't love to hear his mustache looks like a dead caterpillar taped to the top of his lip?" She collapses into a fit of giggles as I groan.

"Stapled," I correct.

"Huh?"

"I said, *'I'm not kissing you and that half-grown Chia Pet.'* And he laughed." Which annoyed me. "And then I said, 'It looks like someone stapled a dead caterpillar to your lip while you were sleeping.'"

"Like I said—classic!"

"Don't." In my imagination, I lean forward and bash my head on the dresser. *Don't. Don't. Don't.*

"That shit's gonna live rent-free in my head forever."

"I can't believe I said it. In front of my clients—his friends! What was I thinking?"

"I bet they thought it was hilarious."

"I suppose Mr. Deubel—Oliver, I mean—laughed." And Evie smiled sort of serenely. Or maybe secretly.

"I bet Fin laughed too."

Did that sound wistful?

"How come he's *Fin* now, and not *Mr. DeWitt?*" I ask.

39

"Because now you've met him," she says, unconcerned. "He's a lot of fun, don't you think?"

He's a lot of something. Trouble, mainly. "You don't mind, do you? That I'm doing this?"

"Mind that you're marrying him?"

"Pretend marrying," I correct. Again. Clutching my robe at the chest, I shuffle around on the stool to face her, struck once more by how beautiful the room is. I've been in a lot of bridal suites, but nothing quite like this. The furniture is a modern take on the region's traditional style: Indonesian dark wood and neutral soft furnishings, intricate carvings and hand-painted artwork. A delicate mother-of-pearl chandelier hangs from a high ceiling, reflecting light in a cascade across the room.

Then there are those breathtaking views—mile upon mile of uninterrupted blue visible from every room. There's a private terrace with sumptuous daybeds and a dark infinity pool to take cooling dips in. There's even a private garden, its high stone walls concealing a small tropical paradise and a sexy-looking outdoor shower that I'd never in a million years be brave enough to use. I'm more of a bath girl, anyway. It's just a shame I won't get to use the tub in this suite, because it looks like it'd be an experience. The black stone looks so inviting and sits in the center of the room like an altar. I'm sure I'd feel like Cleopatra lounging in it.

"Why would I mind?"

"It's just, well, earlier, you seemed very enthusiastic about him. Like you might like him, I suppose?" And there's nothing worse than someone stealing your teenage crush. Except maybe that crush being unrequited. And it did seem unrequited.

"Fin is *flames*," she says, shaking her hand as though her nail polish is wet rather than just glossy. "He's such a zaddy."

"He is?"

"Yeah, he's got it goin' on. Don't act like you don't see it!"

"I've got eyes, Sarai. Even if I don't know what I'm looking at. I mean, what even is a zaddy?"

"Fin is like a daddy but leveled up. He's a little older, super hot, a snappy dresser . . ." She shrugs. "The man has serious rizz."

"This is like another language," I mutter, killing what little "hip" social currency I have. Though maybe using the word *hip* means I have negative social currency.

"Rizz. You know—charisma."

"Oh." Sarai, and Ronny, make me feel ancient. But I suppose I've always been older than my years. "He does seem like he could be charming," I hedge. I have experienced that charm. Not that I'm about to admit it.

"A total zaddy, but in answer to your question, no I don't mind. Fin is old enough to be my dad."

"Is he?"

"Technically, yeah. You bet he knows what it's like to be called daddy."

"You mean he has—"

"In the bedroom." She gives a little squeal. "A zaddy on the streets and a daddy between the sheets."

"This conversation is very inappropriate," I answer, mildly horrified. Mainly because I can see it, but I must ignore it as I press my elbows on the dresser and my fingers to my temples.

More than rizz or good looks, Fin has a gives-no-fucks, *I've got my shit together* energy. And for someone whose life shit is currently falling apart, that could be kryptonite. If I let it, which I won't. I will categorically *not* be hitting that a second time.

Not that we quite . . .

Stop!

The bottom line is there are two very important reasons why I won't be sleeping with my soon-to-be pretend husband. First, it would be unprofessional, especially given he's the close friend of my clients. Who are paying me to pretend marry him. And I am a person who prides themself on their professionalism.

Second is *the fact* they're paying me. I'd have to be completely bonkers to risk the kind of figure that has the potential to turn my life around.

"He totally gives off hot daddy vibes." Sarai sighs. "Like he'd take care of you in *and* outside of the bedroom. Be firm but gentle. Take charge but make you feel safe."

"You sound like you've given this a lot of thought." Like she is crushing on him.

"Nah," she answers with a shrug. "I just spend a lot of time on the internet."

It's probably too late to restrict her internet privileges, I think as I reach for the clasp on my chain and loosen it from my neck. I place it carefully on the dresser and slide my finger over the blue agate eye. The absence of it feels strange, even if it hasn't been much good in terms of warding off ill intentions.

"Obviously, my dad would put me in a monastery if he heard me say any of this."

"Nunnery," I say, massaging my temples again. Maybe I should dig out a couple of the fun-size vodkas I keep on hand for anxious brides.

I'm anxious. And I'm a bride. I qualify.

"No, a monastery. My mom is Buddhist. Dad might run the resort, but my mom rules the roost. All four feet ten of her. But to answer your question, I'm cool with you marrying Fin."

I don't bother correcting her this time.

"Besides, it's not like I can complain when I'm making bank because of it."

"You are? How?"

Sarai gives a defensive tilt of her head. "Hot Mr. Moneybags promised me five thou for helping you."

"Mr. Deubel? Oliver, I mean?" She nods, and I frown. "He probably wanted to make sure I didn't run away."

"Where would you go? We've had all the boats locked up. Seriously, though, I would've been your maid of honor for free, but when he offered to pay . . ."

"It's kind of you, money or not." Can't judge a girl for being enterprising, not when a tiny part of me is still judging myself. That old adage, *Everyone has their price*? Well, it seems I found mine. What I won't allow is anyone else to judge me. Not unless they know exactly what it's like to watch your business collapse. Feel your life unravel.

"Brides are supposed to have loads of attendants and stuff, aren't they?"

"I think that's fairy-tale princesses." I indulge in a small smile. Sarai is like a breath of fresh air. Or maybe a sharp gust.

I never wanted the kind of wedding that comes with a dozen bridesmaids or, worse, hired ladies-in-waiting, which is an actual thing for some moneyed brides. Not that the white-glove approach is my business model, which is why I was surprised when Evie contacted me originally. Given Oliver's status and cash (and her family background, according to the internet), I thought she would've gone with one of London's more prestigious wedding planners. At least, until I met her.

"Two hours in the spa were enough attending for me." I'm not sure about Sarai, but I was rubbed and scrubbed and plucked quite aggressively. They even did my hair and my makeup, though I'm currently trying to tone down the vibrant-pink lipstick and blush.

"I love the color of my nails." She holds out her hand admiringly.

"Let's hope the gel is strong, because it's going to take some oomph to fasten me into that dress." I glance at the delicately beaded ivory gown hanging from the bathroom door. The top is corseted—which will probably make me look like I'm considering an OnlyFans account or just cut off my circulation—and the skirt is tightly fitted before fanning out in a gorgeous mermaid's-tail effect. I can't believe it was Evie's second choice, because it's an absolute showstopper.

I am going to feel *very* uncomfortable wearing it. As a wedding planner, I'm used to being in the background. As a person, that's where I prefer to be. I hate being the focus of attention and have always dressed to blend, not to stand out. Even my own choice of wedding dress was quite plain.

"You're gonna look so hot in it."

Hot, yes. Like a sausage on a grill, threatening to burst from its skin. I can't imagine I'll be able to sit in it, as I doubt Valentino thought to reinforce the seams with steel.

"I hope you know the extension for the maintenance crew," I say with a sigh. "I think it's going to take someone with superior upper body strength to strap me into the corset."

Sarai scoffs. "Bestie, it'll be just like getting into a pair of skin-tight jeans you know you're gonna look as hot as fuck in."

"So you're saying I'm going to end up with a muffin top?"

She laughs, though there's no way she can understand. Maybe in a few years, when her metabolism slows and she's working so many hours she can't get to the gym. Then, at some point, she'll realize she can't afford the membership she doesn't even use and cry over all that wasted money. Or maybe that's just me.

I return to my reflection. I've fixed enough bridal tears over the years to be able to fix my makeup. Not that I have any intention of crying. I'm marrying for money, not for love.

Fake marrying, I mean.

I was never what you might consider a romantic. As a little girl, I hadn't dreamed of being a wedding planner and didn't own a toy box full of Barbie dolls dressed in white. Baba wasn't demonstrative, and love was rarely spoken of. Rather, I fell into the industry after my first part-time job in a wedding shop at the age of fifteen.

Watching brides sparkle and sip champagne as I fetched and carried dresses with extortionate price tags—dresses they'd wear only for one day—opened my eyes to another kind of life. I eavesdropped and was blown away by the figures they expected to spend on their big days. Then I learned how they outsourced the whole thing.

No one I knew could pay for someone to clean their house, much less someone to design, then take responsibility for their wedding. These women made me hungry for another life. I was determined to make something of myself—to make success mine.

I would never have contemplated marrying a man for money, yet here I am.

And while my reasons for choosing the field were pragmatic, it turns out you can't work in the industry without being bitten by the love bug. I adore being behind people's delight, and I've lost count of the number of times I've cried listening to my couples exchange their dreams and their vows. You'd need a heart of stone not to be affected. Not to yearn for the experience yourself.

I thought I had found love, and while my day wasn't to be Valentino and vintage champagne, I was no less seduced by the prospect of the experience. I was looking forward to a wedding of my own, of a future. A promise and a lifetime of love, support, and acceptance. Maybe even a family in the years to come. But it all came to nothing in the end.

"Did Fin seem cool to be marrying you?"

"Pretend marrying." The reminder is important. Even for myself.

"I bet he was amped," she adds.

I pause, eye shadow brush suspended midair. "He seemed okay about it, I suppose. He pretended to be annoyed with Mr.

Deubel—Oliver, I mean. They slung insults for a bit, but they seem to have a really solid friendship."

"Yeah, but how did he look at you?"

"With his eyes?"

Sarai rolls hers.

Well, he didn't run for the hills. Maybe he was pleased to see me again? Surprised but not horrified? I consider that moment, playing it back in my mind, remembering how his gaze lifted and how he slowly took me in, from top to bottom. And how I felt that look every place in between.

It felt as though he was looking at me with intent. But maybe he was just looking at me like I was some random girl he'd gotten to feel up in a coat closet. One of many, by the sound of things. Whatever he thought, I was too busy dealing with my own feelings to guess at his.

"I don't know," I say eventually. "I don't know him, so it's hard to tell."

That's true enough. For instance, I didn't realize, according to his friends, he's no saint as far as women are concerned. But I know he's kind and that he kisses well. And I know he loves his friends. That's why he didn't need a monetary incentive to agree to this piece of unhinged ridiculousness.

"Why do you ask?" I add.

"It's just, when they all arrived, and I was talking to him and you were talking to the couple in the pavilion, his eyes kept straying your way. Like he recognized you. Or maybe like he was into you?"

I ignore the effervescent fizz bubbling away in my chest. "He was probably just trying to work out who Evie and Oliver were talking to."

"It was more than that, it was like he couldn't wait to—" A knock sounds at the door. "That'll be the photographer," she adds.

I groan. This is so ridiculous. I mean, I get it: we should try to keep everything the same to fool those intrusive press idiot shitheads. Which means the photographer, the band, the catering, and the guests (who are now stand-ins from the hotel) are all important props. But this bit—prewedding photographs—who'd know if they didn't go ahead?

Evie said we can just destroy the photos afterward, but it just feels like one more thing. One more reminder of what I didn't get to experience myself.

But that's a *me* problem, not an Evie problem. I need the money more than I hate being caught in a photographer's lens. Even if having my photo taken turns me into a wooden, grimacing thing.

"Hi!" The photographer breezes in, her assistant trudging behind her, weighted down with bags and bags of equipment. "What a fabulous room."

"Isn't it just," I say, playing my part.

"So." She smiles widely. "I thought we might start with the lingerie shots."

What?

Chapter 5
MILA

"I feel like a beekeeper." My bottom lip juts as I blow out a breath that has no effect on the veil that sticks to my face. The dramatic, cathedral-length veil, the thing that protected my modesty in the bridal-lingerie shoot.

Extra points to Evie for choosing a veil with length and volume, as I was able to wrap myself in it. I'd felt sexy, glamorous, and sort of mysterious. *Eventually.* Wearing it now, I just feel overheated.

"Stop complaining. You look hot AF."

"Yes, because I am hot. I'm bloody roasting!"

"Compared to that sack you were wearing earlier, you've had a total glow-up."

"That was linen, not hessian. And the glow is thanks to being sweaty."

"You're delulu," she says with a low chuckle.

Delulu-sional? But she wasn't laughing when I hid in the bathroom after the photographer arrived. Like a four-year-old refusing to go to bed. Or an almost-thirty-year-old refusing to take part in a wedding-lingerie shoot.

"*Get out here*," Sarai had hissed through the closed door. *"You don't want to arouse suspicions, do you?"* She'd sounded very grown up and very bossy for someone of her tender years. Meanwhile, on the other side of the door, I was trying not to rattle my fun-size vodka bottles. Talk about role reversals.

"*I don't want to arouse anyone*," I muttered, staring at my reflection. The full-length view was . . . not terrible. I looked sort of sexy in the tiny ivory knickers and matching balconette bra that I'd packed with the distant (galaxies distant) thought that I might get lucky during my week in paradise. I imagined it would be divine justice that a hot bartender or surfer dude I'd picked up on the beach would peel me out of my wedding-day lingerie.

In hindsight, it's good that I did pack them. I'm not sure the wedding photographer would've bought my *something old* being my wedding underwear.

It's ironic how I seemed to have lost weight, given how I tried in vain in the run-up to my big day. The scales just wouldn't budge. Heartbreak, heartache, and cooking on a limited budget were all I needed, it seems. Although, on reflection, my clothes fit the same, so . . . maybe it's more the case that I no longer hear Adam's nagging voice.

You're eating again? Didn't you just have lunch an hour ago? and *Shouldn't you order a salad? It's up to you, but I hate to see you disappointed when you can't fit into your dress.*

Anyway, I did the lingerie shoot. I held my head high and pretended to be someone else. Someone who didn't need her nerves blunted by a couple of vodka miniatures because she was about to fake a wedding ceremony with a hot stranger. I tried to concentrate on the opportunities the money would bring and not on how Fin's eyes had seemed to devour me. *Or why.*

The path from the bridal suite to the pavilion makes the resort appear deserted, just the whisper of the breeze through leaves and unfamiliar birdsong accompanying us. Even Sarai is quiet as she walks alongside me. There's a slight wobble in my step thanks to the skyscraper heels I'm wearing. *My something borrowed, I suppose, given the Louboutin dupes belong to Sarai.* I'm not sure the vodka helps that wobble, not that I've had heaps.

As we turn a corner, the soft strains of a lone guitar welcome us. At last.

Apt, I think, ignoring the faux leather pinching my toes. The ceremony was supposed to start fifteen minutes ago, but this dress, this exquisite piece of beauty and tailoring, took forever to fasten. As predicted, it was several inches too long, even with the heels. So Sarai, contender for pretend bridal attendant of the year, managed to call in a seamstress last minute. She quickly pinned up the hem, meaning I'll get to spend my pretend-bride fee on something other than medical expenses for a broken neck.

As there wasn't much the sewing magician could do with the rest of the dress, I won't be sitting down. Mainly because I feel like I've been trussed into a medieval torture device. I suppose the one benefit of my boobs sitting so high is that if I feel tired or bored, I can just prop my chin on them and have a little snooze.

No more lonely days. I hum a little to the Etta James classic, before a wave of sadness hits me. That's what marriage is, isn't it? Real marriage, anyway. Two becoming one. Forever.

"Wait." I spin around, only half catching Sarai's frown as I stick my fingers into my cleavage and pull out an emergency vodka miniature.

"Really?" Sarai snipes as I crack the lid. She reaches for it and swipes it out of my hand.

"I'm nervous!" I protest as she shoves it into the pocket of her dress.

"I thought we'd already dealt with that."

"Obviously not," I retort. Sarai gave me something to settle my nerves when the photographer arrived. Something herbal, but it hadn't worked.

"Huh."

"I know this is just pretend, but . . ." I was supposed to do this today. Genuinely. For real. And I feel sad suddenly—not because I didn't marry Adam. A life lived alone has to be better than living a lie. Maybe I'm sad because I might never get the chance again. I can't see myself risking my heart again.

"You'll be okay once you get to the end of the aisle."

Will I? There's so much riding on this, and I know a little too much about my groom. *Like how soft his kisses are and how proficient his finger work is.*

Sarai's hand folds over mine, giving it a reassuring squeeze. The lump that forms in my throat is laughed free as she adds, "Predrinks are meant to be shared."

"I thought my needs were greater." My reply is a little warbly. But then we're on our way again.

"Crunch time," Sarai whispers as we turn the corner and the guitarist transitions seamlessly to Pachelbel's Canon in D.

My lips curve at Evie's solid choice of music. Classic, beautiful. It's what I was supposed to . . . I push the thought away.

"Man, he is flexin' in that suit."

I follow Sarai's tiny nod to the dais, from which Fin watches our progress. His linen suit is somewhere between sand and stone in color, his white shirt open at the neck and unbuttoned a little lower than I'd normally think appropriate. His mouth curls as my eyes lift. They don't hold his gaze due to the albatross flapping its wings inside my rib cage.

"Even with boring hair, that man's kimchi is *extra* spicy."

"What?" I whisper. Then, "Oh!"

His hair is dark—I hadn't realized immediately. It's not midnight dark like Oliver's, but it is much less conspicuously fair. He must've colored it somehow.

My third reaction (following surprise, then eww-me-no-likey) is a pinprick of warmth in my heart. He might be a playboy or whatever, but the man deeply loves his friends.

I wonder what that feels like. To have people who love and support you. I thought I had friends not so long ago, but losing Adam, and the stuff that followed, proved otherwise. Our friends took sides. *His, mainly.* It seems it's hard to remain neutral when that friend group originally belonged to one party. Or maybe it's more a case of it being hard to be neutral but easy to forgive one giant cheating shithead. I doubt he confessed that he was unfaithful at every opportunity that passed his way.

He lied to me, and he probably lied to them. Or maybe they knew. Who knows? But it's no surprise I no longer call those people my friends. The mistake I made (one of many, probably) was prioritizing my relationship over my prior friendships.

But what's done is done. The only person you can really rely on is yourself, anyway. And I've been pretty much on my own since Trousseau began impersonating a beetle spinning on its back. I had to lay people off, and though they said they understood, it turns out their friendships were just transactional.

Other than my grandmother, the only person I have in my life is Ronny, Baba's next-door neighbor's daughter. Bright, caustic, irreverent Ronny. She's an unpolished diamond who deserves better than life on a crumbling housing estate teeming with drugs and knife crime.

Home sweet home. The place I worked so hard to be free of, only to find myself back there again.

I give my head a shake, forcing myself into the here and now. I've done it before and I'll do it again, but right now, it's time to put my game face on. Or maybe something a little softer than grimly determined.

Sarai gives my hand a reassuring squeeze before stepping in front of me, her flowing summer dress perfect for the part. I know Evie didn't plan for bridesmaids, but having Sarai by my side has meant I've been less in my head. She's cajoled and snarked and generally pushed me along, and no one would guess she wasn't part of the original wedding party.

My stomach flips as I follow, keeping my eyes on her slim back as she moves along the flower-strewed aisle. *The effect turned out so pretty.*

I glance at my feet, the punk rock silver-studded tips of my shoes peeking from beneath the beaded chiffon. The flowers draping the dais are gorgeous, and even the hastily added voile looks perfect. Though it obscures those million-dollar views, it also screens us somewhat from those potentially prying eyes out in the bay.

The guitarist plays beautifully, and I find myself thinking what a good decision it was to go with the hotel's choice of vendor. But these thoughts are just a distraction—my mind's attempt to stop me from focusing on my destination.

My pretend groom, that tall drink of water. And possibly the reason I feel so parched.

Step, together.

He's too good looking to be real.

Step, together.

Except I've touched him, so I know he is.

Step, together.

I'm doing it for the money.

Step, together.

For Baba. For Trousseau. For me.

Step, together.

And not because of the way he's looking at me.

Like he wants to open me up and conduct a full autopsy of my thoughts.

I reach the end of the aisle, and Sarai reaches for my bouquet, then steps to the side. Fin takes my hands, and even looking through the veil, I find his eyes so striking. His lashes—long like a camel's—are about the same shade as his dyed hair and curled beautifully. The effect should be wrong on a man, but an unfair god has made sure of the opposite. Then I notice something else, and my hand lifts to his face before I can stop it.

"You've shaved."

Chapter 6
FIN

"Does that mean you recognize me now?"

Her smile falters, the movement of her hand turning tentative. When it looks like she might pull away, I cover her hand with my own, pressing it to the contour of my cheek. As I slide her thumb over the smooth skin above my lip, her pretty eyes widen beneath the netting.

"I . . ." Fluttering lashes and a dash of discombobulation complete such a lovely effect.

"Half-grown Chia Pet" my ass.

I bite back my smile. The 'stache was magnificent, and I was attached to it. *Unless we're being literal, in which case it's more like it was attached to me.* I'd planned to shave it off today as a kind of wedding gift to Oliver. It had already served its original purpose in proving to him he liked me more than he hated it. I considered the threat of it fair punishment after he'd shit talked the 'stache for months, even going as far as making idle threats to replace me as his best man.

But given the change in circumstances and the reduction in my role (or the elevation of it, depending on your perspective) I would've kept it a little longer. I'd grown to like the thing. Sure, some people said it made me look like a 1980s TV detective (Evie) or an aging porn star (Matt), but it had its uses. When asked a question during work conferences and consultations, I'd learned to pause, then stroke it, achieving a pensive kind of effect. It was a perfect cover for boredom, inattention, and general navel-gazing.

I would practice a mediative caress to suggest I was paying attention to a date. That had come in useful, as my love life has been pretty boring lately. It's felt a lot like a repeat of the same scene. Like I'd order a meal from a restaurant, but somehow the kitchen would keep sending me out the same dish. *Night after night.*

Maybe I'm getting too old to date.

Maybe I should take a break.

Maybe I should *actually* get married.

That would break the cycle of tedium, for sure. At least there's nothing predictable about Mila. *My closet-dwelling beauty.* She looks the same as she did, all dark doe eyes and generous curves, but she's feistier than I recall. *And that's not a complaint but a compliment.*

As I watched her walking toward me a few moments ago, a bride in ivory, I thought how it could be any woman under that veil. Yet the tempting swing of her hips seemed to call to me viscerally.

Hello, lover, they seemed to say. *Remember me?*

How could I forget? I've played those moments on repeat.

But curious, repulsed, or ambivalent, women have wanted to touch the 'stache. To experience the brush of it. Often, in more places than just one. It seemed to me as though they'd talk themselves into it, no matter their initial feeling.

So why shave it off? Why not allow Mila to talk herself into exploring its benefits? I guess it seemed like the right thing to do, especially as my presence here on the island seems to have pissed her mightily off.

But more importantly: *Hey, Mila, I've* shaved *a seat for you.*

"May I?" I ask, tentatively reaching for her veil.

She nods and whispers, "I suppose."

I lift and . . . holy fuck. Time seems to stop, the hairs on the back of my neck standing like pins. She is just perfect. Her eyes are so rich and dark, like the color of espresso, just as I'd remembered. Maybe even prettier as the lowering sun brings out lighter striations, the color of a good espresso crema. She takes my breath away, my words, my sense. The setting sun seems to shine brighter, the heady scent of tropical blooms somehow sweeter. *How is that? Why?*

"You're beautiful."

She could've stepped from some heavenly dimension, her cheekbones flushed and rosy and her full lips so fucking tempting.

The night we met, when I opened the closet door, curious as to the noise—and a little buzzed, so why not—I was struck by how exquisitely lovely she was. Her eyes were sad and beautiful, but as they lifted to mine, I felt a jolt of connection. The sensation electric. Undeniable.

We talked. She told me about her ex, and I said something asinine about time healing. And how the universe was full of chance and wonder. *I'd been right, as it turned out.*

"Thank you." She swallows as her eyes slide away, her neck flushing a deep pink. "But you don't need to flatter me, and you didn't need to shave. Not for me."

I'd do more than shave to feel those soft lips again. To hear those tight breaths. To feel her pleasure pulse against my fingertips.

"I'm nothing if not diligent." *Diligent in my pursuit of you.*

She gives a tiny, confused shake of her head. "I just don't know why you would."

"It's not a big deal." *It just means you don't get to ride it later.*

Because let's not fool ourselves: this marriage might be for show, but the sparks that dance between us defy the things coming out of her mouth.

No, there's nothing boring about Mila. And my day is turning out to be amazing. I mean, it's not that I wasn't looking forward to watching my best friend tie himself forever to the woman he fell for.

Tie himself. To Evie. For. Ever. *That shit just blows my mind.*

I love Evie—how could I not? She's amazing. And how she succeeded in molding Oliver into someone almost human, I'll never know. He's her person—the one human in the world meant for her. And she's his. True love is rare, and I think most of us only ever get to feel a facsimile of it. But Oliver and Evie are the real deal. And the things she says to him—the way she busts his balls? That's my favorite thing about Evie. It feels like she's always been part of our friendship group. Me, Oliver, Matt, and Evie. The dream team grown.

I reach for Mila's hands, running my thumb over her dainty fingers. She makes to pull away, so I tighten my grip and give a slight jerk of my chin in the direction of the bay.

"We want to sell this to them, don't we?"

I counted six boats anchored out there earlier. Maybe there's some asshole on the bow of one, a long-range camera lens angled this way.

"Yes, all right," she whispers with a definitive nod. "But just so you know"—she leans in a little closer—"what happened before? That might be a regular occurrence in your life, but it isn't in mine. Don't go counting on it happening again."

And they call themselves fucking friends, I think peevishly.

I like women. I enjoy their company—I can't help that I'm popular with them. But the definition of *player* isn't me, because I'm always straight from the start: I don't play with people's feelings.

"Of course," I reply, a touch silkily. "There are no coat closets in the resort."

She scowls, which just makes my smile a little wider.

I am *so* gonna make the most of this experience.

I know what the issue is. She's embarrassed. Caught off guard and wondering what I'm doing here. What *she's* doing here. I could see it earlier as she negotiated with Oliver, her fingertips white as she clung to elbows and her composure.

But I'm also aware of the way she looks at me when she thinks I'm not paying attention. And when I arrived, I saw her initial expression before embarrassment and reality set in.

So yes, I shaved. I shaved for her. And I'm counting on her being impressed (at least, on some level) that I have. I'd also settle for her guilt that I have, and I absolutely would take that guilt-ridden kiss.

Fuck, this is so trippy! Not just that she's here, but this experience. *One I never thought nor sought to have.* A marriage means nothing. Changes nothing. Is nothing . . . but an experience.

And I'm always down for new experiences.

A few muttered words, a kiss. Maybe a dance or two and an opportunity to make this gorgeous woman laugh again. And who knows? Maybe I'll get lucky. I tend to get lucky at weddings. Who wouldn't get lucky at their own?

Mila's brows knit. It looks like she's having a whole conversation with herself. "I'd really rather you wouldn't mention it again," she says stiffly.

"Oh? Well, that's kind of a shame, because I remember how soft your mouth is." My hand lifts almost of its own volition, my thumb pressing her bottom lip in an echo of something I did all those months ago. I see she remembers too. I feel it in the sharp inhalation of breath—experience the sensation all the way to the marrow of my bones.

I swallow over a sudden tightness in my throat as something nudges me. A feeling. Not a hunch or premonition but something that feels more tangible. Inevitable somehow.

"This is nothing but a job for me," she whispers.

"Sure." I know that's what she's telling herself.

The priest murmurs something low, and we both turn to him, the white of his dress momentarily dazzling. He wears no cassock or chasuble. Just a plain white shirt, a sarong, and a folded *udeng* headdress, but he's no less devout. No less serene, and though his face is creased with age, he seems to shine from within.

"What did he just say?" Mila whispers, her tone low and sweet.

"I don't speak the language."

I sense her gaze and turn to find her staring at me, her expression unimpressed.

"I thought you owned the resort?"

"I also have shares in a sushi franchise, but I don't speak Japanese."

"Stop bickering," Sarai hisses, appearing by the priest's side. Hands together, she ducks a quick bow in his direction, murmuring something with a low deference. "You've been invited to kneel by our priest. So get low," she adds with a wiggle of her eyebrows. "Time to bond with the earth."

"On the floor?" Mila sounds alarmed.

"That's generally where the earth is." The younger woman points to the royal blue pillows set at our feet. "But you get one of those. She'll need your arm," she adds, her gaze cutting my way.

"My hand?"

"Arm. Like an anchor. Her dress is a little—"

"Constricting," Mila puts in as her fingers fold around my forearm like pale-pink talons. "What's one more unanticipated aspect of this piece of foolishness," she mutters.

"That's the spirit," I say through a low chuckle.

Mila angles her head my way with a glare. "I hope you've got decent upper body strength."

"Something wrong with your memory?" My words are a treacle-dripped drawl.

She pauses in the act of adjusting the hem of her dress, but she doesn't look up. Not that this hides the delicious hue that flushes across her cheeks. Then, using my forearm as a counterbalance, she begins to lower herself.

"Thank you," she mutters.

"You can use me however you want," I murmur under my breath. I'm never going to complain about a woman getting on her knees in front of me.

"Do you two know each other?" Sarai is narrow eyed with suspicion.

"No." Mila sends me a warning glare. "Only from earlier."

I seem to forget to reply as I stare down at her. That view. I'm so ridiculously aroused and maybe just ridiculous, because I've never been jealous of a dress before.

Movement catches my eye. Sarai folding gracefully to her knees.

"What are you doing?" Mila whisper hisses.

"I'm gonna translate."

She's an enterprising girl, this one. I bet she's getting paid for this, along with the money Oliver offered her to help Mila. *To keep an eye on her, more like.*

My gaze moves back to Mila. My bride, the picture of innocence dressed in virginal tones and a veil. She's the image of serenity, her lashes lowered in a dark sweep, her cheeks and lips rosy.

"Are you going to stand there all day, staring?" she suddenly snipes.

I might, given the view.

"Just for you," I murmur, folding next to her. She smells like jasmine as I close my eyes briefly, searing the vision of her behind my eyelids. "You know what they say. 'Happy wife, happy life.'"

Her brows lower, but her retort is cut off as a bell chimes, its vibration ringing through the otherwise still air. Our attention shifts to the priest as he begins to chant, the sound low and melodic. The bell chimes again.

"We ring this holy bell to summon good spirits," Sarai declares over its echo. "And to announce this wedding to our deities." Her hands pressed together, she reverently lifts them to her forehead.

The tiny hairs on the back of my neck stand once again—only, this time, a lightning bolt of sensation spears down my spine. *What the fuck?*

The priest's expression is radiant and his voice is resonant as he returns to his incantation.

"We burn bamboo to cleanse these two souls," Sarai explains as she lifts three thin stalks of bamboo from a woven basket. "And to banish evil spirits and remove past sins."

"I hear they might need more bamboo for you," Mila murmurs not *quite* under her breath.

Sarai frowns. I feel myself do the same.

"Oh!" Next to me, my pseudobride startles as the holy man flicks water over her head.

"That's what you get for having impure thoughts," I counter with a quiet chuckle. I can practically feel the heat of her scowl.

I bow my head as the priest moves to me, repeating the action, water droplets falling on my shoulders and head.

"It's obviously not holy water," Mila mutters. "You didn't melt."

"I think that's wicked witches, not wicked men."

"At least you own it," she retorts huffily.

"And you liked it," I reply, quieter still. "You liked it a whole lot."

"*We seek the blessings of the benevolent divine.*" This Sarai delivers through gritted teeth and with a look that's meant to quell. "Get it together, you two," she hisses as the priest momentarily turns his back to us.

"I don't know what you mean," Mila murmurs serenely.

"Neither." My eyes catch hers, and she gives in to a reluctant smile.

Before anything else can be said, the priest turns back. His words rise and fall like a soft ocean swell as he takes my left hand, pressing Mila's right atop it, palm to palm. Like it's the most natural thing in the world, her fingers slide between mine, and, our hands clasped, he begins to bind our wrists in a satin-soft cord.

"We tie you together to symbolize the joining of your lives," Sarai says, her voice following the priest's chanting in a spoken round. "We ask the divine bestow their grace on you both as your paths merge into one."

Mila's dark gaze rises to mine, and like the flash of a car's passing headlight, I find my thoughts briefly illuminated.

Two paths merging into one. Like it's meant to be.

Chapter 7
MILA

"Oh, my God." With a groan, I rise like the bride of Dracula meeting midnight. *So why is everything so blue and so bright?* I shield my eyes from the cheery torment, wondering where the hell I am. Except . . .

Was I at a wedding?

I give my head a shake. *"Oww."* I press my hands to either side of my aching head. It feels like a vodka/dehydration-combo hangover. But I didn't have a lot to drink—that much I at least remember. Then again, I'm not at university anymore, and it only takes a couple of vodka tonics to make me feel like this.

Not vodka tonics. Miniatures.

Was I working a wedding? Yeah, of course I was.

Weddings take up half of my waking thoughts, so—

Not a *wedding,* I realize with a lurch. The *wedding.*

Not my wedding, because that was canceled. And for once, my stomach doesn't plummet with the recollection.

Was it Evie, the American vet, and her scarily posh fiancé? I think so, but even that doesn't seem quite right.

Across the room, something glints, catching my eye: a half-drunk flute of champagne, the bottle lying on its side next to it. Well, that answers some of my questions. I turn my head, and I squint, thanks to the sun glaring from a sea of ivory tulle. A gown. A wedding gown. And what the hell is that on my hand?

I hold it out and stare at the thin gold band on the ring finger of my left hand.

Oh, God. I have so many more questions now.

And, just like that, the details begin to descend into my consciousness like the slow fall of glittering confetti.

A proposal. Strictly business.

A pretend bride. *Me.*

A promise worth two hundred thousand. A lifeline I could never have dreamed of.

A golden groom. The object of my fantasies come to life.

Sarai in a flowery dress. A priest in white robes. Words and chanting, incense burning. A rope binding our wrists. And then . . .

Nothing.

What happened after that? *Clearly something* did *happen,* I think, glancing down and startling at my apparent nakedness. I reach for the sheet to pull it over my chest, the motion filling in one or two more blanks. I feel like I've undertaken a particularly punishing Pilates class, my muscles aching and well worked. But at the same time, I feel languid and sort of sated, swaddled in a satisfaction that has seeped through to my bones.

Clue number two is the spectacular love bite on my right breast, but the ringing bell of absolute obviousness is the very telling ache between my legs.

I've had sex. Enthusiastic sex. Which can only mean . . .

I turn my head and squeak, dropping the sheet in favor of pressing both hands over my mouth.

Sweet Jesus, fucking hell! This is so much worse than I thought.

I fake married a man who's practically a stranger, then went back to my room with an *actual* stranger! Because the head lying on the pillow next to mine—the head attached to a pair of finely defined shoulders and a muscled back—can't be Fin DeWitt's. It's someone with much, much shorter hair.

That's okay. The wedding wasn't real. You're not really a reckless adulterer, I reassure myself, even as I press my teeth to my fingernails.

Bleurgh! Gel nails. Not the same sensation. I glance around the room for something to breathe into instead. But not a condom packet. Or even two of them.

Fuck. Fuck. Fuckity-fuck!

What the hell have I done?

My chest heaves, my breaths too short to be of much benefit. I might not be an adulterer, but I'm definitely stupid. Stupidly reckless! How could I risk the lifeline the Deubels threw me?

God, I hope it was worth it. I hope the sex was amazing—out of this world. And that it'll come back to me in some other way than this dense awareness between my legs. Because, if I've lost the chance to save my business, to give Baba some semblance of dignity in her twilight years, there must be a silver fucking lining! A memory at least of a wild night of sex that happened once upon a lifetime. Something to bring a twinkle to my eye when I'm old and gray. Because, I say again, sweet Jesus fucking hell, what have I done?

I've barely moved, yet the stranger begins to stir, the muscles in his broad back flexing subtly under an expanse of smooth, tan skin.

He could be a soldier. A marine? He's got the buzz cut. Not to mention the physique. It's a wild guess, but it's all I've got, along with regrets; a foggy, empty head; and a case of rising anxiety.

He stretches, his arm extending to reveal a thick tricep, before he turns with the elegance of a breaching whale, landing on his back.

That mouth. Those eyes. And the way he's looking at me. Maybe sex with a stranger would've been preferable.

"You seem to be having a whole conversation with yourself." His voice is thick and husky as his back arcs, lifting from his shoulders with a stretch. There's something entirely sexual about the motion, which I ignore. Along with his apparent nakedness beneath the sheet.

A naked Fin DeWitt is almost impossible to ignore.

"'Conversation,'" I repeat. My thoughts are more like a dissertation. And the title of my thesis?

> Questionable Choices, Lust, and Lapses in Judgment:
>
> An Analysis of How I Seem Determined to Ruin My Own Life

"You're giving off some manic energy," Fin purrs.

I swallow. My throat feels so hoarse, like I've spent the night at a concert, singing at the top of my lungs. *Let's go with drunk singing show tunes as the reason both my throat and my jaw ache.*

"We seem to have had sex," I say, plucking the sheet higher up my chest.

"Does look that way, doesn't it."

He is entirely unbothered. Or entirely satisfied. Whatever that expression is, it causes an avalanche of words to fall from my mouth.

"I don't know whether to flip cartwheels or completely freak out that I don't remember. This wasn't supposed to happen. We weren't supposed to . . . to . . ."

"Fuck?"

Wow. The word throbs like a bruise in my core.

"Exactly. I didn't get paid for this." *What?* "Not that I want you to pay me, obviously. Because I'm not . . . that is, what I mean is, for the record—"

"Whoa, whoa. No one is thinking that. Slow down. Take a breath, wifey."

I rear back so fast, I know I'm giving double chin. I mean, *wifey* is bad enough, but his taunting expression is just too much.

"Pretend wifey," I retort. Yeah, take that comeback . . . because it'll take me a few minutes to come up with a better one. And by that point it'll be too late to deliver it. "And there's no need to keep up the act when we're alone."

"Last night felt pretty real to me."

To me too. Not that I remember. But the supporting evidence is hard to argue with. The heavy ache between my legs, my deliciously soupy limbs. It feels like I've taken part in a sex marathon. Not that I've ever been the participant in a sex marathon before. If that's even a thing. Which I'm sure it isn't. "So we definitely . . ." I give a tiny nod, inviting him to fill in the blanks. "We . . ."

"You don't remember?" he asks, his voice sort of sleep husky.

"Some things." I give a spiky shrug. "I remember we were in the dark." *Where the heck did that come from?*

He leans in, his eyes shining as they meet mine. "What else?"

I moisten my lips as fragments of memory seem to rise like smoke between us. *Taut breaths, quiet moans, the darkness amplifying my senses.*

"You were kissing me," I whisper. *Oh . . .* It's probably best I don't mention which part of me I remember him kissing, because *that* didn't happen during the ceremony.

"And?"

"Was there a bucket?"

He gives a low chuckle, and I gasp, clutching the sheet tighter as my cheeks burn hotter than a thousand suns.

"You know!" I accuse. "You know exactly what happened!"

"Maybe."

"Please be serious. Did we—"

"Oh, we *thoroughly* consummated this union." He moves his hand to his abs and gives a tiny wince.

Lord alive, I had sex with him. And I bet it was worth remembering. What I mean is, I am such an idiot! I make a tiny, hiccuping sob.

"You really don't remember?" Something flickers in Fin's expression: a flash of concern or maybe hurt? Whatever it is, it's fleeting. There and then gone in an instant.

I shake my head. "I remember the wrist-tying thing, and then we drank from a coconut. After that, I just don't know." Is there such a thing as coconut poisoning? I begin to turn toward the nightstand—which is where my phone normally is—to offer my pleas at the great altar of Google. But I realize that would mean flashing him my bum, which is probably a bit like closing the stable door after the horse has bolted. But he's not seeing it. Not again.

"But you weren't drunk." Fin half rolls to face me, propping himself on his elbow, a crease forming between his brows.

My stomach flips as I notice the thin gold band on his finger. "Where did we get the rings?"

"A jeweler. The concierge called for me."

"Oh." Keeping up appearances, I suppose. "Send me the bill and I'll . . . I'll reimburse you for mine." When I get my money from Oliver.

His expression gives a tiny flicker of annoyance. "How come you don't remember? You only had one, maybe two glasses of champagne."

I don't answer as I mentally tally the mini vodkas in my head once again, but I know I didn't have enough to make me black out.

"You were coherent, not messy. Though I was kind of surprised at how you threw yourself into the spirit of things."

"How d'you mean?"

"Dancing and laughing and having fun."

"I can be fun," I say, feeling the sting of my perceived slight. "I know what fun feels like." Life has just been tough lately, that's all. "I'm not always uptight and—"

"Mila." The way he says my name as he reaches for my hand. "I don't think you're uptight. What I'm saying is you weren't drunk. You were lucid and articulate and, quite frankly, a little dominant."

"What if I only seemed okay because you were under the influence of something too?" My attention snaps up. "Wait, what did you just say?"

"You practically dragged me into bed."

"*That* I doubt, sincerely," I retort, sounding like a stuffy old maid. "Not that I hear it's hard to persuade you."

"Slut shaming, Mila. That is *so passé*."

I ignore his mocking expression in favor of allowing my gaze to slide over him. Given the size disparity between us, how would that even work? Unless I rode him into the bedroom.

An image flashes in my head. Oh, God. I think I did. With a pretend lasso and much yeehawing.

"And I'm pretty sure there are photos to prove it."

"You took photographs?" My heart dances a quickstep beat, but strangely, not with fear or offense.

"Wedding-night Mila would've been *so* into that. But I was talking about the wedding photographer. Pictures of you dragging *me* to the dance floor, you climbing into *my* lap. You stripping *me* out of my clothes . . ."

"In public?" I give my head another painful shake. *Oww.* Serves me right for trying to locate that memory.

"We'll leave that one to come back to you naturally."

"No thanks." *Wow, Mila. Another excellent comeback.* Maybe he doesn't remember all of this—maybe he's making it up just to get a reaction. "Look, what I'm trying to say is, last night, something happened to make me behave that way."

"Agreed." A smile spreads across his face, slow and rich, like spilled honey.

"Not you. Obviously."

"If you say so."

Urgh. Why does he have to be so bloody annoying. *And so bloody hot.*

"Why don't I remember?" I murmur to myself. "I'm not hungover." Apart from a sore head, but even one or two vodkas almost always give me a headache the next day.

I sense the weight of Fin's gaze and glance up. His expression makes me feel like I'm being dissected.

"Do you remember any of the night?" he asks, his tone no longer flippant.

"Not much. I have some memories," I admit. "Flashes mostly, but nothing concrete. I do have the sense that I enjoyed myself." In other words, I know instinctively somehow that I wasn't taken advantage of—that none of this is on him. "I have the sense I was happy, and you were . . ." like a dream come to life. The reason I know is because I've spent months dreaming of him. "You were . . . Fin? What happened to your hair?"

"You like it?" He lifts his arm to rub his hand over his head, his kiss-swollen lips fighting a grin. Not that I'm paying much attention, because, holy mother of biceps! *And are those teeth marks?*

He angles his head to look, and my stomach swoops.

Urgh. Whatever is responsible for last night is also to blame for my having said that aloud.

"Huh. So they are." His gaze lifts, his gray eyes sort of silver in a shaft of sunlight. "I think that was the outcome of our pet name conversation."

"I bit you? While we were having a conversation? About pets?"

"*Pillow talk* might be a better description."

"*Pillow—*" I fold my lips inward and start again. "What pet name conversation?"

"We were coming up with terms of endearment, I guess. Names to call each other during the week so we don't use our real names. You didn't like my suggestion," he adds in a low rumble.

"*Wifey?*" I retort. "What a surprise."

"That was your choice. It was *sugar tits* you took exception to."

I gasp and clutch the sheet tighter, and Fin's gaze drops very deliberately from my face.

"I'd say it's a little late for modesty," he purrs, the backs of his fingers a tender caress to my arm. "Given I know how you taste."

Between my legs begins to throb like it's trying to send me a message in Morse code. A really angry message.

"Why was I holding hair clippers?" The question falls from my mouth as a flicker of memory escapes my hippocampus.

"You honestly don't remember?"

My mouth works like a ventriloquist's dummy as another image hits. There *was* a bucket! In the dark, he almost tripped over it.

"*Poor Fin kicked the bucket,*" I spluttered through a giggle.

"There are worse ways to die." I can almost feel the memory of his large hands curling around my hips as he pressed my back to the wall.

"Worse than in here?"

The smell of bleach and disinfectant. The hiss of fabric as he slid down my body.

"I'll find heaven between your legs."

The hot look he sent me before my dress fell like a veil over his head.

"Were we in a cupboard?" I ask, ignoring the continued sensory element of this remembrance.

"The janitor's closet." His mouth tips up at one side. "On our way back to the suite, you decided we should relive our first meeting."

"I wouldn't—"

The velvet brush of his tongue. His hand on my stomach, holding me there. *"Oh, God. Fin, yes!"*

We danced and we kissed under a sky of black velvet sprinkled with diamonds. Happiness and pleasure twining and twirling between us like a ribbon of sweet connectedness. I had the most amazing pretend wedding, and it seems I loved every minute of it. Every minute of my wedding night too.

"Mila?"

I nod and swallow a mouthful of words I can't say, let alone process. I was supposed to get married yesterday. For real. We'd booked historic Islington Town Hall for the ceremony, and I'd bought my wedding dress in the Christmas sales. Knee length and cute, it came with a matching bolero jacket. I'd even ordered a jaunty pillbox hat with a half veil. No princess gown for me, not for the low-key day we'd chosen.

But did *we* choose it, or did I just go along with Adam's plans? It's hard to be objective after seeing myself in Evie's gown. Maybe I sold myself short when I settled for an old-fashioned double-decker bus as transport to our wedding breakfast. *In Adam's favorite pub, beer toasts in the place of champagne.*

Fin reaches for my hand, but I pull it from his reach. "None of this explains why you cut your hair."

"You didn't like the color. Said that it didn't suit me and that it didn't matter if it was just temporary, because it *had* to go."

"So you shaved it all off?" I splutter, incredulous.

"*I* shaved it all off?" There's a note of something in his tone that flusters me.

"Not that it doesn't look good," I add quickly. His shorn head makes him brutally good looking, all tan skin and knife-sharp cheekbones. "You have a nicely shaped head."

"Thanks," he answers, not bothering to hide his amusement.

"It shows off your bone structure."

"My bone structure," he repeats in an entirely different tone. One that makes me feel shivery and hot with a resonance of a night I can't fully remember.

Trust me to have missed out on all the fun.

"I'm just saying it's not horrific or anything," I say, sounding prickly now. "I'm paying you a compliment."

"You did that last night."

"Oh. Right."

"When you told me how good my head felt on the inside of your thighs."

How annoying that he remembers more than me. Or maybe he doesn't and he's just filling in the blanks randomly.

"But why listen to me if it was just a temporary color? Why did you cut it?"

"I didn't."

I press my fingers to my chest in silent question. Fin nods, not bothering to hide how much he's enjoying our exchange.

"That settles it. You might remember more than me, but you must've been under the influence of something too. Why else would you've handed me the clippers?"

He gives a tiny flicker-like shrug. "Maybe I've just never had a naked haircut before."

"Were you naked?" He begins to smile, and my hand shoots out like a stop sign. "No need to answer that."

"You kept your panties on."

But not for long, I recall, as another image rises between us. Fin, bare chested, as I stand between the V of his legs. His hands cupping my hips, his gaze heavy lidded as his thumb skims over my nipple.

"But I think you had to put them back *on* first," he says, pressing his hand to his chin as he feigns deep thought.

"Urgh!" I begin to inelegantly worm my way to the edge of the bed while keeping the sheet banded tight to my chest. "You are the worst," I retort, throwing the words over my shoulder.

Error! Error! my feeble brain offers as the sheet slides from Fin's body.

He makes no attempt to stop it, rather rolling onto his back and stretching out as though enjoying the glide of the high thread count somewhere sensitive. Or maybe to display its effect as the white cotton tents over his groin. *And that is no half-erected yurt.*

"All evidence points to you being correct," he drawls, as he slides one hand under his head.

"Have you no shame?" I mutter, half-crouched, one foot on the floor and one bum cheek still connected to the mattress.

"None," he replies quite happily.

Clutching the sheet at both the front and the back, I stand when the corner of a condom wrapper pokes me in the foot.

At least we were safe, I think, dragging the sheet in the direction of the bathroom.

Safe again, I think as I notice another. And another.

No wonder I'm shuffling.

"You'd better get used to it," he calls happily after me.

"As if," I snark back. "I choose not to be awed by your magnificence."

"Magnificence." The word brims with satisfaction as I reach the bathroom door, where I turn. Just to be sure he feels the full effect of my retort. *Or so I tell myself.*

"Feel free to make yourself decent while I'm gone."

"Oh, it's far too late for that, honeybuns," he purrs, stretching along the bed like a cat.

But I am awed by his magnificence, and we both know it as I slam the bathroom door belatedly.

Chapter 8
MILA

Twenty minutes later, I'm ready to emerge from the cavernous bathroom and face whatever the day—and my new torturer, Fin DeWitt—have to throw at me. I'm pink and scrubbed clean, smelling of expensive bathing products and minty fresh thanks to the complimentary eco toothbrush and paste. As I step gingerly across the tiles, I press my fingers to the sides of my aching jaw, rotating it a little, thanks to whatever went down last night.

Oh, the potential puns.

Fine, so I might not know *what* went down but at least I now know *who*. I push the knowledge away and ignore my stinging cheeks as I cinch the belt on the thick white robe I found hanging on a hook in the bathroom.

I give a quick twirl in the mirror. *Honeybuns,* he called me. Plural.

I pinch in a smile, silently admonishing myself as I slide my feet into an oversize pair of hotel slippers. Taking a deep breath, I pull the door open to . . .

An anticlimactic slump.

The bed is empty, though the room is still trashed. Clothes seem to cover every surface, though they're mostly his, considering I wore only four items of clothing yesterday. Maybe three? I don't think I was wearing the veil when we reached the suite. And definitely not Sarai's shoes.

Speaking of clothing, I don't know how the heck I'm going to get back to my room. I don't have anything to wear other than this robe and Evie's wedding dress.

I turn to take in the stunning view over the Indian Ocean and wonder if I can arrange for the resort's laundry service to clean and repair Evie's gown before returning it to her London address. I've barely completed the thought when something snags my attention, and I do a double take. *Is that my suitcase in the closet?*

I find it is. And that it's been unpacked, the contents now hanging from the rails. *And looking quite sad.* My small travel jewelry box and perfume have been arranged on the glass countertop and my undies and other stuff slotted into drawers.

I snap straight. Nope. This is not happening. I am not staying in the bridal suite this week—there's only one bedroom! *One bed.* Our fake union might've been thoroughly consummated, but there's no way I'm going in for seconds—or fourths? Fifths?

Swinging around, I stomp out of the closet, the slippers making an angry flip-flop sound. I'm so annoyed by the presumption of whoever is responsible for unpacking my small case. It's a gross invasion of my privacy! Not to mention a touch embarrassing.

Whipping the wedding gown up from the floor, I'm hit by a wave of remembrance as I straighten. Fin brushing my hair over my shoulder. Unbuttoning this dress. Each inch of skin revealed kissed and complimented. I almost sense the weight of the fabric falling and hear the guttural sound he made as I turned.

He called me beautiful, and I tried to brush off the compliment, insisting he was the one too perfect to be real. Then I pressed my teeth to his pectoral muscle, as though to be sure he was.

My hand rises to my heated cheek. What must he think of me? I practically pounced on him like some desperate, feral thing.

From the swathes of tulle, something drops to the floor—papers, folded into a square. I stoop to pick them up, and I clamp the dress between my body and my elbow as I unfold the sheets. The first is a document in an unfamiliar script, but for my name. *And Fin's.* And the second is—

"Oh. Oh, no, no, no, no, no, *nooo!*"

I drop the dress, almost tripping over it as I hurry into the living room, the papers clutched in my hand. "Fin? Fin!" I call desperately.

"What is it?" He steps into the suite from the private garden, fastening a downy white towel around his hips.

I halt, like I've slammed into a brick wall, because, horizontal, Fin was a temptation; but, vertical, Fin is a lot in my face. *Almost literally.* He is *so* well put together, every inch of him designed for the daylight. That face, the gold of his skin, and those shorn locks, all glistening.

But those lips of his? They were made for the night.

He reaches for the rope of muscle between his neck and shoulder, his forefinger disturbing the lazy path of a rivulet of water.

Not that I'm awed by his magnificence or anything. I can't believe I said that, and I suffer through a second wave of embarrassment.

"My, my." He begins to move closer with the grace and surety of a jungle cat. "What has your cheeks so pink, wifey?"

"High blood pressure, probably." I ignore the imprint of my teeth and the heat of his sun-warmed skin as I press my hand to the center of his chest. *Stop.* Then I thrust the papers almost in his face.

His brows flicker. "What's this?"

"Exactly. What is it?"

"It's in Indonesian," he says, unfurling the sheets. "And along with Japanese, I can't—"

"This one." Impatient, I pull the top sheet away so quickly, I'm surprised I don't give either of us a paper cut.

"This is a marriage certificate." His puzzled gaze lifts.

"That's what *I* thought! Maybe because it has the words *marriage certificate* printed across the top."

"Cute."

"You know what isn't cute? It appears that I'm married to someone called Phineas."

"Huh."

Why doesn't he look even the tiniest bit uneasy? A man like him, Mr. London Player—wouldn't he be running for the hills?

"So, Phineas would be me."

"Phineas Alexander Gunning Colton DeWitt. Were you a really ugly baby, or did your parents just not like you?"

"I have it on good authority I was a delightful babe. I haven't changed."

I don't so much roll my eyes as my whole body. Like a bad-tempered teenager, I mutter a string of curses under my breath.

"I thought you didn't curse."

"In case of emergencies, break swearing glass." I mime a tiny-toffee-hammer pose. "Extreme circumstances call for extreme words."

"Like during an extremely enjoyable orgasm?"

"Concentrate!" I demand, tapping the paper. "This. This can't be real, can it? It's got to be part of yesterday's"—my eyes skate over him again, without my brain's say-so—"shenanigans."

"There were shenanigans?"

"Pay attention—enough with the flirty eyes and sex voice!"

His mouth lifts in a slow grin. "Sex voice?"

"Stay on topic," I demand, pointing at the paper in his hand. My cheeks feel so fiery, they must be contributing to global warming.

"Well, these are our names, and that's my signature." He gives the paper another cursory glance.

"But it's just something to make the marriage look legit. To make us look—" I shake my head and start again. "To make Evie and Oliver look like they were getting married for real. Right?" Yet the truth of the situation feels like an ache in the center of my chest.

"Our names, not theirs," he says softly. "It looks like we did this, Mila. It looks like we got married."

My shoulders sag. *Just like Baba said.* "But we can't be!" I explode incredulously. Suddenly. But my bubble bursts in the face of his solemn expression. "It was a religious ceremony in a religion neither of us follow, in a country we don't live in. How can that be legal?"

"It wasn't religious, exactly."

"Seemed pretty religious to me! The white robes and the . . . the . . . chanting and burning." Granted, it was a while ago I last stepped into a church, but I see the similarities.

"It was spiritual, which is what Evie wanted."

It was lovely, from the bits I remember. The soft chime of bells and melodic incantations and the elderly priest's serene expression. I was nervous on my walk down to the altar, despite the mini vodkas, but I do remember feeling calmed (once I'd managed to kneel) like I was witnessing a ritual with history and meaning.

"It was a symbolic ceremony that isn't legally binding—"

"That's what I'm saying!" I wish I could say I feel relieved that he's making my point for me. But his expression doesn't exactly help.

"That's why Oliver arranged for a senior member of the civil registrar's office to attend. To marry them legally afterward."

My brows pinch. "I don't remember anyone like that being there."

"You don't seem to remember much though, do you?" His gaze dips to the papers in his hand.

That *can't* be our marriage certificate. Or a translation. It just can't be.

"I think we have to face facts." He lifts his head, his eyes boring into mine, corkscrew sharp. "I signed this. And you signed it too."

"But I didn't mean to." My hands lift, then fall, the motion one of futility.

"It's just paperwork, Mila."

"Legally binding paperwork!" I cry, pressing my hands to my cheeks. "I can't be married. Not to you!"

"Wow." His response is an unhappy-sounding chuckle.

"I didn't mean it like that. But we barely know each other." And then there's the small but very freaky matter of yesterday's date. How can that be anything but a bad omen? *Urgh. I'm turning into Baba.* "I'm sorry, but we just can't be married. It's that simple."

"Saying it, repeating it, won't change this." His grip tightens on the certificate, his tone still even and not at all *I'm sick of your histrionic shit.*

But why isn't he calling for his helicopter and running in the opposite direction? Fin DeWitt isn't the marrying type, according to his besties, who made him sound like the king of commitment-phobes. Which is fine because I'm not interested in commitment. Or men. Or anything other than getting my life and business back on track.

What if being married nullifies the Deubels' agreement—what if they refuse to pay?

"No." I refuse to dwell as I snatch the certificate from Fin's hand. "There has to be something we can do." I spin away and head for the closet.

"Like what?" he calls after me in that slightly amused, half-taunting tone of his.

"I solve problems for a living," I retort, pivoting to face him. "I once wrestled a groom's ex to the ground when she turned up at the church in a wedding gown. If I have to go full WrestleMania to sort this out, I bloody well will!"

In the closet, I rifle through a couple of drawers for my underwear and slip my knickers on under the robe.

"I'd pay to see that."

His voice sounds close, but I ignore it as I wiggle the cotton over my hips with as much dignity as a girl can muster.

"Also, government offices are closed today."

I angle a frown over my shoulder to where Fin stands in the open doorway. He makes no attempt to hide his interest as he leans against the frame, his arms folded across his chest.

"Do you mind?"

"Not at all." He makes a gesture, sort of, *go ahead.*

"At least turn around," I demand in a huff.

"Seems kind of redundant, don't you think?"

His answer and the way he's looking at me make my insides squirmy and hot. It's inconvenient that I find his brand of gives-no-fucks confidence so attractive. In fact, I sort of hate that it has this effect on me.

I've never had a thing for cocky men, and I've met plenty in the course of my job. City jerks and arrogant finance bros dressed in designer suits and expensive watches, their confidence elevated by obscene bonuses and ridiculous job titles. *And sometimes illegal party favors.*

Fin DeWitt is the king of their type—the supreme cock of the walk. And he knows how to push my buttons. It makes not one iota of sense that I kind of like that about him.

I've known rich people. I've run their events. I've often thought how nice it must be to view the world from such a lofty perch, because with money and material possessions comes security. A sense of belonging. I suppose I envy their soft-cushioned upbringings.

It's not like I wasn't loved as a child. But security was scarce, from food to safety. Not that I could've articulated the things that worried me at the time.

I feel like rich people can get away with murder. But someone like Fin, rich and good looking and so charismatic—he could probably make a ritual sacrifice on the steps of Parliament and walk off, unaccosted.

"I don't think it's redundant," I answer eventually. "Just because we appear to be married doesn't give you rights over my body."

"Of course not. Even if you were singing a different tune last night."

"I'm not responsible for last night," I retort quickly.

"And boy did you sing loud and proud."

I narrow my eyes but say nothing as we begin a stare-off. I feel a surge of triumph as his gaze dips first.

"I tell you what," he says, hooking his thumb into the towel. "How about I even things up."

"No!" I whip around just in time . . . just in time to take a mental snapshot. As I stare at the clothes hanging from the rails, my heart flip-flops like a landed fish as I try to process the sight of those long, muscular thighs. *And the hollows of his pelvis that my tongue appears to have sensory knowledge of.* I also now know for sure why I'm a contender for the funny-walk-of-the-year prize.

"Are you always this annoying?" I lift my gaze to the ceiling. This is so disconcerting. I might not remember everything about last night, but it's freaking me out how my body seems to recognize his. How the phantom of his touch seems to be tattooed all over my skin.

I hear the soft slide of a drawer.

"Sometimes I'm worse."

"I should've asked for more money."

"He would've given it to you."

"Why did you talk him up? Why did you help me?"

"It seemed important to you to get back to London. I guess I wanted you to be fairly compensated in the face of that."

"That?"

"Your worries or concerns. Besides, Oliver would do anything for Evie. He'd find a way to give her the moon if she asked for it. Or give you a quarter of a million to make her smile."

Did that sound a little wistful?

"Well, thank you," I reply, still staring at the ceiling. "He does seem to be very in love. They both do."

"What they have is rare."

That was definitely wistful. But I'm not ready to talk love with the man I may or may not be actually married to. Especially when the sounds of his rustling clothing seem to have made my nipples hard.

Think, Mila. Think of something, anything, other than him.

The stairwell to get to my grandmother's home. The pervasive stench of other people's cooking—baked in grease and cabbage and things even less pleasant. The raptor-eyed sociopath who lives on the same floor. The looming date of the housing association's repossession.

Poverty. That'll do it every time. There is nothing sexy about poverty.

My mind drifts back to the question of my fee. Crossing my fingers, I send a silent plea to the universe. *Help me out, please.*

"Why do you suppose my clothes are hanging up in here?"

"Because this is where Oliver and Evie were supposed to stay," he replies. "Best suite in the house."

This is not happening. There must be an alternative.

Unless the alternative is a plane back home after being found out.

"Do you think I've made a mess of things?" I'm not sure he'll hear and I'm not really sure I want to know as I quietly address the meager row of my clothes.

"In what way?"

"After what's happened. Do you think Oliver will refuse to pay me?" I hate how vulnerable I sound.

"I know he seems like an asshole, but you held up your part of the bargain. He'll honor his."

I cross my fingers. So much for not being suspicious. "Are you decent yet?" I ask, tired of talking to my resort wardrobe.

"I guess that depends on who you ask."

Fin DeWitt is nothing if not committed.

Inhaling a deep breath, I turn to face him. I'm relieved (mostly) to find he's at least wearing shorts, a shirt gripped in his hand. That body is such a temptation for a wandering eye, which is why I keep my gaze resolutely on his.

"You can go on and turn that frown upside down. Oliver isn't gonna give a fuck. He'll be too high on life."

I nod, not quite convinced. "I barely remember what I did last night." And the parts I do remember aren't exactly PG rated. "If I signed my name, my real name, to the wedding certificate, what other mistakes did I make? Those things you said about the photographs— what if someone gets their hands on them?"

Panic spikes hard inside. Did I dry hump Fin's thigh when I should've been embodying Evie, who is obviously much classier? I'm sure those are the kind of images she'd like flashed across the internet.

I can only imagine it happened because I've been thinking about Fin for months. Using him as the basis for my fantasies, replaying the

86

way he looked at me in that closet that smelled of wool and leather and spilled champagne. The way his low spoken compliments felt against my skin and how he promised there would come a time when I'd feel whole again. I've reimagined that night so many times, taking it beyond those stolen moments into the realms of absolute fantasy.

But what if I've screwed it all up by making those fantasies real?

"You haven't let them down, Mila. You behaved exactly like a bride should."

But Fin's reassurance doesn't dilute my worry.

"Like a bride should?" I answer distractedly. "According to my experience, that's a wide range of behavior," I say. "I know you think you've been to a lot of weddings, but weddings are my daily bread, and I've seen some things."

"I'm sure you have."

I turn my full attention his way. "I've seen stuff that would make your hair curl. When it's long enough. Like the bride slutdropped on her new father-in-law and two others who were caught in a compromising position. One with her stepbrother. What if I've ruined things?"

"You were the picture of a besotted bride."

"That's not what you said earlier."

He reaches up and rubs his hand across the back of his neck. "I might've been exaggerating."

"Why?"

"You're just too tempting not to needle."

I shake my head as though disappointed. I might've been angrier if I weren't at least a little relieved. "Well, that's good. For Evie, I mean." And for my bank balance. My grandmother. My business's chance of resurrection.

"It was good for me too."

I narrow my eyes. "Maybe not so good for your health." Especially if he keeps mentioning last night.

He slides his hands into his pockets as his gaze dips to his bare feet. "I almost bought into it myself."

I'm tempted to ask him what he means. *Best not.*

"I'd just hate to let them down," I say tersely, hoping my tone signifies a change in conversational direction. "I think we should take the opportunity to get a few things straight between us."

"Sure." His gaze lifts, but not his head.

"I'm sorry about last night, about what happened between us."

"I'm not."

His answer feels like a lick to the inside of my stomach. "Regardless, there won't be a repeat. I'm here to work, and while my role might've turned unconventional—"

"We didn't get up to anything *too* kinky."

"—I take my client's vision very seriously," I rush on. "I under-promise and overdeliver."

"No complaints here," he replies, all silky mouthed.

I close my eyes for a beat, wishing my body would get with the program.

"But you're not my client," I say slowly. *As though speaking to a child. Or an idiot.* "Whatever happened between us wasn't supposed to. Last night was a mistake. I promised Evie and Oliver I'd see this through, and I will. But we won't be having sex again. Further, whether you've seen me naked or not doesn't matter. I'd like you to leave the closet so I can get dressed."

For the first time in our short acquaintance, Fin's expression turns blank. As though he's purposefully wiped all traces of playfulness from his eyes and his thoughts.

I almost feel sorry, and like a bit of a bitch, as he gives a short shrug and turns.

But then, not so sorry again when he says:

"Whatever you say, sugar tits."

Chapter 9
FIN

"So, Mrs. DeWitt."

Ahead of me, Mila makes a sound to convey her continued displeasure. Sadly for her, the sound just makes me think about sex.

No repeats, I silently scoff. Maybe not until she remembers how much she was into it. Last night was the night of my life. Mila writhed like a flame in my arms. Hot, dangerous, and all consuming.

"Wait, thinking about it, you *actually* are Mrs. DeWitt. Trippy."

"What other mistakes did I make?" she'd asked. I could tell her, sure. But then I'd have to admit my crazy part in this. What I did was so out of character for me—just fucking madness. But after examining my feelings this morning, I find I have zero regrets. Which leads me to believe I've either lost my fucking mind or that I've got it bad.

"Can you please stop talking?" She whips around to face me, her dark hair fanning across her face. She angrily bats it away.

"You are as cute as a fistful of buttons when you're angry, Mrs. DeWitt." All kinds of fun and so easy to annoy. Rocking back on my heels, I slide my hands into my pockets and allow my eyes to rake over her.

"In percentage terms, how often does that work for you?"

I'm taken aback by her question. I expected a reaction but not a genuine-sounding inquiry. "What do you mean?"

"And is it because I'm short," she adds, tightly folding her arms, "or because I'm female that you think you can denigrate my ire."

"Your ire?" *Oh, oh.* I tamp back my smile. Talk about a one-eighty.

"Rage. Fury. General"—she makes an airy motion in the air as though the right word might float by for her to grab—"pissed-off-ness. I'm not cute; I'm fucking angry," she annunciates, like the wickedest school prefect I ever did hear.

And there she is again. My girl.

My wife.

"Got it," I say, aiming for and achieving obliviousness. "Glad you're back on the cursing thing. It's good for clearing the old throat chakras, right?" Then I wink.

"This is so wrong," she mutters, her attention turning to a nearby pandanus tree as though she's talking to herself. Or maybe the spiky tree. "This situation is untenable. It's fundamentally fucked up. I'm going to kill him. Or end up in a psych ward." Her attention swings back, her gaze narrowed so sharply, it's almost piercing. "It's annoying, you're annoying, and you're not taking my feelings into account."

"Right. Got it." I bring my hand to my chin. "Honesty it is, then. I guess I just don't feel as horrified about the situation as you do." *Not that she felt that way last night.*

Her gaze flickers as though she doesn't trust what I'm saying.

"And I'm not gonna apologize for calling you cute. You are small, and you are female, but that's got nothing to do with it. I guess I'm just perverse, because the kind of cute you are right now feels more like Medusa."

She throws up her hands. "That's hardly an improvement. Excuse me for remaining unmoved."

The hell she is, because I remember the things she said last night, the way her fingers pierced as she clung to me and how she writhed in my arms. The memories rise with a resonance that I feel deep in my gut. It was more than sex. More than pretend. It just felt right. Beyond that, I can't tell her what happened between us. She wouldn't believe me, and I'd look like a manipulating asshole.

"For what it's worth, your hair is less snakelike," I say, watching a breeze catch the strands, making them dance. "But it does have a life of its own. And the angry looks you throw my way aren't turning me to stone, but they do give me wood."

"Unbelievable!" Yet her eyes still dip as though to check.

"I never claimed to be a poet, but I am honest. I can't help that I find you hot when you're angry, and you're not allowed to yuck my yum, honeybuns."

"I'm not allowed to what?"

"That's a thing. Bottom line, I'm not trying to diminish the way you feel about this situation, but I am goading you. Because your opposition to this inevitability?" I add, moving a finger between us. "It's awesome, like a flavor all of its own. It's goddamn umami."

She stares at me in disbelief, then shakes her head. "You're wrong in the head."

I laugh. Loudly. She might be right on that front, but while I enjoy these interactions and our at-odds positionings, I've also seen the other side of her. The side that wants me. *For me.* But how she gets to the point of realization that she can be raw and honest without consequences, I don't know. But I'm going to find out.

Medusa. What the fuck was I thinking? Couldn't I have just told her she'd floored me? That in her borrowed wedding dress, she'd looked too beautiful for words? That last night—*Fuck, last night*—it was as though she'd been saving her desire for her whole damn life? Saving her feelings, even. She'd had so many feelings, and I'd appreciated each and every one of them.

I've thought of her often since the night we met four months ago. Thought of us fucking, sure, though my imagination didn't come close to the reality. But last night wasn't just sex, and this isn't the start of an infatuation. It feels way beyond that.

To put it another way, I'm an instinctual creature. And this feels right to me.

"You're too fucking cute." I suck in a breath and give my head a slow, appreciative shake.

"Stop calling me that," she demands, through gritted teeth, all piss and vinegar.

God, I'm a fucking simp for this side of her.

"How about *gremlin*," I suggest. "You know, those furry things from that '80s movie? The things you don't feed after dark?"

"I know what a gremlin is," she retorts, folding her arms tight across her chest. *And it is some chest. Eleven out of ten.* "I just have no idea what it has to do with anything."

"Maybe you should come with a similar warning; don't feed Mila dick after dark, because she turns into—"

"Your speaking privileges have been revoked!" she says, springing forward like a cricket to a bush as she squeezes her hands over my mouth.

"—an insatiable entity!" I wrap my arms around her as I tip my head back, laughter leaving my mouth in a joyful spurt.

"Shut up! Shut up!" she demands, not seeming to realize how tight I'm holding her as she continues to try to make me stop. "Why are you so annoying?"

"It's a talent."

"It's bloody annoying," she repeats, seemingly unaffected by the press of my body against hers—hips, thighs, fingers. Chest to chest. My nerve endings sparking like fucking fireworks.

"It's annoying that I'm annoying?"

"Put me down!"

"I didn't even put you here." For shits and giggles, I hike her a little higher up my body.

"The only reason I'm not punching you right now is because we're outdoors. Because someone might see."

"You can punch me if you want."

"Because nothing says love like a bride thumping her groom in the head."

"Some people are into that kind of thing," I say as I set her down.

"Strange, but I can see how," she mutters, pushing her hair from her face again.

"If you don't like *cute* and you don't like *gremlin* and you don't want to be Mrs. DeWitt, just give me an alternative."

"What are you talking about?"

A quicksilver thrill rolls down my spine as her eyes meet mine.

"I can't call you Mila out in public, and calling you Evie just feels weird. Evie's my friend. You're my—"

"Only, calling me Mrs. DeWitt doesn't work," she interrupts with a touch of menace, "because that's not *her* husband's name."

"I never said it made sense." I never said I liked calling her Mrs. DeWitt, either, but I do. I really fucking do. "But this is exactly why we had that pet name conversation last night, sugar nips."

"No." She points a finger my way. "No fucking way!"

"Throat chakra clearing again?"

"You'd make a saint swear."

"And you've got a mouth that would make a sailor blush."

That body part in question falls open as she sucks in an offended breath. "That's a horrible thing to say!"

"Actually, it was a compliment." I try not to smile, because the woman can curse. Oh, yes, she can.

"What is that?" She waves a finger in the general vicinity of my face. "What's going on here?"

"This is a smile. You should try it."

"You're laughing at me."

"Nope. I just don't mind if you only curse around me. Literally *around* me."

"What?"

"*Oh, God. Fin, oh my fucking God. It hurts so good. I've touched myself so many times thinking about this cock.*"

"You—"

"Hottest thing ever. Things almost ended there and then. First time, at least."

"—are unbelievable."

"So were you."

"Urgh!" She pulls away, almost spinning on her heel.

"Come on, honeybuns," I call after her. "We need to decide on a couple of names!"

"You can call me whatever you like." She throws the retort over her shoulder. "Meanwhile, I'm going to find Sarai and get to the bottom of this."

I follow as she makes her way along the path, my eyes glued to the sway of her hips. *And that ass.* "Whatever you say, slut muffin."

She stops so abruptly, I practically walk into the back of her. The only thing that stops her forward motion is the arm I slide around her waist. Her hands fall to my forearm, and I take the opportunity to drop my lips to her ear. "You said whatever I liked. And that's what I like, my little slut muffin."

"That is *not* an appropriate term of endearment."

"I'm allergic to generic," I purr, wondering if she realizes she's forgotten to step away.

"More like you're allergic to behaving yourself. Fine, I'll choose something just as inappropriate for you."

"Mila," I whisper, making a meal of her name. "Don't you remember what you called me?"

She inhales but doesn't immediately speak. But, as I expected, curiosity gets the better of her. She offers me her profile, her mouth such a tempting pout, her lashes a dark sweep as they lower.

"Fine," she says, as though she's doing me a favor. "What did I call you?"

"Daddy."

I feel rather than hear her sharp intake of breath, my arms moving closer with her inhale.

"You can call me *daddy* anytime, sweet girl."

She shakes her head.

"That's a shame." But interesting that she hasn't fought me on it, which seems to imply she's feeling it. Yeah, I think so, given the way her breath caught.

"I'm sure we'll both learn to live with it."

I press my lips to her temples, not quite a kiss, as I loosen my hold. "I guess we'll just go with your second choice. *Thundercock* it is."

Laughter bursts from her mouth in an echo of the woman from last night, blissfully unrestrained. There were quiet moments too—things she said that I know she'd hate to hear me repeat.

She loosens a long sigh and gives her head a long-suffering kind of shake. "You're like the dildo of my life's consequences."

"At least you don't need lube."

"Oh, Sarai!" She lifts her arm and begins pulling from mine. I ignore the instinct to tighten my hold—to haul her in the opposite direction. "Sarai! Over here?"

95

I can't say I've ever been less pleased to see the kid as, on the path up ahead, Sarai's expression lightens. She breaks from her companion with a murmured word.

"What up, lovebirds?" She swaggers toward us, her gait at odds with her traditional-looking uniform. She pinches in a mischievous grin, and as her gaze slides my way, she winks.

I give a tiny shake of my head. *None of that, now.*

"What's up?" Mila briefly folds her arms around herself. "What's up is that I can barely remember a thing about yesterday."

Sarai's brows lift. "I'm jealous."

"What?"

"I mean . . ." Thoughts practically flit across her face, and I feel a slight twinge of panic at where she might take this. "I've heard of passing out from experiencing an intense *O*, but not forgetting the whole night."

For a minute, I think she might be about to reach out for a fist bump. *Un-fucking-subtle, Sarai.*

"What? No!" Mila protests. "We haven't—that is to say, we didn't . . ."

"Really?" Sarai somehow manages to make her tone sound like a singular raised eyebrow.

"I said you were convincing." I clasp my fingers over Mila's tense shoulder, and her eyes dart my way.

"Oh, that. Yes, I suppose I did try my best to look like I was into it. I-into you."

Sarai snorts.

Look like she was into it? I have four condom wrappers, several sucking hickeys, a set of teeth marks, and abs that ache like a motherfucker that say otherwise. That's without the memories seared into the lining of my brain and the fact that I seriously considered icing my dick this morning.

"I was just playing up to my role, right?"

Poor Mila. She'd never be a contender for an Oscar. I give the tight muscles in her shoulder another squeeze. This time, she relaxes into it.

"Huh." Sarai makes a quizzical noise as she tilts her head, adopting a pondering pose. "So were you just tired on your way back to the suite? You know, when you stopped at the janitor's closet. Did you need to catch a few z's?"

"I was just . . . Sorry, I did what?"

"I mean, there must be a reason you asked me to get the keys." Sarai turns to me, her tone just *leaking* with satisfaction.

"I asked for the keys?" Mila's gaze darts my way for confirmation.

I give an apologetic shrug. There was no stopping her—she practically dragged me in behind her. *Practically.* "You said you wanted to re-create our first meeting."

"I thought it was cute."

"Yes," Mila sort of squeaks. "I suppose it might've been, but you didn't need to—"

"'Please, please, please, Sarai!'" Sarai intones, impersonating Mary Poppins. "'I just want to make out with my *gorgeous hubs* in the cupboard again.'"

"Quit being a smart-ass." I tighten my fingers in reassurance again. "She's just messing with you."

Poor Mila glances between us as though she doesn't know which of us to believe. The answer is me, obviously, even if Sarai is essentially telling the truth.

"I knew you'd met before," Sarai crows. "Straight facts—I could see it in the way you were eye screwin' each other from the get-go."

"Look." Mila holds up her hands like she's trying to keep everything away. Sarai's words, the realities of last night, our marital situation. "I don't know what I did last night. I mean, I know some things," she adds as her shoulders begin to creep up to her ears, "but not everything—and Fin says the same! Sort of."

"Really?" Sarai slides me a skeptical look.

I give my head a tiny shake. I guess this is more a case of what Mila would like to believe.

"And that's what we wanted to talk to you about," my wife adds. *Wife. I do like that.*

"You had the time of your life. Lives," Sarai corrects with another hesitant glance my way.

"It's just that—"

"Especially when you did the *Dirty Dancing* lift and Fin held you over his head."

"He did what?"

"Knock that off," I say, though it's more a low chuckle than a warning.

"Did we really?" Mila asks in a faint voice.

"What's a wedding without a little foolishness," I answer, actively rubbing her back now.

And she lets me. In for a dime, in for a dollar, I pull her to my side. And she just fits, like my body was made to accommodate her right there.

"This is all news to me, and all I can think is there must've been something in the coconut," Mila says, clutching at that straw again.

"Coconut?" Sarai repeats in a carefully bland tone.

Or maybe Mila really is onto something.

"Yeah. You know, the things that grow on trees," I put in flatly.

"We drank the coconut water the priest gave us as part of the ceremony. After that, things are vague. I suspect Fin suffered too— maybe not to the same degree. I mean, just look at his hair!" She throws up her hand before it drops in a gesture of futility. "We both did things that just make no sense."

I have to let her think that, for now, at least. But the truth is, everything I did last night, every choice I made, I did stone-cold sober. What's more, I'd do it all again.

I was so happy to find her here on the island, and I put her initial snarky denials down to embarrassment and the setting, then the weird shit Evie and Oliver threw her way.

And I guess, this morning, I put her dismay down to cold feet. The decisions we make in the heat of the night often feel very different in the cold light of day. I was prepared for her feistiness and denials, ready for the challenge that is Mila, and more than ready to remind her exactly what it is she likes about me. But then I realized she was serious—that she didn't remember a fucking thing. It took the wind right out of my sails, so to speak.

But I'm undeterred because I refuse to believe the woman from last night bears no relation to the woman at my side right now. So I'll bide my time, roll with it, and take my opportunities as they arise. She's so determined to discount her attraction, but what she doesn't realize is she already confessed to so much. Last night, she said *the* hottest things. And I was so fucking happy to hear I wasn't alone in dreaming of those stolen closet moments.

Over the months, I'd told myself that my memories were somehow false. That Mila couldn't be as luminous as the image I held in my mind's eye.

I was wrong. And she *was* perfect. Flattered by Fin the man, not Fin the mogul, she had no idea who I was. Yet she put her trust in me. Allowed *me* to kiss away her tears. She left such an impression. *Maybe even on my soul.*

And then last night, I found she felt the same.

"Things happened that make no sense at all." Mila's shrill tone pulls me back from my reveries. "I don't even know where to begin."

Maybe with transcendental sex, janitor-closet fumbles, naked haircuts, and—

"We signed a wedding certificate," she says. "An actual wedding certificate with our own names."

—there was that, obviously.

"How did we do that? How did we make such a huge mistake?"

My heart does a painful little jitterbug, though I force my expression to remain impassive. It didn't feel like a mistake to me, more like the beginning of something new, something wildly exhilarating but real. Fuck, it's hard to know how to explain it. My actions were pure intuition, like I was working with a knowledge that was ancient, primal. From deep within. I knew what I was doing, what I was signing up for, and it felt right.

Sarai's gaze cuts my way. "But when you signed your own name, you said—"

"The coconut," I say, cutting her off.

Her gaze turns wary, but she's picking up what I'm putting down. This is neither the time nor the place to try to explain the unexplainable.

"Look, this had nothing to do with my dad," Sarai says suddenly.

So she does have a part in this. *Fuck.*

"Sarai, the general manager of a prestigious resort knows better than to dose his customers." His daughter, though . . .

"And you can't tell him." This is more of a demand than a request, though she rolls her lips together nervously. "Or my mom."

"Your mom scares the shit out of me," I admit.

"Not even!" She gives a machine-gun laugh. "My mom loves you. Every time she sees you, she turns the color of a tomato and goes all giggly and shit. You ask her to make *betutu* and she runs straight to the kitchen. 'Oh, poor Mr. Fin. He is *hungrrry!*'" she says, imitating her mom, hand gestures and all. "'That man needs a wife to fatten him up. He looks so thin!'" She folds her arms. "But if I ask her to cook *betutu*, she tells me I have to wait until my birthday. And I'm never here for my birthday! Meanwhile, you have her eating out of your hand."

"Like a tiger, maybe," I say with a wry grin. As in, very warily.

"He's really good with people." Sarai directs this Mila's way. "For a one-percenter, he's pretty real, you know?"

"You were going to say something about the coconut?" Mila answers, brushing the weird compliment aside.

"It was shrooms." Sarai says with a defensive flick of her shoulder.

"Shrooms?" Mila repeats. "Who is Shrooms?"

"Not who," I say, tightening my hold on her. I sense this is going to be a little out of her sphere of reference. "What. *What* is shrooms. You sent us on a fucking trip?" I say, turning to Sarai. I'm stunned. And stretching the truth, given Mila was tripping on her own.

"Drugs!" Mila squeaks.

Sarai slides her an unimpressed look. "It was just the local stuff—a microdose at best."

"I can't believe you'd do this," Mila says, sounding genuinely hurt.

"It's not like I didn't tell you."

"Tell me? You didn't tell me!" If Mila's voice gets any higher, we'll be surrounded by yapping dogs.

"Yeah, I did. When the photographer turned up and you wouldn't come out of the bathroom—"

"Because all I was wearing was my underwear and a veil!"

"That was the whole point—it *was* a lingerie shoot," the younger woman snipes.

"Wait. There was a lingerie shoot?" Neither woman looks to me. *That lucky dog,* I think. Then I remember Oliver isn't the groom in this situation. *I guess I could be that lucky dog.* I slot the thought away for examination later.

"I told you, if you came out, I would get you something to help your nerves."

"You didn't say you were giving me drugs!"

"I specifically said *psilocybin*."

"I don't even know what that is," Mila protests.

"Shrooms," Sarai and I reply in unison.

"I would never have agreed to taking drugs—you said it was a local remedy!"

"It is! I gave you the magic mushroom equivalent of baby Tylenol. I was trying to help," Sarai mutters, unrepentant. "You two were not vibing. And the priest might not have understood English, but he picked up the tone. You were totally spoiling his priestly Zen. I was just trying to mellow the situation before the shit hit the fan!"

"Wait." I hold up my hand. "You said you microdosed Mila *before* the ceremony."

"I did. But then I topped her up. During the ceremony. And . . . I might've microdosed you. Inadvertently."

"What?"

"It was the coconut," Sarai adds with a touch of chagrin. "Like, a pinhead of the stuff."

"Sarai." I draw out her name through gritted teeth. "What the fuck were you thinking?"

"I was thinking that Mila had already agreed to it and that you weren't supposed to take the coconut out of her hand!"

"Do you know how dangerous that could've been?" Dosed. She fucking microdosed me! Is this why I . . . No. Mila's been in my head for months—the choices I made yesterday were my own.

But Mila's weren't.

Fuck. My stomach plummets.

"*Please*," Sarai retorts dismissively. "I've heard all the tales of your 'dabbling.'" She physically puts quotation marks around the word. "And you do know I'm a chemistry major, don't you?"

"That's beside the point. And that other shit? That was a lot of years ago." When I was young and reckless.

"You weren't microdosing neither," she mutters.

"What you did was way out of order," I retort severely as I try to reconcile what this means and how I feel.

"Everyone on the resort knows—you used to get high with the head chef, and he'd make grilled cheese when you got the munchies!"

"That doesn't give you the right to decide what's good for me or for Mila. It's fucking irresponsible, Sarai!"

"You were an accident," she persists as tears begin to glisten in her eyes. "I was trying not to blow your covers. You were supposed to be happy and in love, not uptight and scowling at each other." She throws up her hands in frustration.

"You told me it was a local medicinal," Mila begins.

"It is! You just don't get how serious the situation was. The priest sees himself as a channel between heaven and earth. He thought he was there to ask the gods for their wedding blessings for two people planning the rest of their lives together. You were supposed to be madly in love! What would've happened if he'd bailed—walked off? I'll tell you what: buh-bye, wedding; hello, tabloid gossip columns!"

"You could've just . . ." Mila flounders.

"What? What could I have done?" Sarai demands, warming to her dramatic theme. "You tell me. I knew how important this was to you—how important it was to the Deubels. I was protecting all of you."

"Nothing to do with your own fee, huh?" I put in.

Sarai's mouth pinches. "You know that in the States you can get way stronger stuff online. Freeze-dried shrooms, mushroom teas, truffles, capsules, and even candies!"

"That's hardly the point."

The shrooms might be *how* last night happened but not why. Not for either of us. Not that it makes me feel any better about the situation.

"And I hung around afterward like a good little trip nanny," Sarai puts in petulantly.

"What on earth is a trip nanny?"

Poor Mila. She must feel like she's in an alternate universe.

"The person who monitors your welfare," I explain pensively. As though I've never indulged. Like I said, it was a long time ago.

"When you're trippin' balls. Which you weren't." Sarai scowls "Or you wouldn't have been if you hadn't been throwing back vodka."

"Hey—you gave me drugs!" Mila points an angry finger. "You don't get to make me feel bad."

"I asked first," Sarai says again. "And I didn't lie. They do take them in the villages for all kinds of stuff. You must've had way more vodka than the bottle stashed in your cleavage."

"You had a bottle of vodka in your cleavage?" It probably wasn't the best idea to give in to a smile. Or for my gaze to drop to the area in question. But it doesn't linger, thanks to the backhanded slap Mila lands on my chest.

"I was just trying to work out how!" I say with a chuckle.

"Do you seriously think I had space in that dress for a bottle of vodka?"

"Well, there wasn't one in there last night." The dress that clung to her curves like a second skin, the dress I got to peel her out of. "But maybe I should take another look, just to be certain." I playfully reach for the neck of her sundress.

"Hey!" Poking me in the chest, she makes a V of her fingers in the direction of her face. "My eyes are up here, thank you very much!"

"Your gorgeous eyes are the second most beautiful thing about you."

"Rude!"

"Your personality being the first," I answer with mock offense.

She narrows her eyes. God, she's beautiful when she's riled. But it's not her eyes, her personality, or her body that makes me feel the way I do. It's just . . . her.

"Maybe I should give up chemistry and take up matchmaking," Sarai says, with a considering tilt to her head.

"With or without the illegal substances?" Mila snaps again.

"Shrooms are medicinal. They're basically relaxants. I only intended for you to have a good time. The issue had to be your fun-size vodkas."

"I was nervous!" Mila protests. "I always keep a miniature or two on hand."

"One or two?" Sarai pulls a doubtful face.

"At least I only self-administered. It's a perfectly acceptable way to calm an anxious bride. And I *was* an anxious bride. One who didn't want to prance about in her underwear."

"Okay, so I should've checked you knew what I was talking about," Sarai says, her tone almost contrite. *But not quite.* "And I should've asked if you'd drank others when you pulled the bottle from . . ."

"My cleavage," Mila finishes.

"I'm sorry," Sarai mutters.

"You weren't to know," Mila answers with a sigh. Her cheeks flushed, she's no doubt embarrassed now.

"You were okay, though, weren't you, Fin?"

"Don't try recruiting me for your team," I say, sidestepping Sarai's question.

My memory of last night is thoroughly intact, the images filed away under the title "The Night of My Life." That's not to say I was completely unaffected, I now realize. After drinking the coconut water, maybe a tranquilness did seep through my limbs, and maybe, in hindsight, I was a little buzzed. Things were pleasant. Slower and a little dreamlike. But the effects were mild and short lived. I remember everything and I have zero regrets.

"You didn't need any happy juice." Sarai's lips twist into a reluctant half smile. "Bruh, you were stanning so hard last night."

I'm not going to deny it.

"When you said—" Her eyes dart Mila's way before she seems to think better of what she was about to reveal. "Anyway, what you did was dope."

And nothing to do with the shrooms.

I'm disappointed Mila doesn't remember, though it now makes sense. I also know that the things she said last night were the truth, that her behavior, her feelings, were amplified, not manufactured.

The truth and her truth. I heard it in the ache in her words, just as I'd glimpsed it in the closet all those months ago.

"I feel like a dope," Mila says suddenly. "Would you two stop grinning at each other and talking about things I don't understand?"

"Sorry?"

"It's very childish," she continues. "It's like some horrible teenage flashback where I've missed the punch line again and I'm being made fun of for my weird-smelling sandwiches."

Sarai gives a roll of her eyes. "I couldn't possibly relate to being different," she announces. Cocking her hip, she taps a finger to her face to indicate her own sense of otherness. "You've never suffered until you've stunk the canteen out with the smell of fermented fish."

"Ever had knitted lamb intestines?" A smile lurks in the shape of Mila's mouth.

"To wear or to eat?" Sarai asks, mildly horrified.

"*Kukurec* is food." Mila gives in to a reluctant chuckle. "It's a dish with intestines and—"

Sarai holds up both hands and pulls a face. "I get the picture."

"Now you're making me feel left out," I complain with an expansive shrug. "You don't know how lucky you two are. Do you know how monotonous PB&J is every day?"

"I bet you went to some posh prep school." Mila's eyes tighten in the corners. "It probably had a team of chefs, white linens, and silver-service waiters."

"Yeah. No chicken feet in your lunch box," Sarai adds.

The pair exchanges a look of solidarity.

"I *was* just trying to help," Sarai eventually says.

"I know. I accept my part in this too. I should've asked what I was taking—what it was you gave me. And maybe the reason I didn't was because I'd already had a couple of mini vodkas." Mila gives her head a shake and squares her posture. "I suppose we know now how this happened." She folds our wedding certificate again, which means she doesn't see the look that passes between Sarai and me. "We both signed it under the influence."

I nod, because that is true.

But the only influence I was under was you.

Chapter 10
MILA

"What the hell do I know about that?" The phone still glued to his ear, Fin pauses in his pacing to slide me a reassuring half smile. One that seems at odds with his conversation. "Yeah, well," he adds, his attention sliding away, "that's why I pay you. Fine. Sure." His brows pinch, at odds once again as he glances down at the certificate in his hand. *Our wedding certificate.*

I wish he'd taken this call out of earshot, because it's doing nothing good for my anxiety. I'm married. I can't believe I'm really married. And that the object of all my recent fantasies is the man I've plighted my troth (troths?) to.

Fin turns away, allowing me a minor (unobserved) perv of the delectable rear view. His T-shirt stretches tight over his broad back, the short sleeves clinging to the rounds of his biceps. *Can't say I blame them.*

The universe has a wild sense of humor, marrying me to him—a virtual but much crushed-on stranger—on the very day I was supposed to marry someone else. I still can't make sense of how he's here, all the way on the other side of the world at the same time as me.

Six days. I'm stuck here for six more days. With Fin. More specifically, more worryingly, we'll be sharing this space. The bridal suite, with its one bed, thanks to the arrival of a prominent Saudi prince to the resort this morning. His family and his entourage have taken over all the private villas; one each for his four wives and the fifth, the largest of the lot, booked for his own use.

I wonder if the Saudi prince would mind if I bunk with him?

I tip my head into my hands as I try to ignore the feelings, thoughts, and sentiments rioting through me. Conflict seems to be the driving sense, shortly followed by a mixture of nervous excitement. My stomach is a mess of tangled knots, and my nipples are so hard I could probably put someone's eye out.

I still can't believe Sarai gave me an illicit substance. *Yet at the same time, I totally can.* When she said she'd get me something to settle my nerves, I thought she might bring me back a Xanax or something. *Come to think of it, Xanax and vodka wouldn't have been the best pairing either.*

When she'd prized me from the bathroom, she was holding a tiny glass bottle with a dropper set to the lid. I just assumed it was the local equivalent of Rescue Remedy.

It's not *all* Sarai's fault. I should've asked exactly what I was dropping into my mouth.

Of course, topping me up was reckless, and it probably had less to do with the holy man's sensibilities than the money Oliver promised her. But I can't even blame her for that, and on some level, I'm relieved she did microdose me. Because if the priest had walked away, I would have precisely zero to show for my efforts.

Except an annoyingly handsome husband. Or an annoying handsome husband.

Either way, I would've needed to invest in a decent sleeping bag and find myself a bench.

"You okay?"

I spring upright like a jack-in-the-box, yanking my false fingernails from my mouth. "Absolutely!" I reach for my evil eye pendant and rub my thumb over it. I am absolutely a lot of things. Absolutely losing my marbles. Absolutely losing the plot. Losing my shit. All of it. Especially as the images that keep coming back to me are snapshots of our wedding night, and they're so freaking tempting. "What did they say? Your legal people?"

Remember that. Remember the mess you're in. Fin the hot husband is a complication you don't need.

He drops his phone onto the oatmeal-colored ottoman, taking a seat in the middle of the long sofa. Not so close as to make me feel uncomfortable but not so far away as to allow my complete ease.

"Just that the state offices are closed but that they'll try to find out who Oliver dealt with. The thing is, I don't want to call him and ask."

"Oh, no. You definitely can't call him," I say, my words falling quickly. Oliver Deubel seems like the kind of man with very exacting standards (and possibly a vengeful streak), and I desperately need my payday. "You shouldn't text. Or email. In fact, you shouldn't bother him at all—it is his honeymoon."

A faint smile curves on Fin's lips, and my body seems to intuit exactly what he's thinking. Heat kindles in the pit of my stomach. We're both thinking of our own short but seemingly thorough honeymoon.

Did I really call him daddy? Fin teases so much it's hard to tell. I mean, it's entirely possible. I do seem to have developed a thing for being slightly dominated recently. Not in real life, just in my . . . special alone time imaginings. With Fin.

Earlier, when he whispered *daddy* in my ear, heat pulsed through my body. So much so that, when I pulled away from the arm he'd hauled around my waist, I half expected to find my skin seared to his.

"Also," I say, returning to the topic of not contacting the Deubels. "What if they can listen in?" I glance in the direction of the huge wall of window and the bay beyond. "That's a thing, isn't it? Phone tapping?"

"An illegal thing."

"What about seeing in?" My gaze swings back. Do we have to sit together? Cuddle up? There's no way I'm going to voice any of that.

"It's privacy glass. You can see out, but you can't see in. The garden is private too. I guess there's just the pool area we'd need to be careful about."

"Right." I give a nod. "That's good." And mildly disappointing. I was looking forward to swimming. "It must be an awful way to live."

"It has been pretty hard for them."

"I can't imagine having my private life splashed across the internet."

I dread to think what the headlines would read for my own wedding fiasco.

Delusional Wedding Planner Preps for Big Day
While Groom Puts on His Running Shoes

At least Evie got to leave her cheating fiancé. Mine left me. And she did it in style. And while the press may have made her life hell, women everywhere rallied to her defense. I loved reading their supporting comments and laughed so hard at the article that told of her idiot ex suffering a modern-day pillory experience when he was bombarded with rotten fruit in Brick Lane Market.

I would've liked a little support, some female solidarity when times were tough. I give myself an internal shake, moving my mind forcibly back to the present.

"Evie bears the brunt of it." Fin stretches his neck, tilting his head left, then right. Not that I'm watching closely or anything. "Oliver has much thicker skin."

I still feel a little dirty that I watched that awful Pulse Tok video. "If this got out, things would be much worse for her, don't you think?"

"Don't worry. My legal team are on it."

As he lifts his hand to rub the back of his head, my eyes follow the taut line of his bicep. My insides clench, overcome by a wave of sensation as I seem to remember how soft his hair feels. And ticklish. So many taunting fragments of memory. I wish I could remember the whole of it, because then I could move beyond it. Maybe?

"Time zones notwithstanding," I murmur, dragging my gaze away.

"Someone will be hauling their ass out of bed and getting into the office to make that call at the appropriate time."

I send my silent commiserations to whoever *is* making that call. I remember the pain of Zoom calls at odd hours as I liaised with the resort's event staff during the planning of Evie and Oliver's wedding. Or Mr. and Mrs. X, as they were referred to: a high-profile but otherwise unnamed couple. But Sarai seemed to know who they were when I arrived. Then again, she is the GM's daughter. Also, she's not exactly risk averse.

"And we'll take it from there." He stretches out his long legs, propping his heels on the ottoman.

I cross my fingers and send a silent plea to the heavens that I don't end up with my own headline.

My stomach lurches. It might be bad for Evie if the news of this fiasco gets out, but it would be ruinous for me. What bride would want me near her wedding after learning I bagged Fin, one of London's most eligible bachelors, by getting high and super slutty? *A one-percenter* was how Sarai described him. People will automatically assume I married Fin for his money, when in fact, I married him for Oliver's money.

I fold in my pretty gel nails against the instinct to gnaw them. No one will ever take me or Trousseau seriously if even a hint of this is whispered about.

"Do you think we'll get an annulment?" I ask suddenly. "It seems a bit extreme that we might need a divorce for a wedding that was a mistake, doesn't it?"

"I guess we'll find out Monday. The good news is, according to my lawyer, a divorce means you can take me for a lot of money."

"That's not why I asked," I retort, stiffening. "This not only has the potential to ruin my business, but I could end up with people running after me like they do poor Evie. Only they'd be throwing fruit at me instead!"

"Fruit?"

"Like they did her ex—I would be hated. Vilified!"

I find Fin's hand suddenly folded around my thigh, and heat flashes through me. It's not like he's touching me inappropriately—his hand is halfway between my knee and my knickers—but it might as well be inside them for my body's reaction to it.

"I'm sorry I said that. It was a joke."

"A bad one."

"Maybe." His fingers flex a touch.

My skin prickles, and I want to move away. Or climb on top of him. *This is such an odd place to develop a new erogenous zone,* I think as I pause to untangle a clumsy tongue.

"We have to be careful, Fin. What we did yesterday must stay secret."

"Which part of yesterday?" His words end in a playful curl.

"Please be serious. None of this can come out. Not the fact that we may or may not have faked a wedding ceremony. That we might actually be married—that we've potentially consummated that marriage."

"Well and truly," he adds.

"It could look like a stunt—like I've married you purely for the publicity. It would ruin my business, Fin." Once and for all.

"Do wedding planners take a vow of celibacy?" he asks, not quite giving up on his amusement. He just doesn't seem to get it. "Do they swear to remain single?"

"I know it probably looks like I'll do anything for money, but that's not the case." I lift my hand, thinking to move his away, but it would be too obvious—I would look too obviously bothered by it. So I scratch my nose instead.

"I know that." At last, his tone turns serious.

"But how can you? You don't know me. I have my reasons for agreeing to this, not that I ever thought we'd be married for real, but—"

"You don't think I get what kind of person you are?"

I duck my head and give it a short shake. "You barely know me."

His hand slides away, and breath whooshes out of me. And because I can feel him looking at me, I suck another in. I'd rather him think I have asthma than realize I like his hands on me. *That I'm half turned on already.*

"I know enough," he says, his tone serious. "I'm a good judge of character."

I think it's probably more the case that Fin just sees the good in people. He seems the type. To him, everything is easy breezy and nothing is truly serious.

"You don't believe me?"

I make a careless gesture. What do I know? Just that he's a raging flirt and has a black belt in teasing. I also know, according to his best friends, the people who know him best in the world, he's a player. He's super hot and super wealthy, and I'm reasonably sure his tongue game would impress even the most hardcore lesbian. My flashbacks are very comprehensive. *If not in length, then in sensory detail.*

Any of that, never mind all of that, would make him popular. And greedy, I suppose. But beyond all that playboy stuff, I sense Fin DeWitt is essentially a good human. I mean, he's no saint, but at least his life isn't falling apart. And that's sort of attractive.

"I wonder if Evie and Oliver got married," I say, changing the subject. No need to dwell on how not awful he is. Or how his cologne makes me want to bury my nose in his neck to discover its notes.

"They'd better be, after the trouble we've gone to." He pauses, and I feel his eyes on me. "It's been a good kind of trouble. After that night in the closet, I wondered if I'd ever see you again."

I like the sound of that. Him thinking about me.

"I've thought about you," he adds. "Wondered how you were after, well, everything."

I turn to face him, curling my knees onto the seat, pulling a throw pillow into my chest. "You must've thought I was unhinged." My words feel flimsy and inconsequential.

"No. You were just too lovely to be crying. I wanted to make you feel better. Cheer you up, I guess."

"You certainly did that," I murmur, plucking at the edges of the pillow. Until I find the crook of his finger under my chin.

"Just you and me, locked away from the world." He lifts my gaze to his. "I hope you know that moment meant something to me. It was so special."

Oh, Fin, I think about the experience more than the reason I was in there.

"And I'm sorry he did that to you." He briefly cups my cheek, his tone warm but firm. "Hurt you like that."

"I couldn't tell you why I was really upset. It was too humiliating."

"Worse than . . ."

I nod.

"You can tell me now," he says, his voice as soft as an April shower.

I angle my head, and his hand falls away, moving to my shoulder instead. "The party was in full swing, and I was in the hotel kitchen grabbing a coffee when one of the chefs mentioned Adam. He's a wedding photographer, you see, but we'd decided early in our relationship to keep our professional and personal lives separate. Part of that was not broadcasting our relationship at work. We didn't want our clients asking questions, maybe asking for a joint discount, or potentially worrying about us working together after an argument, or whatever. Same goes for the venues.

"Or those were the reasons I thought. As it turned out, Adam's reasons were multifaceted. Anyway, the last time I'd worked at that particular hotel, he'd been the wedding photographer. I suppose that's why the chef thought to mention he'd heard Adam was getting married at all. My heart sort of stopped at the news. I almost told the chef it was old news—that we'd broken up. But then he said something about Adam's fiancée, Rachel, and what a lovely girl she was. Apparently, she used to be one of the hotel's duty managers."

I shrug as I recall how the news had felt like a blow to my chest. I'd suffered the hollow aftermath for months.

"Oh, Mila." Fin's hand tightens as though he'd pull me closer, but it turns to comfort when I resist. "I'm so sorry that he didn't have the balls to tell you himself." His hand slides to the sofa back, his fingers drumming there. "Did you confront him?"

I shake my head. "It's not like we were on speaking terms."

"You don't keep in contact? Not at all?"

"Do you keep in contact with your exes?" I ask pertly.

"Some. But then, I never loved any of them."

"Well, I don't want to speak to him, and I'd live quite happily never setting eyes on him again."

"I hope you told them all what an asshole he really is."

I shake my head.

"Then I hope you slashed his tires or keyed his car."

I almost smile. It's what Ronny wanted to do. *And worse.*

"I told myself that the best form of revenge would be to live well." But then things started to fall apart.

"Living well," he repeats. "That certainly happened in that coat closet," he teases. "Stolen champagne always tastes better."

I tsk. "How would you know?"

"I might've appropriated a bottle or two in my time."

"When you're feeling hard up?" I say with a chuckle. "Or when you've left your wallet in your other ermine cloak and your diamond shoes pinch, so it's too painful to backtrack?"

"An ermine cloak." He nods. "I should get one of those."

"Because you fancy someone chucking a red pot of paint over you?"

His expression suddenly turns serious. "You deserved better. I wish you would've told me."

I shake my head as though it doesn't matter, when the truth is I've reached my limit for sharing. And for feeling like an idiot. "I couldn't." I can't quite bring myself to tell him the whole story now. "I just had to hide. Compose myself, I suppose." I swallow and paint on another smile. *God knows what this one looks like.* "By the time you showed up, I was angry. As evidenced by the bottle throwing."

"I think you left a dent." He grins. "You left your mark on me too."

"I wasn't drunk," I offer quickly. Not because the hot man said a nice thing but because I'd be a fool to believe him. Fin is a decent human; that's all. And decent humans have empathy. I could be anyone recounting this tale to him, and he'd listen. Say the right things.

"Me neither. Except maybe drunk on you."

I say nothing but *feel everything.*

"I'm sorry you had to go through that but happy you're out of it now."

"I don't think anyone has said that before now."

"About breaking up?"

I shake my head. "No. I mean *sorry.*"

"Maybe you weren't listening. It's hard to see the bigger picture, to pay attention to what's going on around you, when you feel like your heart is breaking." His expression barely flickers, but I sense some history in that statement.

"Are you speaking from experience?"

"To be human is to suffer."

"That's deep but not really the answer to my question."

"Have I loved?" He slides me that modest-looking smile. I feel like he's hiding something behind it. "I love. I've just never been in love."

"Been loved?" *I'm sure he has many, many admirers.*

"I thought so once. Thought I was in love once. That I was loved in return." He makes a gesture with his head, the action of a man considering something. "But it turned out not so."

"I'm sorry." I know he's never been married, because it would've said so in our marriage license.

My stomach swoops like a dive-bombing magpie. *My husband.* Why aren't I terrified?

"Life is all about learning," he replies prosaically.

"What did you learn from love? Because all I learned was love sucks hairy arse."

"I learned that the betrayed will betray you and the deceived will deceive you."

Guilt. That's what his response sounds like. But strangely, not his tone. Did he cheat and she repaid him in kind? It's hard to tell. At least his lesson sounds more poetic than mine.

"When you split," he begins again, "friends stood by you, though, right? And family. Didn't any of them want to key his car or maybe beat him to a bloody pulp?"

"I don't really have family. Just my slightly nutty granny, who was convinced . . . well, it doesn't really matter what she thought. And our friends took his side. Oh, they made sympathetic noises initially, tempered with murmurs of *It's better to find out you're not suited now.* As though being habitually unfaithful is something anyone would put on their wish list." I snort inelegantly, still stung by the memories. "Such a joke. Everything went off the rails for a while after that. I got caught up with business trouble, and there were things going on at home. By the time I resurfaced, my so-called friends had stopped being interested. And then, of course, they absorbed the new Mila into their orbit."

"Jesus . . . really?"

"It's a couples group. No one wants exes staring daggers at each other over dinner. But I wasn't around, and that must've been convenient, given my ex's new fiancée now sits in my chair. So I've heard."

"Fuck. Sounds like you're better off without them."

"Yes." Not that I was given the choice. "I'm not saying I wanted people to choose sides." I can hear my voice becoming spiky with anger, but I can't seem to stop myself. "But I couldn't understand it. I still don't. They chose him, and he cheated on me! What does that say about him as a person? As a friend? God, I hate that he wasted my twenties, the best years of my life!"

"Mila." *Oh, the way he says my name.* "Your twenties won't be the best years of your life."

"How do you know?"

"Because I'm heading toward the end of my fourth decade, and it's been a blast."

"No way. No way you're nearly forty." He's obviously older than me, but I suppose I hadn't put a number on it.

"Careful." The backs of his fingers are a tender caress against my cheek. "I might get used to this flattery."

"Hah." The sound is just a breath of air between us, his eyes on mine, mine watching his. It's not flattery, exactly. Maybe I just assumed those laughter lines at the outer corners of his eyes came from his near-constant amusement.

"Unless you're trying to flatter me," he adds in that bedroomy tone of his. "Because where would that leave us then?"

Naked. And in the bedroom.

Fin will be one of those men who grow into their years. He won't have any trouble attracting younger women even when he's old and gray. He has that—what do the French call it? Je ne sais quoi. That certain something. An undefinable allure.

"You told me you like older men," he murmurs as he captures a loose lock of my hair.

"Did I?" I swallow, my breath tight and my response husky.

"Yeah," he murmurs, twirling it around his forefinger.

Maybe it's more the case of liking what Sarai said yesterday. A man who's firm but gentle. A man who'd take you to your limits while also taking care of you. The thought drops into my core, a percussion so tempting that I panic.

"I dread to think what else I said. I'm sure it was mostly nonsense." I give a reedy-sounding chuckle as I pull from his orbit. "Anyway, I don't remember."

"I hope it comes back to you. It was an experience well worth remembering."

"If there was a *Dirty Dancing* lift, then I'll pass."

But it does seem like a squandered opportunity. Fin seems to be a man who takes his craft, and his partner's pleasure, very seriously. So maybe it's best that I don't remember at all.

"Coward," he says, his own amusement low and throaty. "Is your ex older?"

I pull a face. "Maybe the older-men shtick was just flattery."

"You didn't need to sweet-talk me. You already had me."

"Maybe I was just joking—pulling your leg."

His answer is a taunting, doubtful expression.

"It doesn't sound like me is all I'm saying." I give a spiky one-shouldered shrug. "I can't see the attraction, honestly."

"You can't?" he replies, all smirking taunt.

"Older men," I say, digging my hole deeper. "What would we have in common? Tell me a scary story about the last recession," I say, all breathless ridiculousness. "Feed me your butterscotch candies, Daddy. Then let me rub your arthritic joints with Voltaren."

What in the name of all that's good and holy is wrong with me?

"Daddy?" Fin says, biting back a grin.

"That's what you picked up from all that?"

"That and it sounds like you might be into men much older than me. Just so you know, I'm undeterred."

121

"You're a"—*zaddy*—"a mental case," I say, leaning away from his almost embrace.

He stretches his arms above his head, very much unspurned. "Want to take a nap?"

Unspurned and unrepentant.

"Together?" *Clothed or unclothed?* The latter, in Ronny's voice, seems to come out of nowhere. "Why?"

"It was a big night." His hand drops to his abs, and he gives a tiny wince. "A time zone change."

"From Jakarta?"

"I'm kind of tired."

More like pushing his luck. "No. No napping. You can, absolutely, if you like. But we," I add, motioning a finger between us, "can't do that."

"We can do whatever we like."

"Not when we're supposed to be decoys." I hook my thumb over my shoulder. "Thinking about it, shouldn't we be seen out there, in the resort?"

"Seen doing what?" That tone. Does he even know he's doing it—the sex-voice thing?

"We could go to a yoga session?" I suggest. "Or maybe visit the main pool or go for a walk to provide the media a few long-distance photo opportunities. It's not like we can hide out here for the next six days, is it?" More like I won't be able to cope for six days alone with him.

"So . . . yoga and walks and swimming is what you think newlyweds would be doing?"

"Why not?"

His expression flickers as he begins to stand. "I guarantee that wherever they are, Oliver and Evie will barely have left their suite. They'll be too busy enjoying each other, which is the way it should be, bunny."

122

"I don't—*bunny?*" I fill the word with derision.

"Yeah. Let me know when you remember why, and we'll revisit the conversation. Meanwhile," he says, holding out his hand. "I guess I could cope with a walk along the beach with a pretty girl."

Chapter 11
FIN

"You didn't tell me this walk was in fancy dress," I say as Mila appears from the bedroom, because apparently, a walk along the beach required a change of outfit.

I threw on a pair of board shorts, hoping she'd join me similarly. Swimwear, I mean. Purely for aesthetic reasons. Nothing to do with a perv.

Sadly, Mila's beachwear is a little more . . . full coverage. She is a quirky bird, and I find that shit endearing.

"Are you even under there?" I tease, crooking a finger under the straw hat she's wearing. The brim is so wide, it's like its own fucking orbit.

"Har-har."

"Jesus!" I jump back theatrically and grin. *Maybe it's because she makes you laugh.* "I thought I was looking at a giant fly." Because, under the hat, Mila is wearing a pair of huge fuck-off sunglasses.

"Stop that," she retorts, slapping my hand away to tug her monstrous head covering back into place. "I'm going incognito. The hat hides my hair, and the sunglasses—"

"Half your face."

"Exactly. I might be Evie under all this," she adds, plucking at the decidedly unsexy striped garment she wears over her swimsuit. One-piece, I'll bet. Some ugly travesty, when a body like hers should be poured into a tiny bikini.

"Be Evie? For all I know, you might *have* Evie under this," I say, pulling the neckline. Did living with a guy who didn't appreciate what he had make her feel like she should hide in baggy clothes and fucking shapeless dresses?

"Stop it!" She issues another reprimanding slap.

"Where'd you get the tent? I didn't know the circus was in town."

Mila inhales a sharp breath, yanks off her sunglasses, and uses them to point at me. "That is a horrible thing to say."

"And that is a horrible . . . whatever it is. Why would you cover up all this beauty?"

She stills, her head tilting ever so slightly to one side, like she's trying to make sense of what I just said. Stunned? Confused? Whatever that is, it's better than a kick in the balls, which is what I thought she'd choose.

"It's just a beach cover-up," she says, her tone modulated somewhat.

"I'll bet it'll cover the whole thing too. Sea and sand. It might even eclipse the sun."

"Rude!" she explodes, slapping my hand away as I inch the hem up.

"I'm just making sure you don't have Victorian-style knicker-bockers on underneath."

"In-cog-ni-to." She punctuates the syllables with a poke to my chest.

"Ug-ly hat." I tug three times on the brim.

"Hey!"

As I whip it away, the thing sails across the room like a straw Frisbee. "That's much better."

"But I don't look like Evie!"

"No, you look like Mila. And that's the way I like it. I'd just like to see a little more of her."

Something like surprise flickers across her face as the compliment hits.

"That cannot be news to you."

"But we're supposed to *be* them," she says, disregarding the question as she slides the dark sunglasses to the top of her head. "And Evie is . . ." She rolls her lips together and swallows. "We're just built differently." Her words fall in a rush. "And if there are cameras out there, we want them to think we're them—that we're Evie and Oliver."

"You're really committed to this."

"Of course I am. I take my job very seriously. Even the unorthodox bits."

I feel myself frown. "But what happened last night wasn't part of your job description."

"No." Her gaze flickers away, then back. "Not last night. But Evie and Oliver can't ever know what happened. And even if we don't tell them, there's still a chance they might find out," she adds, pointing to the window. "They put their trust in me, and I can't have them think I'm some kind of—"

"Mila." Her name on my lips sounds like an ache as I press my hands to her upper arms, ducking my gaze to meet hers. "They won't hear a word of this."

"You don't know that. I don't think you understand this would reflect badly on us both."

"They'd blame me. You can, too, if it helps. Or Sarai."

"I'm to blame too," she says with a sigh. "I was doing fine until the photographer arrived. Next thing, I'm allowing her to administer narcotics with barely a blink."

"How about I thank you instead?"

"Please try to remember I'm getting paid for this."

There she goes, fooling herself again.

"And you pride yourself on overdelivering," I say without a hint of irony.

"Exactly. Which is why I thought you could wear this." She turns from the waist, turning back with a pink straw fedora in her hands.

I stare at the piece of hideousness.

"To hide your face," she adds.

"You don't like my face?" I know that's not true. Just like I know she wasn't getting paid to ride it last night. An observation I'll keep to myself. "Oh, you're serious." I glance at the hideous hat between her hands.

"Of course I'm serious. You don't look a thing like Oliver." Her eyes dip and slide over me in a way that isn't complimentary.

Does she have a thing for Oliver? I kinda thought she was intimidated by him, like most people. But then my mind jumps to the things she said last night. The compliments she purred while sprawled across my chest. And then the morning came, and with it, her denials.

"*Something happened to make me that way,*" she said. And then she found self-protection in the shrooms, along with the comfort of telling herself that a little vodka stole her inhibitions.

And some of that is the truth, but the rest she pulled deep from her dreams. I know because she confessed she'd been conjuring me in them.

"*When I'm alone and I think of you, I touch myself.*"

Me too. Mila. Me fucking too.

No, she's not into Oliver. Which my skin corroborates as her eyes skate over me a second time.

"You'll wear the hat." She thrusts the fedora into my hands. "And I'll wear this. Then no one will be any the wiser. What are you smiling about?" she demands, suddenly narrow eyed with suspicion.

"The hopefully not-too-grainy images of Oliver Deubel wearing a hot-pink fedora on the *City Chronicle*'s website," I say, feeding the brim between my fingers. He'll blow a gasket. Maybe sue. God, I hope there are photos. "I'll tell you what." I throw the hat into the air, catch it, then flip it onto the top of my head. "I'll wear the hat if you lose the circus tent."

"But they'll know I'm not Evie," she protests, flustered. Or frustrated. Or maybe just plain annoyed.

"They'll probably just print that you—she—had a breast augmentation."

Her hands move to her chest, as though her breasts have delicate ears, and the action immediately conjures an image from my memories. Dark hair and pale sheets, her expression sated, and her eyes heavy lidded. Her hands over her breasts, nipples pebbled and peeking from between her spread fingers.

Fuck. Maybe board shorts were the wrong choice. They don't leave a lot to the imagination. Can't go to the beach half-cocked.

Dick cancer. Prostate exam. The baby's yours. Erection be gone!

I can't go to the beach half-cocked . . . but maybe Oliver could. "I'm sure that will be *super* helpful!"

At Mila's retort, my thoughts snap back.

"Right alongside the story of her recent Brazilian butt lift."

"You don't need one?"

"I know that! It's more that I need lipo." Her lips clamp together, becoming thin, pale lines.

"You leave that ass alone."

"What are you even—"

"That ass is a work of art. Don't you know a man likes a little jiggle when he spanks it."

"Dream on." She snorts. "Because *that* is never going to happen."

At least until you remember it already has.

"And it's very ungentlemanly of you to mention such things." She bristles, her movements jerky and her retort staccato.

"Dammit, you've guessed my secret. I'm no gentleman," I say, dropping my head to roll the ridiculous fedora down my arm and into my hand.

She tsks. "It's no secret, because a gentleman doesn't accuse his companion of wearing a tent."

"Looks like a—"

"My cover-up might look like a circus tent, but at least I'm *not* a clown."

I grin but don't bite, rolling the hat in the opposite direction. Palm to arm, arm to head. A trick my grandfather taught me, back when he was alive and our relationship extended to tricks and light-hearted moments.

"You'd prefer me to lie to you? Just let me know, because I don't want to get it wrong when you ask me 'Does my arse look big in this?'" I intone in Brit-speak and an octave or two higher.

"You are delusional if you think—"

"And you have a glorious ass. I want to squeeze it. Bite it. Ride it."

"I think you're managing that last one quite well already. Talk about reversal of stereotypes, because you're a nag."

"You know that's not what I mean. Let the record show, if it doesn't already, that I'm a fan of your ass. Its number one fan, in fact."

"Delusional and ridiculous. Look, are we going to go to the beach or not?" she demands.

"Is the hat staying?" I point to it.

Mila inhales and pushes the breath forcefully from her nose. "Fine. I'll go and change."

The next time Mila leaves the bedroom, it's in a sarong that's knotted at the back of her neck. It's dark, flowing, and pretty, but still conceals all that goodness beneath. Same goes for the wide-brimmed hat, which she grabs as we leave.

The sunglasses she doesn't take. Mainly because I've hidden them.

I lead her out through the private garden, lush with palm trees and bright tropical plants; citrus-colored gingers, vividly pink hibiscus, and birdlike heliconia sway in the mild breeze.

"The steps are pretty steep," I warn as I pull the heavy wooden door closed behind us. "And there are a lot."

"But the view makes it worthwhile," she answers, gathering the sarong away from her knees.

"Yeah, it does," I say, staring at her ass. "Maybe you should take that off. For safety."

"Good try." That smile, or half of it in profile, twists something deep in my gut. I watch as she holds the rail and begins to descend, to move away, when I'm hit by a wave of sorrow. The sensation is fleeting, the reason not fully formed, as I begin to jog down the steps to reach her.

"I meant to ask," I say, once alongside her again. "Do you think Elton John will want his sunglasses back?"

"You would try the patience of a saint," she murmurs serenely. "Six days. I can cope for six days."

That melancholy tightens in my chest, the unformed thought taking root in my head. *One day soon I'll watch as she walks out of my life.*

"Six days," I repeat, banishing the thought. "What are we going to do with six whole days?"

"I don't know about you, but I'm going to enjoy a little sun, sea, and—"

"Sex?"

Her lovely lips twist. "I was going to say *serenity*, but I realize that's not possible where you are."

"And you can't have a honeymoon without a groom."

She makes an unhappy sound, and we both fall quiet until we reach the bottom step. Mila hops from it like an excited kid, beaming at the stretch of golden sand.

"It's deserted," she says, a tiny bit breathless. Which makes me think about sex. Who am I kidding? After last night, everything about her makes me think about sex. Her hair smells like night jasmine and her skin is so smooth, it's like I can't get enough of her.

"It's a private beach."

"Really?" She turns quickly, and her expression steals my breath, her dark eyes sparkling with wonder and delight. Then, "Oh!" Her foot sinks into the fine sand, twisting in her sandal and making her almost topple. I reach out and grab her arm.

"Careful." Electricity shoots through me at the touch. Our eyes meet, hers umber in the afternoon light as I suffer the strangest sensation. I want her to look at me with that kind of wonder. I want to be the source of her delight.

"A private beach." The tiniest tip of her tongue darts out to wet her lips as her eyes drop to my mouth.

It would be easy to lean in, press my lips to hers, but I won't. I can make myself open to the prospect, but the first move has to be hers. A chance encounter with a stranger in a dark closet is one thing. Getting to know her, feeling something for her—connection, attraction, and more—that all changes things.

"Private. Perfect for a honeymoon."

She begins to pull away. "Pretend honeymoon, so don't get any ideas."

Ah, Mila. It's too late for that. "Wait."

She turns back, her brows pulled in. But I'm already taking her smooth calf in my palm.

"Oh." Her palm is warm on my back as I pull off her pink flip-flops. *One. Two.* I throw them in the direction of the stairs.

"Can't do that on Southend." Her words sound a little shaky, and she shoots me a hesitant smile. "Someone's dog would run off with them."

How easily she makes me laugh.

We walk in a companionable silence along the shoreline. When I reach for her hand, she allows it, but just for the benefit of those who might be watching, she insists. The surf gently rolls in, warm and inviting over our toes as we head toward a dark rocky outcrop. The world is quiet but for the sound of the water and the press of our feet into wet sand.

It's pretty perfect.

"It's so beautiful here." Her attention flits my way. "I can see why they'd travel halfway around the world to get married here."

"It is special." I've always loved the island, though I don't get to spend nearly enough time here. Work keeps me busy. But also, that sixteen-hour flight plus a helicopter flight is a lot. But it's mainly work that keeps me away.

"Do all the suites have access to this beach?"

"Nope. This stretch is totally private to our suite."

"I can't imagine what it must cost to stay here." Her murmur seems a little awe filled. It seems to immediately embarrass her as her lips purse, her attention sliding out over the water. "Not that they have to consider that sort of thing, I suppose," she adds eventually.

"You should come again. On me."

From under her hat, she mutters something that sounds unpleasant.

"I'm serious."

"Seriously smutty."

"I'm serious. And smutty. But I hadn't meant it like that. Although . . ." As she reaches over and playfully punches me in the arm, I react in kind. *"Oof!"*

"It comes as second nature to you."

"Let me rephrase. You can visit here anytime. *Mi casa es tu casa.*"

"That's kind of you."

And that was a very polite English brush-off.

"Hell, if we don't get an annulment, you might be entitled to half the place."

Her hand slides from mine, and it takes me a couple of steps to realize she's no longer walking with me. I glance back.

"Please stop saying things like that. It's not funny," she adds, obviously deciding I'm not taking this seriously enough. "If other people hear you—"

"Who?" I hold my arms wide and glance around the deserted beach. "Who would hear?"

"I don't have a lot going for me right now, but I do have my professional reputation."

"Mila, it was a joke." What hasn't she got in her life? Other than money, which I guess is obvious now.

"I know it probably looks like I'll do anything for money," she said. But if that were the case, we wouldn't be having this conversation. She'd be doing cartwheels along the beach after googling my net worth. So what am I missing here? And what can I do to help?

Is it weird that's what I want to do? Help her. Be useful. Be by her side. Be fucking hers.

"Just knock it off. Please."

"Okay." I give a short shrug and walk back, taking her hand again. "Promise." We begin to walk again.

Women. They usually maintain they're interested in my pretty face, my cock, and my cash, in that order. Though I am aware that, for some—for a lot—the order is reversed. It's not always as mercenary as all that. Sometimes it's my profile, my status, that they're looking to benefit from. I've dated a lot of women, and I've never made a big deal of my background, but when the topic of money inevitably comes up, I've never found a woman repulsed by my wealth.

I guess Mila is a two-out-of-three kind of woman.

And I am undeterred.

"Holding the wedding here was my gift to them," I admit. "It wasn't supposed to cost them a dime."

She lifts her head, her gaze almost apologetic. "That's generous."

"I wish it had worked," I say, shrugging off the compliment. "It's my suite." I glance up at the volcanic rock face, not sure why I feel uncomfortable saying so. I don't normally feel bad for being rich. "The one we're staying in, I mean."

"Wow. Lucky you."

Simply by virtue of my birth, that's true. But I've worked hard my whole life and grown the money I was born to. My share of my grandfather's estate has doubled since he passed, but that's not to say I don't realize how lucky I am compared to most folks.

"And also unlucky, as it turns out," she adds with a hint of malicious glee.

Fuck me, I love that look on her. It seems to say *Look at what I'm about to do to you.* Well, bring it on, bunny, because I want the full experience. "How so?"

"Because I'll be kicking you out of your own bed tonight. That seems *so much* worse than being banished from a random hotel bed to me."

"You think you're kicking me out of my own bed?" The thoughts that flash behind my eyes aren't exactly PG. *Just a husk of a man, discarded after she's had her wicked way with me.*

A man can hope. And this man hopes for a lot of things.

"The good news is you have a lot of other beds to choose from."

"How do you mean?" Is she needling me? *Fucking Oliver.*

"Well, you do own the place," she says, glancing behind us.

"But I only have one bed of my own."

"Pity."

"That didn't sound pitying." I begin to swing her hand, when she slows and turns to me with a small but wicked grin.

"Oh. I do pity you, *and* I feel bad now, because I've just realized you can't really sleep in another room. Not unless you want to run the risk of ruining Evie and Oliver's *actual* honeymoon."

"And that would happen how?"

"You don't want to be responsible for a rumor suggesting their marriage is already in trouble, do you?" She cups a thoughtful hand to her chin. "Though I suppose you could get Sarai to dress up as housekeeping and she could roll you out in one of those industrial laundry hampers."

"I see you've put some thought into this."

Her dark eyes wide, she gives a pleased nod.

"But if we're gonna sneak anyone out, why not you?" My eyes slide over her form. "You'd fit into a hamper much easier than I would."

"You just can't help yourself, can you?" she says, cocking her hip and pressing her fist to it.

"I figure I'd better do it now while I'm still cute. In another few years I'll just be labeled a lecherous old goat."

Her laughter echoes inside me. "Oh, I think you'll get away with it for a few more years yet."

"You mean I might grow into my handsomeness?"

"No, your big head. Anyway, I'm not being smuggled out in a laundry hamper, because I'm far too conscientious to risk my client's future happiness. If you say I can't sleep in the bed, then I'll just woman up and sleep on the sofa." She gives a flick of one shoulder.

"I didn't say you couldn't sleep in the bed. You can. With me."

"Sofa it is, then," she adds with a martyrish sniff.

"Want to step this relationship up a notch?"

"Are your ears pinned on? I'm not sleeping with you!"

"I meant we could have an iconic frolic in the waves," I say. "Fool around in the surf for the benefit of our potential audience, kind of *From Here to Eternity* style."

Her mouth flattens, but her eyes dance.

"Not for the media, the 'Gram, or the grope," she retorts, watching as I pull the ridiculous pink hat from my head. "What are you doing?" Suddenly, she's disconcerted, her attention moving to the ocean and the boats on the horizon.

"Going for a dip." I drop the hat and reach back to the neck of my T-shirt.

"But . . . but the journalists might see."

"Oliver got a haircut, remember?" I rub my palm over the bristles. "And Evie's hair goes really dark when it's wet," I say, whipping the straw monstrosity from her head.

"Hey!" She makes a grab for it. Too late, as I throw it into the air and it's carried from her reach by a sudden breeze.

"Last one in gets the couch!" Sand fills the spaces between my spread toes as I pivot.

"What? No!" she yells. "Fin DeWitt, you are a cheating shithead!"

Chapter 12
MILA

I decide not to chase Fin for the sake of my dignity. Same goes for my hat, and I drop down to the sand and fold my legs to my chest.

He can have the bed. It doesn't matter where I sleep. I probably won't get a wink anyway. Not when he's sleeping just one wall away.

I watch the water splash and glisten as he jogs out, then wades deeper and deeper before diving under the surface with the grace of a selkie.

Mila, mate. You may as well face facts: you are going to fuck him.

"No. No, I'm not," I mutter, arguing with the voice in my head that sounds suspiciously like Ronny's again.

I'm not sure if it's better or worse that I don't remember the first time, though it does seem telling how I almost orgasmed when he placed his hand on my thigh. A slight exaggeration, but it did feel nice. It made me all fluttery. I hate to admit it, but it was as though my body recognized his touch.

I'm so relieved he agreed to keep this whole thing between us, though I felt a twinge of guilt when he said his friends would blame him if they got wind of things. And my heart gave a little pinch when he said I could blame him too.

Fin DeWitt is a perplexity. He's so annoyingly confident, but I think that admission might've been a flash of his soft underbelly. It was almost as though he'd been worn by people's opinions of him.

The man shaved off his 'stache for you—shaved it off to kiss you! And he shaved off his hair because—

I give my head a shake, cutting off that train of thought. *I'm not going to have sex with him,* I silently intone as I aggressively tug the sides of my sarong over my bare legs. Even if he did both of those things for me. Whether he did it to please me or because he wanted to kiss me or get me naked, it doesn't matter.

He can be vulnerable, and he can be sweet. He can have more charisma, more rizz, than anyone else I know. He can make my head swim with desire and my skin prickle with longing, but it makes no difference. I'm just not having sex with him.

Who are you trying to persuade? You remember that prick Adam, right? How he made you feel?

Oh, piss off, not-Ronny!

I can resist. I just need to remember that the longing I feel is often the craving to put my fist in his face. Or maybe his kidneys. His face is too lovely to spoil.

"Come on in!"

My head jerks up at Fin's voice. Sunlight glistening from his wet chest, his smile wide and free. He's so easy on the eyes. Nice to kiss too.

Plus, he has a very pretty dick.

I groan, pressing my forehead to my knees. Why, oh why, has my psyche placed Ronny in the driving seat of my train of thought?

"The water is glorious!"

I sigh, because it was warm on my toes and it looks so inviting.

I watch as Fin throws himself backward into the deep water, commencing a perfect-looking backstroke. His strong arms work with perfect timing, the sun and water creating a glorious effect on his body.

I'm a bit of a water baby myself—I always have been. Last year, when things weren't quite so hectic, I even did a bit of wild swimming. I should be in there, splashing around and enjoying myself. Instead of watching from the sidelines. Or the sand, I suppose, as I dig my toes in deeper.

I was so excited to get this gig, not just in monetary terms, though mostly those terms. It had been a few years since I last experienced a few days in the sun. I was looking forward to a day or two of having fun.

As though my toes pushed into the sand isn't enough of a wedge against the water's calling, I begin to scoop up handfuls, depositing them around my feet and ankles.

The truth is, I would be in the water right now if I wasn't experiencing regret in my packing choices. I didn't have money to buy new clothes for this trip, but I did have a few things I'd bought last year and put away for my honeymoon.

Before Adam decided to drop me like a hot pie.

The swimsuit I'm wearing is . . . honeymoon appropriate. *Very revealing* would be another way to phrase it. A plunging neckline, cutout sides, and cut so high in the leg that a wedgie feels just one wrong step away. It's the real reason I pulled out that awful cover-up, which I brought to use in the place of a beach towel more than anything else.

Fin was right. It does look like a circus tent. But it covered my swimsuit better than I thought the sarong would.

I peel the fabric away from my thigh to examine the other issue with my sarong. My thigh is smudged blue from where I washed my hands and splashed it with water, causing the dye to run.

I cast my eyes to the ocean once more, my stomach somersaulting as Fin jogs toward me, wet and glistening.

James Bond, Casino Royale, *eat your heart out.* Daniel Craig has nothing on him. He totally looks like he should be in a gladiator ring, wrestling lions or something.

"You don't like the water." It sounds more like a statement than a question as he reaches me. He glances down at my sand-covered feet, a tiny smile catching at the corner of his mouth.

"I do like to swim," I answer, squinting up at him. Though his broad shoulders cast a shadow, it's not where I need it to be. I wasn't going to ask him where he hid my sunnies.

"So you just like to turn pink and sweaty."

"Ladies don't sweat. They glisten. Did you miss that lesson in health education?"

"I went to an all-boys boarding school. They didn't seem too concerned about the mysteries of women."

I pull a face—an expressive eyebrow lift. I'm sure it would be more effective if I could get them to work independently, but you've got to work with what you have. "You must've committed to an extensive period of . . . independent study following school."

He chuckles, ducking his head, but I don't believe for one minute he's bashful. Why is it the more charming he becomes, the more uncomfortable I feel?

Because you're afraid you'll give in, and not just to him.

"You like to swim but, what? You're afraid of jellyfish? Sharks?"

"Are there sharks in there?"

His answer is to stare at me as though he might be trying to divine my thoughts.

"I don't like my swimsuit, okay?" I shove my fingers under my knees and prop my chin to the top of them. "I thought about swimming in my sarong, but that didn't feel s'right," I mumble ridiculously. "S'wrong, s'right."

"But no one's gonna see. Private beach." He holds his hands out as though inviting me to check for myself. "You can swim naked if you like."

"You wish," I mutter. Then, "And you'll see."

"So keep the sarong."

"And look like a Smurf?" My toes break their sand shackles as I pull the fabric away from my thigh to show him the blue stain.

"Whoa."

"What?" At the strength of his reaction, I glance down and swiftly pull the dark, flowery fabric back. Hell. I just flashed him a whole lot of hip, cleavage, and maybe even a bit of side boob. "I didn't mean to do that."

"Who's complaining?" His answer sounds a little throaty. "I had you pegged as a one-piece kind of girl."

"It is a one-piece. Pervert," I add with a frown.

"Oh, no." He gives a slow shake of his head. "That's more like a half piece."

"There you go being ungentlemanly again."

"On the contrary, it was a compliment. Good job," he adds, ridiculously holding up two thumbs.

"And you think the sun will turn me pink," I mutter.

"Compliments embarrass you?"

"Compliments make me feel weird." As my confession hits the air, I wish I could swallow it back. I've never been the kind of person who is comfortable with praise. Probably because I didn't get a lot of it growing up. Compliments weren't necessary to survival, and survival was what life was about for a while.

The past aside, Fin's compliments make me feel all squirmy inside. But I'd be lying if I said I didn't enjoy the way he looks at me. *Like he wants to devour me.* I also secretly enjoy the things he says, which aren't exactly a Mr. Darcy kind of admiration.

But I've heard worse things.

"Do you think you should be eating carbs so close to the wedding?"

Go forth and multiply, Adam Wainwright.

"You know I'm only looking out for you, right? You wouldn't like your dress to be too tight on our big day."

I hope your dick shrivels up and falls off.

Fin might not be perfect, but he would never be so crass.

His nostrils flare, and I steel myself against what he's about to say. That I'm being stupid or fishing for compliments, or whatever it is that's making him pull that face.

"You're fun and smart, and you have excellent taste," he says, still frowning. "And I don't just mean in husbands, because the way you dressed the pavilion for our wedding was the best I've ever seen it look."

"What?" I interrupt with little effect.

"We had the most beautiful wedding, even if it wasn't meant for us. And that was all your doing."

"It's my job."

"You care, Mila. You care about people, and you care about their feelings. You're kind and you have a big heart. Look at the way you absolved Sarai of her recklessness."

"I don't think—"

"And you've been kind to me. Once or twice." Amusement flickers in his expression. "You're smart and you're diligent, and I'm not the only one who thinks so."

"What are you doing?" I think my skin is trying to creep back to the subcutaneous layer.

"You're conscientious and a little contentious, and in the event of a zombie apocalypse, I'm voting for you to be on the committee of leaders. I fully expect you to have those rotting corpses doing your bidding in days."

I squint up at him again. "Are you on drugs? Because if you're not, you might want to consider it."

"I'm not done. Your ass is heavenly, your hair moves like snakes, your smile is infectious, and your laughter hits me right here." His conclusion is a fist tap to his chest. He doesn't offer anything else.

We stare at each other in silence. And I don't know what to think, let alone say.

Thanks for seeing through me just enough to pull me out of my own head? Or maybe *Thanks for being so weird you make me feel normal.*

"Right, so . . ." I glance away, my insides a mess of conflicting emotions. I feel icky, but it's a good kind of ick. A warm, gooey ick. And sweet, like caramel. I love that he said those things, even if some of them were plain ridiculous.

"Nice snakes," he says out of nowhere. Amends, I suppose.

"Right," I say again. "Thanks for the clarification."

"You're welcome."

"Do you mind telling me why you said all that?" And maybe why my heart is dancing a rumba and my eyes are a tiny bit leaky.

"Desensitization." He shrugs.

"To you?"

"To compliments. Let's call it exposure therapy, DeWitt style."

"You don't even know me." Not really.

"I know enough."

I make a sound. *Pfft!* All air and derision.

"I'm decisive. I make my mind up about a person quickly, and I'm not often wrong. It's what I do for a living."

"What *do* you do?"

"Primarily investor liaison."

"Sounds like another word for *party boy*."

"Party *man*, smut muffin," he chastises playfully.

I quite like that one, not that I'd admit it.

"Maven Inc. is a private-equity company. Real estate, property development, that kind of thing. Entertaining investors is a big part of that. Reading people is what I do, and I do it well."

"A good judge of character."

"I'm an excellent judge of character."

"Excuse, would you mind moving that bushel over a little," I say making a fishtail motion with my hand. "I think your light might be hiding behind it. *Not.*"

"I think I'll take my bushel with me back in the water." He bends, ridiculously scooping up air. "You coming?"

The answer is yes, if he's got anything to do with it, not-Ronny whispers.

I dip my head, then give the tiniest nod. "You first, though."

"You're right. I'll probably get a better view from out there."

"Wait." Even as I say it, I know I'm playing into his hands. Taking one of them even as it's thrust into my line of vision. Fin pulls me to my feet, and it takes everything inside me not to ask him to turn away. But that only would prolong the agony.

"No commenting," I mutter, reaching behind my neck to loosen the knot of my sarong.

"I wouldn't dream of it."

The fabric flutters in a sudden breeze, my fist at my waist the only thing stopping it from blowing away. Without speaking, Fin takes it.

"We should've brought towels," I say as he balls the fabric and presses it into the pink fedora. We don't need them, really, the late afternoon still warm. I'm just waffling, nervous and waiting for his eyes to rise. For him to say something. Anything.

"Come on."

It's what he eventually says, tugging me behind him and into the water.

I smile as we wade in, the warm water so inviting as it licks up my legs.

"Are there sharks? You didn't answer me before."

"Just reef sharks."

"Do reef sharks have teeth?"

"They stay out on the reef and eat the fish. The reef is why there's so little surf."

"Miles of sky; endless beauty; calm, warm waters; and no sharks. Remind me, why do you live in London again?"

"Can't have too much of a good thing."

"Said no one ever."

"And I didn't say there were no sharks." He turns his head to slide me a wicked grin.

"Just reef sharks," I say. "Dwellers of the reef."

"And bamboo sharks."

"Which are obviously vegetarian," I say hopefully. "Like pandas."

"There's a shelf," he says as he turns to face me, his hands reaching for my waist. Behind him, I can see the water turns a deeper blue farther out.

"I'm okay. I'm a pretty experienced swimmer. I've even done a bit of wild swimming back home."

"Sharks should be no problem for you. Not when you've dealt with water cold enough to turn your extremities blue. Not to mention floating condoms."

"Ew!"

"And killer ducks."

My hand lands on his shoulder quite naturally as he pulls me closer. I sense him push off from the ball of his foot, his back gliding through the water as I follow on my side. In my mind, I imagine myself as graceful as a ballerina, though the reality is probably nothing near that, even as my hands glide through the water.

"I forgot the hammerheads." His lips wrap in the shape of a smile as he moves away from me. "Hammerhead sharks."

"I think I've changed my mind," I say, using my hands and feet to tread water, keeping me in one place.

"Don't go."

We're suddenly back to touching, his hands on my waist, his eyes a mixture of storm clouds and silver.

"Jokes," I whisper, resting my hands on his shoulders. Then I shriek as he pulls me under.

Bubbles, air pushed from my nose, before I burst from the water, slicking back my hair. Then I chase after him. We roll, hands touching, skin sliding against skin. We're like a couple of carousing dolphins twirling, turning, playing.

"Monster!" I eventually say as we break the surface at the same time. "You pinched my bum!"

"Sharks," he says, sliding water from his face. "One probably couldn't resist a nibble."

"You!" Using both hands, I drive a wave over him. I don't know what devil possesses me next as I duck under the surface and yank at his shorts.

Oh, my days! I *so* wasn't imagining things.

"I'm sorry," I splutter as I surface. "I didn't mean—"

"Mila," he growls in reprimand.

I squeal, overcome with excitement and his darkened expression and the way his hands disappear as he yanks his shorts back into place. I use the pause in proceedings to duck under the surface and power away.

A quicksilver thrill courses over me as I glide through the water, making for the shore. I imagine him behind me, his fingers reaching for me, just inches away. Exhilaration floods my bloodstream, my fight-or-flight instinct fueling my swim as my legs power me through the ocean's resistance. I'm a decent swimmer, though I don't have Fin's strength, but as something brushes my ankle, my excitement peaks. My heart beats wildly when it happens again. Then Fin pulls me back—pulls me under. Our eyes meet under

146

the surface, air bubbles streaming from our noses before we break together.

"You pinched my bum!" I protest breathlessly as I swipe back my hair, the tips of my toes grazing the sea floor. "You deserved—"

He yanks my body closer, no small feat given the water's resistance.

I gasp as our bodies connect.

"Fuck, Mila, you make me not want to be a gentleman."

That is possibly *the* hottest thing I have ever heard. And this might be the hottest version of Fin, his gray eyes storm cloud dark and his expression hungry.

I wrap my arms around his shoulders, ignoring the warning bells going off in my head. "What does that look like? You not being a gentleman. Seeing as you've such a strong sense of propriety, ordinarily."

His chuckle sounds almost tortured, but that might be the result of me sliding the inside of my knee up his thigh. "No one likes a tease," he utters, gripping it and holding it there.

"Which is exactly what I've been trying to tell you."

"What am I gonna do with you?"

"Leave me alone," I whisper, sliding my finger around the glistening shell of his ear. A shiver-inducing caress.

"Not a chance."

"Maybe stop looking at my boobs, then?"

"I'm not looking at your boobs. I'm looking at your swimsuit. Didn't I tell you I have a kink for swimwear?"

"Kink?" I repeat, but not because I don't understand. I just wondered if it would sound the same if I said it.

"A *huge* kink."

I know something else that's huge, not-Ronny whispers.

"There's just something about the wet look that does it for me," he adds.

"Does what, exactly?" Like I have to ask. Like I can't feel what it does, thanks to the close press of our bodies.

"Revs my engine."

"I'll leave it out for you tonight, if you like. You can use it in your special alone time."

He laughs, throwing back his head, exposing the strong line of his throat. Why does it seem erotic, that stretch of him? Skin and tendons, the muscles working with his swallow.

"It's gotta be wet."

"You can dunk it in the pool."

"Wet hair too. It looks as sexy as fuck on you."

"Better than snakes?"

"I like snakes."

My eyes dip, along with his, and I watch as the tip of his forefinger glides over the soft swell of my breast.

"See how shiny your skin is?"

I nod but—holy moly—cool water, LYCRA, and nipples do not make a modest trinity. *Quartet, if I include the main reason for their stiffness.* I can't seem to help myself as I repeat the stroking action across his glistening cheekbone. "You could sharpen knives on these."

"What's the necklace." Is he interested, or is it just another reason to touch me? I'm not complaining, either way.

"My grandmother gave it to me when I was small. It's to ward off trouble. Ill wishes and evil spirits."

"Doesn't work, huh?"

"Idiot," I chuckle. My bloodstream feels like it's been filled with champagne bubbles as he continues to finger my pendant.

Maybe you should ask him to finger—

Not-Ronny has such a mouth on her.

"These cheekbones are wasted on a man."

"Meaning?"

"I'm jealous of your bone structure."

"Your bone structure gives my bone structure," he replies with perfect seriousness.

Mila girl. You might as well whip off your knickers and hit that good and hard!

"Swimsuit," I say, correcting not-Ronny's admonishment.

"*You* make the swimsuit work. You're built like a goddess, and you're so beautiful, and I fucking hate that you don't think I'm being serious when I say so."

"I don't—"

"You pull a face or roll your eyes. I'm not even sure you know you're doing it."

But he's right. I brush off even the mildest of compliments.

When did I learn to dislike myself so much?

Chapter 13
MILA

The question sticks with me, annoying and embarrassing, like a seed stuck between my front teeth.

Has my self-confidence really eroded away to nothing? Did I do it to myself? Have I allowed my experiences to grind me down?

"You okay?" From across the table, Fin watches me, his glass paused in the air.

"Sorry." I pull my head from my thoughts. "I zoned out. Watching the sunset." The sky is beautiful, not that I was paying it my full attention, my thoughts turned inward, rather. But I am looking at the sky now, the expanse a wash of watermelon and violet as the sun's hazy tangerine orb descends over the horizon.

I thought he might kiss me as we frolicked in the ocean. And despite all my protestations, I thought I might let him.

We dragged ourselves from the water, wrinkled and breathless, and I forced myself not to reach for my sarong. *No need to channel Smurfette.* Plus, I decided to make the effort to be braver. I definitely feel braver after absorbing his praise. Fin swiped up the pink fedora and stuck it on my wet head, announcing, "You wear the hat, you ride the cowboy."

I didn't like to point out that the hat was mine, which would surely mean . . .

No need to mention that.

When he suggested a walk along the beach, we moved toward the volcanic outcrop. I found myself gasping, and for the briefest moment, I forgot I wasn't on my *actual* honeymoon. There, just beyond the dark rocks, in an Instagram-worthy setting, was a white-muslin-draped pergola. A uniformed server waited to seat us with a warm deference and champagne cooling in a silver bucket.

Dinner on the beach, watching the sunset. How dreamily romantic, right?

"I wonder who did the rose petals," I say, now glancing down at the sand. Was this preordered for Evie and Oliver? Or did Fin do this for me? I mean, for our ruse.

"Looks a little like a pentagram," Fin replies at the precise moment I bring my champagne glass to my lips.

I cough-swallow a mouthful of bubbles. Pressing my fingers to my chest, I try not to die due to a lack of air and an excess of bubbles as they burn my throat. Fin frowns and makes to move, aborting the movement when I give my head a tiny shake.

"I'm okay. But, yuck! A little of that came out of my nose." I glance down at the petals again. "I was wondering what the pattern reminded me of."

The petals are red and laid out in swirls, not quite a geometric pattern, but the addition of strategically placed candles does give it a *let's summon a demon for shits and giggles* effect.

We're served dinner as though dining in a MICHELIN-starred restaurant in the middle of London, not sitting in our damp swimwear, hair wild with seawater and salt. *Mine, anyway.* The food is amazing—grilled lobster with a side of melted garlic butter. French beans and dark rye bread, and whoever said you don't make friends with salad never had one that tasted like spring rolls in a bowl. I need the recipe, because that salad and I are destined to be besties.

"Try this." Fin holds out a delicate cake fork with a morsel of chocolate torte balanced on the tines. The waiter offered us both a trio of miniature desserts, though I declined mine. The bread—I ate so much of it.

"Why do you keep trying to put things in my mouth? First it was the butter," I add quickly, flustered by his incendiary expression. I couldn't resist as he offered me the morsel on oven-warmed bread. My thighs can attest I'm a sucker for fresh bread.

"Was I wrong about the butter?" he asks, lowering the fork a touch.

"It was the best butter I've ever tasted. So salty, rich, and creamy."

"Stop that," he says in a low, warning tone.

I give my lashes an innocent flutter. "I don't know what you're talking about."

"Sure you don't." He gives his head a slow, disparaging shake.

"Fine." I drop my gaze to the fork before lifting my eyes. "Just this one time I'll let you put it in my mouth."

Fin barks out the kind of laugh that feels like a glug of good whisky in my chest. He lifts the fork again, and like a good baby bird, I open.

"Oh, my days," I practically moan—and not to tease him either! The mouthful is light, a fluffy—a chocolatey—heaven.

"Good, right?"

"*Mmm*," I agree, pressing my fingers to my lips.

"Eating is one of life's great pleasures. After sex, of course."

I roll my eyes despite loving the way he's watching me. *Like he's the one enjoying dessert.*

"So eat the damn torte," he says, pushing his dainty dessert platter to the center of the table. "Then try the citrus tart."

"But I'm full!"

"Then why were you eyeing my plate like it owed you money?"

"I can look. It doesn't mean I have to taste."

"Yeah. I feel that," he says in that low tone again. "Suffer it anyway."

I frown a frown that's in total opposition to the sensations rioting through me. Once more, I'm sure my nipples could put an eye out. I hunch forward in my seat.

"Come on. Just a little more," he cajoles as he forks the torte. "You can take it. For me."

"When you put it that way, how can I resist?"

"Beats me," he murmurs, leaning closer.

"Oh, my God." I press my fingers to my lips as I slide the fluffy sweetness around in my mouth. "That is just . . ."

"The result of a French pastry chef."

"Is he single?" I ask, pressing my hand over my still-moving mouth because, the flavors!

"You're not."

"What? Oh." I appear to consider his answer. "Only for the purposes of this visit. But I think I could be really into a man who can cook."

"Did your ex cook?"

I give a theatrical sigh. "He tossed salads."

Fin appears to choke and, grasping his napkin, coughs into it. "What?"

"What?" he answers, his eyebrows almost hiding in his hairline.

"What was that? What's funny about tossing salads?"

"Nothing," he says, more composed now.

"Because I did all the chopping and stuff, and . . . eww." I pull a face as the penny drops. "You're nasty!"

"Hey, I'm not the one talking about—"

"Nasty!" I repeat. Balling up my napkin, I throw it at him and half expect him to make me a tactless offer, when the tone of our conversation changes.

"Was he a chauvinist or just not very adept in the kitchen?"

I pause to consider this. "A chauvinist. No. He was controlling. Covertly controlling, I now realize."

"How so?"

"His actions were stealthy." My mind turns inward as I consider my lack of friends. I had friends before I met Adam, and I socialized with them in the early days of our relationship. And then I didn't anymore, without even grasping what had happened. Granted, I had a lot on my plate with Trousseau and Baba, not that she was showing full symptoms of her illness. In the early days I put her erratic behavior down to quirkiness and just old age. I wasn't living with her, so I suppose it was harder to spot.

"I don't actually have any friends," I begin again, ignoring the sharp poke of shame from my admission. "And that's down to him." My tone is pondering as I piece together my thoughts. "It's not as though he ever said 'I forbid you' when I wanted to go out with them, because that would've been too obvious. He would've been rumbled, right?"

Across the table, Fin says nothing but observes all, his expression inscrutable. I press my elbow to the table and my chin to my palm.

"He slowly isolated me from them. Pouting and giving me the silent treatment if I made plans. Making comments about how great it was when just the two of us were cuddled on the sofa on Saturday nights, and how girls out together are only interested in the attention of men." I shift uncomfortably in my seat . "I fell for it, like a Pavlovian response, and that's why I have no friends. I just didn't realize what was happening at the time."

"Manipulators go out of their way to make sure you don't notice. They're experts at using guilt and manipulation. Gaslighting the hell out of you, making you question yourself. Don't feel down on yourself," he adds, probably reading my expression. "It's because you're a good person you didn't realize how fucked in the head he is."

"How do you know?"

"I was raised by a manipulator," he replies, reaching for his glass.

"Oh." That's quite an insight. There's obviously more to Fin than meets the eye. I mean, of course there is. But it doesn't mean I should examine it—him—because this isn't real. But still, being manipulated as a matter of course by a caregiver seems much worse. I might not have had the easiest time growing up, but at least I knew Baba put me and my well-being first. "It's insidious, isn't it, how it happens?"

"Manipulators are cunning."

"He'd oh-so-subtly try to control me, bringing up my insecurities, making me feel horrible about myself. The things he said—the salad obsession and 'You're eating chocolate? Again?'—never came from a place of caring or concern. It wasn't even about my health or fitting into my clothes. It was just to make me feel bad about my appearance."

"To knock your confidence," Fin adds. "Because he had to make himself feel better somehow, right?" He takes a mouthful of his drink and puts down his glass. "He was intimidated by you."

"I don't know about that."

"People only put others down because they're insecure. The smaller you feel, the less confident and competent, the better they feel about themselves. Your ex did a damn good job of making sure you wouldn't leave him."

"Ah, but he left me."

"Then he did you a favor in the end."

"I know that, but . . ." My chest feels tight, and I realize I'm fighting tears. "His timing could've been better, given he almost made me homeless. I feel so supremely stupid when I think of how I trusted him and how he treated me. Why did I put up with that?"

"Like you said, it happened without you realizing. And I'd like to correct you on one thing. You do have a friend. You have me."

"My accidental husband," I say, biting back an awkward smile. "I'm not sure our friendship will thrive, let alone survive this experience. You're very annoying, you know."

Fin settles back in his chair. "I'll take that over ambivalence."

My gaze dips to the remains of Fin's dessert. I scoop my finger through the rich chocolate torte and bring it to my mouth. "I think I could cope with a gay husband if he made me food like this."

"Is that my cue to take a culinary course?"

"Cute." The word hits the air in a small huff as I dig in a second time. This time, when I look up, Fin's gaze is dark. Hungry. And not for torte. Flustered, I reach for my champagne glass.

"It might be worth it," he murmurs. "Watching you eat feels like a sexual experience."

"That's . . . weird."

"Is it? I guess I just like to see you enjoying yourself."

My body heats, flushed with pleasure. Yet I feel awkward and self-conscious at the same time. Not because he's watching but maybe because he's paying attention. *Caring.* The word whispers in my mind. Reaching for my champagne glass, I bring it to my lips. "Enough to let me marry a gay pastry chef?"

"We could just take him home?" Leaning back in his chair, he makes an expansive motion.

I pretend to consider it, tilting my head. Then I imagine Fin kissing another man. *Hot or not?* It's hard to tell, given my brain seems to have made *me* the other man. "That sounds a bit kinky," I find myself answering eventually.

Fin laughs. Smuttily.

"I meant I could employ him back in London. While I'd love to make all your fantasies come true, maybe we can table that one for a special date. Say, our thirtieth wedding anniversary."

"Very funny." But again, I'm pink with pleasure. The man is very practiced in his craft. And I need to remind myself of that. "I think I'd rather have cake than sex, anyway." My hand flies to my mouth as I chuckle behind it. "Is there truth serum in this?"

"Not by that answer."

"Shows what you know," I retort smoothly.

"I know you like sex, same as I know you like cake. But it seems to me you enjoy one more over the other."

"I'll have to take your word for it, because last night doesn't count."

He slides me a doubtful look.

"Because I don't remember."

"Want a reminder? Right here? Right now?"

I pull a face. "Tempting, but I'm sure the sand would be uncomfortable."

"Say the word, and I'll carry you back to the suite."

"You'd have a heart attack carrying me up all those stairs. I'll just stick to cake, thanks."

"And what about the closet?" he all but purrs.

"We didn't have sex there."

"And you didn't enjoy it either." He gestures to my glass. "That's not truth serum."

Just as well, not-Ronny whispers.

"But getting back to the other thing." He leans a little closer across the table. "What the fuck." His dark tone sends a beetle skittering down my spine. "He made you homeless?"

"I couldn't afford the rent on my own." Thanks to Trousseau's downturn. "I didn't know how he'd manage it either. Obviously, because I didn't know he had another woman waiting in the wings." Maybe I shouldn't be telling him any of this. He's not really my friend. I don't want his pity, and I'm sick and tired of feeling like a blind idiot.

"What a fucking asshole."

I startle as Fin sits suddenly forward but release a long breath when I realize he's just topping up my glass. The angry look on his face is real enough, though.

"It's not as though I found myself on a park bench or anything."

"I'm gonna ruin him," he says, leaning back in his chair.

I make a weird *ha ha* sound, because that's just nonsensical. Even if he looks like he's enjoying the prospect. "I just moved in with my grandmother."

"Baba Roza, right?"

"Yes," I say, slightly disconcerted. "How do you know?"

"You mentioned her name last night." His expression doesn't flicker. It doesn't reveal a hint of what else I might've said. "You told me your father's family is from Macedonia and that your mom's people were from Cornwall."

I nod, not sure what to say. This feels so unnatural. We've had sex; we're married, even; but we barely know a thing about each other. *Well, he seems to know a bit more about me.* Did I tell him I had to put Baba in a care home? That guilt gnaws at my soul?

"I lost my parents when I was young," he says. "We have that in common."

I bite my tongue against asking if he's reading my mind or my face. I bet his grandmother wasn't almost sixty when she took over his care. Or an immigrant with an accent as thick as her saggy woolen stockings.

I used to feel deep embarrassment when she'd come to my school's open evenings. Her headscarf would be fastened tight under her neck and her darned cardigan buttoned right under it. When times were tough, I wore shoes with tattered toes and cardboard-stuffed soles, and I felt ashamed. But Baba had a deep fear of the state, I now know. I'm sure we would've been entitled to government benefits, but she feared they might take me away. So we made do. I wore other children's castoffs and would open my lunch box to cold toasted sandwiches filled with feta cheese and marinated bell peppers. Sounds quite bougie by today's standards, but back then, all I wanted in the world was a little plastic pot of Kraft's Lunchables.

I know Baba was doing her absolute best. She just came from a different time and a different place. She uprooted her life, moved from her village—the only home she'd ever known—to look after me. The least I can do now is repay that care.

"Do you still live with your grandmother?"

Can't we go back to laughing over misunderstandings and threesomes with the French pastry chef? It's hardly a sexy question. The answer even less so.

"I'm still living in her flat. But not for much longer." Under the table, I cross my fingers. *Please let it be so.* At least now I'll have money, which means I'll also have choices. "My business was struggling." I shrug.

Fin's expression turns pensive, which is better than sympathy. "Breakups are a lot."

"True story." My gaze dips as I draw my finger through the condensation on my glass. "It wasn't because of the breakup, though I'm sure it couldn't have helped. I didn't cancel on my clients. They canceled on me." I feel my brows knit, my mind wandering down that well-trodden path of *how*. "Now that I think of it, the cancellations began not long after we met."

"Maybe the financial downturn? It's been hard on people."

I give my head a quick shake. "Not the kind of people I was dealing with. Money wasn't an issue for them. Some of them even forfeited their entire fees. There are no refunds after a certain period in the contract, you see." At least I still got paid for those.

"Did you have many cancellations?"

"Yes," I admit, glancing up. "And then future bookings started to fail."

"Did you ask your clients why they canceled?"

"The ones who would return my calls," I reply. "Not that they were very forthcoming. The ones I managed to speak to were cold—icy cold, come to think of it. But I had other things going on. I didn't have the brain space to dwell, because my grandmother . . ." There are too few words and too many thoughts for me to adequately explain.

I knew Baba's health was beginning to fail, but it took living with her again to notice that her mind was failing too. There was, and there is, a lot of guilt with those realizations. She gave up her life to look after me, and when the time came that she needed me to pay attention to her, I was too wrapped up in my own problems to notice.

"Tough times," he says softly.

"Yeah. It sounds strange, but I wondered for a time if what was going on with my business might somehow be linked to the night we met."

"How do you mean?" Fin tilts his head as though he doesn't want to miss a thing.

"I'm not sure, really. The timing, I suppose. I know it was just a coincidence, but I did consider it. Remember I told you how I heard about Adam's engagement?"

"Yeah."

"So I was hiding in the closet after one of the chefs told me Adam had just proposed."

"Because he didn't have the balls to tell you himself," he repeats, his disgust still very evident.

"Well, I suppose I lost my composure."

Lost your shit, more like, not-Ronny counters.

"I can see that happening."

"The news of his engagement was just the tip of a very nasty iceberg. You see, as far as they were concerned—the kitchen crew and the waitstaff, the management, even—Adam had been single the whole time we were engaged. And that's why the chef added how surprised they all were that Rachel, the ex–duty manager, had accepted his proposal." I inhale deeply. "You see, Adam had boned half of the hotel's servers that year."

"Oh, Mila."

"So not only did I find out he was engaged just weeks after our split, which was suspicious enough, but I also discovered he'd been chronically unfaithful. It wasn't just that hotel either. He'd been flaunting his infidelity right under my nose. Probably for years."

"Ah, shit."

"It was a bit shit," I answer breezily as I ignore my burning cheeks and the poke of discomfort in my chest. I feel like such an idiot recounting this. "He let me get excited about our wedding. He let me waffle on about colors and flowers, make a down payment on catering, and even buy a dress. And all the while, he had no intention of getting married. Not to me, anyway."

"That is fucked up. So fucked up."

"So I wondered . . ." I straighten the dessert plate an inch, move my napkin from the right of the table to the left. Anything rather than see his pity. "Wondered if the news somehow got out that I'd completely lost it in the hotel kitchen. That I shouted and I cried and cursed and basically made a holy show of myself. I wondered if that's why—if I'd been deemed mentally unstable. I mean, it was completely out of character and so unprofessional. I was mortified the next day, and for many days afterward."

But in the moment, I was just unhinged. Crazed. "Hell hath no fury" and all that. Even later, when I found myself accompanied in the coat closet, the experience felt unreal. Like an out-of-body experience, almost.

"You didn't hear anything about it by any chance, did you?" I ask, meeting his gaze finally.

Fin shakes his head. Pissed on my behalf, he's all dark, stormy eyed and tense jawed.

I try not to like his reaction too much.

"It was just a theory," I say with a small shrug. "A brief theory, but none of the guests can have seen or heard, really. It was after dinner, so most of them were already smashed."

"Were you hoping you could patch things up? That he'd change his mind, maybe?"

"God, no. We'd been over for a few weeks at that point. I wasn't grieving him, because I'd already begun to examine how he'd manipulated me." How I'd misconstrued his behavior for love in the beginning and how it had just become the norm. How stupidly willing I was to overlook all that just because I didn't want to be alone. No friends, barely any family, and lurking at the back of my mind was the realization that, once Baba left the world, I'd have no one. I shiver as though something unpleasant has just scuttled down my spine. Death is a part of life, but that doesn't mean I want to think about it.

"Good," he says. "I'm glad."

"It took a little distance to truly see, but in that moment, I was so angry. How fucking dare he? After my outburst, I just wasn't in the mood to deal with a wedding and all that outpouring of love."

"Drunken or otherwise," Fin puts in with a sad smile.

"Exactly. The wedding was over, but for sore heads and next-day regrets. So I swiped a bottle of champagne and hid in the coat closet where no one would find me."

"No one but me."

I give in to a small smile. "You were the highlight of my night." And I'd been living on that memory since.

"And the dread of it when I turned up here again."

"I thought I'd hidden my feelings quite well."

At this, he laughs.

"It's strange how things turn out sometimes."

"And sometimes, though they hurt, they turn out for the best in the end."

"I suppose. The night we broke up, Adam said he loved me but that he wasn't in love with me."

Fin grimaces. *Such a terrible cliché.*

"I asked him why he'd proposed when he didn't love me, how he could let me plan my wedding. But he just kept banging on about how he'd been lying to himself. No mention of lying to me. Or even an apology." I roll my suddenly tense shoulders, my anger rising like a spark from a tinderbox.

Enough. I can't believe I just spewed all my personal ick. My deepest, darkest secrets. How I was taken in by Adam for all those years.

"Story time over." I give a brittle-feeling smile. I sit straighter in my chair and try to decipher Fin's expression. There's sadness and, *urgh*, pity. "You don't have anything to add?" I ask lightly. "No quip to make me laugh?" *Please make me laugh.* "Maybe you'd like to offer me a quick shag, just so I can kick you under the table?"

"You can kick me if it makes you feel better."

My heart plummets, and tears suddenly prickle.

"Your ex isn't just a manipulative asshole. He's fucking cruel."

I grab my napkin and twist it between my fingers, forcing back the ball of emotion creeping up my throat. "I bet you can't believe we're having this conversation. I know I can't. I feel a bit like a geyser—not a *geezer*," I amend in my version of Cockney patois. "This is the first time I've really talked about it. With anyone."

"We can talk about it for as long as you want."

"Why are you so nice?"

His face. It's like I've insulted him.

"What's wrong with *nice?*"

"It's what every man wants to hear." His reply sounds like a roll of the eyes. He rocks back in his chair and stretches, clasping his hands to the back of his head.

"I'm sorry. Did I tweak your masculine sensibilities with a compliment?"

"*Nice* is not a compliment."

"Yes, it is. Being called *nice* is nice. I like it when someone says I'm—"

"Nice? No, honeybuns. *Nice* means you can't come up with anything more positive. And I know you can." His eyes move hotly over me.

"*Nice* is good," I protest as my heart begins to canter.

"So I'm nice?"

"That's what I said, didn't I?"

"Nice what? Nice looking? I have nice manners? Nice teeth? A nice cock?"

"You're nice when you're not talking," I retort.

"How about this for an entirely *nice* proposition?" His voice is all husk and gravel suddenly.

I hold up my finger—*pause, please*—reach for my glass, and drain it. Something tells me I might need it. "Go on."

"I'm so nice, I think you should consider having sex with me."

I snort. "That is not news."

"I'm serious."

"Of course you are." Why do I sound like an indulgent aunt?

"I think you should have sex with me for no other reason than you want to."

"*I* want to?"

"Sure, I do too," he admits, with a flick of his shoulder.

"Of course you do!" I find my hands in the air, my amusement feigned. Because what I really feel is a lot more complicated. What I remember from last night makes me want to press my lips, my fingerprints into his skin.

"Meaning?"

"That's you. You're all about casual relationships," I retort, twirling my hand in the air like I'm winding a bobbin. "And hooking up."

"Only, we're married." He's all lounging, tawny, and relaxed. Like a lion pretending he's not about to pounce.

"Well, I'm not your pity project."

"I don't pity you, sweetness. I want to fuck you. This is about you and me and how amazing we were together. I got the sense it was cathartic for you, that maybe you needed it. You deserve to let go, and you ought to be desired. And I want and desire you like nothing else."

"No one needs sex," I say, trying not to hang on to his reasoning like it's a lifeboat. *I am my own captain, dammit.*

"We all need connection."

"Some of us more than others," I add under my breath. "Thank you for the *very nice* offer, but no thank you." This wasn't as easy to say as my delivery made it sound.

"Just think about it. Five whole days and five nights to realize all those fantasies."

"I don't know what you're talking about." The words come out of my mouth with horns.

"Yeah, you do. You're just a little surprised that I know too."

"Shrooms must make a girl fanciful."

"I could be your holiday romance. The one you packed your fancy wedding panties for."

"Oh, yes," I splutter, "because boffing for five days solid sounds *so* romantic."

"Come on, honeybuns. You know better than that."

"Stop calling me that! I'm still trying to work out why *bunny*," I add in an unhappy mutter.

"I could tell you. If you ask me. Nicely."

"I'll pass, thanks."

Despite my dismissive words, I get a shimmery feeling in my chest when he laughs.

Sex with Fin would be amazing. I remember enough to know that without a doubt. Why else would I have spent months thinking of him and a dark closet?

But I can't say yes, no matter how tempting he is. Five days might not be long enough to fall in love, but it's perfectly long enough to ruin things. *If Oliver Deubel finds out, one night might already be enough.* I push the unhelpful thought away. I'm so close to the end of my troubles, and sex with Fin is not a chance I'm willing to take.

But when I think about returning to London, everything seems so gray and heavy. Hard and inevitable, like my choices will be stripped away. Right now, I'm living my version of champagne wishes and caviar dreams. I just can't afford to indulge.

This golden man and his golden existence can't understand. Not even in his worst nightmares could he imagine what it's like to live my life. He probably couldn't even name a social housing estate in London, let alone have stepped foot in one. He can't know what it is to run the daily gauntlet of street-dwelling criminals, their presence frightening and their catcalls predatory. I'm certain that, in his perfectly posh corner of London, wherever that is, he's never heard his neighbor beat his wife to a bloody pulp through an adjoining wall.

There can be no fantasies realized for me, no holiday romance. I need to grab this opportunity, not risk it. Grab it with both hands, claw my way out of this life for the second time.

I clear my throat, suddenly realizing Fin is watching me.

"Maybe I should just call you *puddin'*."

"Like dessert?" *Because I ate too much of it?* I think darkly.

His gaze moves over me in something that feels like a promise. It leaves every inch of my skin tingling and wanting as my foolish body fights my brain.

"Because you're the dish I want to lick."

His words make me feel like his tongue is already inside me.

"I imagine that sounded better in your head," I lie as I sit forward to ease the empty ache between my legs. "Maybe the problem is yours. Could it be the thought of not having sex for a whole week?"

A tiny crease forms between his brows.

"Is that why you're relentless. Are you feeling a little desperate, Fin?"

"I had sex yesterday, so . . . there goes that theory."

God, I am *such* a sucker for those hot, intense looks of his. "I'm just sorry your come-ons have no discernible effect on me," I say, leaning back in my chair once more.

He sighs as he puts his elbow to the tabletop and his chin to his fist. "Then I guess only your nipples are into me."

Chapter 14
MILA

Wifey. Sugar tits. Sugar nips. Medusa. Gremlin. Honeybuns—plural. *Slut muffin. Smut muffin. Bunny.* And now *puddin'*.

I shouldn't be flattered by all that, should I?

I'm not sure if he was serious about *daddy*, but *thundercock* suits him. *Anatomically, at least.* My shoulders creep up under my ears as I give in to a giggle that Muttley, the cartoon dog, would be proud of. I think my blush might run all the way to the roots of my hair. *What an eyeful that was.* I can't believe I (underwater) pantsed him—what devil possessed me?

As my giggle recedes, I give myself an internal shake. All the things I told him, all the cringe-inducing failures of my life. Was I trying to put him off?

And why didn't it work?

It doesn't matter. I can't get caught up in this, I decide as I pull my feet up onto the sofa and curl them under my bum. My phone sits on the sofa arm, charged and connected to the Wi-Fi, but I'm trying very hard to ignore it. Same goes for listening to Fin moving around in the bedroom. Bare padding footsteps and toneless humming, and the odd question he calls out that I can't ignore.

Such as: "Wanna come watch me shower?"

"No thanks!" I call back.

Maybe it's more that I was trying to make it so awkward that I'd be too embarrassed to even think about sleeping with him. Not that it worked. Memory fragments from our wedding night don't exactly help.

You could be his little puddin'. The dirty vessel he'd like to lick clean.

I absolutely ignore not-Ronny's words, even as between my legs thrums at the thought.

The truth is, I've never wanted anything as much as I want him. But I can resist—I don't have poor impulse control!

I will not jump Fin DeWitt's bones.

I will reside serenely next to him until Friday without giving in to temptation.

I should write it out five hundred times. I just need to find a pencil and notebook. *And some self-control.*

Fin is a whole lot of man and a whole lot of fun, but this isn't just about me. It's about Baba, about securing both our futures. I want fun in my life. I want a relationship and love and a family of my own in time. All those hopes I put into Adam haven't gone away. But Fin is too much of a risk. A wedding certificate does not a marriage make.

Okay, Yoda.

Ignoring not-Ronny, I decide I need a distraction. I swipe up my phone, only to tap it absently to my chin. It would be absolutely wrong for me to google Fin. First, I don't need to know anything else about him. In fact, the less I know, the better, right? Second, it feels a tiny bit hinky. Like an invasion of his privacy. Even if the information is in the public domain.

It would be wrong—all kinds of wrong. Especially after watching how distressed Evie was before she left. I mean, Fin wasn't chased out of a church by a vengeful fiancée, but I bet there are still things on the net that he'd prefer weren't there.

But maybe the fact that he wouldn't want me to know is the exact reason I should know. Sensible women google men before they meet them for dates.

But we're not dating.

We're . . . something else. Something that defies all logic.

I've confessed all my ridiculousness to him. *Well, not all of it.*

I wonder how many of Fin's dates google his net worth first. Not that I'm interested in his wallet. What he has in his pants, however . . .

It's a very good thing I have self-control, I decide as I slide my thumb over the lock.

The screen lights up.

And I quickly type out a text:

Miss your face.

My phone vibrates with a message immediately.

RONNY: New phone. Who dis?

She deleted me? I've only been gone a couple of days!

Not that we're friends. Maybe we are sort of friends, even if I'm ten years older than her. Ronny's popped over a lot since Baba went into the nursing home. But she's just a kid—nineteen—it's not like she's the type to listen to me pour out my heart over a bottle of rosé.

Actually, she probably would. Though I'm not sure she'd be much good for advice. You can't take dating advice from someone whose own dating life comes with a curfew.

Almost immediately, my phone vibrates again.

RONNY: Lol/jks. What's up?

ME: I thought you'd forgotten me!

RONNY: How could I forget my fav neighbor and potential boss-lady?

Ronny is looking for a summer job, and this is another of her not-so-subtle hints. At least I'll be able to help her out on this front now. Doing what, I'm not sure. Ronny is a little rough around the edges.

ME: I might just have something for you.

RONNY: That news is so hype! Can I call round?

ME: Not yet. I'm still in Indonesia.

RONNY: Flexing! I like.

ME: Not so much. I'm here for work, remember?

At that very moment, my work project walks into the living room in a pair of thin cotton shorts. *Hello, thundercock . . .*

"Did you only pack one T-shirt?" I ask pertly.

"Sorry?" He glances down at his chest. To be fair, so do I.

"You had a T-shirt on earlier. Did you forget where you put it?"

"You should be thankful I'm not free ballin'," he replies. "That's my usual vacation style."

I close my mouth and dip my eyes back to my phone.

ME: Something came up and I have to stay longer. I'll call you when I'm home.

RONNY: Want me to call in and see Roza?

ME: Would you? That would be great.

Relief floods through me. Despite my reasons for doing this, it's been almost impossible to ignore the guilt of not being there.

RONNY: I'll take her some Turkish Delight.

ME: Thank you so much x

"What's got you smiling?" Fin asks, throwing a white pillow to the other end of the sofa. "Is it my magnificence?"

"You're not going to let that go, are you?"

"Nope," he says, popping the *p*. "I might even get it in a tattoo."

"Knock yourself out," I say, unfolding my legs to stand.

"Don't you feel even a little bad for kicking a man out of his own bed?"

"Also *nope*." Taking hold of my pendant, I shuffle my way around the ottoman.

"Hard woman."

I startle as Fin suddenly takes stock of my hips from behind. Startle and almost melt. "The bed is big enough for us both," he says, his voice low and sort of raspy. His fingers flex, like he's trying to restrain himself. "It's a California king."

My shoulders begin to shake with a silent chuckle.

"My bed is funny?"

"Your pleading," I say over my shoulder. "I said I'd take the couch. I don't mind."

172

With a groan he tips forward, and I think he's about to kiss me, everything inside me tightening in preparation. Instead, he presses his nose to my hair. And inhales. "What kind of man would that make me?"

"One who really likes snakes?" I whisper.

"I really do." He straightens, his hands falling away as he takes a step back. "May your dreams be plagued by me."

"Not possible," I say, turning and tapping my pendant. "The eye protects me from evil."

"Hard and harsh," he replies, but I hear his smile even if I don't look back.

I make my way into the bedroom, feeling only slightly guilty as I close the door behind me. The room is quiet. So quiet. But for the loud thud-thud of my heart. It smells like him, his cologne and soap and something uniquely Fin.

I pull back the crisp white covers and slide in between the cool sheets, my phone still in my hand. And then I do what I was really going to do all along.

I open a Google search page and type in Phineas DeWitt.

The search bar autofills with What is Phineas DeWitt's net worth.

Nope right out of that!

Wikipedia comes up first, so I give it a quick scan.

He has two sisters, both older.

Parents deceased. Like mine.

Raised by his grandparents in moneyed Westport. Similar to my upbringing. If you cross your eyes.

Schooling. All-boys boarding, as he said. Ivy League university and postgrad at LSE. Clever man.

I move back a page and scan my results. No Bookface. No 'Gram. No Pulse Tok. No social media whatsoever.

There are mentions of his name on several business and entrepreneurial sites, plus interviews with journalists. *Forbes*. *The Financial Times*. *Bloomberg*.

I scroll and scroll, so much of the same. Nothing salacious, which is surprising. *Disappointing?* His name comes up in lots of society news pages. Tabloid stuff, mostly. I open one or two. Then four or five. Then a few more, all of them in the same vein. A photograph of Fin looking movie-star attractive, a leggy looker on his arm. A byline that names the event, sometimes his companion, but the snapshots provide no more insight than that.

No damning indictments of his character. I'm not even sure why I'm looking for it.

Then I note a Blogspot entry, way down in the list. I open it up. It's a screenshot of an article from the *City Chronicle*, dated last year.

A Little Bird Told Us . . .

news that makes a Little Bird's heart *and* wings flutter.

Evelyn Fairfax, our poor Pulse Tok bride and virtuous doggy doctor, is sitting in a swanky Kensington restaurant right now with none other than Fin DeWitt, the handsome darling of London's gossip columns.

Get you some, girl!

Fin and Evie? It's a wonder he's still breathing. Unless they were a thing first.

The screenshot of the article goes on . . .

If a Little Bird needed a broad shoulder to lean on, party-boy Fin's would be top of the list!

Check out the pics. She looks so happy!

#Finlyn

There are no images attached and no mention of this coupling anywhere else on the internet. Not when I google their names together. In fact, the article isn't listed in past posts from the *City Chronicle*'s website.

So if it isn't housed in the archives there, does that mean it was retracted? Did Oliver threaten to sue? Either way, I can't see it being true, not having witnessed their interactions. As a trio, they seemed far too solid. Evie and Fin's exchanges seem more like that of siblings. No animosity, but lots of insults.

I flip back to the article with the screenshot and holy moly! How many comments?

251 comments

HideYoKids: She deserves a ride on all that fine after what she's been thru. Go get you some, gurl!

FloozyLoosie: Oh, Evie. Out of the frying pan and into the fire, luv?

AmaraKarna: That man *is* fire!

EllenDeGenerate: Tru dat. I'd make his thighs my earmuffs.

HollyBloLightly: I'd make my thighs *his* earmuffs.

Aunti_Depressant: Wasn't he shagging the blonde from Made in Chelsea?

MisAnnThrope: No, it was her from *Made in RICHmond*. The one who looks like her horse.

FloozyLoosie: He's banging them both. He's a total man ho.

AmaraKarna: I'd be okay with that. I'd totes be his side ho!

Thots.an.Prayers: I was working a wedding where he shagged a pair of bridesmaids at the back of the marquee.

AmaraKarna: Lucky bridesmaids

Thots.an.Prayers: Another time, it was the mother of the bride.

AmaraKarna: Doesn't put me off. It just says he takes his craft seriously.

Load more comments . . .

"Fin the playboy" checks out, according to the anonymous horde and not just his friends.

Even more so when I google the TV show mentioned in the comment thread. The woman from *Made in RICHmond* looks nothing like a horse, unless we're talking thoroughbreds. She does seem a little familiar, but I expect I've seen her on TV. Not on that show, though. I'm not a fan of reality TV, but the *Made in RICHmond* cast do seem particularly vacuous.

I change my search terms:

Who is Fin DeWitt dating?

Dozens of A Little Bird Told Us posts pop up. If he was dating this much, he'd never make time for the office, let alone get any sleep. The press seem so invested in him—the posts in various publications going back years! It looks as though he only has to be seen standing next to a woman for it to be rumored they're together. As for the alleged dalliance with a mother of the bride, I will say the women Fin has been linked with aren't all dewy-eyed starlets under the age of twenty-five. The man likes a little variety.

He's so photogenic, though. Dapper in a business suit and hot in a tux. Zaddy energy, Sarai would say. And the women by his side are all drop-dead gorgeous.

I sigh, ignoring the fleeting thought that notes me as the anomaly. I'm not being all boo-hoo about it; rather, I'm a realist. I'm pretty and I'm personable. I'm just not going to be walking any catwalks or winning any beauty pageants.

There is one weird find on my internet search. It's a link to a social media platform that seems to be the kind of place that took over from old-school chat rooms. Not that there's anything weird in that. *Weird* isn't even in the name of the group, or *server*, as it's called—StarsInHerEyes. The weirdness is in the name of a locked thread. FindingPhineasDeWitt.

I can't dig any further without joining the platform and then applying with the moderators of the server. Which I'm not going to. I don't need to dig anymore, because I already know getting involved with Fin is a bad idea.

Unless—

I block out not-Ronny's smutty suggestion and set an alarm on my phone before placing it on the nightstand. I pull the satin-soft sheet up to my neck and snuggle in. Then sit up and turn my alarm off again.

I'm on vacation for five more days. The least I can do is try and enjoy myself.

Chapter 15
FIN

Hey, let's have a vacation relationship!

I blow out a breath as I stare up at the darkened ceiling and the woven fan as it lazily rotates. She might just have a point—none of that sounded romantic, but that was the point. What I thought she'd prefer. Obviously not, because it made no difference to the outcome.

The thing is, I want more than sex, but I thought that news would frighten her off. I'm not a raving maniac who turns rabid at the first hint of abstinence or blue balls. Despite my friends' near-constant teasing, I don't fuck anything with a pulse.

I don't *need* to have sex.

I can go without it.

And I have done. Just not often.

But I've never tried to convince a woman another man is gay. *Threatened by a fucking pastry chef?* Whether he's gay or not is purely academic—she's a married woman!

And by that reckoning, I have problems. One thing is for sure, I have never worked so hard for any woman.

"You're a fan of the low-hanging fruit." The recollection is unwelcome, but timely, I suppose, the echo of Matt's soft Irish lilt somehow softening the insult. *Even if it landed true.* Oh, I protested, but he was right. I don't chase women. And I'm well aware of why, even if no one else is.

Rolling onto my side, I punch my pillow a couple of times, then nearly fall off the edge of the couch. Fuck, I can't believe I'm here. My bed is huge—I would've made a pillow wall if she'd wanted.

I thought for sure she'd change her mind. Not for sex, although obviously I hoped. Which is pretty much all I am at the moment. Hope. And skin and bone. And dick. Which I'm trying to ignore right now.

I roll onto my back again and shove my hand behind my shorn head.

I wish she'd open up. I know there are places we could find common ground. Our childhoods, for one. *Because nothing says soulmates like dead parents?*

There's something she's not saying. Maybe about her grandmother? I guess she's not the only one. In my case, I was fucked over by my grandfather. Did that experience make me the way I am? Probably.

And there I go, spoiling my mood again.

Hey, Mila, if we're both fucked up, then maybe we belong together!

Rotating my shoulders, I tweak my neck, turning it this way and that, trying to move a little of the tightness out. I am single by choice. Thus far. And Mila hasn't been single for some time. The circumstances are hardly ideal.

It would be one thing if she were to say that it's too soon, that she needs to heal / smell the daisies / screw a whole soccer team. Then I wouldn't be sleeping on the couch. I'd be in there, working as hard as eleven men.

She'd been lied to for years—I understand her reluctance. But I also get some sense of *less than* from her, especially in relation to her body. Her hot, heavenly body.

"Fuck." With that groan, I kick my feet from under the sheet. She's built the way a woman should be, which is . . . any fucking shape a woman wants to be, in truth. But all that shit she told me, was she confiding in me or trying to put me off?

You'll have to try harder than that, my delectable wifey.

She has money issues, as far as I can make out. I can help her there, because the only issue I have with money is what to do with the stuff. I'd offer to help her in a heartbeat, but I like my teeth where they are.

But there's also something else going on under the surface. Some other reason behind her reluctance. It feels kind of familiar. Self-protection, would be my guess.

I just wish she'd let me in. I could try to make it better. Make her feel better, at least.

I lift my fist, and when I should maybe hit myself in the face, I use it to rub the sudden ache in my chest. I see her in my mind's eye, her dress white and her eyes bright. Pen in her hand, the official in his lightweight summer suit standing behind.

I sigh and swallow over the sudden tightness in my throat.

It wasn't a conscious thing that made me do what I did in that moment. I didn't reason it out or weigh up the pros and cons. I just knew it felt right. That in the depths of my heart and to the very marrow of my bones I'd follow her to the ends of the earth.

I groan again, the visual of Mila in the ocean rising like steam. Hair, swimsuit, and skin slick, her nipples as hard as diamonds. Fuck, how I wanted to press my tongue to them.

How I loved watching her movements turn languid with her second glass of champagne during dinner. Her laughter a little throatier. Her words a little naughtier.

I know she's into me. It's in the way her breath holds when I touch her and how her eyes darken at what they see in mine.

I sigh again, and shift, my body taut with tension.

I want what I can't have, and she wants what she won't let herself have.

"It's so fucked up."

We've both been traumatized by life. We were both raised by our grandparents, and we both bear some scars.

We both like champagne. And swimming.

And neither of us can keep our eyes off the other.

We're both excellent in bed. *And so fucking compatible.*

Hell, I've seen relationships start on less than that.

I bring my hand from behind my head, cupping my balls as I kick the sheet from my body, fighting to untangle it from my feet. I lift my cock from my shorts with a groan. One slide, and moonlight emphasizes the drop of moisture on my slit, turning it the color of a freshwater pearl. I drag my hand up my hard length, squeezing the crown with a hiss as I pinch the sticky bead.

I ought to be disgusted, lying here, abusing myself while on the other side of the wall lies the woman I want to be with in so many ways.

My eyes spring open at the sound of something hitting the floor. Heart beating hard, I lie in the darkness, my senses alert. *Mila?* I sit, trying not to groan, but I'm not twenty anymore. Can't get a good night sleep lying on a fucking couch.

"Baba, please slow down."

Mila's voice. Other words I can't make out, but I intuit the tone just fine. Distress.

A strip of light is visible from the bedroom door. *She closed it, right, when she went to bed?* I know she did—the thud a sign of finality.

Maybe she came out to wake me.

I swipe the sheet away, more concerned for Mila than I am for propriety, though I pause at the door. I'm not eavesdropping, I tell myself. I'm just concerned.

"Baba, please." Mila hiccups, then sniffs. *Tears?* "I know, my darling, but you can't come home." Pause. "Because the doctor said so."

I tentatively push on the door, my heart instantly aching at the sight of Mila crying, tears running down her reddened face.

"Are you okay?" I whisper. "I heard a noise." It's a pathetic excuse, but it's all I've got. But I'm not leaving her. Not until I know she's all right.

She points to the floor where a can of mosquito repellant lies, and she tries to smile. A terrible, beautiful, wobbling thing as she swipes the heel of her palm against her cheeks.

I step closer and loosen the gauzy mosquito net. I hadn't unrolled it last night. Maybe I should've showed her how. I pull the swathes over the mattress as Mila continues to croon into the phone.

"I'm sorry, Baba. I'll be back soon, back from work. And Ronny's coming tomorrow. She's going to bring you Turkish delight. They're your favorite, right?"

The responding voice sounds sad—full of despair—as I shake out the netting.

"Baba, please don't cry, my love. I'll be home soon. I promise."

Before I make to pull the sides of the net together, I scoot lower and take her hand in mine and give it a reassuring squeeze.

"I'm sorry," I whisper, my words warm against the back of her hand as I dust my lips across her knuckles. Fuck, I just want to make

182

this better, but how can I? I couldn't have guessed her grandmother was the reason she was reluctant to stay on the island longer. And if Evie had known, she wouldn't have asked. Oliver, though, probably wouldn't have given a fuck. Still, I feel bad—culpable somehow.

Maybe if she'd just let me in.

"I know, I know," she croons then, "Don't cry, Baba, please." Then, "Oh!" Breath rushes from her chest in a relieved gust. "Thank God, Sarah. Yes, of course. Good night, darling. I'll see you very soon."

A pause. Gentle voices. An angry, unforgiving one. And then a burbling laugh and a different voice. "We'll take it from here!"

"Thank you, Sarah," Mila replies. "Some days she struggles to remember who I am, yet today, she not only remembered how to use her phone but she found my number too."

"The mysteries of the mind. What time is it over there?" the tinny voice on the other side of the line asks.

"I don't know. After one?" Mila glances down to where I hold up two fingers. "It's gone two. That makes it about eight in the evening in London?"

"Cocoa time!"

"Please wish her good night from me when you tuck her in."

"I will, my love," the voice returns. "See you when you're back."

"Wait, Sarah? That other nursing home you told me about? I think I'm going to be able to swing it. I've had a bit of a windfall."

Something pinches in my chest as it all begins to make sense. Fuck. What rich, self-absorbed assholes we must seem.

"Right." Mila's hand slides from mine and she covers her eyes while massaging her temples. "How long do you think before it goes? Oh. Okay." Her teeth worry her lip at the answer to that. "Thanks for letting me know."

The call ends, and Mila just stares at her dark-screened phone. Cicadas chirp in the garden. The bed creaks, or maybe my knees. I reach for her hand again.

"That was my grandmother." She gives a shrug that hurts my insides. "Baba Roza." And then she bursts into tears.

"Mila, darling." I'm on my feet and on the bed, scooping her into my arms immediately. "It's okay."

"I know," she says, swiping at her tears. "It's just, Baba has dementia."

"I didn't know." Because she didn't tell me. She didn't confide in me. But why would she?

"Usually, she can't remember how to use her phone, but tonight she managed not only to turn it on but find my number too."

"That's good, right?"

"Not really," she says, allowing me to pull her closer. "Dementia doesn't work like that. It's a thief, stealing bits of the person you love until all that's left of them is a husk. I hate it. I fucking hate it! As if I don't feel bad enough for not noticing how ill she was sooner. As if I don't feel wretched enough that I had to put her in a nursing home after she fell. It's a horrible place, Fin. But I had so little choice and even less time to find somewhere, because the hospital couldn't release her to my care."

I don't know what to say. For the first time in forever, I don't have a thing to offer—not a suggestion or thought. But the one thing I can do is hold her tight. "I'm so sorry, darling."

"Mila, Mila," she whispers, pulling away. "You know, all those nicknames you tried—you could've just called me *darling*."

Using my thumbs, I wipe the rivulets of tears from her cheeks. "I didn't think you'd like it."

"But it's my name." She gives a watery laugh. "It's what *Mila* means in my grandmother's language. *Darling*."

"My parents might've saddled me with an ugly name, but yours, at least, got it right. Here." I chuck her chin and, reaching across her, pull a tissue from the box on the nightstand. "Blow," I instruct, pressing it to her nose.

"You wish," she says, pushing my hand away to do just that. "I hope these aren't your masturbation tissues. Oh, God. Don't listen to me."

"Never grew out of the habit of a tube sock," I respond.

"Don't make me laugh," she says, doing a little of that. "Thank you." She balls the tissue in her hand. "For the tissue. And for the cuddle."

"Anytime." I pause, then dip to bring my eyes level with hers. "Is there anything I can do? I mean, I wish I had the cure for dementia . . ."

"That would be so good. This role-reversal shit is hard. God, what am I doing? I should be at home."

My heart gives a little pang at her desolate words, her tear-streaked face.

"I can get you a flight." I don't want to, but I don't want her to be sad right now.

"I can't. If I leave . . ."

"I'm sure Oliver will—"

She reaches out, grabbing my hand. "Promise me you won't tell him—I won't risk it."

"I promise." I turn my hand under hers, linking our fingers.

"The silly thing is, she'll be tucked up in bed now and likely have forgotten she's spoken to me. I could be back in London and walk out of her room—just for a minute—and she'd forget I was ever there. She'd greet me with a hug and an admonishment for not visiting more often, even though she'd seen me just moments ago."

"Shit, Mila. I'm so sorry." Useless words, even if I truly mean them. I can only imagine what she's going through.

185

"No. Being here is the right thing." She brushes at her cheeks, her tone resolute. "Because I'm going to get her out of that place to a nursing home that can offer her dignity. Maybe a bit more stimulation. The home she's in—the nursing staff do their best, but . . ."

It all makes sense now. And it doesn't make me feel great. "Can you arrange to move her now?"

"Once I get Oliver's money—my fee—I'll do it then. Hopefully, they'll still have space," she says, her tone less certain.

"You're worried about timing, about the money coming through?"

"It's fine," she says, brushing away my concern. "It'll all work out. It has to."

"Why don't I help? I can do that for you, for Roza."

"There's no need," she says in that stubbornly prim tone I haven't heard since before we got hitched.

"But you want Roza in a better place, right?" Low. But I'll go lower. "And you might not secure it in time."

"It'll be fine," she insists. Then rubs her lips together nervously.

"Let me help."

"I can't."

"Why not?"

"Because this is not your problem! She's *my* responsibility."

But you're crying in my bed and you're wearing my ring, I almost say. But I don't go with that, because the observations wouldn't help anything. *Least of all me.*

"Then let me loan you the money, at least," I offer instead. "For Roza. For your grandmother. And because I'm your friend."

"We're not really friends, Fin."

"You know how to crush a man. A fucking loan, Mila. The world won't stop moving on its axis if you let someone help you."

"But it wouldn't be *someone*. It would be you."

"Ouch," I say with a stuttering laugh.

"I don't mean it like that, but things are already so bloody complicated. I can't borrow from you," she repeats adamantly.

I throw up my hand. "Want me to draw up a contract? Give you a sixty-day line of credit? Charge you interest? You're not being fucking fair here, least of all to Roza."

At this, she frowns.

"You know, pride is a terrible sin."

"I'm surprised you can see my pride for your own hubris," she counters with a glower.

"You did this for her, Mila. Let me do this for you."

Cicadas and silence and dirty looks.

"All right," she eventually says. Because she's smart and because she loves her grandmother. "I'll take you up on your offer. For Roza. And with no strings attached."

"Damn." I move my head slowly from side to side. "You got me. I was gonna make you my sex slave and everything."

"Idiot."

That's me. I'm just an idiot for her. "Give me the name of the place. Your grandmother's name and anything else you think I might need."

"It's gone eight—I mean, two. You should get some sleep."

"I will," I say as I stand and tug back the sheet before drawing it over her knees. "AirDrop me the details. I'll go make a call. You know, it's been at least twelve hours since I pissed someone off at work."

I pull the mosquito net closed and swagger out of the room, against every physical instinct I have. Her red eyes, her flushed cheeks, the hair I want to smooth and pet. Her sleep-creased pajamas and the heat of her body as it touched mine. Touch, sight, smell, taste—all those senses want to stay.

My brain, though—my heart—they know I need to play a longer game.

Chapter 16
MILA

"You're a good dancer."

Dancing. That perpendicular expression of a horizontal desire, so obvious in the hypnotic sway of our hips.

"You know what they say about good dancers." My husband presses his answer into the soft skin below my ear, the sound waves causing a ripple of *Yes please* through me.

"No, but you can tell me." My answer sounds thick with suggestion.

"They practice." His voice is deep, his intent clear as he takes my hand, twirling me before him. My dress flares outward from my knees, the long train held like a bracelet to my wrist. I'm dressed like a princess, held in my prince's arms as he pulls me back, our bodies flush.

I remember now. It's my wedding day. My Prince Charming is a husband.

"Practice," I whisper, smiling secretly. "I see."

"Now feel."

Oh, I do. The hard press of his body and our hips swaying in time to the music.

"Dancers are also flexible." I give a small sigh as his lips caress the sensitive spot where my neck and shoulder meet. "They have exceptional stamina."

"Lucky them."

He makes a husky sound of agreement. "But it's a double-edged sword, because they'll work their partner so hard. Get them so . . . *hot*." His words are a heated burst in my ear that is somehow connected to my core.

"Sounds terrible," I answer as we move, oblivious to everything around us.

"A good dancer starts slow, finds his partner's rhythm. He discovers what you like, and the more time you spend dancing together, the more proficient you'll become."

I suck in a sharp breath, his whisper like a sensory trip wire as my body floods with a liquid heat. I know he senses my reaction as his arm tightens around my middle, his body so hot and so ready.

We're going to have sex.

"Yes, yes we are."

I smile to myself. I'm almost giddy with want.

But then the landscape around us changes, and it's suddenly dark. Or almost dark, as my eyes adjust to the lack of light. The noise of the door closing registers distantly in my brain, the sound of Fin's breath and his footsteps a little more so.

"Fancy meeting you here," he purrs in a change of tone.

I chuckle, the sound low and sort of sexual as his hands capture my hips.

"Yes, fancy," I whisper as he moves me backward and my bare shoulders meet a cool wall. *Yes, please. Yes, more of that.* My insides heat with longing, my silly gel nails catching his shirt as I reach for him, every inch of my skin alive and wanting.

Fin palms my breast, almost as though to hold me in place.

I arch, silently begging him with my body as I whisper breathless-sounding encouragements. "God, I want you. I've thought about you so, *so* much."

"Tell me."

"Like this. I imagined you just like this. The room dark, you on your knees, getting me off."

"Just like old times," he murmurs. "Did you touch yourself while you thought of me? Did you make yourself come for me, Mila?"

I reach for his neck, seeking to pull his mouth closer to mine. *"Always."*

"You're such a good girl." His words—his praise—light me up inside. His words dance across my lips. We're not quite kissing; more like sharing air. "Do you know I have a thing for good girls?"

I hear the smile in his words as my hand glides down his chest, and over the demarcation of his leather belt. "I wonder what that thing could be."

He makes a rough masculine sound as I wrap my fingers around his hard length.

"Please say it's this," I whisper, adding brazen to wanton and not caring one jot.

"Would you like me to give it to you?"

"I thought only girls could be a cocktease."

His chuckle vibrates across my skin, but any further response is cut off by his kiss. Slow and thorough, he devours me little by little. My jaw, my neck, my breast as he palms again. Clasping it tight, his strong fingers slip into my neckline.

"Too tight. My dress is too tight."

But my nipple is already free and at the mercy of his mouth. A throb of pleasure radiates from my core as his tongue swirls the hardened tip. I moan as he sucks, the noise changing in length and depth as his cheek, rough with stubble, brushes my breast. It seems only moments ago that his face was as smooth as silk.

He shaved for me. Made sure I'd want to kiss him.

The realization is heady. Powerful. I want him to mark me. To bite. To suck. To leave some lasting sign that I was his. That he wanted me. Even if just for a little while.

The sudden wave of melancholy recedes as he takes my face in his hands.

"Look at my hands, Mila. They're shaking, I want you so much. Let me take you to the room."

"Let's stay here." My eyes fill with silly tears. This man makes me want things I shouldn't. The wedding of a lifetime was enough. I can't allow myself a perfect wedding night.

"You're sure?" He pushes my hair from my face.

I nod. *You can be mine for a little while.*

His kiss is pure perfection, his tongue licking into me, rich and clever. My pleasure quickly spirals, my need along with it. I whimper as he begins to pull away.

"Hush now. Just a taste," he whispers as he begins to lower.

I gasp at a sudden loud noise—something scraping over stone. Then something begins to topple, a metallic sound ringing out. Moments later, a broom handle falls and wallops Fin across the back.

I giggle. He makes a frustrated huff, but it doesn't stop him from beginning to gather my dress, pushing it up my legs.

Amusement dies, and I gasp as his hand slides between my knees, his rough fingertips tender against my skin. My body bows, my thoughts wild as I arch and meet his touch. *There. Yes, there.* Aching, pulsing, I'm reduced to nothing but sensation, no longer skin and bone.

But then the backdrop changes, the light suddenly so very bright against my eyelids. I inhale deeply, because this smells right.

It feels real and heavenly as I run my fingers along his neck. His stubbled cheek.

I must've been dreaming, or maybe it was a memory. Outwardly, things have changed. Internally, my body is still crying out for him.

"You're here," I whisper, sliding up Fin's body to reach his ear.

"Mila?"

I purr and run my hands over him, unable to touch enough to meet my satisfaction. It was a dream. It was a memory. But I'm *so* ready to make it real.

"You're so warm," I whisper, pressing my teeth into the corded muscles of his neck.

"Fuck."

I smile, biting my lips as though to contain it.

"Mila, are you—"

Fin's voice is husky with sleep, and his skin smells so damned delicious. Warm and musky and like lemon verbena. *Which is oddly specific.* Is it his cologne? Whatever it is, it makes me want to lick his skin. So I do.

I deserve this. I want this. He is such a good man—and he wants this too.

"You smell amazing," I whisper, spanning my hand across his chest. Smooth skin. Hot man. "You taste so good."

"Mila, love."

I've never loved the sound of my name as much as I do right now. Full of aching want. I could bottle the sound, stock up on his masculine moans, and huff them like a gateway drug when I'm alone.

Because I will be alone, I know. But I don't have to be now. I can take what he offered. It doesn't feel as though he's changed his mind . . .

His hand curls around my shoulder, moving me, and . . .

We give a joint groan. I'm so slick, and he's so hard. And I appear to be riding him. Not full penetration, but enough to feel how hot and hard he is. Enough to make me pulse and ache for relief. It's good—*so* good. And so tempting as I adjust my position, and—

"*Oh!*" The wet slide of him, the bump of his crown against my clit. "I need you," I whisper, pushing my hand between us as I suck the salt from the skin, as I undulate, seeking relief. "So, so much."

This is what I wanted. My wedding night. What I wanted to remember, to feel him beneath me, shaking with desire.

His arms come around me, and he's panting so hard, I'm pretty sure his breaths could blow a little pig's house down.

"*Fuck.*" The ache in his words. A pleasured hum in my response. "Please, *please* tell me you're not asleep. That I'm not dreaming."

"I'm not asleep, but it feels like a dream."

"It feels like heaven."

"I want you, Fin. Can't you feel it?"

His thick swallow. "You're the only thing I can feel right now. I can't believe I slept on the couch when we could've been doing this."

Finally, his hands find my hips, and he rocks into me.

But. *But.*

He was on the couch, making a phone call. I fell asleep. I had pajamas on.

Baba. The nursing home. The loan. I can't have sex with him— it would muddy the waters!

I jerk upright; only, that's not quite right, as Fin's hands tighten. How come he's naked too? Why's he underneath me? Hell, how come he's in this bed!

"What . . . what are you doing here?"

His sleepy expression firms, arousal replaced with confusion. "What?"

193

"What are you doing in this bed?" I repeat. I sound a little shriller the second time.

"I don't rightly know. But Mila, I'm not the top in this situation."

The top. I'm on *top*. My hand is on his hard chest, my thighs spread wide over his, my intimate bits touching his. *Soaking his.*

"I don't know what you're doing here—in this bed." A wobbling panic fills my voice as I grapple for the sheet, but it's wrapped around his legs. As are his cotton sleep shorts. I—we—didn't even pause to take them fully off. And that's the crux of my panic. I might not know how or what he's doing here, I just know I can't be here too.

Not given what I was about to do.

He's loaning me money. He said we could be friends.

I can't do this. I shouldn't.

I yank the sheet again, the movement causing a wave of contact between us. Fin groans, and I gasp, between my legs pounding like footsteps on pavement.

"I went to bed alone and woke up dry humping you!" Only I'm not dry. I'm wet. *So wet.* And my heart is banging against my ribs like it's trying to crack them. "How? How did this happen?"

He swallows audibly, his expression sort of tortured. "I can't concentrate when your nipples are staring at me."

I immediately give up on the sheet and cover them with my hands.

Fin groans, angling his head so his gaze is on the ceiling. "I can't believe you thought that might help." His words are like a whispered prayer for deliverance.

I slide from his body, another wave of *Oh my God, do that again* washing through me. My cheeks are burning hotter than a thousand suns as I tumble from this bed, dragging the sheet with me a second time. I slam the bathroom door behind me, but I can't even do that right because the sheet is caught in it.

"Mila, please," Fin calls after me. I fancy I can hear the quick pad of his feet against the tile. I yank the sheet, slamming it shut properly as his hand hits the wood.

Hands pressed to the cool vanity, I stare at my wild reflection as I try very hard to ignore the gnawing sensation the ache in his voice causes me.

I almost screwed my husband. And the worst of it is, out of the five words in that sentence, I regret only one of them.

Chapter 17
FIN

"Mila?" I rap my knuckles on the bathroom door. "Tell me you're okay."

"I'm fine," comes a little squeak. Does it sound as though she's crying?

"You don't sound fine."

"I am," she answers, her voice a little stronger. "Except the part where I woke up being molested."

My stomach plummets. What the fuck? "No. Mila, that's not what happened."

"I know. I was joking."

I frown. "It was a really shitty joke."

"I know. I'm sorry. I say stupid things when I'm . . . when I'm embarrassed. I thought you might've realized that by now." A pause. "Chia Pet?" she adds in a warble.

I smile. Despite my flagging hard-on and the ache in my chest. "There's nothing for you to be embarrassed about."

"Easy for you to say."

I glance down at my dick as I murmur, "It's not. Not really."

"You weren't in the bed when I went to sleep. Did you come back in after you finished on the phone?"

"No, but not because I didn't want to." Gripping the sides of the doorframe, I rest my head against it. "I must've been on autopilot after I took a leak during the night."

"Oh."

"I'm sorry."

"It's okay. Understandable, even. It is your bed. You might even be a hero."

A half dozen things flash through my head, none of them making any sense. "I don't . . ."

"You probably saved a pillow from my unwanted advances."

I give a breath of a laugh, hot air bouncing back from the door into my face. "Not all heroes wear capes," I say softly.

"Some of them don't even wear pajama pants."

"I *was* wearing them." Only out of deference to her.

"That was my fault too. But I'm telling myself I was doing us both a favor—that the room was too hot."

"It was hot." So fucking hot I thought I might melt under her hands.

She could've killed me, and I wouldn't have complained. I would've just enjoyed every minute of it.

I thought I was sleeping, that I was having *the* horniest dream, when I woke to her tight, frantic breaths; her hands; and her wet pussy sliding the length of my dick. It took me a minute to realize that Mila, my goddess of a wife, was getting herself off. I was just a means to an end. Her sex toy. And I had never been so aroused in my whole goddamned life.

But how do I tell her that? How do I say I can give it to her however she needs. That I long for her touch. That I'm rock hard again just thinking about it.

What I settle on is: "You okay in there?"

"Yes." Her voice, while still soft, seems a little louder. Like she's just on the other side of the wood. "But I can't come out yet. You see, I seem to have melted my face off."

"No, love. You have nothing to be embarrassed about."

She gives an unhappy laugh. "Oh, I beg to differ."

"I guess we'll just have to agree to disagree, because what just happened was one of the hottest experiences of my life."

"I doubt that very much. Not with the size of your fan club," she says, her annoyance piqued. "I wish you hadn't followed me, because I was just going to compose myself, then come back and tell you I have sexsomnia."

"Sounds . . . like something I might have the cure for."

"There he is." She gives an unhappy-sounding chuckle. "The man I've come to know. And assault."

"Is it assault when the other party wants it?"

"That sounds a bit dubious."

"I have to agree to disagree. Consensual nonconsent. Or plain old ravishment. I'm down for either, because the thing I have for your ailment is a willingness."

"You're daft."

"Of course, I prefer *ravishment*." I glance down at my cock. *He's so down for that.* "In fact, when you come out of the bathroom—"

"Didn't you hear me? I'm never leaving this room again."

"That might be problematic. My heart medication is in there."

"You have a heart problem?" she squeaks.

Only that I've lost it to you, maybe. "Bad joke," I whisper instead.

"I might just stay here until you've gone, in that case."

"Or maybe you could come out and we could talk about what just happened. We don't have to . . ." I find myself pressing my hand to the wood, as though I could draw her out by touch alone.

"I think I'd rather eat my own feet."

"If you don't want to talk, we could just . . ." Fuck it. "Come out, and we could pick up where you left off."

No answer.

"I can't be any clearer. I want you, Mila. I want you so much it hurts."

I turn from the bathroom, leaving her there. For now. I'm so fucking frustrated, because it seems there's nothing I can say or do to make her believe me. Or to gain her trust.

I make my way into the compact kitchen, pulling out a carton of juice. I inhale a glass, unable to get my thoughts to stick. Unable to chase this low-grade ache from my gut.

Shower or swim?

Or take the bathroom door off its hinges and kiss the strength of these feelings into her.

Consensual nonconsent. What was I thinking? That's not her bag.

She's so self-reliant, so unwilling to accept help. And I get it: her experiences with her asshole of an ex would make anyone lack trust. But it feels deeper than that. Like it's a reflection of her life somehow. Her current existence. A place where she has no choice in the matter but to close herself off. But in her deepest, darkest fantasies, I know she enjoys letting go of that control.

She's so fucking strong, a fighter. And she doesn't even realize. The world likes to overlook the strength in women, yet they carry the weight of it quietly in the background, mostly without realizing it themselves. Fucking period pain, childbirth to keep the damn species marching, fear of men, workplace bias, pay gaps, power imbalance, yet they keep on trucking. *Resilience*—that's the word I'm looking for. My wife has reservoirs of the stuff. And I find I just want to walk alongside her. Maybe carry a little of that load, if she'd let me.

I know what she wants in the bedroom. What she needs in her life. *Love. Support. Trust.* And I'll give it all to her gladly. I want the whole package. The real deal.

With that thought, I drop the glass to the sink and put back the juice as I adjust my crotch. What a shit show. She's tearing herself up. Meanwhile, this thing just wants to tear her up.

It looks like I'll be jerking off in the shower.

I don't make the decision lightly, and while it's not quite a necessity, I find it's more pressing than a want. Post-nut clarity is an actual thing, not an excuse to touch yourself, as some might think. Given I'm about to spend a day with Mila being all in her head, I could do with the clearness of mind that jerking off will undoubtedly bring.

I don't want to spend the day salivating and imagining her unclothed. I want her to feel heard, not just seen, even if she has the kind of body I want to lose myself in. At this rate, it's not likely to happen again.

Like a sad sack, I make my way through the suite, pausing as I pass the bedroom door. When there's no sign of Mila, I carry on, pushing the glass door open and stepping out into the walled garden. The air is already sultry as I open the outdoor cabinet and grab a hotel-amenities pack; the eco toothbrush and tube of toothpaste, adding one to the other and shoving it into my mouth. I grab a towel from the rack as I pass. When I say *grab*, I mean *lift carefully*, because a snake once fell from between the folds of a towel I was just about to dry my nuts with.

With a deep sigh, I step onto the black rock shower platform, and flicking the dial, I tip my head under the waterfall-effect spray.

The water is instantly hot and the fall of it against my body delicious as I twist my neck this way and that, simultaneously moving the toothbrush over my teeth. The heat unknots the tension-filled coils in my shoulders as I press one palm to the stone wall, letting the water cascade. Letting it sluice my troubles away.

Only it doesn't, because my mouth still feels full of her, and I still have this need clawing in the pit of my stomach.

I felt like I awoke in heaven, Mila's wild hair like clouds spilling over my chest. I didn't know what to think as she pressed tiny licking kisses to my skin. Scratch that—I couldn't think as all the blood in my body drained to my cock. She looked so fucking hot, undulating over me. And I just lay there like a landed fish, straining my brain, hoping—wishing—she'd make that one slick slide and put me inside.

She was so wet and I was so hard.

And now I'm terrified we won't ever get to that point again, let alone make this a lasting thing.

I could make her feel so good, if she'd let me. Make her see what I see, show her how she deserves to feel good. *To feel loved.* She ought to be worshipped, and I should be the one to make her feel that way.

I feel like such a fuckhead. I don't know what I did to spoil the moment, other than being in the bed in the first place. I ought to have made sure she wasn't asleep. But as she worked her sweet body over mine, I found I couldn't care—my need overruling my brain.

Why do I keep saying the wrong thing? Doing the wrong thing? Calling her names just to get a fucking reaction like we're grade school kids. It's like I can't help myself, like my brain switches off when she's near. I'll take any kind of reaction from her—a roll of her eyes, her disdain and distaste—as long as she's next to me.

I stand straight with a growl, slicking the water back from my face. I'm so frustrated, so fucking annoyed with myself, I can barely stand it. And I'm so fucking hard, my idiot body at odds with my fucking brain again.

There's only one thing for it. Well, I guess there are three.

Cardio. Meditation. Masturbation.

When the monkey brain is in charge, you've gotta pick an outlet.

I can't go for a run and leave Mila to find an ominously empty suite, and I'm too amped for meditation. Not that it's really my bag, anyway. So I take the option left to me.

Time to work out those kinks with my cock in my hand.

Then maybe I'll get to move on with my day with a little more sensitivity.

Every male, from the time he hits puberty, is aware of the benefits of masturbation and the ease of cleanup when in the shower. Soap, shower gel, bodywash—whatever ruffles your fun-time feathers.

I drop the toothbrush onto the ledge and slick a dollop of bodywash to my hand, smear it down my chest, then farther to the base of my cock. My palm plenty lubricated, I make a pleasantly soapy upward stroke.

God, I wish Mila was here with me. She looked so fucking hot, all wet and glistening, dark strands sticking to her cheeks. If she was here, I'd press slippery kisses to her slick skin and lick at the drips.

I groan softly. It feels so good. Not as good as having her under me, or over me, but you've got to work with what you have. My eyes fall closed as I imagine her here, her dark hair streaming down her back. I'd turn her to face the wall and take her hips in my hands. Maybe twist her hair in my fist instead. Her fingernails would scrape the stone when I smack her ass, just for the hell of the moment. Just for the joy of watching it.

Mila has a body built for sin. Only, marriage is supposed to be a sacrament. The act of giving yourself to another. I tighten my grip and angle my thick crown to the teasing fall of the water, each touch blending into another.

A sacrament, not a sin. I guess it makes sense, given fucking her feels like a religious experience. She feels like heaven.

"Fuck."

My wife. I love fucking my wife. And I love it when my wife gets off on me. In my mind, I hear the sound of our bodies joining. Skin against skin. Moaning and taut, tortured breaths.

What I wouldn't give to have Mila on her knees in front of me, her fingers digging into my thighs and her pretty mouth stretched wide around my crown.

I tip back my head and groan her name, the rough sound echoing, and the sky above the only witness to my need.

"Fin."

I press my hand to the wall and drop my head. I've got it bad. I'm so obsessed I can actually hear her.

"Fuck. Oh, fuck." My arm works a little harder. *Her mouth. Pussy. Nipples diamond hard.* A familiar sensation begins to build in my core.

"Fin."

The second time, her tone sounds less tentative. In fact, it prickles down my spine. I run my fist to my crown and squeeze, turning my head over my shoulder just to indulge my curiosity. Because she can't be . . .

Here.

Yet she is.

Twice. She called my name twice. This is no accident.

Her eyes dip deliberately to my ass, her full bottom lip tortured by the press of her teeth. I take my chance, my heart beating so hard I can hear it.

"Have you come to watch me shower? Or to watch me get myself off?"

"I didn't know." Her cheeks flame. "Are you . . ."

"Hard?" I turn to face her, my cock pounding as her eyes dip, then widen. "Am I fucking my fist while thinking of you?" I give a husky groan at my next slow, torturous stroke. *Not entirely for her entertainment.* "Look at me. I'm so fucking hard for you, Mila." Her eyes are wide as I press into my hand. "You did this to me—made me like this. You were whispering my name, so wet and so ready for me. I'm sorry it freaked you out. But I'm not sorry I'm in your head. Look at me," I demand. Her eyes rise to mine as the water continues to cascade behind me. "I'm a man on the edge. Take fucking pity."

"You want me to pity you?" Her voice is 90 percent purr as she steps closer, her hips a hypnotic sway. It's around about then I realize she's just wrapped in a towel, my brain working on a fucking delay.

My cock is so engorged, I'm maybe just a few minutes from blacking out.

"Or are you asking me to pity *fuck* you?"

Joy bursts from my chest. Her question, her conflicted expression, and her *come fuck me* body language. How did she get to be so perfect? Like she has one thing to be insecure about.

My laughter eases. My smile falls. She's in touching distance, but I don't reach out. "I'd take your pity fuck, but not your regret."

Not again.

"You called me a good girl." Her lashes are a dark sweep as she keeps her gaze from me, her finger tracing the vivid-orange birdlike head of a heliconia. "In my dream, I mean."

"Maybe it wasn't a dream but a memory."

"I liked that you said it," she admits without lifting her gaze.

"I know." A pause. "Tell me, Mila, why did you come out here? To watch. Or to be part of this. I need to know, sweet girl."

The flower bobs as her finger retracts. She takes a step, a provocative goddess with hips built for that sway. I tighten my grip on my cock, so fucking ready for this. I'll take the dregs—if she wants to watch, I'll give her such a show.

Another step as she reaches for the fold of her towel.

Then she pulls.

Chapter 18
FIN

"Damn." I shake my head as though I might be seeing things.

"I don't want to watch." Her tone is cool, her delivery supremely confident, but the tilt of her chin betrays her nerves. "I want you to touch me. I want to feel you inside me. I don't want to just imagine it anymore."

I give my head a shake, overstimulation causing a break in my neural wiring.

"Fin . . . please say something."

"Have I blacked out?"

She glances away, hiding a shy-looking smile.

"Mila . . ." I make a groan of her name, drinking her in. "You look like a fucking dream." She has curves for days. Silky skin and jet hair. I feel like I should drop to my knees, humbled in the face of all that is her—that I should give thanks *for* her.

She steps onto the shower platform. I suck in a shocked breath when our naked bodies collide as she slides her arms around my neck.

"A holiday romance," she says softly, her cheek pressed to my chest.

My heart dips, then rallies, banging so hard that I wonder if she can hear its bass *thump thump thump*, the sounds of the shower its backing track.

"Five days. Two people just enjoying each other, like you said."

She's shivering. Is it with nerves or desire? *Either way, that's not gonna cut it,* my brain supplies. I manage to halt the message before it reaches my mouth as I fold my arms around her, grasping for something else to say. Something that isn't going to frighten her the fuck away.

How about yes. *Say yes, fuckhead.*

She feels like she belongs in here, in the circle of my arms. Can't she feel that? Can't she let her guard down? Let me in. Not just into your body, but your heart. Let our skin meld and our souls fuse.

"It's what you offered," she repeats, filling the pause, as though I need persuading.

I stifle a sigh. I may be rock hard, but I know we're destined for more. That we deserve to be more.

"Yeah, I know." I also know that sex can be a gateway to more. Just look at Evie and Oliver. Despite the official story behind their meeting, I know they fucked the day she said "I don't" to the tool she was previously engaged to.

"Don't worry," Mila whispers. "I won't get attached. I know you're not the type to settle down. And I have too much going on in my life right now to be serious about anyone."

I know she's pressed herself this close to prevent me from seeing her face, from reading her expression. But that works both ways, because that arrow landed hard.

Fuck me, but don't love me. That's usually my line. It's what I tell women up front. What a turnup for the books. Or a kick in the guts.

"Not that I'm suggesting you'd be interested in more," she adds softly.

I tighten my hold on her, mentally kicking myself for not answering. "Hush. Any man would be honored to be part of your life. You're special, Mila." I feel her bristle, but I carry on anyway. "You need to believe that about yourself."

"You're sweet."

"Sweet *and* nice?"

Her body moves against mine with a giggle. I close my eyes and swallow back a moan.

"What if it turns out to be more than sex?" says sad-sack Fin as he finds his voice.

"It won't be," she says, pressing her lips to my still-slick chest. "Because it can't be. We're just too different, you and me. Beyond the physical, we don't even like each other. Not really." The latter falls flat, despite her joking delivery.

My heart dips. Is that what she thinks, or is it what she's telling herself? People who don't like each other don't behave like we do. The opposite of like, of love, is indifference, not an electric attraction.

"I thought we were friends."

"Well, maybe you like me just a little bit," she says, tracing the outline of my nipple. "And I've already told you what I like."

My cock throbs, and I swallow thickly. This is going to be over before it begins, if I'm not careful. It's been years since I was reduced to distracting myself from nutting by silently reciting multiplication tables.

"The things that I think about," she whispers. "The things I haven't . . . Would you . . . would you do those things with me?"

My brain shuts off. Shuts down—a misfire in its cerebral wiring as I imagine just that. Before it can reboot, Mila pulls back. Her dark lashes flutter as her fingers, five points of aching-hot contact, sear my skin. She tips onto her toes, and I groan as she presses her soft lips to the base of my throat.

"Teach me how," she whispers. "Please?"

I feel it all—feel everything. Her breath before it leaves her lips. The brush of her hair under my chin, the press of her fingers and the skim of her hip.

Her touch is tender as it slides down my chest. Then farther, causing my abs to tense, my mind going hazy around the edges, my whole body quivering like a struck tuning fork.

And that's before she takes my cock in her hand.

"Tell me what you like," she murmurs, teasing my crown with the tips of her fingers. "I want to make this good for you."

Jesus Christ. Who's teaching who?

I come back to myself and fist my hand in the back of her hair. Her eyes turn to night, her shocked gasp reverberating through to my bones. "If your hands are on me, if you're touching me, I like it. Got that?"

She nods her agreement—winces—her posture softening as I lower my mouth to hers.

"Anything I do that you don't like? You only have to say so."

"Five days," she whispers, her words feathering my lips. *And mine hers.*

"Five days," I agree. "I'm going to pick you apart bit by bit. Find out what you really like." Become your new addiction and never let you leave.

I slide my lips over hers, inhaling her soft sigh of acceptance. Light touches and caressing tongue, I stoke this fire between us as her hand slips around my neck once more. Her hips tilting to the hard press of me, light turning to dark, heat flaring between us as I deepen my kiss.

"Are you wet for me, Mila?" My free hand roams, the other holding her in place by her hair. I give and she takes, and she likes it enough to moan into my mouth as I do. "Answer me."

"Fin," she admonishes, laughing a little as I turn us.

"I asked you a question."

With her back to the shower, I step into her, pushing her under the water. Her expression as the spray hits the top of her head matches her stunned gasp. But she isn't under long, as, water cascading down her body, I follow her, backing her up against the wall.

"That was a shock!" She laughs, free and loud, sluicing water from her face.

But I don't answer as I bend and lick the glistening beads from the tips of her hardened nipples. She moans as I capture each in turn with a soft, sucking tug. Water flows down my back as I take her hips, pulling her closer to slide my thigh between hers.

"You're wet now." A smile pulls at my mouth as I dip a little, slide my tongue over the seam of her lips. My cock throbs as she tentatively sucks on my tongue, and my hands slide across her hips. I take her breasts into my hands—her nipples into my mouth. I can't feel enough, touch enough, not as she moans softly and begins to rock against me. Taking her pleasure where she can.

"Are you going to come like this?" I press my thigh tighter into the heat of her pussy. "Are you gonna get yourself off riding my thigh like a good girl?"

Her cheeks color, her rhythm faltering.

"You have my permission, Mila." *Fuck, I think you might just have my heart.*

"Oh, God." Her lashes flutter, the ends beaded with moisture from the shower as stray droplets of water bounce from my shoulders onto her. I want to lick her clean. Lick her dry. Feast on her until all that remains are her sighs.

"Show me, darling. Show me what you can do. I get so fucking hot when I think about you getting yourself off."

"Oh, my days." Her head tips forward, pressing to my chest. "I shouldn't have told you." But she doesn't stop.

"But you did. And now it's all I can think about."

She undulates a little harder, her soft moan bouncing off the shower walls.

"Yeah, just like that." My touch is one of reverence as I take her face in my hands, brushing away her hair and keeping her eyes on mine. "You're so, so beautiful," I croon, not sure how a moment as hot as this hasn't dissolved my brain. "You're such a good girl for me."

She whimpers, so conflicted, so lush and so ripe as she rolls against me again and again.

"That's it. You can take it."

Her attention turns inward, her eyes glossing with pleasure.

I kiss her, one quick slide. I want to watch. I also want to swallow her whole. "You're so, so sweet, doing this for me. Doing all the hard work for me."

"Fin. Oh . . ." Her body bows, as though she can't contain what she's feeling, as though the sensation is too big to fit under her skin.

"Good girls get rewarded," I croon. "Good girls get to come, Mila. Show me how good you can be."

"Oh, Lord . . ."

I laugh, the sound low and dark. "God isn't making you come. But you bet he's watching."

"I . . . I . . ." Her mouth falls open as she hits that point.

I hold her there as her body contracts. My mouth against hers, I swallow her cries.

Chapter 19
MILA

I swallow thickly, unwrapping my arms from Fin's neck. Aftershocks of pleasure pulse through me so hard, I'm surprised I can coordinate my limbs.

"You're so beautiful when you come," Fin whispers, pressing his lips into my hair. I hear the smile in his voice. Feel it pulling at my heartstrings.

I'm a good girl. The thought drops into my chest in a wash of confliction. I'm embarrassed, but I clearly liked it. Oh, hell. I got off on it.

"Well, that was . . ." I begin as I pull away, but I don't get very far, as something blooms hotly inside me. And, *oh*, his fingers grip my bum. They grip it so tight, I feel like his fingertips might become embedded in my skin. I like it a lot.

"Did I say you could go somewhere?"

His low tone causes a ripple of pleasure across my skin. So *this* is daddy energy. I like it. I like it a lot. Oh, hell.

"I just thought we were . . ."

"Done?" There's a note of dark amusement to his tone. "Not even close, honeybuns."

"No, not done, not exactly," I say, ignoring his taunt. "I just thought that I could . . . that I could . . . because I can't . . ." *say those words out loud!*

"Mila." He makes a warning of my name, and I just about melt. "Spit it out."

"I don't *come*," I whisper as my face flames. "Not very often." I give a tiny apologetic shrug that he can no doubt feel. "I probably should've mentioned that before. Not that it wasn't a good orgasm . . ." My words trail off when he presses me back to better see my face. Which is probably puce because—how mortifyingly uncomfortable.

"You don't come." A statement, not a question.

I shake my head. "Not easily. Open your ears, for God's sake, Fin! Stop trying to em—"

"You don't remember how many times you came on our wedding night?"

"Don't tell me," I retort tartly. "Dozens? And don't expect me to believe it either." My mouth tightens, and his expression changes too. Only he looks like I just reached out and tickled him. *Rather than the other way around.* Though the brush of his still-hard cock isn't exactly a tickle. It also doesn't make me want to giggle. Which brings me to my point. "It's just, with Adam, I'd usually—"

His happy expression dissolves. He suddenly swoops, and I find myself hauled unceremoniously over his shoulder.

"Oh!" My stomach flips with surprise. And pleasure. Not that I'd admit it in a thousand years. And never to him—I'd never hear the end of it!

"Don't tell me what Adam did," he grates out as he turns and carries me through the garden.

"Not much, actually. I meant more what I'd do for him." I swipe my damp, dangling hair out of my face and use my other arm to try and support the girls, before my body stiffens. "Hey!" I shout—yelp—as his hand swats my bottom.

"I said *don't* tell me."

"I was trying to suggest I might reciprocate!"

"That's very decent of you." His amused drawl still makes me feel hot all over, and my bum cheek tingles, not unpleasantly.

"I don't feel like it now." My words come out snipey from embarrassment.

"The stone would be too hard on your knees, anyway."

"Oh." The fire drops out of me. But what kind of man doesn't want a blow job?

"And I plan on taking my time with you," he adds, his tone annoyingly conversational for someone walking through a garden stark naked with a woman draped over his shoulder like a side of beef.

His feet stop quite suddenly, and my damp hair swings in my face.

"Pfft!" I swipe at it. "What is it?" I ask, trying—and failing—to see around him and not enjoying how my boobs peel from his skin.

His answer is to stroke up and over my backside, the caress soft yet possessive. With just a hint of a squeeze.

"What—ouch!" My right bum cheek immediately stings.

"Keep still," Fin reprimands as his hand strokes, elevating the sting to a tingle. "I caught a glimpse of your reflection. I had to pause to appreciate it. My wife's ass is like a work of art."

"Like a bag of laundry, more like." The words leave my mouth without thought. Fin's hand comes down again, sharp and swift.

"Cut that shit out," he growls. "You don't get to insult my little slut muffin."

"*Your* slut muffin?" I ridiculously repeat. Though I appreciated his "little" prefix, my bum wobbled, and I should *not* be fine with

214

that. But his growling reprimand and the throbbing between my legs seems to drown my indignity out.

"Mine for the next five days. That's what we agreed. And don't tell me you don't like it," he adds as his fingers tease . . . where they have no business teasing, sliding along the crease where my thigh and bottom meet.

"Of course I don't like it," I whisper.

"Oh, shame." His voice is so soft as those teasing fingers slide between my legs.

I say his name on a gasp, wriggling as though I want to get away. But I don't want to get away, just as I don't want to acknowledge how I've eased his access. I screw my eyes tight against the pleasure of finding Fin's finger inside me.

"Such a shame you don't like it, Mila. Right? Such a shame you don't like me fucking you with my fingers."

I shake my head, liar that I am, my trailing hair swinging this way and that. In my head, I see the image of us so clearly. The reflection of Fin's expression as he adds another finger, twisting his wrist to stroke me intimately. I pant and I squirm with a mixture of indignity and hedonistic pleasure as heat reddens my skin.

But the moment is over as quickly as it began, and I stifle a moan as he slides his hand away.

"*Fuck*. Look at that. You're so sweet and sticky between my fingers, Mila."

How can something that sounds so conversational make my insides ache and flame? But then we're on the move again.

"This is so undignified," I whisper, sticking to my unimpressed theme as I stare down at his sculpted butt cheeks. I wonder how many squats he does to keep them in shape.

More intelligent thoughts might center on why I'm doing this. How I changed my mind. But as I stood in the bathroom earlier, my heart beating wildly and my senses jangling like keys on a chain,

I listened—really listened—to what Fin was saying from the other side of the door. I realized he was trying to make me feel better about the way I woke him. *All over him.* He was absolving me of blame, trying to get me to laugh, even. But if the shoe had been on the other foot, if I had woken to a mauling, might it have been a different story?

At the very least, I would've been as prickly as a hedgehog. At the other side of that scale might've been some scary accusations. Potentially, at least.

I want you so much it hurts.

The longing in his words broke something open inside me. I realized it was relief. Fin is unlike any other man I've ever known. Under that licentious facade, the playboy image, he's just so decent. Last night, he not only offered to pay for Baba's room, but he even let me be ridiculous about it for a while. In fact, his response made me realize how absurd *my* behavior was.

I'm heading for thirty, and this might be the nearest I ever get to marriage. It could take me years to rebuild my business, and I want to devote as much of my time to Baba as I can. She won't be here forever, and her mind will leave me sometime before her body finally does.

And if that's not a wake-up call for grabbing life while you can, I'm not sure what is.

Which is why I decided to make the most of this opportunity, of this honeymoon. I'm so stupidly attracted to Fin, we're both single, and we're sharing a bed in paradise. So what if he's king of the commitment-phobes, because I have no space in my life for a man.

In a few short days, I'll be back to London, and if I'm really lucky (thanks to my bonus wedding fee), life will be boring, humdrum, and gray. Because boring and gray are better than a white-knuckle existence any day.

I might never find a man I can trust my heart with, but I know I can trust Fin in this experience. *If not this marriage in the traditional sense.* He's made our relationship a safe space, and after what I've been through lately, that means everything to me.

The light dims as he steps into the suite, the soles of his feet slap-slapping the tile before he dips and sets me down in the bedroom. The sheet I snatched earlier lies in a heap at the bottom of the mattress. Maybe I should've straightened it before he—

All thoughts, distracting and otherwise, dissolve as I find my face in his hands. *Like I'm something to treasure.* He holds me there, his eyes drinking me in with a kind of soft-eyed wonder. Oh, yes. I like this.

"Hey, beautiful." His words stroke like a caress. Whoever said romance is dead never had a man look at them this way.

"Hello," I whisper a little breathlessly as champagne bubbles pop in my bloodstream. But this isn't real romance, I need to remind myself. At least, not in the love sense. This is the romance equivalent of fake fur. From a distance, it looks real. It might even feel similar when you brush it the right way.

Who are you trying to convince? PETA?

Not-Ronny can . . . go away.

His thumb presses my chin, angling my mouth for the brush of his. Or maybe I'm overthinking it, as he doesn't move in for that kiss.

"You're frowning," he says as his thumb gently boops my nose. "I'm not."

Did he *actually* just do that? Like I'm a golden retriever and not a woman standing in front of him, naked. *Physically and emotionally.*

"You're not what?" I ask as my brows knot.

"Frowning. Ask me why."

"Okay." I roll in my lips, moistening them. "Why aren't you frowning?"

"Because I'm too fucking happy."

"Right." So bloody well do something about it, then!

"Do you want to tell me what's going on in that head of yours?"

"I thought you were going to kiss me." *And I'm crawling out of my skin with need, and you just booped me.* "And I suppose just standing here feels a bit of a waste when there's a bed—"

I twist from the waist in the direction of said bed, when Fin turns me back, pulling me against him to fasten his lips to mine. He kisses me, really kisses me. It's a kiss that's neither frantic nor frenzied, but slow, and thorough, like he's been waiting to kiss me for years.

His broad palms coast down my sides and slide around my back as he moves closer—moves into me, deepening his kiss. He steals my breath and feeds me his, as his fingers curl around the soft flesh of my hips, pinning me in place as he pulls away.

His features sort of hazy and indistinct, his face is so close to mine like this. But I don't need to see to know he's still smiling. And so am I. *Relief. So much of it.*

"Mila?"

"Yes?" I answer, a little dazed.

"Lose the fucking attitude."

My spine stiffens, but that's as far as I get as Fin presses his thumb to my kiss-tingling bottom lip. Everything inside me seems to contract as he pushes it into my mouth. My brain switches off, my mind now completely blank as he pulls my lip down.

This shouldn't feel sexy but, *oh*.

"You're all in your head." His tongue coasts over the exposed skin. "Do you know what that means?"

I shake my head, my movement limited.

"It means I can't enjoy your body." His pulls away. I rub my lips together, a little dazed. "Because your body is mine, remember? That's what we agreed."

My body likes the sound of that, of being owned. Being coveted. Not that I have time to fully process as he spins me around to face the dark wood dressing table. The top is cluttered with cosmetics; a brush thick with my dark strands, a bottle of my perfume, and me, naked, in the mirror. *And not just to the skin.*

"See how beautiful you are." His words are a bare breath across the back of my neck. "Look at yourself, Mila. See what everyone else sees. What I fucking see."

I see . . . me. I've been seeing me in the mirror for almost thirty years, and I'm no great shakes.

"Why can't we just move to the . . ." As I turn my head over my shoulder, my words trail away.

"Bed?" His breath is hot and his lips a flirting tease as his hands skim my body, taking in the shapes of my breasts, my hips. "I love how those big brown eyes watch me," he murmurs as his fingers loop my wrist. "Just taking everything in."

I straighten as he pulls gently, settling my fingers to the back of his neck.

"You make me so goddamned hot." His tone all husk and want as his knuckle brushes from my wrist down.

I not only feel but see my reaction as my gaze moves back to the mirror without really noticing. My breasts rise and my nipples tighten as I sink into him. Sink into the solidness of his body.

"Yeah, like that." His hand snakes around me, heat rising through my skin. Capturing my nipple between scissored fingers, he gives a soft tug.

My reaction is multidimensional. The sensation, the way I arch into his caress, and the sight of myself in the mirror. It's all so much.

"I want you like this." His eyes meet mine, as dark and as somber as thunderclouds. "I want you to see what I do to you. What you do to me." His hand flat to my stomach feels as hot as any brand when he presses me between his palm and his cock. "I want you to take your pleasure, Mila."

I whimper as his free hand cups my breast.

"See it in the color that rises on your skin."

"Touch me," I plead, need surging through me. "Fuck me."

"Mila." He makes a warning of my name. "An offer like that, and I might not be a gentleman."

My head floods with such images. His thumb in my mouth. His cock. His hands in my hair, his gratification as he holds me there.

"Please," I whisper, sliding his hand lower, pressing it between my legs. Because the woman in the mirror looks like the kind who knows what she wants. Such dark, languid eyes, and a soft sigh of relief as Fin's fingers part her flesh like a piece of overripe fruit.

His bicep flexes against my side, the veins in his forearm standing proud. All that heavenly musculature, that movement just for the pads of his fingers to circle my clit.

"You're so pink and so pretty and glistening for me."

I sigh, elongating my body and widening my stance to deepen the heavenly contact.

"Do you like that, darling Mila?" He smiles as though remembering. *Double darling.* His fingers slide lower, gathering my wetness to paint over the rise of my clit. "Shall I slide my fingers inside? Fuck you with my fingers?"

I nod, feeling as though I might burst from my skin, and I give a taut gasp as he does just that.

"So fucking beautiful," he purrs as we both bear witness to my pleasure in the mirror. "Watch. See how you glisten."

And I do. Oh, God, I do. I watch as he makes a V of his fingers, exposing the velvet skin to the mirror. He begins to circle, pet, and strum that tight bundle of nerves as the sounds of my pleasure rise through the room. My cries become louder, bouncing from the walls as my fingers tighten, my nails piercing on the nape of his neck.

"Oh, God, please . . . please let me, Fin!" I tip onto my toes, chasing his touch.

"Are you putting on a show, darling? Do you think the journalists will see?"

Something spikes through me, my heart misfiring as my gaze slides to the wall-size window. A sensation swims through me. It's panic. It's power. It's something I can't make sense of, even as I remember Fin's earlier words.

Privacy glass. We can see out, but no one can see in.

"Maybe you only hope they will." His harsh whisper curls around my ear before the realization of what this is echoes in my head. I told him—this is one from the vault of my secret reveries. A fantasy too sordid, too dirty for actual words. *Yet I must've whispered it to him.*

"They'll be so jealous. This lush body, this perfect pussy. This hair and this ass—only I get to touch them. Because you're all mine."

I make a velvety groan of his name as pleasure begins to violently pulse through me.

"Maybe they'll take photos and show their friends. Print them and keep them for their special alone times," he says, using my own words.

An incomplete fragment of memory pulls at me. He had been inside me on our wedding night when I whispered my fantasy. That I sometimes imagined being watched; fucked and coveted at the same time. His rhythm faltered; then he whispered a harsh curse as my fantasies drove him deeper.

"You'll be so shiny and slick when I get my mouth on you. You're a feast, my love. And I'm going to devour you whole."

My body spasms around his fingers, a reaction to this invasion, to his words. My climax detonates like a bomb, my body twisting as I grip the back of his neck and come undone.

His arms come around me in an honest-to-goodness bear hug. Solid. Fortifying. Safe.

"Thank you," he whispers, pressing his lips to my hairline.

"You're welcome," I answer ridiculously, my wits still loose and rolling about my empty head.

Twice. I came twice in pretty quick succession. A first for me. *The first I remember, anyway.*

"Three for three?" he asks with a wicked grin, either intuiting my thoughts or maybe reading them on my face.

"Three?"

His hand curls around my shoulder, encouraging me forward. My palms flatten to the dresser top, cosmetics rattling and rolling as he pulls on my hips, and my bum thrusts out. *Like my body was made for this. Made for him.*

He's so large behind me, all hard angles and slopes, every muscle clearly defined in his reflection. But it's his expression that takes my breath. So focused. So serious.

I roll my lips inward as his hands slide over my cheeks. As they caress, as they squeeze. As he drops to his knees with an awe-filled "You're so, so pretty, just . . . everywhere."

His appraisal brings with it a disgraceful wash of pleasure. Every inch of my skin seems to inexplicably tingle.

"What are you . . ." *Why are you? And how can I like this?*

"You're not the only one with fantasies to fulfill," he purrs.

"I don't know what that means."

"So many questions," he taunts as his thumbs slide to part me to his gaze.

I close my eyes, the sensations too large to process; mewling— yes, mewling!—as his thumb slides over my flesh. My insides throb as his hot breath hits me, my body bucking wildly to the press of his tongue. He slicks through my wetness with a groan of appreciation, licks as though I am *the* tastiest dish.

I've never done anything like this—never had anyone go down on me while standing. *From behind.* It feels so dirty. So wrong. And yet so utterly wonderful.

"Wider, love. Spread yourself for me."

How, at the age of almost thirty, am I discovering this is even a thing?

"Don't make me ask twice."

"Oh!" And, apparently, I enjoy being spanked. And having my bum squeezed by big, possessive hands.

"That's my girl."

That shouldn't press my pleasure buttons, but it does. I screw my eyes tight against the sight of my pleasured expression, my nails scraping the wooden top as Fin buries his tongue so deep, I swear I can feel it behind my belly button.

It seems like no time at all before that familiar sensation begins to build. A sweet and urgent kind of agony.

Already? Really?

Yes, really, as I begin to pant like a wild thing.

"You're so fucking delicious." His words, their low vibration, rock me to my core. I grind back against him—against his face— moaning like I've been paid to do so.

There can't be this much pleasure in the world.

And yet there is, as Fin doesn't so much savor as devour, twisting my orgasm into something otherworldly, his tongue and fingers plucking me apart. *Just as he'd promised.*

With a frenzied cry, I drop to my elbows, my arms giving out as something swift and sleek rushes through me, from me. I collapse in a heap on the now-messy dresser.

Seconds, maybe hours later, Fin's hand grazes my waist, my skin reacting like fire to the brush of it. He presses a kiss to my head as he opens a drawer, pulling out a square of silver foil.

I watch as he lifts it to his mouth, his lips shining in the bright sunshine, smeared lewdly with my pleasure.

Three orgasms and nothing yet for him, the whisper of not-Ronny supplies.

Every moment so far has been about me. About my pleasure, not his. Conjuring my fantasies with his dirty whispers, the command in his tone, the way he's touched and held me. And it's all brought us here. To the point where I want—no, *need*—to reciprocate, as I turn and push him backward in the direction of the bed.

I see in his expression when he realizes what I'm about. See that he likes it. He lowers to the bed, pressing his hand to the mattress behind him. *As proud as a pasha,* I think, as I take the condom from between his fingers and drop it onto the mattress. I fold to my knees, and I wonder if he can feel it, this connection throbbing between us.

As I bow my head, he gathers the dark strands over my shoulder.

"Thanks," I whisper ridiculously.

"You're welcome." Eyes dark and smile lurking, he watches as I moisten my lips and wrap my fingers around him.

"Thundercock," I whisper, the thought escaping without thought.

He runs a tender finger across my cheek. "You prefer that to *daddy,* huh?"

Daddy is an energy. He's firm but gentle. He's bossy in the bedroom. He takes charge but makes you feel safe. A daddy cares.

Daddy suits him. Not that he'll ever hear those words come out of my mouth.

He gives a moan that's ragged around the edges as I press my lips to him, then slide down.

"Mila. *Oh, fuck.*" He falls back on his palm once again, his mouth slack as I hollow my cheeks and slide back to suck and lick his silken crown.

"Jesus! Keep doing that. I'll be putty in your hands."

My mouth comes off him with a sucking pop. "You know there are pills you can get for that," I say, my voice soft.

Laughter bursts from his mouth like honey from a squeeze bottle.

Oh, my. I love that. But it doesn't last as I lower my mouth with a soft sucking kiss. He hisses, his thigh tautening under my fingers, our eyes locking as I slide my tongue along the underside of his wide cock.

"I love how you watch me, Mila. Like you're staring into my soul . . ." He swallows thickly, not quite as unaffected as he might try to seem. "I love how you watch . . . watch what you're doing to me."

The sweet agony in his words. *I did that.*

"Fuck!" His head drops back, the muscles of his shoulders so taut.

I did that too.

"Yeah, like that," he whispers, staring down at me once more. "That's right, love, get it nice and wet."

I make a noise. The aural this man gives . . .

"You look so, so pretty sucking me."

I almost swallow him.

"You like that, don't you? You like a little instruction. A little praise."

I moan around him, not quite an agreement, but I can't help the effect his low, rumbling commentary has on me. As Ronny would say, "I high-key love" what it does to me as my insides throb like a poked bruise.

225

"That's it, take me all the way in. *Fuck!* You look so hot, your mouth stretched wide around my cock."

I moan again. Fin DeWitt doesn't play fair, and my movements become messy as I take what I can, working the rest with my hand. I work him from root to tip, loving the tight breaths of his seductive commentary.

"Mila, darlin'. You're gonna make me come."

His assertion makes me lose all composure. I begin to work him wetly, with gusto and zeal, wanting to get there, wanting to feel—

His hand slides under my chin, pulling my mouth away.

"Isn't that the point?" I wipe the back of my hand across my mouth and notice his chest moves as though he's been running.

"Maybe next time." He grabs the condom from the mattress, pressing it to my hand. "I need to be inside you the first time I come."

"Oh." My. Days. I wonder if he knows how powerful his words are.

Fin watches intently as I tear the corner of the foil, then leans back on both palms as I begin to sheathe him. Then, with an inciting look, he whispers, "Climb on."

Chapter 20
FIN

I close the door behind me, leaving sleeping beauty curled up in my bed. I could've stayed there all day, lying next to her, just studying the nuances of her loveliness. The tiny REM flutter of her dark lashes, the beauty mark behind her left ear. Her violin curves, and her dainty fingers and pink-painted toenails. But the longer I watched, the greater the temptation grew to kiss her. To pull her close and just fucking hold her. As though it might contain the enormity of my feelings.

In other words, post-nut clarity just wouldn't let me sleep. And my girl needs her rest, given she pretty much passed out after she climbed off my dick.

It was amazing to touch her before, to kiss her, to taste her tiny whimpers. But there's something about her taking charge that elevated the whole experience.

Wife, my mind whispers. It blows my mind.

A grin suddenly creeps across my face. I love Evie for Oliver, but I couldn't quite believe that anyone would tie themselves to another for life. It blew my mind trying to understand why, let alone how they could be so certain. What blows my mind now is that I'm in the same place—that I understand and feel those same certainties. Mila is the one for me, and I know now the whole point is *not* to get it. Until you do. Because that's how you get to be so sure.

Five days. We're on the same timeline, just not on the same tracks. I'm sure Mila thinks she's getting her freak on—getting her groove back. While I'm down to help her with that, I do so with the plan to ultimately, matrimonially, lock her down.

I know it's crazy, and my feelings might seem over the top to anyone else, but the way I see it, I've been falling in love for months.

I've got it bad, and I don't give one single fuck.

For almost twenty years, I've actively avoided relationships and pushed away any possibility of love. *Who would've thought I'd find it in a coat closet,* I think with a wry smile.

Mila is unlike any woman I've ever known, and she treats me like no woman has. I just want to walk by her side. Be hers—be part of all her life stories. And her, mine.

I make a call to the concierge, order some food for when Mila wakes, then dunk myself in the outdoor shower, which isn't nearly as much fun the second time around.

Then I pick up my phone.

"What the fuck time do you call this?" Matt, the third of our trio in Maven Inc., doesn't bother with niceties, his usual soft Irish lilt leaning more toward aggressive. A tone not often heard from him.

"What do you mean?" I don't bite. I'm too blissed out to be annoyed.

"I emailed you hours ago. Hang on." The loud trundle of wheels over gravel and the beep-beep of a reversing construction vehicle sounds through the handset. A door opens and bangs shut, footsteps, and then, "What's going on with the Dildo?"

I'm confused for a second. I know I've recently had sex, but post-nut clarity isn't extending that far. Then I remember. The building.

"Nothing, as far as I'm aware." It hasn't even passed planning yet.

London has the Gherkin, the Cheesegrater, the Boomerang, and the Walkie-Talkie, which are all actual buildings, even if those aren't their actual names but the ones Londoners have christened them with. Soon to join their ranks will be the Dildo, as it's been referred to internally (ahem) by Maven Inc. It's touted to be the tallest building in London, once it's built, topping the Shard by seventy meters, sprouting from the skyline like a great phallic beast.

I really hope the nickname sticks. Especially as I came up with it.

"We really need to start calling the place by its actual name," I murmur, dropping to the couch.

"It might not need a name, given the word on the street."

A cube of ice drops into my warm mellow. "I don't know what you're talking about."

"Then you should maybe read your fucking emails."

"I'm on vacation." *Honeymoon,* my mind supplies as I pull a throw cushion from behind my back and launch it to the ottoman. "I haven't opened my laptop since I arrived. Give me the highlights."

"Fuck off with your vacation," he retorts. "It wasn't even scheduled in."

"Take it up with Oliver." As the major shareholder, he likes to think he's boss. "I don't suppose you've heard from him."

"Not since Wednesday, when he told me not to bother turning up to his wedding."

That asshole. So much for their plan not being a solid one.

"At least he told you. I flew in from Jakarta for the wedding that never was." I can't really complain. Not when I also got the girl. The girl who fake married me to help her grandmother. *Then found herself real married to me.* My mellow returns as I think of how she allowed me to help secure Roza's new home. That has to be a step in the right direction, right?

"Well, it's a wedding that has been now," he says. "I met Lucy for a quick cuppa yesterday. The deed was done in Saint Bart's. How he pulled that off on such short notice, I'll never know."

"I expect the conniving shit planned it this way all along," I say with grudging respect.

"Good fella you are for helpin' them out, all the same. I'm not sure I would've been so keen in your place."

"You know me. I'm all for helping out a friend."

"Especially when there's a pretty girl involved."

"Lucy told you, huh?" I rub my hand up the back of my neck. Lucy would be the one person Oliver let in on his plans. The one person who would've been present. I mean, the three of us have always been tight—Oliver, Matt, and me—and we've become a quartet since Evie joined our squad. But Lucy is different, because she's Oliver's blood. They've suffered enough bumps in the road, so I know he wouldn't have kept this from her.

"Aye, she did. What a harebrained scheme, eh?"

"It's pretty nuts," I agree, setting my shit-eating grin free. "So, what's going on with the Dildo?"

"There are whispers of insider trading with the Deux Toi lot," he grumbles. "And if that turns out to be true, we know the Qataris will pull out, and then we'll all be fucked."

"Leave the Qataris to me. As for the French crew, I'll make a few calls and see if I can find out what's going on."

"Tongues are wagging, Phineas," he says in an ominous tone. "And you know what a bunch of auld wives they are in this game."

"I'm on it. I'll stomp out any flames I find."

"Thanks. I appreciate it. You know that shit's not in my wheel-house," Matt adds, clearly relieved.

Maven Inc. is a private-equity company that primarily deals with real estate and property development, and within it, each of us has a niche. Oliver is the dynamics. Always ahead of the trends in both equity and capital investments, he has a nose for making money, which keeps our investors happy. *Along with the rest of us.*

My responsibilities lie with our investors and maintaining strong working relationships with them. And yes, that includes wining and dining the big players, which is why I've been dubbed the party boy. I prefer to say I'm paid for who I know, not what I do. And not for *who* I do, which the assholes rag on me unfairly for. *You make a mistake one time . . .*

Matt, meanwhile, is in deal origination. He's front line—grass roots—and, truthfully, he does way more than he should. Which is why I heard construction noise on the line.

"So." His tone turns expansive in that one tiny word. "Work aside, how's the Oliver-mandated vacation going?"

"Technically, it was Evie mandated." *Oliver just stumped up the money.* I find myself frowning. I don't care that he paid Mila to be here, but I do know it weighs on her mind.

"You're with the wedding coordinator, I hear."

"That's right." There are no fucking secrets, though I'm not sure I appreciate his tone. "She's great. Really great."

"And pretty, no doubt."

I frown, as though he's said something wrong.

"But a week, Phineas? That's not your usual MO."

"What's that supposed to mean?"

"Come on. A week with one girl?"

"I'm hardly railing a different woman every night of the week."

"No," he concedes. "You usually have Wednesdays off." His joke falls flat, not that he pauses long enough to realize. "One girl in close confines for a week? Things are bound to happen."

"Could that be a *wee touch o'* jealousy in your tone?"

"That is a terrible attempt at an Irish accent. Never injure my ears thusly again. And no, fuckface, I'm not jealous. I have a third date with Isobel on Friday."

"Third date." I whistle. "You know what that means, don't you?"

"That you can fuck right off with your insinuations. If I had to spend a week with you, I'd probably drown you in the swimming pool."

"I'm not dead yet."

"Anyway, some of us have got standards. I wouldn't spend a week shacked up with a stranger, pretty or not."

"Says Maven Inc.'s only bachelor."

"I mean, I know you've done Oliver a grand favor—" His words halt, and I'm pretty sure I can hear the cogs of his brain turn over.

"I said what I said."

"No." One incredulous word. Then, "No fucking way!"

"I got married Saturday. Got the ring, certificate, and everything." I lift my left hand, examining the thin gold band on the fourth finger.

"In me bollix!" he scoffs, which is followed by another pause. "It was all pretend."

"Until we changed our minds and fell madly in love." So I'm stretching it, but fuck him.

"Jesus, Mary, and Joseph. And the little fuckin' donkey! You're being serious?"

"Congratulate me," I say, kicking my bare feet onto the ottoman. "For I am a married man."

"This is not an episode of *Bridgerton*!"

"What's *Bridgerton*?"

"Doesn't matter," he mutters. "Let me get this straight. Oliver asked you to *pretend* to be him."

"Yep."

"And to pretend to get married to the wedding coordinator, who was pretending to be Evie."

"That's right."

"But you got married for real?"

"Yep." A pulse pounds low in my belly, and my eyes fall closed as an image flashes in my head. Her dainty fingers wrapped around my cock, sunlight bouncing from her gold wedding band. I'd almost busted a nut right there as the word *mine* echoed in my head.

"Right there and then? In the ceremony meant for Oliver and Evie?"

"Was that the sound of you clutching at your pearls?" I retort, yanked back from the heavenly recollection. Mine to love and mine to fuck. Mine to spoil, to drip in diamonds, if I want. *Oh, she is gonna hate that.* The corner of my mouth hooks up at the thought.

"Were you still pretending to be them at that stage?"

"What?"

"Because that mad fucker will kill you if he's finally gotten Evie pinned down and you've somehow made him a bigamist."

"Don't be an asshole. I got married in my own name. It's not like it was planned, but I'm happy about it. In fact, I'm fucking ecstatic."

"And what about the girl—is she happy with her choice of husband?"

I pause. I know I've made her happy a few times already today. As to the deeper meaning, she just needs to let go and relax into it a little.

"Fuckin' eejit. What did you do?"

233

I should've just said yes—*Yes, my wife is deliriously happy to find herself married to me.*

"I didn't *do* anything." Which might turn out to be part of the problem when she finds out. *If* she finds out.

"So, what? She's got cold feet?"

"No."

"So she's sick of you already?"

"I didn't say that."

"Doesn't she know women have been tryin' to put a ring on it for years? And by *it*, I mean your nose?"

"Does my reputation precede me, you mean?"

"You've got more chance of nailing shit to a ceiling than this working out. You know that, right?"

"That's where you're wrong."

"Except for the huge-arse pregnant fuckin' pause just now. What's the issue? Is she not into this marriage quite as much as you?"

"Yet," I mutter, staring up at the ceiling fan. "She's not as into it *yet*."

Saying the truth aloud makes me feel a little ill. "Look, she means more to me in a couple of days than—" A couple of days, my ass. I've been falling in love with her from the fucking coat closet.

But what if I can't ever get her to the same point? I push the thought away.

Is it me? Is it her? Is it because her ex fucked her over and all men are scum?

A little of the first, thanks to the internet and my so-called fucking friends. And a little of the second, which ties into the third, I guess. And the third deserves my boot in his face.

I know what it's like to be betrayed and what it takes to heal. I thought I had. Twenty years playing the field. How is that healthy? *How is that supposed to make her trust me?*

I have none of the answers. Except one. And that's Mila. Every place I look, every path I consider taking, she's at the end of it.

Another thought, another scenario, hits: I loaned her money—not that I want it back. Other women have considered me good for nothing but my cock and my wallet. What if she thinks this is my MO? What if she decides all I'm good for is throwing my dick around and throwing money at problems?

Matt makes a noise, long and low, pulling me from my unhappy musing. "I never thought I'd hear the day. Wait, this has got to be a first for you, right? First love?"

"Fuck off," I drawl. No way I'm baring my soul to him.

"You can't make someone love you, Fin."

"Maybe you can't. Besides, it's not like that." Or so I tell myself. I'm not used to losing, to struggling, so maybe that's just my ego talking. My fall for Mila has been like a drop from a sheer cliff. Mila, meanwhile, is still standing on that edge. Will her fall be a slow tumble, or will she leap and soar someplace else?

Maybe now *the shrooms are taking effect. That was some God-awful analogy.*

"Well, I suppose there are worse things than getting married. Like getting married to a woman who isn't into you."

"I didn't say that she wasn't into me, asshole." She's into me, all right. I just need her to get to the place where she can see me in her life, beyond endless sun and tropical climes.

See me for who I really am.

A man who hasn't had a serious relationship since he was still wet behind the ears. A man who's used to getting what he wants, using his charm and his smile to make sure he comes out on top. *What a fucking catch.*

"Or contracting smallpox. Or Ebola. And what was the last one? Ah, that's right. Gettin' your dick caught in a meat slicer."

"Yeah, okay. You've made your point." I said all those things at Oliver's bachelor party, though I use the term *party* very loosely. I'd been up for a weekend in Ibiza for the celebration, or a week-long blowout in Vegas, though the latter wasn't Oliver's style. Matt suggested a Dublin pub crawl for the excellent *craic*, and I even threw in Prague as a second and more cultured attempt. But Oliver rejected any and all plans, adamant he'd be in bed with Evie by the end of his bachelor night.

So, dinner it was. At his own fucking hotel.

Wild, right?

I ribbed him about it all night. Told him he was pussy whipped. The irony is, I get it now. There was just a wall between me and Mila last night, and I wanted to tear that fucker down.

"I said that shit, but as it turns out, I'm happy to be proven wrong. I feel this, Matt. Feel the rightness in my bones. And she's not a stranger. I've spoken to you about her before."

Matt groans down the line. "It's not that horsey-lookin' one from that shite TV show."

"Who?"

"You know the one—she always seems to surface when we're out. Hanging around when the photogs are about."

"The woman from *Made in RICHmond*?" I feel my expression twist. "Charlotte something or other?"

"That's the one. She can't take a hint, which makes me think she hasn't enough brain cells to start a fire. You need two to rub together."

"I haven't spoken to you about her."

"Aye, you have. Complained, more like."

"I've never touched her," I reiterate. Not that she hasn't offered.

"I should've known it wouldn't be her. Evie wouldn't have that fame whoor anywhere near her big day."

"Evie likes my girl." That much seemed true.

"*Your* girl?"

"I'm fucking married to her!" I protest. "Her name is Mila."

Matt falls quiet. But just saying her name sends a wave of sunshine through my chest.

"Mila," he repeats.

"You remember, right?"

"Yeah," he says. "I remember. I just can't quite believe it."

Chapter 21
MILA

"Hey, pretty girl."

My eyes flutter open, and I'm momentarily unsure who the compliment belongs to. But then I remember the voice from my dream. And how his touch became my reality.

"Hi." I smile, the buttery light in the room making the color of his eyes meltingly sexy. "What are you doing?" My question is soporific, my movements sort of liquid as I stretch out along the mattress.

"Just watching you."

"Creeper." A flight of butterflies sweeps through my undies. "Any particular reason you're watching, Creepy McCreeperson?"

"I've been waiting for your eyes to open. So I can make them roll back in your head again. Cool trick, huh?"

"You're hilarious," I say, sounding the opposite, though I wouldn't be surprised if they had. I think I was even speaking in tongues at one point. "How long have I been asleep?" Because I feel *amazing*. I'm not sure how laughter can be proclaimed the best form of medicine when Fin has made me feel this wonderful.

Maybe life would be simpler if great sex was offered on prescription.

"Smiling girl." But Fin is smiling too. "Wanna share those thoughts?"

"Not with you."

From where he's seated on the edge of the bed, Fin brushes a few strands of my hair away from my cheek. "You've been out a couple of hours."

"You weren't sleepy?"

His response is a little enigmatic. And a lot out of character.

"Was I snoring? Because I don't snore," I tag on quickly, hoping that Adam was lying. Just being cruel.

"Nope. That would've put me off counting your eyelashes." But then he grins.

I make to stretch the sleep from my limbs, when I remember I'm naked under the sheet. Again. My heart gives a one-two thud, my arms dropping back to the mattress as my sympathetic nervous system turns over and does its awkward thing.

But when I find the ends of the sheet folded neatly just under my neck, I stifle a smile. Fin obviously went to the trouble of covering me before waking me up. Not because he doesn't want to look but because he wants me to be comfortable.

That previous unhappy thought, one about Adam, suddenly feels like a poke in the middle of the forehead. How different this experience is. Or maybe all relationships turn toxic at some point. Does familiarity breed contempt?

No. The reason I've been so down on myself, so down on my body, is because Adam wore me to that point. I lost myself in that relationship, but I think Fin is helping me find myself again. Just a few hours ago, I was naked and spread-eagled in front of him—I know he likes what he sees, and I don't just have to take his word for it. *His huskily delivered, heart-stoppingly dirty compliments.* Because

239

I also see how he watches me, how he pays attention. How his eyes drink their fill when I'm undertaking the most ordinary of tasks. And then there's earlier, when he studied my reactions and seemed to get off on my pleasure, postponing his own.

To think I might've missed out on that experience.

To think we could've been going at it like bad bunnies since Saturday.

Sex. Wow. That tiny word doesn't even cover what he did to me. What he did *for* me. What we experienced together. He pushed me out of my shell, showed me who was boss . . . while making sure at all times I was happy to hand things over.

How did he know to do that? Intuition, I suppose, just like now, covering me with the sheet. He pays attention.

"Thank you for covering me," I whisper.

"Wouldn't want you to get cold." His eyes dance with humor.

"How long did you look before you covered me?" I ask as I reach out to cup his cheek.

"That would be telling."

"I don't look like your usual type." I silently curse myself for the brain fart that burst from my mouth. Wow. I so need to adjust the dial on my internal self-love barometer.

"Stalker, much?" His words end in a playful curl.

"You wish," I say, ignoring my stinging cheeks, because that wasn't the answer my subconscious was looking for. "I just had to make sure you didn't have a wife and a boatload of kids." And absolutely nothing to do with my insecurities.

"You think I might be a bigamist?" His expression—it's like he can't decide whether to laugh or be annoyed.

"You know what I mean. Anyway, it turns out you don't have a harem, but you also have a fan club," I retort, thinking of my internet stalk.

"I wonder who's collecting the membership subscriptions. I should get a cut, right?"

"You're ridiculous," I whisper, stretching my arms about my head. As the sheet grazes my nipple, I realize I'm experiencing my very first nipple slip . . .

"You're the sexiest woman I know."

"Is that so?" I whisper, sliding my fingers from neck to sternum, dragging the sheet lower as my fingers traverse my ribs.

He hums a sound, low and long, his gaze turning my nipples to hard points. Oh, my days, pushing through your insecurities—forcing yourself to relax into your own skin—is sort of empowering. Look at me and my blooming sexuality, and my power over him.

I make a tiny noise of pleasure as Fin slides his thumb across my exposed nipple.

"You know, I never considered myself to have a type before," he says, watching my body undulate under his touch. "It turns out I do." His eyes are so dark as they lift.

"You don't look very happy about that," I say, arching into his hand.

"It's not that," he murmurs, bending to press his lips to the hard bud. "I'm kind of conflicted. I ran you a bath—I thought you might like that—but now I just want to lick you clean myself."

The man ran me a bath. I am ridiculously touched by that.

I was also physically touched. Because we fooled around a bit. *And it was heavenly.*

He touched me here, here, *and* here, I mouth silently in the mirror, examining the evidence. A patch of stubble rash. A sucking bite to my chest. He might praise my bum, but he also seems really into my boobs. Actually, I think it's more the case that he's into the whole package. I love that for me. All this pleasure *and* a bath!

It might sound stupid, given I've got hands that work, but no one has ever run me a bath since I was a little girl. A bath is a treat to me as an adult—a moment to indulge in a little relaxation. It's like a sign that says *Go on, take some time. Treat yourself.*

And I never treat myself.

So I appreciate this so much. I also appreciate how Fin didn't wait around, allowing me a few moments alone in the bathroom to do what a girl must. I leave the door open afterward as a sign that I wouldn't mind his company, pushing myself a little further out of my comfort zone.

It's where the rewards are.

And I'm just sinking into the fragrant water as Fin appears on the threshold. *Shirtless, just how I like him.* I like that he doesn't ask permission, just drops his shoulder against the doorframe and watches.

"How's the water?"

His appraisal causes heat to flare and swirl through my core, even as that voice inside triggers those familiar sentiments. *You're too short. Too round. You want too much—you are too much.* Yesterday, those thoughts would've hit me hard. Would've caused something prompted or pointed to shoot out of my mouth. Today, I choose a new path. If I'm too much for you, too bad. Because I'm just who I need to be for myself. Or at least, I'm learning to be. And I revel under Fin's attention, because it's clear he doesn't find me lacking.

The thought shimmers across my skin.

"It's perfect. Look, my skin is all silky." I lift my arms, sliding my hands over each in turn. "I don't know what you've put in here, but I'll smell good enough to eat."

His eyes darken and he folds his arms across his chest. "Looks to me as though someone's decided to be a naughty little strumpet."

"A what?" I ask with a delighted, stuttering laugh. I sink deeper into the tub.

"And it sounds like someone is angling for a spanking."

"Wait, wait, wait," I say, ignoring the flush of heat his words cause. "Let's back it up a bit. Who, under the age of seventy, says *strumpet?*"

"We have established you like older men." He pushes off the doorframe and stalks toward me. My insides flip. "Maybe I can borrow a walking stick, and we can indulge in a little role-playing, Mila style."

"First of all, *eww.* Second, what even is a strumpet?" As I speak, I turn my head, following his path as he moves behind me to the top of the bath.

"A very bad girl," he says, drawing the words out as he encourages me to lie back.

And I do, jumpy and sort of nervous as I force my arms to remain by my sides. My body is such a pale contrast to the dark water.

"A strumpet is a very wicked creature." He dips his hands into the warm water, and I bite my bottom lip as his bare chest brushes my shoulders. His hands skate up my arms, the bath oil aiding their slick slide. "Who loves to tease."

"Sounds like you might be a strumpet."

His laughter sounds so dirty as his hands swipe across my shoulders before making a return journey. They move momentarily away, returning with a natural sponge. This time, he reaches over me, dipping it into the water before showering it over the tops of my breasts.

"Sit up. I'll wash your back."

The fact that this isn't a request makes me tingle all over. It's a good thing he's behind me, because it's not the heat from the bath that's making my face hot. I do as I'm bidden, the water sluicing up the bath's sides before Fin begins to soap me up, drawing soft circles over my skin.

"I've got some news."

I turn my head and watch him in profile as his words echo in the cavernous room.

"We're not going to be able to go down the annulment path," he adds, his expression unchanging.

I turn away, not sure what to say as my mind struggles to process, jumping from pleasure to uncertainty. "You spoke to your legal team again?"

"I just got off the phone with the head guy. There's no space for wrangling, legally speaking. But I'm assured it'll be easy to fix once we're back in London."

"How? How easy can a divorce be? Because that's what we're talking about, right?" My mind begins to run through the implications. Married. To him. But not really. There are bound to be complications, even if the marriage is just on paper.

Baba's nursing home, for one. The thought brings with it a sinking feeling. As she has no assets to speak of, the local authority—the state, I suppose—is responsible for the fees of her current nursing home. My upcoming windfall, the reason I'd supposedly fake married Fin, means I'll have the funds to contribute—to *choose* to place her somewhere and pay the shortfall. That was the plan, at least.

But if I'm suddenly married to a wealthy man, a man who has already contributed—because that's how his loan will appear to the authorities—might I then become liable for the fees? Her current (mediocre) nursing home charges thousands a month.

My new nest egg isn't going to get us very far.

"Try and relax, Mila. I promise I'll fix things."

I snap out of my thoughts, relieved at the interruption. Not that I can tell Fin any of this.

You could try, not-Ronny suggests. But I ignore her.

I've stood on my own two feet my whole adult life, through good times and bad. I'm not about to get out my begging bowl now.

"Your legal people, they won't blab, will they?"

"Lawyers have a code of ethics they're bound to."

"Oh. Of course. But—"

"And watertight NDAs."

I frown and nod at the same time. "We can't tell anyone. Not even your friends."

"Still want to keep me your dirty little secret?"

I ignore his teasing. Wouldn't that be more the other way around? "I'm serious. You especially can't tell Evie and Oliver."

"I know, you already said." But his tone sounds uncertain.

"I mean it." I turn my head over my shoulder as I make a grab for his wrist. "Promise me, Fin."

"Sure." He doesn't get it, judging by his expression. "This isn't the big deal you think it is."

"That's easy for you to say," I murmur, turning away again. "I doubt you've ever had to wear the weight of other people's judgment."

"Fuck what people think. I should've said that before. I never judged you, not even before."

Before he knew about Baba, he means. Maybe he'd judge me if he knew what Baba had predicted. He might even think I did this on purpose.

"I don't care that Oliver offered to pay you. That was business, nothing more. What happened after was apart, and nothing to do with anyone but us."

I huff a breath. It's not quite a laugh. It all sounds so fucked up. Oliver, his best friend, paid me to fake marry him. Not to real marry him. Not to have lots and lots of sex with him. Not to fall in love with him. Which I won't. Still, I can't help but think how people would twist this, make it sound as worthless as Oliver buying his best man a lap dance.

"You shouldn't give a fuck what people think—not that Oliver and Evie would judge you."

"You can't know that, and it's a risk I can't *afford* to take."

He doesn't answer immediately, so I hope my meaning is sinking in. But the silence feels so uncomfortable.

"I need the money," I whisper. "And I haven't exactly met my part of the bargain."

"Some would say you've overdelivered. Transcended . . ."

"It's not just the money," I admit. "It would be bad for my business if news of our marriage gets out."

"You know, you didn't answer when I asked if wedding planners have to take a vow of celibacy." The sponge circles, his words turning teasing and light. "Are they not allowed to take part in the blissful state themselves?"

"Please be serious. You were there, you heard Oliver promise to get my business mentioned in some magazine articles. I could really benefit from the exposure. It's not that I need Oliver's help; it's that I'm desperate for it—that I refuse to risk it."

"Won't I do?"

"By recommending my services for a wedding where I'm the bride? *Your* bride?"

"Yeah, I see your point."

But I'm not sure he does. *Fin DeWitt, consummate bachelor and alleged playboy, would like to recommend the services of Trousseau, a boutique wedding-planning service.* It would be like Sweeney Todd recommending Mrs. Lovett's pie shop, or a pyromaniac a brand of matches.

"I'm sure we could come up with another angle, PR-wise," he adds.

"It looks bad, Fin. I plan a wedding for Oliver and Evie and snag their best man, one of London's most popular bachelors, in the process? Marrying him within days?"

"We might've fallen head over heels for one and other."

"And out of love again once the divorce is finalized? No," I add softly. "That's a plan with very little long-term appeal. I won't risk Trousseau. I think it's best no one knows."

A silence falls between us, but for the ripple and drip of water.

"*One* of London's most popular?" he says, moving the conversation back from the topic of us, perhaps being careful not to point out he's technically no longer a bachelor.

"You already know I looked you up."

"Which is my point," he says softly.

"I don't think your profile will be good for my business." Or my heart.

He doesn't answer as he begins to rinse away the suds, squeezing the wet sponge over my back and my shoulders before encouraging me to lie back again.

"I'm sorry if I sound harsh. There's just such a lot at stake for me."

"You don't have to explain."

But I feel like I've hurt him. We fall quiet again.

"What's your favorite color?" he asks as the soapy sponge slides down my arms.

"Why?"

"We've got a few days. Can't spend every minute of it fucking."

I actually laugh at that.

"I thought we could get to know each other. We *can* be friends."

"Okay," I answer uncertainly. It's a nice sentiment, but it also feels a little like a trap. "Probably blue," I say, though I almost answered *gray*. "Yours?"

"I like pink," he murmurs, sliding the sponge between my breasts.

"Do you wear a lot of *pink*?" The word hits the air in a hard puff as the sponge glides over my nipple.

"Not really. But it's still my favorite color," he says swiping again. I let out a shaky breath as the sponge moves away. "How did you get into wedding planning?"

"The official story is I'm a sucker for a good love story. That I'm efficient and goal oriented just means—"

"I can vouch for you there." I tilt my head to find his lips already near my ear.

I don't have an answer. Not a verbal one, at least, as he traces the sponge over the rise and fall of my chest.

"You were saying? About your job."

"I worked in a wedding-dress shop as a teenager. After school came a succession of admin jobs. Then I ended up helping a neighbor with her wedding after her mother died quite suddenly. I was between jobs," I whisper. Between jobs and a little listless. I'd forgotten about my earlier dreams of living like those women in the shop.

"A new direction." Fin dips the sponge under the water and over the softness of my stomach, grazing the top of my pubic bone before sliding back.

"Yeah. Baba volunteered my services, and I just sort of learned on the job. It turns out, one of the bride's guests worked for a small magazine publication, and the wedding ended up being featured."

Fin repeats the motion, and I release a shaky breath as he dips a little lower, coasting over my pussy.

"And a legend was made," he purrs.

I don't answer as my body strains to maintain the contact, my back arching and my breasts rising from the water.

"What about you? Do you en-enjoy what you do?"

"I like people, and I like money, so I like my job," he murmurs, continuing to swirl the sponge over my skin in soft, teasing circles.

I bet he's never liked it so much, needed it so much that he'd consider marrying a stranger.

"I think it's time to wash this soap away," he says as he reaches toward the tall tap. Which turns out to have a detachable showerhead. Warm water suddenly rains down on my breasts, and I make a startled noise, my arms rising from the water to reach for his.

"Hush now," he whispers, leaning closer and pressing the showerhead between my legs. "Open your legs for me, sweet girl."

And fool that I am for his touch, for him, I do.

Chapter 22
FIN

"Fin?"

Busted.

I get a little twinge in my gut as Mila pauses at the other side of the tiny kitchen, her head tilted like she's an inquisitive terrier. An adorably sleep-mussed terrier, dressed in the obnoxious Hawaiian shirt I was wearing this morning. I love the sight of her in it, and I just know I'm staring at her like a man starved.

Not that she'd admit it, but she's eyeing me just the same. She might complain about my lack of shirt wearing, but she fucking loves it so much, she deprived me of that one.

"What can I do for you, gorgeous?" I turn to face her, leaning my hip against the countertop.

"I was going to ask you what you've done with all my underwear, but . . . What are you doing?" She scrunches her nose adorably.

"Your underwear is missing?" I tap the spatula to my side as my gaze falls over her. "So what are you wearing under my shirt?"

Pursing her lips, she sends me a look that says: mind your own business.

"I was making pancakes. Trying, at least. But the fuckers won't stay up," I mutter, hitting attempt number five with the spatula. I'm unsurprised when it improves its appearance.

We barely moved from the suite yesterday. Hell, the bedroom! We fooled around and fucked, taking naps in between. We'd wake glued together, Mila spread across my chest. One trail of her fingers, one slide of her foot along my calf, and we'd be off again.

Or maybe we'd wake spooning. Mila is the best little spoon. And you know what they say about spooning. It usually leads to forking; I can confirm.

We paused only to eat and walk along the beach at sunset, followed by a midnight skinny-dip in the pool. Mila is so fucking beautiful, but wet and glistening in the moonlight? I barely survived that round.

"Fin?"

"Sorry, what was that?"

I watch as she steps up to the small breakfast area, her legs lithe and her dainty toes painted pink.

"Why are you making pancakes?" she asks, waving her hand over the food laid out.

I want to fuck her. Right here, in the kitchen. Bend her over the countertop, turn her ass pink with the spatula. Cover her tits in chocolate sauce and lick her clean.

She'd taste better than the crap on this skillet, anyway.

"Pancakes were supposed to be the centerpiece. The pièce de résistance," I complain, indicating the space in the middle of a round platter left for said pancakes. The perfectly spherical space is as hollow as my attempt to impress her, but surrounded by artfully piled berries, papaya, mango, and banana, along with tiny containers of chocolate chips, tiny pouring pots of dulce de leche, two kinds of chocolate sauce, and other fucking bits of breakfast perfection.

"But aren't these pancakes?" she asks, pointing to the tiny puffs in one corner of the platter.

"Those are *poffertjes*," I mutter, waving the spatula vaguely while briefly considering taking the credit for it all. "Dutch pancakes. That shit is all from the kitchen."

"The churros? Waffles too?" She sounds confused.

"Yeah, they made those. I had them put the platter together and send the ingredients for pancakes," I say, gesturing behind me with the spatula, only now realizing what a mess I've made. The soles of my feet are gritty with sugar, and the countertops are covered in flour and steel mixing bowls, whisks, and other stuff I don't know the fucking names for. "I guess the chef must've realized I'd be shit at it when they sent so many fucking bowls." Along with a recipe and step-by-step instructions that a toddler could probably follow. *Yet I still got it wrong.*

"You made breakfast," she says, a tremulous smile playing across her lips.

I mean, technically, it's not even brunch. *We've mostly skipped food in favor of devouring each other.* I wanted to do something nice for her, find some other way to make her eyes roll back in her head. As much as I enjoy fucking her, I wanted to show her I can be more. Do more. Hell, I wanted to woo her, so I thought I could best a not-gay fucking pastry chef? *Talk about desperation.*

"Go on, yuck it up." I toss the spatula into the sink behind me. "Some fucking breakfast. I can't even—" My words cut off as I turn back and feel her arms wrap around my waist and her face press into my chest.

"Thank you," she whispers.

"For ruining breakfast?"

"For even thinking about making me breakfast."

"Right," I mutter. Some idea this was. I should've gotten the kitchen crew to make it all and just be done with it.

"Shut up," she says, tightening her grip. I feel her smile against my skin, and the sunshine peeks out from behind my gray mood.

"Fine," I mutter, submitting to my failure. I guess I can stand anything as long as she's touching me.

"You know, the last person to make me breakfast was Baba. And I was probably eleven or twelve."

"Yeah?"

"I bet you have a private chef who feeds you."

"I'm a protein-shake man." I mean, I do, for dinners and stuff. I obviously haven't picked up any of his skill.

"Thank you for doing this. For looking after me. It feels . . . nice."

I feel the loss of her heat as she pulls away, her gaze averted.

"In this case, I'll take *nice*."

"Oh, will you now?" she replies pertly.

"Yeah." I flick a lock of her hair over her shoulder, then press my lips to her forehead so she can't read the rest on my face. *I want to look after you so damned well—and for the rest of your days.*

"Time to dish up those pan crepes," she says brightly as I pull away. "I'm so hungry, my bum is eating my knickers."

My chuckle sounds kind of filthy.

"Yes, okay. It would be eating my knickers if I could *find* my knickers. I don't suppose you know anything about that, do you?"

"Do I know anything about your panties?" I repeat pensively, rubbing my hand across my jawline. "I know I like to see them 'round your ankles. I also like to see them licked to transparency and sticking to your pussy."

"Stop that!"

I catch the dish towel she throws at my head. "They also looked pretty good stretched to one side while I—"

"La-la-la-la!" she sings loudly, pressing her hands over her ears. "No distracting me from my meal," she says, waltzing around me to gather a few of my sad fucking pan crepes, as she called them—more like pan craps—from the plate next to the stovetop. "I'm so starving."

"Me too," I rasp, sliding my hands around her. My palms gravitate to her tits. "I just can't seem to get my fill of you." I can't touch enough, can't fuck her enough, can't make her laugh enough to my satisfaction. But I intend on making it my life's work. *If I can.*

"Sex maniac," she says, laughingly pulling away.

Mila maniac, more like. And I do love her exasperation.

"You've gone to all this trouble to feed me," she adds, dropping the sad offerings to the middle of the laden platter. They look so out of place. "So feed me."

I adjust my crotch, my thoughts instantly X rated.

"Not that." Her gaze drops pointedly.

"I didn't say anything!"

"You didn't need to. Pervert," she adds as an apparent afterthought. Or maybe a compliment.

"You weren't complaining about my perversions this morning." God, I love this. Banter. I've never had a relationship with a woman I could have this kind of fun with. She dishes it as well as she takes it. And my God, she takes it *so* well. It's like being with the guys—and Evie—only better, because I don't want to fuck my name into any of them.

"Shall we eat on the patio?" she says, picking up the napkins, side plates, and silverware that arrived with the platter.

"Sounds good." I lift the platter. Because I'd follow that ass, *that woman,* anywhere.

◆ ◆ ◆

"You like what you see?" I give a comic waggle of my brows as I catch Mila eyeing me from across the table.

"I was just thinking you look like you should be lounging on a yacht on the Côte d'Azur. Well, except for your hair."

"Which makes me look like I should be on a prison ship?"

"I bet you'd be really popular on a prison ship," she says with a snicker.

"I'd prefer Portofino."

"To a prison ship? Who wouldn't?"

"I'd prefer Portofino to the Côte."

"Oh." Her eyebrows lift. "Of course you do."

Shit. She didn't like that. So maybe I won't offer to take her with me next time. At least, not yet, as I watch her use her fork to move pieces of pancake around her plate a little more.

"You don't have to eat it."

Her gaze lifts.

"No need to fake a dolphin sighting so you can drop it into the potted palm behind you."

"I wasn't going to," she says with a frown.

"But I wouldn't blame you. They're fucking awful."

"They're not that bad," she murmurs, moving her attention back to her plate. "Eggs," she adds curiously.

"What about them?"

"How many did you add to the batter?"

I already know where I went wrong. I just wasn't looking to broadcast it.

"Well, there were eggs mentioned in the recipe, but I dropped them."

"You dropped the eggs," she repeats, amused.

"That might be an understatement. There was egg and shell and goop everywhere," I say, miming an explosion. "That shit was in the cabinets, all over the floor, on my T-shirt, and in my hair. It was *everywhere*."

"Sounds to me like just another excuse for not wearing a shirt."

"Do you know how hard it is to clean up cracked eggs?"

"Yes. Everyone over the age of five knows how messy a cracked egg is." She begins to laugh.

"What's so funny?"

"The fact that you only found that out today," she says, sliding those awful fucking sunglasses from her head. Folding them, she places them on the table. Next time I'll find a better hiding place than behind a throw pillow. Maybe she'll let me take her to buy new ones sometime in the not-too-distant future. Maybe we could take in an afternoon of shopping in Covent Garden. Or better still, spend a weekend in Paris. We could take a stroll through Saint-Germain-des-Prés, book one or two private boutique appointments, where I could spoil her a little. Mila could try on some clothes, maybe even a little lingerie, while I sit back and drink champagne.

I'll shower her with gifts, if only to let her throw them back at me.

"Now I'm going to turn that question back at you," she says, reaching for her glass of juice. "What's making you happy?"

"That's easy. You." *And the way you'd react if I told you I was thinking of showing you the world. Making you my world.*

"So, tell me, if you don't cook, how do you eat? My guess is you don't subsist on toast and noodles."

"I like toast, and I like noodles," I say, shoving a lump of bacon into my mouth. It's cold yet still crispy and delicious.

"But do you make them yourself, or do you have a chef?"

Because *that* didn't sound like an accusation.

"Don't be embarrassed. You can say!"

"He's part time," I admit. No need to mention the rest of the crew. The housekeeper, the groundskeeper, and the gardening teams at my place in Florence. The cleaning service, my personal assistant, my personal shopper, and so on.

"And the rest of the time?"

"Eat out, I guess."

She frowns, but it doesn't last. "Well, thank you for going to the trouble to cook for me. I appreciate it."

Sunshine fills my chest. And more bacon fills my mouth. "Can't fault my enthusiasm," I say around it.

"Ten out of ten for effort."

"You know I always try my best," I kind of drawl, unable to help myself.

"Do you remember when you said you were always a groomsman and never a groom?"

"I kinda tempted fate with that one, didn't I?" I offer happily.

"Why do you say yes?" she asks, sounding genuinely curious. "To being a groomsman so often? Do you just really like wedding cake?" The latter she adds flippantly.

I'm such a good groomsman, I'd be an asset to her business. I almost said as much when she was soaking in the tub. And not for my experience either. Married to me, her profile would hit all the news channels. But that would be a worry in itself right now. So I kept it to myself.

"Sometimes it's just good for business," I admit instead. "A big part of my job is building relationships. I get to know our clients pretty well. I've even been instrumental in getting one or two of them together. When they ask me to take part in their wedding plans, I feel like I can't say no."

"So, they become your friends?"

I give my head a shake. "More like acquaintances. My friends are Oliver and Matt, and Evie. And, of course, my beautiful new wife."

"Don't," she says softly.

"It's what you are," I remind her just as softly.

"I thought we were making do with *friends*."

"And I thought you said I'd be bad for your blood pressure. When, clearly, I'm so good for it."

"How'd you make that out?"

"All those feel-good endorphins I induce." I give a playful leer.

"And all the cortisol and stress hormones you induce the rest of the time."

"You know what the answer to that is. More sex."

"You're sure sex isn't why you like being a groomsman?" Her words are lighthearted, but I feel the barb in them. "Weddings are a hotbed of hookups—not that there's anything wrong with that. I mean, it's bound to happen, isn't it? The combination of so many single people all in one space, flowing wine, champagne, and pheromones. There's love in the air and lust—not murder—on the dance floor as the single ladies congregate and get their flirt on. Honestly," she adds, sliding her hair behind her ears, "David Attenborough should narrate a documentary about the mating rituals demonstrated at weddings."

"I guess the reason I like weddings is that I like seeing people happy. Being in love."

"Even when love isn't something you're looking for, yourself."

"I never said that." My answer sounds a little sharp, and Mila looks slightly taken aback.

"Sorry, that's right. You said you'd loved once. I guess I just assumed once was enough."

"I never closed myself off to the possibility of it." Maybe I just took care not to find it.

"Well, I suppose weddings are as good a place as any to look for love. Or whatever," she adds.

"Two things," I say, making a peace sign with my fingers as I lean in, covering her hand with mine. "One, I found you at a wedding. At two weddings." As Mila makes to pull away, I tighten my hold. "And two, you shouldn't believe everything you read about me."

"What about when the words come from your best friends' mouths?"

"Sometimes people only see what they want to see."

"Not that it matters."

"It shouldn't." I lean back in my chair again. "But getting back to the topic of food, there's this place in Chelsea that does the most amazing breakfasts. We should go when we get back. Maybe Sunday?"

She shakes her head.

"Or we could do dinner instead."

"No. No breakfasts or dinners." Her tone is soft, her delivery careful.

"Are you breaking up with me already?"

"Fin, be serious."

"Okay." But I'm as serious as the fist currently crushing my heart. "Look, I know you don't want anyone to know we're married, and I get that. But we've had fun, haven't we? We've gotten on well. Wouldn't you like to see where this goes?"

Before the words are out of my mouth, she's shaking her head. "That's not what we agreed."

"Will being my friend also be a risk to your business profile?"

"That's not what I'm saying."

I might be "*one of London's most popular bachelors*," but I recognize a brush-off when I hear one.

"Plans change, Mila." Sometimes, people even fall in love.

"Well, my plans haven't changed."

She looks so sad, I change tack, forcing a smile, when what I want to do is throw my arms around her.

"I really like you, Mila." Understatement of the fucking year. "I think it would be a mistake not to get to know each other better. It doesn't have to be all about sex." Or only about sex. "And we don't have to do this publicly."

259

She pauses for a moment, blinking as though absorbing my words.

"I don't think that would be wise."

Just . . . fuck that noise. We're fucking married, and as crazy as it sounds, it's going to stay that way if I have anything to do with it.

"I'm sorry," she whispers, studying her plate again.

My heart isn't breaking, and I'm not hurt. Or not exactly. I expected her reaction. I guess I just hoped for better. Maybe it was too soon to bring this up, but I thought . . .

Fucking pancakes. It was just meant to be breakfast—maybe even a breakfast fueled by jealousy—but I see it for what it is now. Breakfast is the least of what I want to bring to her life. I want to shower her in riches, shower her in my love. Walk alongside her in life and share her load. Carry it when she'll let me. Scoop her up into my arms when she won't.

I'm undeterred. I have no choice in the matter, not with feelings this real.

"Don't you feel that spark between us? The connection?"

"It's just a holiday romance." Her eyes lift to mine, almost pleading for understanding. "We can't trust what we feel in this setting."

"Maybe you can't."

"When the holiday comes to an end, so will this," she says quietly. "It has to."

"Why? Tell me why it has to be that way." Hooking my foot around the empty chair between us, I pull it out and lift my feet onto it. *Spell it out for me, love. Is it me you don't trust, or just yourself?*

"I've got a lot to deal with when I get back. A lot to think about."

"I know."

"I have to find a new flat, and I have my business to concentrate on—"

"I can help," I persist. Pressing my elbows to the arms of the chair, I steeple my fingers. "I'm not just a pretty face."

"I'm going to be busy. So busy," she says, disregarding that. As she probably should.

"Let me be your friend. I can be a good friend. Whatever else they say, Oliver and Evie can vouch for that."

"But I won't, and friendship is a two-way street."

"I'm kind of low maintenance. No need to worry about upsetting me."

She tips forward suddenly, pressing her hands to her face. "Look," she says, red cheeked and wild haired, when she emerges again. "I've never done this before. I don't know how to navigate a friendship with someone who knows how my body works. Or even a situationship—a friends with benefits deal—which is what I assume you're really talking about."

"Why would you assume that?"

"Because you're almost forty years old and you've never had a long-term relationship, as far as I can make out. You're a regular feature in every gossip column in London. The women by your side change as often as the weather does! I can't do it—I can't take a risk on a relationship or even a friendship with you."

"Well, thanks for your honesty," I grate out. This one isn't an arrow but an axe that lands hard. And also, with respect, fuck that noise. This isn't about before. This is about now.

"I'm sorry if I didn't make myself clear, but I don't have space in my life for a friend, benefits or not. I've just gotten out of a relationship that I'm coming to realize robbed me of my self-esteem. Made me feel less than me."

"You're fucking amazing," I mutter begrudgingly. Not because I don't want her to know it, but way to go, calling me an aging playboy! And maybe I am—maybe I have been—but I only want to be hers. Her husband, her lover. Her fucking everything.

"I'm so grateful to you, Fin."

I feel my expression twist. *Thanks for the memories?*

"You've taught me so much. Shown me parts of myself I didn't know I possessed."

I groan and drop my head back, like a truculent teen. "Stop. Just stop trying to flatter me." She'll be back to calling me *nice* next.

"If I was trying to flatter you, I would've paid your cock a compliment."

"And what would you have said?" I know, I know. I can't seem to fucking help myself. Not with her.

"Probably that it's pretty."

I fold my arms and slide her an insightful look. "My cock is not pretty, Mila."

"It's pretty huge." She bites the corner of her mouth as though to countermand a smile. "In fact, sometimes I find myself thinking it must be so heavy."

"Yeah?"

She nods, all pink cheeked and adorable, her dark hair alive in the scant breeze. "Yes. And I think you should let me help. I could . . . I could hold it for you?"

"If I let you hold it, what would you do with it?" My gaze lingers speculatively where she toys with the button of my shirt. *No panties. Not for the rest of the holiday.*

One-handed, she flicks the button open. Then another.

"I think it's more a question of . . . *where* I would hold it," she whispers, her cheeks gloriously pink as she trails a finger between some stellar cleavage. The feet of her chair scrape against the sandstone tiles as she stands. "Would you like to come with me and find out?"

I know I'm being played—being distracted, like a kid with the promise of a shiny toy. *But I do so like it when Mila is shiny and slick.*

I push my own chair back, feeling the brush of her gaze over my chest as I stand. It seems we're both suckers for that part of the other.

"You know," I begin, unable to stop myself from trying one more time. For now. "It doesn't have to be complicated. It could be just as good as it is right now. Just without the sunshine."

"We're married, Fin. And we shouldn't be. Isn't that complication enough?"

The answer is no. Being married to her isn't nearly enough. I want her heart, and I won't be satisfied until it's love that binds us.

Chapter 23
MILA

Our final night.

When Fin suggests dinner at one of the hotel's restaurants, I jump at the chance. I think his offer is a kindness to us both. I know he's full of feelings—we both seem to have a lot of them. I see his in the way he studies me when he thinks I'm not paying attention. It's like he's logging every facet of me for later inspection. For me, these days have been a dream. But now reality awaits just around the corner.

Fin insists I choose a restaurant from the resort's offerings, and I opt for Japanese. Though I wonder if I've made a mistake when we walk into the space and I find it to be all low lighting, dark wood, mirrors, and quiet intimacy.

We're offered a private dining room, and when Fin looks to me, he declines without needing to ask. We follow the hostess to a table on the main floor instead.

Out of all our days, today is not one where we need to be alone. Somehow, the second-best seat in the house still leaves us feeling like we're wrapped in our own little world.

Conversation happens. It's not easy. And though I have difficulty swallowing my food, let alone tasting it, I manage. Fin recommends we dine *kaiseki* style, which turns out not only to be a multicourse dinner of delicious small plates but also the experience of *omotenashi*, which means "wholehearted hospitality," as he explains.

The food is a treat for the eyes, the courses served on hoba leaves, slate, and shell, each serving decorated with watercress and tiny edible flowers. And while the dishes look like works of art, the tastes and textures are where the real art lies. We're served dainty dishes of tuna tartare and wasabi, seared lobster dressed in coral sauce, and a crab croquette in a sweet-and-sour sauce. Wagyu beef in miso nut next, and *unagi seiro*, which turns out to be grilled eel. The latter is a little out of my comfort zone, but Fin manages to coax me into trying a little, served from his chopsticks.

We eat sushi to round off our main course before moving on to share our desserts: tonka bean ice cream infused with cherry blossom leaves and a deliciously light chestnut tart. I don't put up a fight this time, and our dinner passes in a blur of polite interruptions, delicious sake pairings, and carefully curated conversation.

And then it ends. And we walk hand in hand back to the suite, under a velvet curtain of twinkling stars. It's not quite the perfect ending, until the door closes quietly behind us.

"I might not be able to cook your dinner," Fin purrs, backing me up against the wood no sooner than it's closed. "But I hope I've showed you a good time."

I shiver, need blooming deep inside me, my eyes fluttering closed as his lips lightly brush mine.

"Dinner?" I swallow, my voice already husky with need. "You can't even scramble an egg," I tease, pressing my hands behind me, mainly to hide how they shake. I want this so badly. Need to feel him over me, owning me, making me forget what's to come.

Parting is such sweet sorrow?

No, parting just hurts. Even when you know it needs to be that way.

"That's true," he agrees as he presses his forearm above my head. He stares down at me with such incitement as he begins to slowly flip open the buttons on my dress. One, two . . . five—he flicks the sides open all the way to my waist.

He gives one of the many smiles in his arsenal, this one seductive, the kind that probably moistens underwear in a five-mile radius. Fin DeWitt could seriously be my undoing.

If only I could let him.

Since our conversation the day before yesterday, I've played his words over and over again in my head. What if he wasn't trying to wangle a situationship? What if he was being serious? About being serious?

Did I get it wrong that day in the outdoor shower? Was I not clear, or did he deceive me? It's not like I asked him to sign a contract or swear his allegiance to singledom.

Imagine if I'd asked him to promise not to make things complicated?

Hey, Fin, I'll fake marry you, but you've got to promise not to fall in love with me, m'kay?

He probably would've laughed in my face.

Not that it matters, because it's just the setting that makes things feel like this. It's the magic of the island keeping reality at arm's length. Our close confines that muddy thoughts and skew feelings. I tell myself that if Fin had felt any sort of attraction to me, he would've sought me out after our closet interlude.

"What is it?" he whispers, staring down at me.

"I was just thinking you can't scramble an egg but you can certainly scramble my brain."

With a throaty chuckle, he lowers his head, his mouth meeting mine, this time in a slow, teasing kiss. I twine my arms around his neck, my head tipping back as he shifts, the tenor of his kiss changing. His lips chart every inch of mine, his tongue encouraging me to open wider, to accept the seductive brush of it.

"This mouth," he whispers, but he doesn't finish his thought as his broad palm slides up my body: hip, ribs, the side of my breast. His thumb coasts across my nipple, the nub tightening under that tiny press.

I whisper his name as I pull him closer, my breasts aching and heavy as all those feel-good potions begin to swim through my veins. He's my champagne wish and caviar dreamboat. A dream, not because he's a little bit posh or too rich for my tastes, but because I just can't afford him in my life.

"I love how you touch me," I whisper boldly. "How your big hands hold me. You make me feel like I'm yours."

"You are mine," he says, pulling back. The low light turns his face all angles and shadows. "You're my wife."

"Only for tonight."

His jaw flexes, his tone low and husky. "Better make it memorable, then."

As if I could ever forget. As if I ever will. It's like he's carved away a piece of me that I'll never get back. But for now, I'm all his and he's mine, and we feel it everywhere. Skin touching skin.

"Pretty," he murmurs as his fingertip charts the scalloped edge of my bra, his eyes following the motion.

"I'm glad you think so. Matching knickers too."

"So I see."

"Though I think it was unfair of you to only return them to me in exchange for a kiss."

"A kiss per pair."

"Opportunist."

A pulse thrums in his throat as his touch coasts down the valley between my breasts. "Ingenious. Fuck, Mila. You're truly beautiful."

My chest heaves, my body straining closer, my sighs all desire and building desperation. I want him to hold me, bend me. I want his rough whispers in my ear and his thick solidness between my legs. I want him to touch me everywhere, and all at once. And then I want to do it all over again until I forget that tonight is all we have.

He cups my breast, his spread thumb and forefinger the perfect frame as he lowers his head, sucking my nipple over the fabric. Need spikes inside me, and I whimper as he curls his thumb inside the lacy cup, exposing my nipple to his view.

"I love your tits." His base compliment hits all my pleasure buttons, my body reacting viscerally as his thumb glides back and forth over the sensitive peak. "At some point tonight, I'm going to slide my cock between your pretty lips. You're going to make it nice and . . . *wet*." Had a word ever felt so seductive? "Then I'm going to fuck you right here."

It's not a question, and I'm okay with that as he holds me. Whispers. Squeezes. Sensation layering sensation as I pull his head closer, desperate.

"Fin." His name aches from me.

"You want my mouth?" His breath is a hot burst against my nipple.

"*Yes*. Touch me." I shiver as he presses the flat of his tongue to my nipple, swirling it across the tip.

"You're so sensitive here, aren't you?" His eyes shine as they lift to find mine, his body an elegant arch as he pulls my nipple into his mouth. He sucks as though desperate, his attentions rougher than before, but the tide of his actions matches my need perfectly.

"I bet you could come like this." His assertion is hoarse. "I bet you'd come so hard without me touching you anywhere else."

The way I feel, it's entirely possible, and I encourage the return of his mouth.

"Yes, oh, God. Like that." In his mouth, my nipple is a taut, aching point. My nails tighten against his shoulder as I share this pleasured pain. "Take me to bed."

"No, darling. I want you right where you are," he whispers, words peppered in the space between his kisses. "Just. Like. This."

I watch through watery eyes as his large hands curl around my bare hips, his thumbs caressing my hip bones. He lowers himself to his knees.

"You're so lovely, Mila. I'm going to miss holding you." He tips forward, pressing his mouth over my underwear. "And I'm going to miss this pussy." He inhales so deeply and presses his tongue to my lace-covered slit. "So, so much."

"Oh, God." My words are sandpapery as I arch away from the wall, my hand clasping his head, holding him there. Hot breath and soft lips, my insides throbbing needily for this. *For him.*

His eyes catch mine, his thumbs curling into the sides of my underwear. "Look at me, Mila. I want to so badly, I'm shaking."

I whimper, loving this. Loving how open he's being. As he yanks the gossamer fabric to my knees, my body bounces from the wall with the motion. I inhale a sharp gasp, twisting, as I seek to fill the space between us.

"Can I touch you?" he murmurs, watching as he presses his thumb to my slit.

"Yes." I swallow my gasp as the tip slips inside. Consent might be sexy, but I crave this.

"You're so fucking beautiful here." His thumb swipes through the already slick ribbon of my flesh. "Mila." His whisper sounds awe filled as he rubs my arousal between his forefinger and thumb. "So sweet," he adds, sucking those digits into his mouth.

How do I feel that so viscerally? "Fin, please."

"Show me where you need me, love."

My hips begin to buck, meeting his movements.

"Here, is this the spot?" he purrs, bringing my wetness to the soft rise of my clit.

It feels so desperately dirty like this, pressed against the door, half-undressed, my underwear stretched wide between my legs.

"You like that, my wife? Does that feel good?"

"Stop playing."

"I'm not playing, love. I'm making dreams come true." His whisper is hoarse as he pressures and pets, as he swipes and swirls, as he steals my breath, making my body shake. "Such a good girl, getting yourself off on just my thumb."

"More . . ." My fingers still tremble as I reach for him. "I need more."

"You need me to kiss you here? Suck on this clit? Do you need me to fuck you with my tongue until you come on my face?"

"Yes!" My answer leaves my mouth in a tight, tiny sound. "Please, Fin. *Please.*"

"Then when I kiss you later, you can taste yourself. Because you get off on that, don't you?"

I roll my lips together to suppress a moan, his gaze dragging liquid fire across my flesh. The pictures his words paint slide another layer of sensation to the experience as he presses his tongue to my swollen clit.

"Oh, God, yes!" My hips meet his tongue as he licks and laps, and he sucks, not to savor but to devour.

"There's my good girl. My sweet, filthy girl."

I cry out, relief and sheer bliss washing through me as Fin whispers such wicked words, such filthy things.

How delicious I am.

How he can't wait to fill me.

To feel me throbbing around him.

How he owns me. Completely.

And in that moment, he does.

But I fight the sensation—I'm not sure I can do this standing up, my legs shackled by my underwear, my body weak and shaky.

"Oh, God, Fin, please. I can't. Not like this."

"Stop wriggling." His teeth are a sudden reprimand, pressed to my thigh.

"Oh!" The smarting throb seems to fall in time with the desperate beat of my body as Fin slides my underwear the rest of the way down my legs.

"Or I won't let you come until I'm inside."

"I don't think you'll be able to stop me."

His attention flicks up, humor and wickedness shining there. I smile, hoping it doesn't look too wobbly. This right here, good sex and connection, laughter when you least expect it. It could be real. *If only I could trust it.*

The moment breaks as Fin takes my ankle, sliding the scrap of abused lace from my foot. He discards it behind him somewhere but doesn't lower my foot again. Instead, he lifts it to a leather box that wasn't in the hallway last time I checked.

He slides my dress out of the way as he presses my thigh open. I feel so deliciously exposed. Powerful somehow.

"So fucking pretty." His gaze lifts, but not his head. "I'm going to destroy you, Mila. Fuck you so well that I'll ruin you."

"Do it," I whisper, my breath taut, aching. I want him so much, I shake with it. Every second of tonight has built to this. Our final night together before tomorrow, when we'll leave behind this perfect messy moment of us. It's the way it must be. The adult thing to do. We're just too different. Too separate. We're no dream come true.

"There will be no other men for you." His eyes catch mine, and he watches my expression as he drives two fingers between my legs, the motion slow and rhythmic, illuminating just how wet I am. I arch as his head lowers, and as his mouth meets my pussy, he sucks my swollen clit between his lips.

Tomorrow, I'll be back in London, worrying about my life and my choices. So tonight, I'll just switch off my brain and revel in this.

His mouth meets my pussy again, the vibration of his groan vibrating to my bones as he presses his tongue to my clit, painting a wet stripe across it.

"*Oh!* Fin . . ."

He begins to feast on me—there are no tentative tastings or licks as he devours me, piece by piece.

"That's it—you make those fucking noises for me," he says as his lashes flutter closed, and his tongue licks into me like I'm a pudding bowl.

My hands scrabble for purchase, the wall, then his shoulders, using them as leverage to move my hips. To fuck his face. I'm writhing and desperate as Fin takes ownership of my body. Licking and swirling, lapping and sucking, he peels me apart with his tongue until I'm begging for more. Which he gives. And gives. Until it all feels too much. Until I'm bursting from my skin.

I make to move my leg, not sure I can stand it, or even just stand, when his hand tightens on my thigh, pressing it back.

"Open your legs. Open your fucking legs right now."

My reaction to his command is visceral, my body throbbing and twisting with need. I shouldn't be turned on, not at the rasp in his tone or his command. But I can't help it. I can't help but give in. I spread my knees wider and beg him with my body and my words.

With a grunt, he drives two fingers deep inside me, aiding this spiral of pleasure. A brush of his stubbled chin and the barest threat of his teeth draw me higher and higher until I'm fit to burst from my skin.

"Yes, come for me, Mila. Come for me as I suck on this clit."

I cry out, my hips arching away from the wall for the last time.

"That's it, beautiful. Come on my fucking tongue." He slides his hand behind me, pulling me to his face, where he just . . . inhales me.

My whole body twitches—like I'm suffering a seizure. I press the back of my hand to my mouth, my throat hoarse thanks to his torturous assault and an orgasm that seems unending.

◆ ◆ ◆

FIN

I tilt my head to take in all this loveliness. The rounds of her pale hips marked red by my hands. Her head tilted skyward, her eyes closed, her hair tumbling around her shoulders. Her nipples pink and hard, her chest rising and falling as though she's been running.

"You're so beautiful when you come for me." As I press my lips to the soft pout of her inner thigh, Mila tilts her head, committing my kiss to memory. The slide of my hands to the past.

Or so she thinks.

Her lashes flicker closed as I stand, her bottom lip trembling. I press my mouth to the corner of her eye, and one salty tear transfers to my mouth. "Hush now."

She nods but doesn't reply, choking back the things she might say as she lifts her hand to my neck.

"I'm going to fuck you now," I whisper as I brush my thumb across the wing of her collarbone. "I'm going to make you feel so good."

"Yes, let's do that." Her chest moves once with some semblance of a laugh, the words lazy and long.

"Then I'm going to take you into the bedroom and start again. From the tips of your toes to the top of your head, I'm going to worship you, Mila."

Her lashes flutter, her eyes dark inky pools. But she says nothing.

"You're going to cry out my name so the whole resort knows who you belong to. And when you're back in London—"

Her finger finds my mouth. I bite the tip in admonishment.

"When you're back in London, you'll think about me. You'll remember the way I touched you, and you'll miss me."

"Fin, don't."

I reach for my fly, but Mila pushes my hands away. My heart beats like hooves as her fingers fold around my cock, pulling it out.

"You'll remember how I made you laugh." My words come out husky as she swipes my silky crown with her arousal, making herself shiver. "You'll think about the times I held you, the shapes I bent you in, and you'll realize that no one will ever fuck you better. Hold you better."

Let me in, Mila. Let me in, please.

"Yes." A sibilant hiss as she presses me there. *I need you.*

My pulse pounds so hard it echoes in my ears. I tighten one hand on her thigh, lifting, spreading, my other finding the base of her throat, where I feel her gasp. As I drive myself inside, her cry vibrates through my hold.

"Mila." I press my cheek to hers, her walls a tantalizing throb. Breaths mingle, our bodies fused as I hold her there, just absorbing the moment. "You'll miss me. And you'll call me." I slide the damp strands from her face when she closes her eyes, denying me.

Veiling her thoughts.

"You'll call me," I persist, pressing my lips to her chaotic pulse. "Because you'll realize what we have is too good to let wither."

"And too hard to make work," she whispers in response.

My curse is delivered through gritted teeth, the grip of her body around my aching cock enough to make me burst. I flex my hips, and she groans, undulating into my next thrust. "Wrong, darling. I'd work so hard for you."

She makes a noise, a tight breath, something inside her opening.

"I want to be inside you so deep."

"You are," she whispers, her lips by my ear. "So deep. I'll remember this time until I'm old and gray."

And I'm sitting in the rocking chair by your side, my mind supplies.

"Goddamn," I moan, grinding against her. Pleasure crawls along my spine, tightening my balls, making her grunt as I thrust harder.

"It hurts so good." Breath more than words. She grazes my earlobe with her teeth and shatters the last vestiges of my civility.

I give a long, raspy groan. I can't think or process as a wave of *Fuck yes* ripples through my insides, pleasure coiling so low. A second later, everything becomes urgent and frantic, the darkened hallway filling with the sounds of our coupling.

"Don't look away." My fingers unfold to find her chin. "That's my girl. That's my good girl. Watch me, Mila. Watch how I make you mine."

My heart feels like it could burst, my mouth meeting hers on an upthrust; our wet, messy, tongues twining as this need, this desperation to have her, own her, fills every inch of my being.

"Oh, God, Fin . . ."

Her body begins to throb my name, milking me for all I'm worth.

"I've got you," I rasp into the soft skin of her neck. "Let go. I've got you, my darling girl."

Still holding her wide, holding her eyes on mine, I drive myself inside her one final time.

This woman is mine. She's not just my wife, but my *why*.

Tonight, or forever, I'm not letting go.

Chapter 24
MILA

Sarai was right. The food on a private jet is amazing. At least, it looks amazing. Sadly, every bite I slide into my mouth tastes like cardboard.

My decisions taste like cardboard, too, and my sadness like a paper cut to the tongue. At least it stops me from speaking. So here I sit, cocooned in the jet's plush leather seat, probably the most comfortable place ever. Save for being cradled by the hands of God. Or the arms of Fin.

Oh, I am *miserable*.

Last night . . . I will remember last night for the entirety of my life. How Fin held me. How he treasured me. How he wiped away my tears, never pausing in his quest to fuck his feelings into me.

I'm not sure there has been a word invented to describe how the experience made me feel. Bittersweet touches and brain-melting inducements. It was like nothing I've ever experienced. *And nothing I'll ever experience again.*

This week has been like living in an alternate reality, from Oliver's offer of payment—which felt like a dream come true—to claiming back a little of myself, of my autonomy and my self-worth.

And then Fin. He helped me discover the parts of me I never knew existed.

Watch me, Mila. Watch how I make you mine.

But they're just words. I'll get over them. Besides, the only person you can truly rely on is yourself. *Though Fin was an excellent crutch while it lasted.*

My gaze slides to the tiny window, the sky beyond pitch, as I recall waking Sunday morning to find myself in bed with Fin. I hoped it was worth it, that the sex had been amazing, and that it would come back to me as the silver lining of what seemed like the ruination of my escape from poverty.

I was possibly being a little dramatic, but I don't think I'm being so now when I say I've changed my mind. I hope I forget the last five days. I hope the memories fade as quickly as my tan. Because, as I said the morning I woke to find I was Fin DeWitt's wife, *"Sweet Jesus fucking hell, what have I done?"*

I told myself we'd have great sex with little connection, but it's been so far from that in reality, and I'm a little scared. I let my walls down with Fin, but I just need to remember who I am—who I really am. Or who I was before life kicked me down. I'm as capable as I am determined. As professional as I am thorough. So shields up and armed. I'll just ignore how my soul hurts in the meantime.

I won't regret my time here, though I know I'll pay for it, because despite the things I told myself—despite the things I said to him—of course I want to see him again. As he sits across from me tap-tapping on his laptop, I want to touch him so much that my fingers ache.

But I can't lose my heart to Fin, and pretending I could settle for being just another notch in his belt would be foolish. I'd be lying to myself, and to him, because I'm just not built that way. And even if, in some strange, alternate reality, there's a chance Fin might be the one, I have too much going on in my life to be distracted by love.

Not that I love him. I esteem him. Like him. I fancy the rotten pants off him! I've gotten off on our interactions. *Sometimes quite literally.* But I don't love him. I can't love him. And that's the end of that.

I ride the Tube to get around. He has a private jet. We wouldn't last in the real world.

"May I take your plate?"

I glance up into the purser's smiling face.

"Yes." I give myself an internal shake. "Please. All finished!" I paint on a polite smile and stop short of asking her if she'd like a hand with the dishes. Anything to distract myself from these thoughts. Thoughts that drift into memories. Memories that pierce like claws.

"May I refresh your drink?"

Because on a private jet there's nothing so gauche as a *refill.*

"Thank you, but no."

I watch as she folds away the tiny white tablecloth that was placed across my half of the table. Fin declined food, though he is nursing a whisky.

"Thank you, Agata," Fin murmurs, glancing up. "How did your granddaughter's rehearsal go? Sophie, right?"

Agata, an attractive sixtysomething, beams. "She got the part!"

"That's great!" Fin says, his genuine pleasure evident.

"We're so grateful for—"

He makes an almost indiscernible motion of his head—barely a tilt. "I only picked up the phone. Sophie did the hard part. Please pass on my congratulations."

"Of course." Agata inclines her head before disappearing to the back of the jet.

I stifle a sigh. Like I needed reminding how not awful Fin DeWitt is right now.

As though sensing the weight of my gaze, he glances up from his laptop and gives me a sad-looking smile. We've been sitting like this for what feels like hours, him supposedly catching up on work and me with my nose buried in my phone as I read. Which is more a case of staring at the same page as my mind tortures me with impossibilities.

Maybe turning cold toward him this morning was a step too far. He probably doesn't realize that I said my goodbyes while he was still sleeping. How I lay in his arms, marveling how, in the space of a few days, he'd become my cave of safety. Every morning we'd woken the same way, his body curved around mine, his arms holding me tight. I can imagine how, after a bad day, a girl could retreat into the cave of Fin so easily.

But not a girl named Mila. Not anymore.

"We're gonna pretend you're by yourself, enjoying your . . . special alone time. That's right, sweet girl. I'm gonna watch, and you're gonna play. Not over there. Come here. Bring that sweet pussy over my face."

I come to with a start, the light brighter and a soft pillow under my head. It takes me a few moments to orient myself, the thrum of the plane echoing inside my aching hollowness. I struggle upright, reaching out to stop a cashmere-soft blanket falling to the floor, when Fin beats me to it. As he would, given he's sitting next to rather than across from me.

"Did you say something?" The words come out accusingly as I glance up at him, wiping the back of my hand across my mouth. *Classy, I know.*

His mouth tips, and he reaches out, tugging gently on a lock of my hair. From the corner of my eye, it seems to have turned springy from being squashed to my head.

"What's wrong? Did I invade your dreams, beautiful?"

"No," I answer far too quickly. I blink, pushing the wayward strands away. "You've moved."

"I know."

"Why?" Another accusation.

"You looked cold," he says, with a look of benevolent patience. "I covered you up, and you reached for me. Maybe you were uncomfortable."

"I'm not sure how. These seats are so comfy. I wondered earlier if this is what it must feel like being cradled in the hands of God." I pat my hand against the backrest and plump the square pillow, as though to support my point.

"Maybe you find my arms preferable to the hands of the Almighty."

The story checks out, thanks to the patch of drool on his chest. He must've changed while I was sleeping, as he's no longer wearing the shorts and T-shirt he boarded in, but a pair of crisp, dark jeans and a pale-gray fine-knit sweater that looks so soft and makes his eyes look like rain clouds.

I don't point that out, of course, as I stretch the sleep from my body and try not to enjoy how his eyes sweep over me.

"We'll be descending soon," he says, with a casual glance in the direction of the window.

"Really?" My hands drop to my sides, disappointment filling my chest. *Stupid chest.* "How long was I asleep?"

"Almost eight hours. Comfortable, see?" he says, kicking out his long legs in front of him.

He might be right, but I'm also worn out. I haven't had a lot of sleep this week, every night and every afternoon siesta interrupted by touches, by kisses. Sometimes intentionally, sometimes during our slumber. It's as though even our unconscious selves were reluctant to waste a moment. As though my body has been making up for lost time as well as stocking up for the future.

My future will be one of focus. Of dedication to my grandmother's comfort and to my success.

God, I can't wait to move out of Baba's tired flat. It'll be hideous being back there.

"I'd say that's reason enough to keep in contact."

"Sorry?" My brain connects the dots a beat too late.

"I'm a good place to land, Mila."

"Fin," I murmur sadly, my gaze sliding away. "Please don't." I can't move on and keep him in my life. Cold turkey is the only way to go. The seat belt clunks as I loosen it, though he catches my wrist as I try to pass.

"I'll say it again, Mila. This doesn't have to be complicated. It could be just as good as it is right now."

But I don't trust myself, and I shouldn't trust him. I know he wants me, but for how long? How quickly will his interest wane when he finds out I live like a trash rat? When he learns I eat my feelings and then skip meals, that I bite my fingernails down to the quick when I'm stressed, and that I have one-way conversations with the teenage girl who seems to reside in my head.

"No, Fin. It's already too messy. We can't. Not anymore."

He nods, as though he finally understands. Or is finally giving up on the idea of us. Giving in to logic, I suppose. And that doesn't make me feel glad. Which is absurd. *Please let go of my wrist.*

"Then I'm sorry, Mila."

"Me too. But—"

"No, I'm sorry that you might not have any choice in the matter."

My brow furrows as I begin to shake my head, but I abandon the action when I can't make sense of what he means. His tone isn't threatening, but there's a finality to it. A hardness. Why would he say such a thing? I pull again. This time his fingers loosen.

"What is it? What do you mean?"

"That it might not be entirely in your control." His words, not his tone, are what sound vaguely threatening. "Sit down."

"I don't want to."

"Sit down, Mila." The phrase *brooks no argument* flashes in my head. That tenor. It's not one I've heard from him before. And I don't know how I feel about it.

"Okay." I shoot him a cool look and make to move to the seats opposite. He reaches for my wrist, making me still.

"Sit here."

"What difference does it make?"

"Would you just fucking listen? Sit your ass down next to me."

"What has gotten into you?" I mutter, lowering myself to my original seat.

"I just think you should be close when you see this."

He hands me his phone, and my heart sinks as I read the heading.

Chapter 25
MILA

A Little Bird Told Us . . .

news that will rock the London dating scene. Lean in my little cluckers, because do we have juicy news for you!

Fin DeWitt, our favorite man about town, the darling of the gossip columns and one of the head honchos over at Maven Inc., is officially . . .

OFF THE MARKET!

Yes, you heard it here first. Fin and his dark-haired mysterious mate were spotted getting spliced at the jewel in the crown of the DeWitt resort hotel chain's exclusive Indah Atoll on the weekend.

"Oh, no." I press my hand to my mouth. "Oh, no, no, no." I glance up, my gaze finding Fin's. "What the fuck? How did this happen?"

"I guess someone tipped them off."

I can barely process his answer, let alone make sense of his expression, my eyes drawn to the rest of the article. *Like a car crash in the making.*

You might remember last week a Little Bird reported Fin's partner in crime, Oliver Deubel, and his fiancée, Evie Fairfax, were seen climbing aboard Maven Inc.'s private jet at London City Airport, but we had no idea it would be to attend Fin's nuptials.

A Little Bird would like to pass on their congrats to him and his new wife, twenty-nine-year-old wedding planner Mila Nikols . . .

"They know my name!"
"I know."

. . . while also offering commiserations to the rest of us.

"Well, that's just charming," I mutter without looking up. Why not just print *Congratulations, you bitch!*

Single women everywhere will be crying into their G&Ts tonight, along with a few of the married ones, who may or may not include Princess Marta of Castile before her divorce came through. *Allegedly.*

And what of posh girl Charlotte from the TV sensation, *Made in RICHmond*? We recently reported the previous beauty to hold Fin's attention was snapped trying on wedding dresses. Though the plummy reality-TV star and sometime influencer has yet to make an official response, a source close to her has confided that she's "heartbroken."

A Little Bird feels you, hon. We really do.

Don't forget to check out the exclusive images! We especially like the one of Fin wearing a bright-pink fedora while frolicking on the beach with his curvaceous wife. We're happy to see his porn-star 'stache is no more, but the jury is out on that haircut.

Meanwhile, a Little Bird is trying to work out why Mila—a native of London's East End and the owner of Trousseau, a boutique wedding-planning company—was hired by Evie Fairfax and Oliver Deubel to plan the pair's upcoming nuptials.

Which a Little Bird thought was happening on the DeWitt resort . . .

Mystery or coincidence? Watch this space for more details as they come!

#TheEndOfAnEra #SadFaceGirls #ThanksForTheMemories

I'm going to cry. Or scream.

Actually, I can't quite make out how I'm feeling. *Curvaceous*? That's just internet speak for fat. What the hell? What did I do to them?

But they did mention Trousseau, so that's good. Except for the other implications. Stealing the nation's favorite bachelor is one thing; to have (allegedly) stolen him from another woman—well, that's the kind of smack talk that gets you (virtually) pilloried!

"This is going to ruin my business." My words sound eerily calm. So matter of fact.

"I don't see how."

My head turns his way, anger flaring inside my chest. "Did you not read this?" I say, holding out his phone.

He takes it from my hand and slides it away. "I think you came off quite well. It's me they made sound like an asshole. For what it's worth, Princess Marta is an investor in a couple of Maven projects."

I hold up my hand. "I don't care." *Do I?*

"As for Charlotte, I've seen her around, sure. And I'm pretty sure we interviewed her brother for a position with Maven, but that's it."

I huff but don't look up. *There are enough images of them together on the internet.* "Yet she's 'heartbroken'?" I say, making physical and very snarky speech marks around the word. My God, am I jealous? I think I am—jealous and annoyed that she might've had her paws on this man. Of all the ridiculous . . .

286

"I'm sure she could squeeze out a few tears for the cameras. Isn't she on some reality TV show?"

"So I've heard," I mutter. Maybe he really doesn't know her.

"I guess some people will do or say anything for publicity."

Publicity.

Pub-li-city. The exact thing I demanded (nicely) from Oliver as part of our deal. My name in a few choice publications, with the aim of drawing in business—drawing in brides, if not ones from Oliver and Evie's circle, then those who aspire to live the high life.

I suppose I was so annoyed (and secretly jealous) reading that article, that drivel, that I failed to see the bigger picture. I didn't want anyone to know Fin and I were married, or to learn the story behind it. I wanted to claim success on my own terms.

But what's done is done, and the genie is out of the bottle, so I may as well put him to work! Because, as it turns out, being married to Fin might not be so bad after all.

Women—brides—whether wealthy or professional, social media influencer or social climber: come one, come all. Don't just book me to plan and implement the wedding of your dreams—aspire to be lucky in love, just like me. The wife of London's most popular bachelor.

Until our amicable split, I guess.

"That was a big sigh." Fin takes my hand. "You're convinced being married to me is going to be to the detriment of your business, aren't you?"

"No, actually." I don't sound happy about it. Mainly because I don't want him to gloat. "Being married to you might just be the making of it."

"The bigger picture, huh?" His mouth hooks up in one corner as though pulled by an invisible piece of string.

"There's no need to be smug."

"*Moi*, smug?" He presses a hand to his chest a touch theatrically. "The man who's fucked half of London? The man who the other half of London would just *love* to fuck?"

"I'm sure I didn't say that."

"Maybe you didn't, but the press? They make shit up. I know you were worried about people finding out, and I know you're stressing about your fee. But you met your part of the bargain, and Oliver will meet his. If he knows what's good for him," he adds in a mutter.

"I'm not going to come between you and your friends. And I didn't want people to know, because they'll assume I've married you for your money!"

"So let them. There's no such thing as bad publicity. There's just the way you spin it."

I'd like to spin him sometimes. On the end of my foot.

"You mustn't have spent much time on social media," I retort. "Oh, I forgot." I give a superior sniff. "You're old."

"Old enough to know better and not give a fuck. Mila, I don't care if you climb out of this plane and announce to the world you only married me for access to my cock—"

"Shush!" I hiss, my gaze sliding to the galley, where Agata is likely to be.

"—because it won't stop people thinking what they want. Or what's most entertaining to them. And Agata has worked for us for years. She's a good woman who signed a watertight NDA."

"Fine," I mutter. "Thank you." My lips draw together like the strings of a purse.

"You're welcome," he replies, making a flourish like he's *Aladdin*'s Jafar. "Oh, suspicious one."

"This is all a joke to you, isn't it?"

"On the contrary," he says, reaching for my hand again. "I might be the only one of us taking this marriage seriously."

I pull from his hold, biting my tongue against asking what he means. "I've been in this business for almost ten years. I know what people are like. I've spent most of those years bending over backward to cater to people's whims." Ten years of anticipating my Monday-morning emails—I swear the process has aged me. Monitoring the comments on my social media accounts. More often than not, it's praise I receive, but when the complaints come in, people can be really savage.

"Maybe from today you won't have to worry about that anymore."

"Yes, I'm sure people will stop complaining once they hear I'm married to a legendary *cock*."

"For better or for worse," he says, purposefully misinterpreting the insult.

"You just couldn't resist sticking that in, could you?"

"I suppose you're gonna tell me *that* wasn't a Freudian slip?" he all but purrs.

"Let's go with *worse*," I retort, folding my arms. Mainly because his tone feels like the brush of his thumb across my nipples. How can he simultaneously annoy me and make me hot? But I haven't fought this hard for this long to watch my business get flushed down the pan.

"Nah, not when your profile will increase with me on your arm."

"Oh, listen." I hold up my finger—*hush*. Then I turn my head as though straining to catch something. "Did you hear that?"

"It's just engine noise."

"No, I'm pretty sure that was Emmeline Pankhurst turning in her grave."

"A high-profile husband," he repeats.

"You mean *a notorious playboy*," I counter.

289

His playful expression falters, and I'm immediately apologetic—I'm angry and lashing out when none of this is his fault.

"That was unfair," I say. "I'm sorry."

"Apology accepted. If you want to make it up to me, there are still twenty minutes before we land."

"You wish." Maybe I do too. But only couples in a real relationship have makeup sex. "Can we really do this?" I begin again. "Pretend it's real, the same way as we have been?"

"Sure we can."

"But we won't be doing it for Oliver and Evie. We'll be doing it for my business."

He shrugs, unconcerned.

"Why? Why would you help me?"

"Because we're in this together." He reaches for both of my hands.

"But what about your friends? What do we tell them?"

"We can tell them the truth, or we can say we're in love. That's up to you."

"You'd lie to them? For me?"

"You've got more to lose, so yeah, I'd lie to them. If you want me to."

"I think that might be best," I whisper, feeling like such a shit.

He gives a decisive inclination of his head. "We'll issue a press release. Post the news of our wedding in *The Times*, saying we met months ago, which is true. We're basically sticking to the facts."

"Minus the closet interlude," I add. "That wouldn't help."

"We'll say we've been keeping our relationship under wraps. That we weren't ready to share any of the details. Also somewhat true."

"But what about your dating life? The women you've been seeing in between then and now. Will they be as discreet, do you think?"

"I guess we'll find out."

"And then what?" I ask, not quite understanding why he'd go along with this.

"We'll stay together at least until your business has recovered. Keep the divorce plans on the down-low in the meantime."

"No more jokes about settlements, please. You've done enough for me."

Fin is a lot of things. Annoying and irreverent. Insanely good looking and super hot. Kind and generous. Sweet sometimes. Infuriatingly maddening. But I still don't get why he'd do this. *Other than amazing sex.*

Agata suddenly appears by Fin's seat, her expression giving nothing away as she does a surreptitious seat belt check. "Is there anything I can get you?" she asks with a smile. "Last chance saloon before we come in to land."

"Thank you, Agata. We're fine."

She smiles and leaves again.

"*Fine* will do," Fin adds, turning to me once again. "*Fine* is making the most of the situation. But what that situation is, is up to you."

Chapter 26
MILA

"I'm not sure that's a good idea," I say for what feels like the thirteenth time since we entered the terminal. Unaccosted, I might add, because rich people don't have to clear immigration. Or collect their own baggage. And neither does a rich person's spouse. *Winning?*

"I mean, sure, it's up to you," Fin says, his hand tightening on mine. *For the sake of appearances, I allow it.* "But I'm not sure how you expect people to believe we're in a real marriage if we're not living in the same house."

"One of the Kardashians doesn't live with her husband."

"I don't know who that is. But I'm guessing they aren't trying to fool half of London."

"And I'm pretty sure I read Gwyneth Paltrow and her husband don't live together full time," I say in lieu of an answer.

"As newlyweds? Wouldn't that kind of arrangement go against everything your business stands for? Love, togetherness, forever?"

"*Forever* means no repeat customers," I repeat disingenuously. "Look, I'll think about it," I add as I begin to dig in my purse for my phone, eventually pulling it out from the depths.

"What are you doing?"

"Booking an Uber," I say, pointing the screen his way as though the answer is obvious.

Fin expels an exasperated huff. "My driver will be outside. He can drop you off wherever."

"No need," I answer quickly, pulling the sides of my cardigan closer. I already feel so out of place in my leggings, T-shirt, and Converse. "It's fine. An Uber is fine." And much more my style. *Some might even say an upgrade,* I think as I flick through the app, mostly to avoid his gaze. There's no way he or his driver is taking me home. Not to Baba's flat. Even if I could convince him to stay in the car and not walk me to the door, which I know I won't manage, the experience would still be mortifying. The whole place is a dump.

"You're not getting an Uber home," he says, leaning into that bossy thing. *The zaddy thing. Or maybe the daddy thing.* Whatever. It's like he's guessed what it does to me. Which is simultaneously turn me on and piss me off.

"Married or not, this isn't the 1950s. If I want to get an Uber, you're not going to stop me." *Even if it is going to cost me an arm and a leg to get home.*

"A little louder, love," Fin says, leaning in. "Then maybe the porter can sell the highlights of this conversation to the *City Chronicle.*"

"Fine." I almost bite my lip as I spit the word out. "We'll discuss this outside." Is this what my life is about to become?

"Or maybe not."

I angle my gaze his way as he lets go of my hand in favor of pulling me into his side. I follow his gaze to the glass doors and the small crowd of people outside. My first thought is it might be a family waiting for the arrival of their loved one. But then a flash goes off. Then another. And another.

"Fuck," he grates out, swinging us both around to face the other way.

"Are those . . ." I glance over my shoulder. Then my stomach hits the tiled floor. "Please don't tell me you have photographers following you all the time."

"Not as a matter of course." He nods at the porter, handing him a folded bill almost by sleight of hand. "What are you doing?" he asks, as I move to take the baggage cart.

"What does it look like?"

"You can't use that as a battering ram. Not in today's litigious society."

"Says who?"

I pivot in the direction of the loud Irish voice before its owner backslaps Fin.

"Mila, right? I hear congratulations are in order." The man turns suddenly, enveloping me in a short but expensive-smelling hug. His cologne is expensive smelling, at least. And his shirt feels pretty nice against my cheek. As he pulls back, amused green eyes stare down at me.

"Yes, th-thank you," I answer, my gaze darting between the pair.

"I'm Matt," he offers. "The better third of the Maven unholy trio."

"My ass." Fin scoffs.

"Did you lose your mind when you lost your hair?"

"Real funny." With the reminder, Fin slides his hand up the back of his head.

"What happened to it, anyway? Lose a bet?" He glances my way.

"It's a long story," I offer, and the man grins.

"Knock that off," Fin complains.

"Maybe it's commiserations I should be offering, if she's married you." Matt winks, and I decide I like him. "Car's waiting."

"Bob?" Fin asks, taking my hand.

"Oliver, in his infinite wisdom, gave your driver the day off. He's arranged transport himself."

"A welcoming party?"

"A welcoming party," Matt confirms. "Are you ready for the circus?" he says, turning to me again.

"That depends. Do I get to be the lion or the clown?"

Flanked by both men, I make for the glass doors.

"Was it planned, Fin?"

"No comment," Fin says to the journalists who accost us as we exit the small terminal.

I blink as a camera flash goes off in my face, and I hold up my hand, dots dancing in my line of vision. I'm sure my feet would slow if it weren't for Fin's hold on me as he tows me along.

Now I know why celebs keep their sunglasses on.

"Did you tell Charlotte?"

"Has she given her blessing?"

"Is she gonna sue you for breach of promise?"

"Did you take back the ring?"

"The ring?" I repeat, glancing up at him.

"Not here," he sort of singsongs. "Not now."

He pulls me tighter into the shelter of his arm, Matt flanking my right. I mean, it's not like the paparazzi are out to get us—there are only four of them. I've felt more threatened walking home from the Tube station on occasion. But then an honest-to-goodness limo screeches to a halt in front of me, and Fin yanks at the passenger door handle.

"A limo? Really?" he says as Evie's happy expression suddenly emerges from the darkened interior.

"Of course a limo!" she trills, unrepentant. "Quick!" She makes a circling motion with her hand. "Get in."

Fin presses his hand to my back, and for once, I feel not that subtle thrill of his touch but a solid shove. I burst into the interior and almost tumble into the lap of Oliver, who eyes me like a rotten kipper someone just hurled at him.

"Allow me," he murmurs, pulling me deeper into the bowels of the vehicle before settling me on the leather seat next to him.

The limo door clunks closed behind me, the interior lights brightening to illuminate Evie's expectant expression and Oliver's mildly bored one. I glance at the door I was just shoved through, my stomach flipping at the opaque shape of Fin as he's bombarded with questions.

"Is she pregnant, Fin?"

What? I pull my purse onto my knee, not quite sure if I should be offended or if Charlotte from *Made in RICHmond* should. Maybe she is pregnant, but that doesn't mean it's anything to do with Fin.

"Don't listen to them," Evie says softly, as though intuiting my thoughts.

"I wasn't," I say far too quickly, then I swallow over the lump in my throat. I think that might be my heart trying to escape, which isn't helped as Oliver moves to the side-facing seats, placing himself next to his wife.

Maybe I smell like a kipper too. I resist the urge to stick my nose into my armpit to check.

Evie grins quite suddenly. "You know, the last time a woman burst into Oliver's car, he ended up with a wife."

As he reaches for her hand, she holds the other upright, the diamonds in her wedding band sparkling like stars.

"One wife is enough for one lifetime," he murmurs.

"Congratulations," I offer as I slide my left hand under my purse and use my thumb to pull my sweater over my knuckles, hiding my own slim wedding band. *It's a good thing I hadn't thought to take it off. But why hadn't I?* "I'm so happy to hear it went well for you both."

"Thank you. And thank you for your help," Evie adds. "I want you to know how grateful we are. We couldn't have managed any of it without you."

"The money should already be in your bank," Oliver adds, not realizing his wife is looking at him like he's grown another head. Or maybe horns.

"Sometimes you make me truly wonder," she murmurs almost to herself.

"What? I was merely advising Mila that I'd held up my part of the bargain."

"*Part* of your part of the bargain," I can't help but add. No need to be coy just because I've married into the friendship group, sort of.

"Yes, well." His brows pull in as he studies me. "That might take a little creative accounting."

"I'm sorry?"

"It will be hard to convince people that we were married on the DeWitt estate when the images on the internet are of you and Fin getting married there."

My heart hits my boots. Or my Converse, rather. "Yes, I see your point. I suppose it will."

"We'll work something out," Evie says. "But for now, remember that Mila just married your best friend."

Oliver frowns, his hand scratching his chin in consideration. "You're right. She deserves a bonus."

"That is not what I'm saying, Oliver. Jeez, pull your head out of your ass!"

"Honestly, it's fine," I put in. I'm too tense to enjoy their domestic disagreement. Though it does occur to me that maybe they don't have it all figured out. But they do have love, I see, as Evie's expression turns indulgent when her husband presses a kiss to the center of her palm.

"I'm dying to find out how it happened," she says, her attention swinging my way. "Fin is so—"

Both passenger doors are suddenly flung open. To my right, Matt climbs in at the same time as does Fin from the other side.

"What a feckin' circus," Matt mutters, dropping into one of the seats opposite Evie and Oliver.

"I had no idea it'd be like this," Fin says, reaching for my sweater-covered hand. Then frowning at it.

"You're sure your life isn't like this all the time?"

His brows lift, his answer amused. "This isn't about me."

"Well, it's not about me," I retort unhappily.

"It's about both of you," Evie puts in. "Congratulations! I'm so happy for you both, I could burst!"

I say nothing. But I'm probably doing a solid impression of a koi carp as my gaze bounces between the pair, not sure who to look at. I thought I could do this—lie to them. But Evie looks so genuinely happy, I suddenly don't think I can.

"I should've known there was something behind you recommending Mila for the job," her effusiveness continues. "Not that I wasn't impressed with your portfolio," she adds.

Her words are like a needle scratch on one of Baba's old vinyl Edith Piaf LPs.

"You did what?" My head whips around. "I got the job because of you?"

"I only gave Evie your card."

"I didn't give *you* my card," I retort.

I know this is neither the time nor the place, but my heart is banging against my rips like a two-year-old with a mallet and a xylophone.

"No, the concierge at the hotel did. I found it in my jacket pocket not long after Evie mentioned their wedding plans. I just passed it on, that's all. The night we met, I was so impressed—"

Now my heart gives a discordant twang, and my jaw drops open as though it's unhinged. He is *not* about to mention that night in front of his friends.

"—by the job you'd done, I suggested to Evie that she check you out. Right?" He turns to Evie, who confirms with a vigorous nod.

"There was nothing more to it than that," she insists. "I added your card to my list of possible planners. Then we met and gelled, and the rest is history."

Do I believe her? Or do I think these two conspired to get me to Indonesia? And if they did, how the hell did I end up married? That can't have been part of their plan.

"Fin is invited to more weddings than most," Evie puts in, eyes wide and innocent looking. "I'm sure I already said." The color in her cheeks deepens, no doubt remembering what else she'd said.

"Most people decline and send a gift," Oliver adds dryly.

"No, that's just you," Evie says, patting her husband's hand. "Kismet brought you both together. I just helped her along."

"Did kismet bring you and Charlotte together?" I could bite off my tongue. My head swims with thoughts. How I got here. How I got Evie's wedding. And underneath it all, there's that inexplicable swirling of jealousy.

Fin's brow flickers, but I'm already turning away, embarrassed.

"We're married," I begin, without looking at any of them. "But we're not in love." Beside me, I feel Fin stiffen. "The whole thing was an accident—a freak accident. Sarai, she—" I halt, not sure why I'd defend her, given her role in this. "There were shrooms," I add, my words halting and disjointed as I stare at my own palms, as though the rest of my explanation might be written there. "It was a mistake, and we can't get out of it without a divorce."

"Oh. I thought Matt said . . ." Evie's words trail off.

"The media stuff was a shock." I glance up, pasting on what remains of my professional smile. "And what has happened has the potential to ruin my business, so Fin has kindly offered to stay married to me for a little while. Which I think might help. Help me get back on my feet, at least."

"That's about the strength of it," Fin ends, always ready with a quip.

I even allow him to take my hand between his, because the sudden silence in this vehicle is deafening.

Chapter 27
FIN

Mila is largely silent for the rest of the ride home as Evie and Matt pick up the conversation, filling the holes. I watch her from the corner of my eye as the sun lowers and the streetlamps flicker on and intermittently wash her in a sickly yellow light only to steal her from my gaze again.

Fuck, I wish I could read her thoughts.

The limo pulls to a stop at the front of my building. It's gone ten now, but London is never really dark. Or silent. Even in the parks and the quietest streets, the hum of traffic is ever present in the distance. Not that I'd have it any other way. I love it here.

I invite my friends in for a drink, not blaming them one bit when they decline. The ride was awkward enough. I can only assume it was Evie's idea to be at the airport. I expect she was ecstatic to hear the news of my marriage. She's always teasing me, insisting my life would remain hollow until I found myself the love of a good woman.

My stock answer has long been that I was happy for bad women to fill those holes in the meantime.

Matt beats the limo driver to the bags, pulling them from the trunk before grabbing me in a hard, manly backslapper of a hug.

"I don't know what the fuck you've done," he says, his arms still around me, "but I expect you'll fix it, as per usual."

"Everything I said on the phone was true," I say, pulling away. "I've got it bad, but Mila . . ."

"Ah, jaysus," he mutters accusingly. Then he eyes me as though I smell unsavory.

I glance at my shoes, feeling so fucking dumb. "I don't even think Jesus is going to fix this one. Didn't you hear her?"

When I told her on the plane I'd do this, that I'd fucking "pretend," I said it was because she had more to lose than me. It was a lie, a great big fucking lie. Because I've lost my heart to her.

"You said I couldn't make her love me, and I laughed it off, remember? Now *that's* hubris."

"Get out of it, you miserable fucker," he says, dismissing my words.

"I mean it," I say, rubbing the back of my neck. "I've got nothing."

"I've never known you to give up. Not without a fight. A dirty feckin' fight."

"I'm beginning to wonder if you were part of the same ride."

"That's the jet lag talking." His eyes slide behind me, and I turn, following them to where Mila stares up at the imposing edifice of my apartment building. "It's not the size of the dog in the fight but the size of the fight in the dog. And that there is some scrappy wee terrier."

My eyes cut sharply Matt's way, because that is no *dog*. That's my—

"Or to put it another way, the lady doth protest her disinterest a bit too strongly, I reckon. I thought she was gonna bite off your head when she mentioned that fame whoor Charlotte."

302

"You think she's jealous?" It's probably more that she's pissed by the implication harming her business plans.

"Cop on to yourself, man. Of course she's jealous. Just get yourself a good night's rest. Things will look better in the morning."

"Sure thing, Uncle Matt."

"You look like boiled shite. Like you haven't slept a wink in days." His eyes narrow, and he pulls an unhappy face. "Are you blushing?" he asks incredulously.

"Don't be an asshole," I retort, grabbing the bags. But, yes, I think I am.

"Get fucked yourself," he mutters as I pass, and he slaps my back.

"Good evening, Mr. DeWitt." The doorman reaches for the bags as the bronzed glass doors slide almost silently open.

"Thanks, Pete. I've got them."

"As you prefer, Mr. DeWitt. Madam." He inclines his head in the direction of Mila, who murmurs a quiet hello.

"You live in a hotel?" she asks once we're out of earshot.

I shake my head. It looks like a fancy hotel, and it does have links to the nearby Mandarin for room service and shit, but no. "This is my apartment building." Which is just a stone's throw from Harrods and Buckingham Palace.

Matt and Oliver heaped shit on me for buying this place off plan, comparing my tastes to the oil sheikhs I'm often wining and dining on behalf of Maven. But the joke's on them, because I could sell this place tomorrow for double what I paid.

We cross the lobby, the low tasteful hum of music overlaid by the slap-slap of Mila's Converse and the trundle of her trolley bag. I try to see the place from her eyes. The onyx marble floors, the plush velvet couches, and the concierge desk and the welcoming smiles of the staff stationed there. Chandeliers like art installations; lush greenery; bronzed mirrors reflecting our path to the elevators; the doors that open before we reach them. The car that moves without inputting our destination.

"A place so posh you don't even have to push the buttons?" The reflection of her smile is unsteady.

"It's a private car. One destination. I bought the place as an investment," I add. *Weird.* I've never sought to explain my life or my decisions to anyone before now.

The door opens into the small hallway. Shiny floors, more plants, and another couch, as though a short elevator journey might be fatiguing. I input the code at the ebony front door, and it opens.

"After you," I say, ignoring the insane urge to carry my bride across the threshold of what I hoped would be her new home. *Rather than the place she has to stay to save her business.*

"Oh, my days." She makes a beeline for the wall of windows. The lamps are on in the living room, and though it's dark outside, you can still see the tops of the trees. It's like looking over a field of darkened broccoli in the middle of the city. "Is that Hyde Park?" Her voice sounds doubtful, her eyes widening as her gaze turns my way, and I nod. "Wow. Those are some views." Her smile barely holds before she turns away again.

"Yeah." I stifle a sigh. "A view." Fuck me, that ass was made for leggings. My eyes slide over the flare of her hips. In my mind's eyes, I press my palm to the sinuous arch at her lower back as I bend her forward. *Palms against the glass.* "What did you tell them for?"

She swings around, her smile nowhere to be seen as her gaze skims over the room, the color palette a repeat of downstairs. Amber and bronze and dark wood. Opulent accents and tactile soft furnishings. *All chosen by a decorator.*

"I couldn't lie to them," she says, linking her hands at her front. "And I couldn't make you lie to them. Not for me."

"You didn't make me," I answer wearily. "I choose to." *For you.*

"I just panicked, all right? Evie is so kind and so nice, I just couldn't do it!"

"Well, they won't tell anyone, so no need to worry on that front. As far as the rest of London is concerned, we're still married. We're still in love. That is, if you want to stick with the plan."

"Do you think they might think, or wonder, if they've been paying me to sleep with you?"

Despite her worried tone, my own words hit the air with violence. "Do you think I need to pay women to sleep with me?"

"I can't be the first woman who took offense to your . . ." Her eyes flick to my lips before she drags them away. "Your mustache."

Her eyes widen as I round the sofa setting, before I pause at the polished walnut cocktail cabinet, pulling out my wallet and flipping it to the top. "You mean *'half-grown Chia Pet'*?" I slide her a provocative look over my shoulder as I open the small door.

"Sorry. I told you I say inappropriate things when I'm—"

"Are you sorry for saying it or sorry I shaved it off?"

"What does it matter?"

"It doesn't. Not really." I reach for the tantalus, which once belonged to my grandfather, and select the decanter of single malt. "Other than you didn't get to ride it."

She huffs audibly. She might say stupid stuff when she's worried or nervous, but me? I prefer to dig my holes a little deeper as I lean into the lascivious character she's made me in her head. Or maybe that really is me. Fuck, I don't know anymore. I don't know whether I'm on my ass or my head. Not with her. All I know is she can flay me with one look and turn me on with the next, and I just can't stand the thought of her walking away.

So I'll do what it takes to keep her. *Stick to the plan.*

"Can I get you a drink?" The scent notes of earth and peat rise as the liquid hits the bottom of a lowball glass.

"No. Thank you," she says stiffly. "I'm tired," she adds. "If you just tell me which room is mine, we can talk tomorrow."

I press the lid onto the decanter and slide it back in. Close the doors.

"Any of them." I turn to face her and lean back against the cabinet, hooking my elbow over the top. "Doesn't matter which if it isn't mine."

"I'm not sleeping with you. I thought I'd made myself clear."

"After your earlier one-eighty, I thought I'd just put it out there."

I thought I could make this work without telling my friends the truth. *That she doesn't love me. That I'm maybe just useful. That I thought I could make her fall in love with me in the meantime.* Not that her admission changes anything. Not for her, at least. My friends are more like family. They'd help bury the bodies, no questions asked. I know they'll extend this to Mila. *For me.*

"I'm sorry I blindsided you. Lying to them was more difficult than I thought it would be."

I tilt my glass to study its contents in the lamplight. "It doesn't matter."

Mila's eyes drop to my lips as I tilt my head, savoring the subtle slide of burning liquid down my throat. She folds her arms across her body, its language turning electric, kindling a spark of fury that could light a fire. Maybe she's angry at herself. Maybe it's me.

"Did you know I'd be on that island when you arrived?"

Well, that answers that question, I guess.

"How could you not tell me? Didn't I deserve the truth?"

"The truth that I handed Evie your business card? It didn't seem important. And no, I didn't know you'd be there. But yes, I hoped."

"It seems like too much of a coincidence, you and me being there at the same time, all the way on the other side of the world."

"I didn't ask her to hire you, Mila. I can't say it any plainer than that."

"I believe you, even if—"

"You want the truth?" I move from the cocktail cabinet like a striking snake. "The truth is I carried your business card in my wallet for months, too chicken to call you myself. I was so goddamned into you that you plagued my fucking dreams. But I couldn't make myself call because what happened between us wasn't some hookup. It felt real. Too real. So I gave Evie your card and let fate take care of the rest."

"No, not fate. Magic mushrooms did the rest. It's all such bullshit," she spits, her eyes glittering as they move over me with revulsion. "You should've told me, Fin. I've never been so embarrassed as I was in that limo."

"Aw, babe," I say with an exaggerated pout.

Her eyes harden. Out of all the things I've called her, I'd never gone generic.

"You should take a leaf out of my book. Just don't give a fuck what people think about you."

"That's exactly the kind of thing I'd expect a man like you to say."

"A man like me?" My voice is quiet, my tone hard.

"A fuckboy," she says, emphasizing the fricative with vitriol.

With a low, guttering laugh, I throw back my drink then set it down, the glass connecting with the walnut harder than I anticipate. "A fuckboy," I repeat, as though trying the title on for size.

"Yes. The top-shelf version."

"Tell me, what is that?" I step closer, not threateningly, but her eyes still narrow. "A man who doesn't respect women?" I ask, coming to a stop in front of her. "One who's selfish? Who doesn't care who he hurts?"

307

"A fuckboy," she enunciates, "is a man who only cares about getting his dick wet, whether with Princess Marta, with me, with Caroline. Whoever."

"I think you mean *Charlotte*." Worse, I say it with such soft familiarity. What the fuck am I doing? I know what I want to do—shake Mila for her ridiculousness. "As for getting my dick wet, my preference would be with my little slut muffin," I add, my words turning to a taunt. "Because, *babe*, your pussy got me plenty wet."

"Not anymore." Her hand twitches by her side, and for a minute, I wonder if she'll lift it to slap me.

"The thing is, whatever happens between us, I'd do it all again," I whisper as my mind races a mile a minute. "I'd go back if I could, rewind and live those days again and again. Even with the same painful outcome. I'd do the same things. Say the same things. Because I will never regret you."

"Fin." My name sounds like regret as it falls from her lips.

"Should we? Do it again? Maybe we go farther back and find a closet. We could climb in and let our bodies do all the talking. It doesn't seem as though we're doing so well by ourselves."

"You're a mental case," she whispers, her eyes glistening. "Absolutely crazy pants."

"Yeah, I know." *I'm crazy for you.* "Should we? You could dry hump me into oblivion. Or stick a spiked heel into my ball sack."

"What?"

"Or whatever. Whatever it takes to turn the clock back." To take away this ache, the sense that everything is slipping away. "I'm not that man, Mila. I'm the guy who makes really shitty pancakes because I want to take care of you. I'm the guy who loves your ass, loves your laugh. The one who doesn't wear shirts, just for your entertainment."

"It's not that entertaining," she whispers.

"Then why do you stare so much?" I lean forward, the space between us a yawning gap. Or a small madness to close, not that I expect—

Madness might be contagious as Mila throws herself at me. The force of her makes me stagger backward as her arms come around my neck and she practically scales me.

"I'm sorry." Her fingers curl in the shoulder of my sweater. "I know that's not you, even if part of me wishes it was."

I grip her ass and make a groan of her name as her legs close around my waist. She reaches down my back, gripping my sweater to pull it over my head.

"Please, Fin." Her whisper is frantic, her lips trembling against mine. "Please fuck me."

"So you can tell me it's my fault in the morning." Despite my harsh words, my hands—my arms—couldn't hold her any tighter right now.

"Never." Her lips a hot press over my hammering pulse. "I'm sorry. I need you." And so goes her litany as I strip her one-handed from her cardigan, pressing her to the back of the couch to pull off her T-shirt.

Chaotic hair and grasping hands, her legs still linked behind me as she toes off her Converse. Leggings next, panties with them. We work my fly loose together, the gold of her wedding ring glinting in the lamplight as she wraps her fingers around my cock.

"I fucking love that," I rasp, watching as her thumb swipes over my crown, the pulse there pounding *mine, mine, mine.* "I like the way it shines when you're touching me."

"My ring?" Her brow flickers.

"It makes me feel something I can't explain."

She takes my hand, pressing her lips to my wedding ring. Then my hand to her breast. "I need you." She gives a soft vowel sound as she rubs my smooth crown through her wetness, her breath catching on her next words. "Like nothing else."

Positioning myself, I thrust upward and, *"Fuck!"*

I'm in so deep, and so close to her, as I bring my hands back under her ass, tumbling us onto the couch. My back against the cushions, Mila undulates over me, making my vision go hazy around the edges.

"Ride me," I rasp, all gasping demand. I take her hand and press her fingers to where, with each flex of my hips, I move inside her. "Fuck me, Mila. Make me yours."

And I thank the stars when she does.

Even if it's only for a little while.

Chapter 28
MILA

Fin's kitchen is huge and largely unused. Like the rest of the penthouse apartment, its color palette is moody—matte-black cabinetry and marble countertops veined with gold. Its high-end appliances include an unused professional range and a Sub-Zero fridge, a central island as large as the bow of a ship, and pendant lighting that looks like alien spaceships.

I run my finger over the silky petal of a potted orchid, artfully arranged in a shallow silver urn topped with moss. It's an odd thing to have on a kitchen counter. But then, so is the stylishly arranged stack of cookbooks, all tonally monochrome, and all unused. And the shiny balloon dog that's an original Jeff Koons. According to Google, it's worth twenty thousand big ones. For an ornament.

It's like another world.

Minutes ago, while drinking my coffee from the built-in Italian coffee machine, I recalled an article I'd read last year about orchids and how some wealthy people—billionaires, I suppose—employ an orchid keeper. That's an actual job. Someone who tends to the potted pretties, swapping them out for other orchids of the same color and size when the plants go into their vegetative state and stop flowering. For nine or ten months of their lives.

How crazy is that?

I was trying to convince myself that wasn't Fin, that he wouldn't be so wasteful. So shallow, I suppose. Then I picked up the balloon dog, googled it out of curiosity, and discovered what it was worth. To borrow a Ronny phrase, I was shook.

I still am, but I'm trying not to hold it against him as I rifle through the kitchen drawers looking for a pen and paper.

It's like no one even lives here. Where's the junk drawer?

I'm being unfair, I know. Especially after I acted like such a bitch last night. It's his money, and I'm sure he works hard for it. But when there's so much poverty in the world, it's hard to stomach. To think my fee might only buy me ten of these stupid balloon dogs!

An objet d'art *or maybe an* investment piece, *I'm sure the interior designer would've called it.*

It might only be a drop in the filthy lucre ocean to Fin, yet this money is a lifeline to me. I'm so grateful to have it—and I have better plans than spending it on bits of shiny rubbish.

Ah, good. A pen and paper. I pull them out and flip open the pad.

I was a total bitch as a defense mechanism, but I apologized for calling him a fuckboy. I know that's not him. I apologized with words too. Not just with my body. *That wasn't my intention when I flung myself at him.* I think, in the moment, I just needed to be held. And I wanted to hold him.

My cave of safety.

The thing is, I don't think I'd ever need to be on the defense as far as Fin is concerned.

"We need to think about our sleeping arrangements."

Last night, as Fin's chest rose and fell under my mine, our bodies still joined, his back sprawled across the sofa, he seemed to think I might need an excuse to sleep with him after I said I'd take another room.

"What do you mean?" I was seminaked and sprawled across him. Wasn't that hint enough?

"I have staff. A housekeeper, a cleaning crew."

"An orchid keeper?"

"A what?" He lifted his head and stared at me as though I had two heads.

"It's a thing. Apparently."

"If we sleep in separate rooms, we might set tongues to wagging."

"As long as they only wag in this apartment," I said, my eyebrows riding high on my head. "Because surely a smart man like you had them sign NDAs." So he wouldn't see my amusement, I pressed my lips to his chest. His skin was salty with sweat and a musk unique to him.

"I did. They do." I could hear the smile in his voice as I struggled upright and he slid the hair from my face.

"So what's the problem?"

"The press gets their information from somewhere."

"You have a leak?"

He shrugged, not quite committing himself. "Who knows? But do you want to take the risk?"

"If I didn't know better, I'd say this has the very strong flavor of you angling for a thing."

"A thing?"

I heard his reply like a lift of questioning brows.

"A fling. A situationship. A relationship. A something."

The backs of his fingers coasted down my arm. "Or like a husband and a wife enjoying their marriage."

"Fin." His name ached from me quite suddenly.

"We could just not name it and see where it goes."

Until it burns itself out and one of us loses our heart?

I slept in his bed. In his arms, in my cave of Fin. And all those noises, all that confusion, it still chattered as I sank into oblivion.

He woke me before he left for the office this morning. He had a meeting he couldn't miss, he said. He'll be back before lunch. But I won't be here, so I scribble him a note to say not to expect me back for the rest of the day.

My heart tells me I should stay far, far away, but my head knows that if I want to hang on to what's left of my business, that's not going to be possible.

Keep a business, lose my heart?

My body sways in time with the carriage. This morning's mammoth trek from Fin's swanky Knightsbridge address to Baba's nursing home in the outer reaches of East London has included two Tubes and a train. The carriage is packed, though the motion lulls my tired soul in a song of *get in, get out, get in, get out.*

I pull my phone from my purse as it buzzes with a call—an unknown number. I don't bother answering. I can't imagine it'll be important. Besides, I hate taking calls when I feel like people might listen in. The call rings out, and I stare at the screen, the temptation to reread that stupid article so hard to ignore.

"No one hears good at a keyhole." My grandmother's words echo in my head.

But still I type.

A little bird. The search bar autofills, and I select the first search: the latest post.

A Little Bird Told Us . . .

Loved up and super casual!

Check out the footage of our new lovebirds arriving at the private terminal in City Airport last night. Fin DeWitt looking snatched as ever—we're kind of digging the haircut now, brutal chic and cheekbones for days! Meanwhile, his new wife, Mila, was casual in black leggings and Converse. We like your thinking, Mrs. D. Comfort over style for those long-haul flights.

Why not go the whole hog and call me frumpy.

Fin declined to comment when asked about Charlotte, his reality TV star ex, but was all smiles as he and that other piece of deliciousness, Matías Romero, helped a startled Mila into the waiting limo.

They make me sound like a piece of baggage.

To be fair, the accompanying footage makes me look like a bag too. Not that I look much better this morning. I'm wearing jeans and a hoodie I pulled from Fin's walk-in closet. The place looks like a fancy menswear store, the kind that shuns price tags and mannequins and has amazing lighting.

But I digress, because A Little Bird's latest post includes images of Fin and Charlotte dressed for some swanky event a couple of months ago. He's dressed like James Bond, and she's wearing a couple of Band-Aids masquerading as a dress that my own boobs would absolutely fall out of. The caption reads:

> Fin DeWitt attending the Nexus Charity Ball, his companion, social media influencer Charlotte Bancroft, cutting a stunningly svelte figure in TOM FORD.

Companion. Fin made it sound more like a chance meeting, or even a series of them.

I think about the language used to describe me. *Casual. Comfort. Startled.* While *snatched* and *delicious* were reserved for Fin and his friend. I know I shouldn't pay attention—the intelligence in me says I shouldn't believe the media, even as the woman in me studies the image like an FBI profiler. Why are they standing so close? Could his arm be behind her?

"The betrayed will betray you, and the deceived will deceive you." Fin's words from the resort suddenly come back to me. He said this is what he learned from love. Whatever it means, it must've put him off trying to find love again. *I can't say I blame him.*

Pushing the recollection away, I scroll to the comment section while knowing I should just move on. But it's like a grazed knee I can't resist picking.

181 comments

Innit4theD: THAT'S his new wife?!?!

Fast&Curious: What's wrong with her? She looks like a regular girl to me.

AmaraKarna: Exactly. I'm thinking there's hope for me and him yet!

BadKarmaKitty: Except he got MARRIED.

AmaraKarna: That man can't keep it in his pants. I give them 6 months.

Aunti_Depressant: Poor Charlotte. She'll be crying into her new TV contract.

AnonEmouse: No wonder he left her. She looks like she could hula-hoop with an onion ring.

Susie_Choosie: Skinny shaming is a thing.

AmaraKarna: I wish someone would skinny shame me.

Thots.an.Prayers: The new Mrs. D has got BACK!

Taylor_Drift: She's got front too. Do you reckon she'd give me the name of her plastic surgeon?

Load more comments . . .

No thanks.

◆　◆　◆

As I emerge from the bowels of the underground station, I blink into the sunlight like a newborn soul. And like a newborn, I want to wail. I didn't sign up for this. For people to comment and pick fault with my clothing, my body—my bloody life! I have eyes in my head; I know I don't look like the women Fin usually dates. *Is photographed with or whatever.*

Who do these people think they are? These journalists and anonymous commenters—don't they understand words have power? That they hurt?

I felt bad when Evie was upset, when she described her experiences. But I didn't really get it. I do now. Boy, do I get it.

Pulling my hood over my head, I put my head down and join the hordes of similarly unhappy souls, blank faced and gray looking, rushing to work or getting kids to school. Regular Londoners living on the edge of poverty.

It could only be worse if it were raining. Though I suppose I could also be in the city, being jostled by finance bros far too important to pause a moment in the sunshine. Or silently cursing tourists for cluttering up the sidewalks with their suitcases while they gawk at their camera phones, not really paying attention to the things around them, just snapping images as proof of their being here.

It's such a strange world we live in, everyone desperate to appear interesting to their peers.

I should take a leaf out of Fin's book and not give a fuck. So that's what I do. *Fuck you, journalists! Fuck you, Charlotte! Fuck you all for trying to make me feel less than.*

I denounce my insecurities forthwith!

If nothing else, my silent conversation makes me smile, when my phone rings again. It's another private number, but as I'm almost at the tiny hole-in-the-wall coffee shop, I let it ring out. I've got other things to concentrate on today, and nothing is spoiling my Zen.

I order two Turkish coffees and a pistachio pastry and turn left out of the shop for Baba's nursing home, when my heart sinks to my Converse.

"Mila?"

My feet slow, my eyes shuttering closed. All the way out here? There are nine million people living in London in an area of over six hundred square miles. I might as well be on Mars as way out here—no way this speck of East London is Fin's normal patch.

"Hey." I paint on a small smile as I turn. My Zen is wobbling but not yet gone.

"What are you doing here?" we both say at the same time.

"You first." I rub my nose with the back of my hand, conscious of how quickly these tiny coffees cool and how much I don't want to have this conversation. Especially not here—this place is about as unlike Knightsbridge as you can get. And he looks so out of place in his bespoke suit, pristine shirt, and shiny white shoes. He's an invitation for a drive-by mugging.

318

Give me your wallet, watch, and shoes. Handmade Italian leather. There's bound to be a market for them.

"I'm here with Matt." He gestures behind him to where a 1960s concrete shopping center stands. Beige pebble-dashed concrete, abandoned shop fronts, and unimaginative graffiti. "We were on our way back to the office but stopped to look at an investment opportunity coming up. It's a shopping mall and business center that he hopes to get our investors interested in."

"It's about time gentrification spread this way."

"It'll be more like demolition. The whole area is to undergo a regeneration package."

I think about the block of flats I grew up in. I hope they raze it to the ground. I can't wait to move out. Move on. Again.

"So, what are you doing here?" He glances at the coffees and the brown paper bag containing Baba's pastry.

"I'm going to visit my grandmother," I admit, my heart heavy as I prepare to see her, wondering what kind of a morning she's having.

"Baba Roza." His inflection turns his statement into a question. I nod. "She lives around here?"

"Yeah, her nursing home isn't far away." *Vague. Keep it vague.*

"Oh." His expression flickers with something that looks like sympathy. "I didn't know."

"Because I didn't tell you." I fold my lips together against any other escapes and make a gesture with the coffee cups. "I'd better get going before these get cold."

"Can I . . ."

My feet shuffle but don't move, though I cringe as he starts again.

"Can I come with you. Maybe meet her?"

"I don't think that's a good idea." In fact, as I turn warily, I think it's a terrible idea. Possibly the worst I've ever heard.

"We don't have to tell her we're married. You can just introduce me as a friend."

"My grandmother has dementia, remember? New things, new people, confuse her. I really don't think it would be a good idea, especially as I haven't seen her myself this week."

Fin slides his palm over the top of his head, and my treacherous body reacts. "Yeah, sorry."

"Well, I'd better get going." I lift the paper cups as though in explanation. *Or excuse.*

"Let me walk you there, at least."

"Not necessary!" I sort of sing, like the backdrop is less *Trainspotting* and more *The Sound of Music*. I don't want him anywhere near the place. The facility is far from pretty. I mean, I'm grateful for the care they provide, and the staff are great, but it's not how I envisaged Baba ending her days.

"Come on. I'm done here. Let me just walk you to the door."

I stifle a sigh and nod, knowing he's not going to give in.

We take a right, cross a road, and weave through the car park. A few minutes later, I press the buzzer on the hospital-style doors and turn to him. "I'll see you later, yeah?"

"Sure."

The buzzer sounds, and Fin pulls on the handle before I can get to it.

"Thank you." I step inside, intending to put down the coffees to sign the visitor book, when pandemonium hits.

"Shut the door!" one of the nursing assistants calls as a large and seminaked male patient makes for the outside world.

I pivot as Fin steps inside, closing it behind him, but I can't concentrate on that as I sidestep the escaping motion machine.

"Thanks." The nurse smiles apologetically. "The inner door lock popped." Her attention turns to her charge. "Come on now, Harry, your son will be here to visit you shortly. Why don't you come back inside and we'll get you dressed, ready to see him."

"Get me my teeth!" Harry demands. "I'm gettin' outa this fuckin' madhouse," he explodes.

"Now, Harry . . ."

The man pivots, his hands landing heavily on Fin's shoulders. "Son, have you ever been in prison?" he asks earnestly, spittle lashing his captive's face.

Fin, God bless him, doesn't flinch. Instead, he holds the man's gaze without recoiling from his aged, dangling almost-nakedness. Meanwhile, I don't know where to look. Time is not easy on the body. But this is what I mean about changing facilities. The staff are great here, but there aren't enough of them. This door breaks regularly, and the whole place is just tired. Baba deserves better, and I want to give her that.

"I can't say that I have," Fin answers calmly.

"You'd be popular there," Harry says, patting his cheek. "I've been in the clink," he adds, his tone confidential. "And I'm not going back."

"Harry," the nurse cajoles. "He's a former lay preacher," she adds as a quiet aside. "He thinks this is prison, bless him."

I give a tiny nod in understanding. But also, I see the similarities.

"Lack of inhibition and sensory issues are classic dementia symptoms," I offer Fin's way. Like I just read it from a piece of frightening literature, the kind they supply you with at a diagnosis.

"That's right," the nurse says. "Come along, Harry. Let's go and get you dressed." With that, she turns Harry in the opposite direction. "You don't want all the ladies ogling, do you?"

"Dead birds don't fall out of their nests," he mutters in response.

"I'm sorry about that," I mutter to Fin, then I roll my lips inward. I'm not laughing. What I want to do is cry. Dementia is so cruel, stripping people of their dignity. But I also can't help but wonder how Oliver Deubel would've reacted to this situation. Something tells me it would not have ended so well.

"It's not your fault. Is there a washroom?" he asks, pointing to his face.

My heart sinks. I suppose it looks like he's coming in.

"I can leave," he offers, coming out of the washroom and wiping his palm across his face. He obviously doesn't want to, and I'm not sure why. I sometimes wish I didn't have to come here myself. Harry's outburst isn't the worst I've seen. At least it was mildly humorous. Sometimes, a dementia patient's outburst can be traumatic for all concerned.

The facility is understaffed and underfunded. It's all flowery wallpaper and cheap melamine, and though they're mostly cheerful, the staff wear the strain of their jobs on their faces without realization or intent.

"It's okay." He's here now. He's seen the place. He must've noticed the pervasive scent of cabbage and disinfectant already. I suppose all that remains is to see what kind of day Baba Roza is experiencing.

"This way." I glance down at the paper espresso cups. "She'll complain this is cold now." If we're lucky.

"Do you want me to go grab fresh ones?"

"It's okay. Thanks, anyway." And he hated the label *nice*. Maybe I should've said *decent*. Because he is.

I knock softly on her door, which is already open (and never locked), and find Baba sitting in her facility-issued chair, dozing.

"How long has she been in here?" Fin asks softly. He looks too big for the tiny room.

"Not so long. She'd been diagnosed more than a year ago but kept it secret. It wasn't until she fell and had to be hospitalized that I found out. I didn't have any choice but to put her in here."

Put her in here. Like a pet in a boarding kennel. Unlike a pet, she won't be coming home after the holidays.

I glance around the room and try to see it with his eyes. The hospital-style bed with the flowery duvet cover from home. The cream crocheted doilies she made years before. The religious icons on the walls and the framed pictures of passed loved ones.

"Your grandfather?" he asks, pointing to a black-and-white photo of my stern-looking grandfather.

"*Dedo*," I say, using the Macedonian name for *grandfather*. "I never met him."

"You look a little like him."

"I look like my mother, but I have my father's coloring. And his peasant DNA."

Fin gives a tiny frown, but it's true. No matter how much exercise I undertake or macros and calories I count, my body is always preparing for a harsh winter or a drought, hanging on to its fat cells, just in case. Yet the way he looks at me makes me feel like a goddess.

"*Zdravo!*" My grandmother comes to life like a jack-in-the-box, all arms and smiles and warmth. "My Mila!"

She lets loose a string of Macedonian I can't even guess at.

"English, Baba, remember? I don't understand."

"Yes, yes. I remember. Ah!" Her eyes widen and sparkle like diamonds. "You have brought Alexander," she announces, holding out her hands. *Aleksander*, it sounds like in her accent, a hard *k*.

"No, this is Fin. My friend." I don't know any Alexander. It was weird when she came up with the name, and weirder still that she keeps mentioning it.

"Come!" She makes a grabbing motion in the air, which is my cue.

Relief and love flood my system as I lean in for a kiss and she takes my face in her hands. She smells of flour and tomatoes and lavender water, the very singular scents somehow ingrained in her skin. "How are you, my love?"

But she doesn't answer, reaching now for Fin. Those grabbing granny hands must be universal, as I find him next to me. We swap sides, and Baba takes hold of his face.

"Aleksander, you cut your lion mane!"

"I did. But it was for a good cause." Pressing his hands over hers, he drops to one knee in front of her chair.

"For my Mila?"

"I like to think so."

"It's Fin, Baba," I interject. I know I'm not supposed to correct her, but I find myself doing so anyway.

"Yes, yes. Aleksander. Like the conqueror."

"Alexander the Great?" I screw up my face. The ancient Macedonian king from way back before baby Jesus hit the scene?

"He looked like a lion. So handsome."

"And you know that how?" Because when we watched the movie starring Colin Farrell, she tutted and complained about his terribly dyed hair.

"Because he is here!" she says—sort of, *you silly girl.*

"Alexander the Great?"

"No, your husband. He looks like lion. But where has his hair gone?"

"Baba, what are you talking about?" A frisson, something uncanny, washes over my skin, making the hairs on the back of my neck stand like pins.

This is so freaky.

"You married her, huh? You married my Mila in the sunshine?"

"Yes, that's right. Just like you told her I would."

Like she . . . oh, my days.

"You will look after her," she says, turning his left palm in her hand.

"Always."

She begins to study his palm, and I feel my cheeks heat with the silly, old-country-ness of it as she runs her finger along the lines. "Many, many lovers," she says, her eyes dancing as though to say *Lucky you!* "But that stops now. Here." She taps his palm. "One love, your whole life. And you will be very, very happy."

"That's good to know," Fin says. "Thank you."

"Baba." I make a noise; frustration mixed with pain, though I don't know why. It's not as though she'll remember this conversation. Or at least, not verbatim.

Or maybe it's because Fin will.

"Money, children." She glances my way. "Two. The girl you will call Roza."

I don't think so—on either front.

She lowers her head, then lifts it immediately again, as though struck by a sudden thought. "Oh! Lucky Mila. Your Aleksander will keep you very happy in the bedroom."

"Baba! There's no way you can see that on his palm." But I look anyway, as though I expect to see some kind of phallic symbol.

"Your grandfather, Stefan." She shakes her head. "I was not so lucky."

"I think that's enough for today."

Baba reclines a little in her high-backed chair, her face wreathed in a smile. "I told you, darling. I saw your husband in the coffee grounds. This one," she says with a waggle of her finger. "This one, he is a good one."

Chapter 29
MILA

He knew about it all along. He knew about her silly premonition, and he never breathed a word—never said that I told him.

Cringe. Cringe. Cringe!

Bloody shrooms. I'm so embarrassed. Not that Baba's words can have *anything* to do with our marriage. It's just a coincidence, that's all. She didn't even get his name right *and* she thought he was Alexander the Great! Not that I would mind seeing him in a toga.

We leave Baba dozing in her chair, though she made him promise to bring the backgammon board next time he visited. Not *a* backgammon board but *the* backgammon board. I really want to ask him if he owns one, but I don't really want to know the answer.

"Where can I take you?"

"I'd really rather make my own way." There's a lump in my throat the size of a tennis ball, and I'm worried it might shoot out. I'm going to Baba's flat, and the place is a dump—it all got too much for Roza, and I never realized the extent of her difficulties until I had to move back in. It's not like I abandoned her when I moved out in my early twenties, but I'd take her for lunch and days out rather than visit. Christmas and Easter she'd come to us. I wanted to treat her, but in doing so, somehow I missed her illness.

But if the flat is a dump, the building is a dumpster fire. In an island of dumpster fires. I don't want Fin anywhere near the place.

"Seems unnecessary. I have my car, and you're clearly in a hurry to go somewhere."

"I'm always in a hurry to get out of that place," I say, glancing behind me. "I hate it in there."

"Yeah, I get that. It's not the nicest facility, though you're pretty lucky with the nursing staff." A smile curls in the corner of his mouth, but I'm not going to comment, even when he pretends to hide it by scratching the tip of his nose. "It was nice how they congratulated us on our marriage."

I still say nothing, and I step back as a woman with a twin stroller barges between us, narrowly missing my toes. How did they even know? It wasn't the gossip column, because there were no funny looks. No sly suggestions that I'd bagged myself a rich man. Just smiles and congratulations.

Ah! The realization hits. We're both wearing wedding rings. Coupled with Baba's confused mutterings, that was probably it.

"So now you've seen for yourself why I agreed to fake marry you."

"But not why you real married me. And now you know you told me already about Roza's coffee premonition."

"You must've thought I was crazy," I say. "I can't think how I brought it up."

"It was a really sweet moment. Even when you explained how you thought she was confused about the date."

I say nothing and hope he'll do the same.

"We got married on your original wedding date." It's a simple statement, though a tiny spark of humor lurks in those gray eyes of his.

"The date, yeah." I scrunch my nose.

"It must've felt pretty wild for you."

"That's one way to put it." *Freaky* would be another. "But it's just a coincidence. Thank you for humoring her. You know, with all that palm reading and woo-woo stuff."

"No problem." Still with the amusement. Amusement restrained.

"Well, I'd better be off. I need to get back to Baba's flat ship-shape." I throw my thumb over my shoulder, though that's hardly the direction I'm headed.

"Today?" Fin's brow furrows briefly.

"Not everyone owns their home," I begin, my words spiky, "and the housing association wants the place back. Which is another reason I said yes. To Oliver and Evie's scheme, I mean." There's no point hiding this stuff anymore. Not now that he's seen where I come from. Though he hasn't (and won't) see the worst of it. "It's. . . been a time. I got dumped. Baba lost her marbles and moved in there," I say, throwing my thumb behind me. "Which meant I was about to become homeless a second time. My business went wonky, which you know, and all that together made for a very trying time." Understatement of the century. "But things are looking up now." I smile—staple that sucker on.

"Because you married your grandmother's dream man?"

"No, that's Alexander. Why are you pulling that face?"

"Reasons," he replies enigmatically. Or annoyingly.

"Anyway, we should probably talk about our exit strategy at some point." I sound so clinical, but it's the best way. Right?

"From marriage?" He pushes his hands into the pockets of his pants, his gaze dipping briefly.

"Well, obviously, I have to find *my* Alexander at some point," I mutter, slightly caustically.

"Of course." He gives a huff of a laugh, that twinkle in his eye coming back.

"Look, Fin, I'm grateful for your help, and I'm sorry if it doesn't always seem that way. I know I wasn't very gracious before, but I would like to be your friend. If you think that's possible still. You're on good terms with your exes," I add as an afterthought. A slightly desperate sounding one. "Not that we'd really be—"

"I'd like that. To be your friend."

I thought I might feel relief, or comfort. I do not. "I'm going to be busy over the coming months. I'm sure we both are. And I expect, for appearances, we should probably be seen together. Sometimes. Maybe?"

"I think that would be best. Neither of us would benefit from being outed in a lie."

"True. I think what I'm trying to say—and making a mess of—is that I don't think we'll be spending a lot of time together. But I'd like to—well, if you'd like to too . . ." I take a deep breath. "I want to sleep with you—in your bed. To be intimate."

"Be intimate?" he repeats with a twitch to his lips.

"Have sex. And not just because there's a chance someone on your staff might tell the tabloids." A smile tugs at my lips, because we both know that was nothing but a ruse. A silly excuse. "I want you. And I want to."

"I guess it *is* Roza sanctioned."

"Can we not talk about my grandmother and sex in the same breath?"

"Can I ask what made you change your mind?"

"Last night, I came to the conclusion that, if we're staying in the same house, I won't be able to keep my hands off you."

A fact I find mortifyingly necessary to admit.

◆ ◆ ◆

In the end, Fin insists on taking me to the flat, and short of tripping him and making a run for it, I don't see how I can get out of it. But it turns out, he's not driving. Bob is. Bob is Fin's sometime driver.

"If Bob drives, it means I get to work," he explains with an apologetic shrug.

I give Bob the address, and I know by his blank expression he's heard of the area. I mean, most Londoners have. The place is notorious. Knife crime and drugs, gangs, addicts, and police raids. I'll be so glad when I never have to climb that concrete staircase again.

"Take a left here, please." I direct Bob to the car park nearest to Baba's building. If you read about the area, you'll learn the sprawling towers include over three hundred homes and that the building style is something called *postwar brutalism*.

I would say living in the shadow of these towers is brutal, if nothing else.

"Right." I reach for my seat belt, my tone determined. "I expect I'll see you later."

"I'll come with you," Fin says, doing the same.

"No," I bite out. "No need," I add a little softer. "You'll just get in the way."

"I get that you want to do this alone, that you feel like you need to do everything unaided," he adds with consternation. "But I can help."

My eyes slide to the driver, who does a solid impression of being inanimate. But he's got ears.

"I can," he repeats.

"No, you can't. Not with this. This is personal. I don't want you there." I feel cruel saying so, even if it is the truth.

"Fine. Then I'll just walk you up."

"I knew it," I say under my breath as I reach for the door handle and yank it open. I'm out and almost at the stairwell, my cheeks burning angrily and my head thumping, as he catches up.

"Wait."

"I've been climbing these stairs for years. See?" I make a couple of ridiculously exaggerated steps. "I don't need your help."

"Oy, mister!" Our heads simultaneously turn to the voice from the other side of the car park. "You need someone to look after your motor?"

"He means your car," I mutter, eyeing the gray-tracksuit-, black-hoodie-wearing group of boys. Men? They might be ten years old, or they might be in their twenties, it's hard to tell. They could be kids messing about, or they could be gang members. "You'd better go back. We don't see many Bentleys around here." I turn away, only to find his fingers wrapped around my upper arm.

"No, thanks!" Fin yells back with an affable wave. "Bob will look after it. It's an ugly car, anyway," he adds just for my ears. "Part of the company fleet."

"But still—"

"That fat fuck?" the voice yells back. "Is he carrying?"

"He means—"

"You don't have to translate for me," Fin answers, amused. "I'm sure he'd invite you to find out!" he then calls over his shoulder.

"Fin!"

"They can take it up with him just fine."

"But he's—" old.

"He's ex-military," Fin replies. "Like, serious shit."

"Whatever!" the voice yells back. "I bet he's not fire retardant."

"You should go."

"And leave you here?" he says, as though I've lost my mind.

"I *live* here." Shame pokes at me, though I know it shouldn't.

"Not anymore," he grates out. "And not if I've got anything to do with it."

"Well, guess what? You don't," I retort.

"Okay." He holds up his hands. "Let's just go upstairs," he adds, instantly calmer. And ignoring the threat.

"Fine. On your own head be it. Or poor Bob's," I add in a mutter.

"That was quite a sophisticated choice of words for an idiot," he says, trudging behind me. *"Fire retardant."*

"They're not idiots," I say, whipping around. "They're poor. There's a difference."

"Okay?" Fin holds up his hands. "But they're probably also criminals."

"That's what happens to the disenfranchised. A lack of choices leads to a life of crime and violence." I sound so sanctimonious and feel like such a hypocrite.

"That's not true for everyone."

I don't answer as I turn away, not even sure why I said those things. I might've agreed with him five minutes ago, but that doesn't make it right. Any of it. Just because he can afford to waste tens of thousands on a stupid balloon dog, it doesn't mean he's any better than us.

Them and us.

We're worlds apart in life and experiences.

We're just too different.

But for what?

"Someone said you got here in a Bentley this morning," Ronny says, as I open the front door to her smiling face an hour later. The same door I closed (not quite) in Fin's face when it looked like he wasn't going to leave.

"No secrets in this building," I mutter, closing the door behind her, bolting it too. The scent of the hallway is stale, though the rest of the place still smells like home, the scent of a thousand tomato dishes having seeped into every nook and cranny.

"With walls this thin?" Ronny grins as she sets her can of energy drink on a doily in the center of a small nest of tables. "Who was it, then?"

I swallow back a sigh. *May as well get it over with.* "My husband."

"What?" Her eyes fly wide. "Spill the tea, sis!" Then she playfully punches me in the arm.

"That's all I'm saying." I pivot and make my way into the kitchen.

"Nah. No way!" she says, bounding in behind me. "Is he a big-time dealer?"

"A drug dealer, Ronny? No!" I turn to the pantry, pulling open the yellowing melamine door.

"So, he's like, just rich?" Her expression scrunches. "Regular rich. Come on, he must be rich if he drives a Bentley. Did you get hitched on holiday?"

"Do you know that spices were first brought to England in the Middle Ages?"

"What?"

"I'm pretty sure there are some in the back of this cupboard with date codes from then."

"Oldies, man." She shakes her head. "They keep everything. My nan has jerk seasoning from way back when."

I'm pretty sure Ronny's gran is about fifty-five. At least, she looks around that age. And so glamorous.

"I have a job for you," I begin, knowing that'll catch her attention before it spins elsewhere. *Whirlwind Veronica—so her mother calls her.*

"Yeah? What is it?"

"Business is picking up." Seriously. I was amazed when I checked my message bank to see I had three messages. Three booking inquiries! And now I have three introductory meetings next week. Yippee! The downside is I'll have to schlep them, as I no longer have an office but each couple (or bride, in these three cases) preferred an actual meeting to a virtual one.

"You never explained what happened to your business. You know, why you moved in with Roza and gave up your flat and stuff."

"I had a run of bad luck after me and Adam split up." I pull out the first of a dozen tins of tomatoes. Checking the dates, I sort them into two piles on the two-seat kitchen table. *Bad date code and donate to the food kitchen.* I turn back to the pantry, which is filled to the brim with tins and packets and boxes, some of which are a dozen years old. Treacle might not go out of date, but crackers go soft. She can't really have been eating these, can she?

My heart is heavy as I glance around the small space. There is so much to sort through before I can hand back the keys, and yet another letter arrived from the housing association while I was away. I haven't opened it, as I know it's just another threat.

"Seems a bit sus."

My attention drops to Ronny. "Sorry?"

"A bit suspect." She shrugs and begins sifting through the old foodstuffs. Picking up a packet of single-serve oatmeal, she screws her nose as she reads the date. "The wedding industry is booming," she says, dropping the oatmeal back. "I don't see what luck has to do with it."

"Booming?" I try to keep my amusement from my voice.

"Yeah. I've been doin' a bit of research. You know, after you said you might have something for me. Beats working in a factory."

"You work in a sports shop. Part time."

"Selling running shoes." Her lip curls. "And you know I hate feet."

Ah, Ronny. She makes me laugh.

"Anyway, the revenue for the wedding industry is up twenty-two percent on last year." As she says this, she swings her backpack from her shoulder, pulling out a notepad. "Do you know the vicar charges when you get married in church?"

"Yeah."

"If there's a God, I hope he's paying tax."

Ronny pulls back a kitchen chair and opens her notepad, all business, as she slides away my neatly stacked piles with her forearm, oblivious. She goes on to explain how she's been hanging around some of the online wedding forums, taking notes of trends and what brides are looking for. I take the seat opposite, impressed. A lot of the information she's gathered doesn't really pertain to me; I have my preferred vendors and venues, but Ronny wouldn't know that.

"What was your wedding like?" she asks quite suddenly, reaching up to tighten her ponytail, jet spirals spilling over her shoulders as she does.

"It was beautiful." What I remember of it. And what I remember most isn't the decor or the setting or even the dress. It's the way Fin looked at me as he lifted my veil. My heart hammered, and my knees were shaking like crazy, but that all faded when he took my face in his hands and whispered how beautiful I was. It went a bit pear shaped after that, but it was mostly nerves.

Specifically mine, which he seemed intent on getting on.

When I think about Fin . . . I quickly remind myself not to.

"The ceremony was held in a place overlooking the ocean. The sun was shining, and everything was just perfect."

"I expect so. It is your job, after all."

"Yes." The reminder is a good one. It was just a job.

"So you didn't have a job to do over there," she says with a grin. "You went and got secretly hitched!"

"Surprise," I say weakly.

"Do I get to meet this husband of yours, then?" she asks, pressing her chin to her hand.

"I'm sure you will." Fin was great with Sarai, so I know he'll be good with Ronny. I bet he builds a rapport with everybody he meets. *Decent, kind, sexy Fin.*

"That's not him downstairs in the Mercedes people carrier, is it?"

"What Mercedes?"

"The bloke driving it looks like a policeman, but the wheels are too posh for him to be a copper," she adds, using the colloquial term for a policeman. One of the more polite ones, at least.

"That's nothing to do with me," I say as I pull out my phone to check the time. Or to see if I've received an alert for a new post on that awful gossip column. And what do you know? I have. A fist grasps, then twists my innards, but I won't look at the post now.

"Is that A Little Bird?" Ronny peers over the top of my phone, so I flip it over.

"Yeah. I was just checking something."

"It's so trashy," she says with a laugh. "But it gives me life."

"What?"

"I love it. It's, like, a guilty pleasure."

"Reading about . . ."

"What's going on in London. How the other half live and all that. Like, last year, when that woman trashed her wedding after finding her man had been cheating."

"I read about that. It was awful."

"I watched the Pulse Tok," she says, beginning to rummage through her backpack. "I high-key loved it."

"But the bride was devastated."

"She served him his arse," she says, her tone making it clear she disagrees. "Then it went viral, and that man was tortured! The best part was he was so salty about it, which just meant he was heaped on even more."

"I didn't see any of that." *But he deserved it,* I think as she pulls out her phone. She'll just be checking her texts. *I hope.* Or her Snaps. She's obsessed with Snapchat.

"Gossip is, like, so nourishing it should be its own food group." But then her eyes widen, and I realize my thoughts were just wishful thinking as she scrolls. And scrolls. And then suddenly sits back in her chair.

"Sis," she admonishes as she sets down her phone. "I am *shook.*"

And I've been busted, it would seem.

Chapter 30
MILA

"Have you read this? Read what this skank is saying about you?" she says, brandishing her phone.

"No, and I'm really not interested."

"I get it. You're too classy to spill the tea. Congrats on your new man, though. He is *fine*."

"Thanks." I think. As if this wasn't an awkward enough exchange.

"I can't believe she's sayin' this shit, though."

"What?" Okay, so that didn't last very long, I think as I flip over my phone.

A Little Bird Told Us . . .

Oh, what a tangled web the gorgeous Fin DeWitt weaves, according to his former love interest, reality TV star Charlotte Bancroft. The saga continues!

Blond Charlotte took a break from filming the new season of *Made in RICHmond* to confide that she was "rocked" by the news of his sudden wedding, adding, "It was only three weeks ago that we had dinner together. He's been working in the Far East, and I was looking forward to being reunited with him." She added that his new romance must've been "a whirlwind affair."

"Affair!" I spit.

"She is, like, so main charactering right now," Ronny adds angrily. "As if this is even about her! You're the one that married him. A hard launch too."

"Yes, I suppose our marriage was a hard launch. A surprise, anyway." Most of all to us. "But the tabloids can't be trusted for real news," I add, trying to temper my anger as I lower my attention once more.

The svelte Surrey native added that she harbors Fin's new bride no ill will and wishes her luck in keeping her man's eye from wandering. "He's a very generous man, both inside and outside of the bedroom. Of course, we can all see her attraction."

"What the fuck!"
Oh, well. That didn't last long.

And as the spokesperson for SynCycle, the latest gym sensation to hit the UK, she added she'd be willing to introduce curvy Mila to the worldwide craze. "I can tell it hasn't hit the poor girl what it takes to be in the public eye, but she can rely on me to show her the ropes." She just needs to "reach out."

"Reach out and throttle her, more like," I mutter. "Don't for a minute believe any of this." I hate the post's accompanying image. Charlotte Bancroft doesn't look pregnant. In fact, she looks like she barely eats. It was obviously me the journalists were talking about at the airport. *Just because I've got a bit of a tummy.*

"What a bitch," Ronny adds. "She's just some fame whore who's pedaling hard to stay relevant."

I'd like to pedal her right off a pier, I think. Stick the SynCycle so far up her skinny . . .

No, stop, Mila. Those thoughts just make you as bad as her.

"What kind of woman says that sort of stuff about another woman? What happened to sisterhood?"

"All's fair in love and war," Ronny says. "Especially when we're talking TV deals."

"I don't follow."

"*Made in RICHmond*—which, by the way, is the worst TV program I've ever watched. The so-called stars are like, so cringe."

"I'll take your word for it. I have no desire to watch it."

"You won't need to. It's been canceled. The current season is its last. She'll be trying to create a name for herself, and she'll use you as drama, if you let her."

"I'm not letting her. She's just doing it," I mutter.

"Stay classy," she says. "Don't get pulled into it."

"I have no intention of getting involved."

"But if you do, show her who's the fucking wife, yeah?"

"Okay." I eye Ronny from across the small table.

"Why are you looking at me like that?" she demands, her tone still mildly belligerent.

"I was just thinking that I've missed you."

"Aw, sis! That's, like, so nice." Her expression softens.

"Sometimes, I feel like you're with me even when you're not." She nods, impressed.

"And I find myself thinking, what would Ronny do?"

"Yeah?"

"And then I usually do the opposite."

"Piss off!" she says, throwing the singular packet of oatmeal my way. "Was Charlotte Shit-for-Brains his ex?" she asks suddenly. "Or were they just hooking up?"

"Neither. They just happened to be in the same place a few times. Photos were taken, and that's about it." I mean, why would he lie about it?

Ronny's mouth twists pensively. "She must have a thing for him, though."

I make a gesture—kind of *so what?* "I'm sure she's not alone."

Ronny grins as she holds up her hand for a high five. "My girl Mila married the GOAT!"

"Did I?" I answer, meeting her hand awkwardly.

"The 'greatest of all time,'" she supplies. "So, when did you meet him? Did you meet him before, or was it a case of instant island love?"

"We met about four months ago. At a wedding." It's the truth, and I'm sticking to it.

"Cool," she says before falling quiet.

"What's with the face?" I ask, waving my finger in front of hers. "What's going on in this head of yours."

"I'm just thinking."

"You're not thinking about doing anything, are you? To Charlotte, I mean."

"Like what?"

"I just remember how you wanted to send your mates around to trash Adam's car."

"That was just in the heat of the moment," she says. "And he is a cheating scumbag. Charlotte is just a loser. So no, I wasn't thinking about retribution."

"Good. Because I don't want you to get involved in any of this."

"Meels, you're so suspicious," she admonishes.

"Promise me you won't."

"Course. Honestly, I was just thinking about the research I did."

"Well, that's good. I'm impressed."

"That was my aim. And I hope to find it reflected in my wage."

◆ ◆ ◆

"You look very happy this evening."

A few days later, I'm pouring myself a glass of celebratory wine when Fin walks into the kitchen.

"I am. Very!" I brandish the bottle. "Want one?"

"Not a whole bottle, but I could go for a glass."

"Fun-ee," I reply in the opposite tone.

But I'm super peppy today. Everything seems a little brighter because business is booming. Earlier this week, I resolved to stop reading posts from A Little Bird, and I've managed to get Baba's kitchen almost clear. Though there's a lot of stuff in boxes and bags that I need to somehow get down three flights of stairs. I was going to ask Fin's security guard—the mysterious man in the Mercedes—but we're both pretending we don't know anything about him.

As in, I haven't noticed him, and Fin hasn't sent him.

As Ronny would say, *lol/jokes.*

I get that he's there as a precaution, especially after those kids got mouthy. But that's all they turned out to be in the end—teenagers looking for a reaction rather than pyromaniac extortionists.

"I signed another client today. Woot!" Being married to Fin is wedding-planner gold dust.

"Congrats."

Our marriage, our names being linked in the press, and Fin's status, his high profile, have been such good news for me. Whether it's curiosity (get to meet the woman who caught the man) or aspiration (meet the wedding planner married to a wealthy man) or something else, I don't care. Whatever gets them to pick up the phone I'm okay with, because the bookings are ultimately my doing.

"It's just a cheap bottle," I preface as I reach for another glass.

"I said yes, Mila," Fin replies with a soft, slightly exacerbated smile. He strips from his jacket and drops it to the back of one of the stools before his gaze flips down to his chest. "Did I spill something earlier?"

"No." I'm just staring, because yum! "You're wearing braces—suspenders, I think you call them."

"That's it?"

"I've just never seen you in them before." I hug the wine bottle to my chest. For reasons.

"And you like them, I take it?" His voice drops lower.

"They're okay, I suppose." I flick my shoulder, then remember I was supposed to be filling his glass. "You don't often wear a tie either." A dark tie and suspenders, a silver tie clip, and a brilliant-white shirt. He looks so very sexy, but I can't stand here gawking. "Have you had a haircut?" Twisting off the bottle top, I splash a little into his glass. I set it down beside him as I round the island.

"Just the back and sides." He gives a soft chuckle as he rubs his palm up the back of his head. "I was starting to look a little like a fuzzy tennis ball."

My skin shimmers with that sensory memory of it as I lean against the marble. It's not like I need to cast my mind back very far to remember the circumstances. *To last night, that's all.*

"So we're celebrating?" he asks, taking his glass.

"Absolutely. The wedding isn't until May next year, but it's a start."

"Well done," he says, tipping the rim of his glass to mine. "Here's to many more."

"Yes, more of those, please, powers that be." I bring the glass to my lips and sip without really tasting, because the way he's looking at me means all I can taste is him.

Fin leans closer, feeding his hand under the weight of my hair. He cups the back of my neck, his fingers warm and comforting. "You're the power, and it will be. Because you deserve great things."

I've never considered myself the addictive type, but the risk feels real with him. The thought ripples, like a stone dropped into the mellow warmth of my chest.

It's just sex, that's all.

We're the king and queen of commitment-phobes.

It's just, his shirt and that tie, the one I feel my hand gravitating to, is so attractive. Settling my palm against the center of his hard chest, I decide they'd look even more attractive someplace other than on him.

Fin's glass makes a tiny chink against the marble as he sets it down, before taking mine. I giggle, ticklish, as his hands link around my waist, and he lifts me to the countertop.

"Did you go to see Roza today?" His cologne is heavenly and his features hazy as he rubs his nose against mine.

"It was one of her good days." The new nursing home is trialing her on new meds, which make her a little sleepy, but sleepy is better than agitated, for her state of mind.

"Did she ask after me?"

"She asked after Alexander," I say, pinching in my smile.

"So she did."

"Get a toga and a breastplate, and then maybe we'll talk."

"You'll get it." Pulling back, he slides me a sultry smile. "Sometime."

"Sounds promising," I say, wrapping his tie in my hand and pulling him closer, until his lips are pressed to one corner of my mouth. *Then the other.* I sigh at the gentle press of his teeth against my bottom lip. "What if I don't want to wait?"

"I have something I want to talk to you about."

I make a sound of pleasured inquiry as his lips brush mine once more.

"I want you to let me hire in a clearing service." I still, but he doesn't seem to realize as his touch feathers down my neck. "Sorting out the flat is taking so much of your time. It makes you sad, so I thought—"

"No," I answer softly. "Thank you, but no."

He pulls back to look at me. "It could free you up to concentrate on Trousseau, the business that makes you happy."

"Clearing Baba's house is my responsibility."

"Yeah, I know, but—"

"No," I reply firmly, sliding from the countertop.

"Mila." He presses a hand to his hip, his expression one of consternation. "It makes no sense, you spending all your time doing that."

"It doesn't take up all my time." Though it probably should, because the housing association is breathing down my neck. It wants to place a new tenant, and I'm not working fast enough for them.

"But it pulls you down. Why make yourself sad like that?"

"It doesn't have to make sense to you. I know what I'm doing."

"Do you? I called the housing association today."

"You did *what?*" I make it to the other side of the island, instantly annoyed.

"I wanted to see if there was something I could do to help."

"Unbelievable," I mutter. "Why would you think that's even appropriate?"

"It's just as well I did," he retorts, "given what they had to say."

I stalk out of the kitchen before I say something mean. Because Lord knows my head is full of mean right now. And my chest feels tight. He's stepped way over the line.

"Don't you want to know what they told me?" he calls after me, his shoes echoing on his shiny marble floors.

"No!"

"They've written to you a dozen times."

"That's not news," I retort over my shoulder as I storm into the bedroom. I swing the door closed behind me. I hear it slap against his palm as he catches it, then his footsteps as he follows me in.

There's something about this exchange that feels familiar. Maybe that's why my head and my chest hurt. It feels . . . controlling. Am I overreacting? Fin isn't anything like Adam. *Is he?*

"They're considering court action, Mila. Do you know that? Every week you keep the place on is another week's rent overdue."

"That's fine. I can afford to pay it."

"But why delay? They want their property back."

"I have it under control!" I stalk to the window and stare down at the Hyde Park treetops below. My blood feels like it's boiling in my veins. He just doesn't get that I owe it to Baba to ensure her possessions, her worldly treasures, are treated with the utmost respect. The contents of that flat are our history, and I became her sole purpose within those walls. I can't let some stranger tear through the place. Yet I can't seem to say any of that, the meaning behind the words too large to spit out.

Do I even owe him an explanation, the way he's behaving right now?

"Why won't you let me help you?"

"But you're not trying to help. You're trying to take over. In fact, this feels like you're trying to control me!"

"Control—" He swipes his hand through his hair, then presses it to his mouth. "That's not what this is," he answers. "I'm just

346

trying to help. I'm doing my fucking best to keep you out of the shit!"

"I don't need your help," I snipe, hating how it makes me feel to see him like this. *This other side of him?*

"Well, fuck," he says, leaning back against the dresser as though I pushed him there. His expression turns so cold, he looks almost unfamiliar. Un-Fin. "Only, that's not quite the truth, is it, honey-buns? You need me for your business—need my name. Not to mention my notoriety, because that shit's good for the ladies, right?"

"Your notoriety has nothing to do with me." My mind instantly fills with the thought of that fucking influencer, or whatever she is, and the things she spouted to the press. I hate the power I've given it in my head, and I hate how I feel right now.

"And my cock. You might not need it, but you sure like it being part of the deal."

"There's no need to be so crass." My heart echoes in my chest. Or maybe it's the truth in those words. *His hurt.*

"Is it crass when it's the truth? 'Help me Fin,'" he says, sweeping his hand through the air, "'but only in the narrow areas I say. Fuck me,'" he adds, sweeping it back. "'But don't care for me. And whatever you do, don't love me.'"

"That's not—"

"I don't know what to tell you, Mila. I'm feeling more than a little used."

"I didn't ask for any of this," I retort as I begin to tremble. When he puts it that way, it sounds so bad. He doesn't deserve that.

"No, but you did ask me to keep on fucking you. As long as I don't fucking fall for you!" This he almost yells, his composure finally breaking.

"Because *love* means *betrayal and lies* to you. Why would I put myself up for that?"

"What the fuck?"

"Those are your words," I spit. "So don't pin this on me."

"You have no idea what you're talking about." By his sides, his hands tighten into fists.

"Of course I don't, because I'm *that* shallow. So shallow, in fact, what I ought to do is take this *curvaceous* body the press loves to hate and set myself up an OnlyFans account. Cash in and create my own notoriety, because I'll do anything for money, right?"

"That's your hang-up, not mine. Money is just a means to an end, not something to set us apart."

"That's easy for you to say," I murmur as I stare at my reflection in the darkened glass. Behind me, Fin folds his arms across his chest and tips back his head. I don't understand how we've gone from kisses and sexy suspenders to this—to hurting and throwing insults.

"Not everyone in your life is going to fuck you over," he says so softly, I wonder if the fight has drained out of him. "You're just scared. And I get it. I really do."

I pivot and glare at him. I want to believe he's nothing like Adam, that he truly thinks he's helping, not controlling. That his past is just that, and that when he talks about love he's being serious. Because, God help me, I think I want that. I want him to love me, but not like this. I won't ever make the mistakes I did before. I won't ever settle for someone who makes me feel less.

The thoughts swirl and tumble and turn, and I just can't stand it. I cross the room so quickly—as though I can escape them—only to find him in my path. He takes me in his hands. *His hands, not his arms, pressed to my forearms.*

"I'm done talking about this," I mutter. My thoughts and my feelings are too tangled to untie.

"Admit you're scared, Mila. Scared of your feelings."

"What I am is hurt, and I can't do this right now." Pulling away, I leave the room.

Chapter 31
FIN

"What are you doing sitting in the dark like a sad ball sack?"

I squint as Matt turns the light on in my office. It's early evening and the shutters are drawn. I thought everyone had gone for the day. "I'm thinking," I answer with a sigh.

"I wondered what that smell was." He sniffs. "Like burning. You ought to oil those cogs before you use them. They get rusted up without use."

"We're talking about my brain, not your pipes. And if you must know, I'm avoiding going home."

"You've only been married two minutes."

"Feels a lot longer today." But that's a lie, even if it's hard to remember a time before Mila was in my life. Mila, my maddening, stubborn wife. The reason I can't bring myself to go home right now. I don't want to fight with her again—I didn't want to fight with her three fucking days ago! And now she's so closed off. My stomach cramps, because I feel like we might be days away from her calling this whole thing off.

I counted on her wanting to stay. Counted on her needing me a little longer, which would give me time to get her to open up. For me to woo her. Time for her to see that I fucking love her!

Need. She doesn't *need* me. I accused her of needing just the idea of me, the outward persona. Because that's my fucking fear. Not that she heard it that way, given the pile of cash on the kitchen countertop this morning, a pink Post-it Note stuck to the top, which read:

> THE MONEY I OWE YOU FOR ROZA'S
> NURSING HOME.
> I APPRECIATE YOUR HELP.

Fucking appreciates my help. I was glad to give it. But the note and the money felt like a big *fuck you*.

Three days of her not being around. Three days of her sleeping in another room.

It could be worse, I suppose. She might have gone back to her grandmother's flat. Then I, rather than a security team, would be sitting outside it in a van.

I just want her to be safe. Happy. I want her to fucking love me!

In the periphery of my vision, I note Matt shaking his head.

"What?" I ask wearily.

"I was just wondering if I should call a chiropractor. Slunk low in the chair like that, you won't be able to walk when you stand. Posture is important at your age."

But I'm not in the mood for shit talking.

"I asked what's changed, fuckhead."

"Everything," I mutter. "And nothing."

Matt folds his arms. "Well, that's helpful. Maybe you should wait until your hair grows and then get Josie to order you some frilly shirts. Maybe some quills and a pot of ink. Some parchment

350

and shit. Better to look the part if you're aiming for brooding romantic poet."

"It's not gonna work."

"Not surprised. I've heard your limericks. Your poetry would be truly shite."

"With Mila. She doesn't want anything to do with me."

"What did you do?"

"Why does it have to be something I did?" I pull myself up straight in my chair. He's right about my back, though I won't admit it to him.

"Because you know how women work," he says, making an awkward gesture. "But also, you don't *know* how women work."

"And you do?"

"I've got sisters."

"As have I."

"I've got more than you. I've also got a million female cousins, and I'm still as lost as the next fella when it comes to trying to work them out. But what I will say is we've all seen the way you look at Mila. And the way she looks at you. You used to be the last man standing at work dinners. Lately, you piss off home before dessert."

"You might see a little more of me now, because you were right. I can't make her love me. And I can't get her to accept my love."

"Have you tried? Told her you love her?"

I shake my head. "She isn't interested in any declaration." Worse, she's actively avoiding me. If she's not with her grandmother, she's working. And if she's not working, she's clearing her grandmother's flat. So much for making this work. So much for making things easier for her.

"*Controlling*," my arse. Can't she see that it's love?

Matt's brows hit his hairline. "Here's an idea. Why don't you just tell her how you feel?"

I tip back my head and stare at the ceiling. "I told you. She isn't interested."

"Have you tried?"

"Of course I have." *Haven't I?*

"Well, can't say I blame her." Matt sniffs.

"Remind me not to come to you for sympathy."

"No, I mean from what you said about her last fella. She's gonna find it hard to trust anyone after the way he fucked her over. Maybe even confuse caring for control. Or who knows, maybe you confused one for the other . . ." His words trail off, his expression bland.

"I'm not him," I retort. "I'd never hurt her."

"But how does she know that after all the shite that's written about you on the internet?"

"Everyone knows it's bullshit."

"Ah," he says, holding up a pondering finger. "Is it, though? You've been a mad shagger as long as I've known you."

"Thanks."

"If you're different from her ex, you need to prove it to her. All the ways he fucked her over, you have to show her you're not like that."

"By not sticking my dick in other women? Too easy."

"She was jilted, arsewipe. That's going to throw anyone's center off balance. Meanwhile, that fame chaser is telling the world Mila's not good enough, that you're still that mad shaggin' man whoor."

"You don't read that Little Bird bullshit, do you?"

"Well, you obviously have. So much for the *'I don't give a fuck what people say about me,'*" he retorts with a dismissive wave.

"I'm just keeping an eye on it. For litigation purposes."

"Oh, aye. That's bound to help," he answers heavily.

"It might. It's just inconsequential bullshit."

"It's easier for people to believe the bad, though. Especially if that's been their experience." He pauses for a beat to study me. "Have you done anything that might make her doubt or mistrust you?"

"No, I—" I would hardly give Machiavelli a run for his money. I might've manipulated one or two outcomes. But that's not what I was doing when I suggested a house-clearing company, and she almost bit off my head. *She called me controlling.* And maybe it seemed that way, but . . .

"You're either a really bad liar or just relationship dumb."

"I thought you came to help."

"This is me helping!"

I rub my hand through my hair. "Can you just fuck off elsewhere? Please?"

But Matt just folds his arms and stretches out his legs. "Take Oliver. A shrewder fucker I've yet to meet. Every move he makes, he's already calculated three possible outcomes and at least that many moves ahead. But look at the mess he made of things with Evie. That eejit ended up chasing her halfway across the world, taking himself off to a jungle where he could've easily been bitten by a snake or sold to rebels to be ransomed back to us piece by bloody piece."

"I wouldn't have paid," I mutter.

"So I say again, what might you have done to make her mistrust you?"

"Nothing."

"Apart from the shit you pulled with Evie, giving her 'Mila's business card.'" He encloses the final three words of his statement in physical speech marks.

"That wasn't underhanded. I didn't even know if Evie would bother looking her up."

"Sure." His expression twists. "You would've made some sign to Evie, and she would've gone off on one of her do-good quests like a terrier down a rabbit hole. She would've found out what her ex had done, and Bob's your uncle—as well as your driver—and Mila is suddenly Evie's wedding woman."

"*Her* wedding woman. Coordinator. Whatever. Nothing to do with me. Like I said, I just gave Evie Mila's card."

"And a hint. And that's all it would've taken."

"Stretching, Matt."

"Is it, though?" He pulls a superior expression. "It put her in your path. The question is now, What are you gonna do to keep her there?"

I'm still pondering the question long after he's left my office, when I pick up my phone. And do the opposite to his advice. It might look like another case of control, of manipulation, but it's desperation that turns me mildly Machiavellian. Or so I tell myself as I make that call.

I might lose everything. But I'll risk it all for her.

Chapter 32
MILA

"It was lovely to meet you both," I say, shaking hands with the couple of my fourth introduction meeting this week, this one nothing to do with my marriage to Fin but a referral from a wedding I planned last year. They've also booked a date, woo-hoo!

"Thanks for making time to meet us at the venue."

"It's such a perfect hotel," I offer. "Space for the ceremony, the gardens, the private cocktail bar. It really does have it all."

It is a lovely place. And I'd found myself standing outside for a moment or two before coming in, and my reflection in the glass doors made me smile. My hair, though a little wild, looked good on me. My new pantsuit smart and functional but also stylish. I'd looked good, and I'd felt good too. And it had made me realize I hadn't felt like that in a while.

And then I'd had the strangest thought. A few weeks ago, before my recent adventures, before Fin and the wedding and all that has entailed, I probably would've paused in a different way. I would've seen my reflection and felt . . . not enough. Not *good* enough.

Business is good, and I'm obviously feeling that success. But it's more than that. I just can't quite put my finger on it.

"We do love it here." The couple exchanges a fond look. "And thank you again for seeing us so soon. We just left everything so late, and we're scrambling to catch up."

"Don't worry. It'll all come together beautifully. Life usually does." Even as I say the words, I feel a pang of regret. If life always works out, why aren't Fin and I speaking yet?

Because we're both smarting still is the obvious answer. Because neither of us wants to make the first move. We left things at such a bad point the other night, and now we're like ships passing in the night in his beautiful home. He's taking care to keep out of my way, and I'm taking care to be busy. *While trying not to overthink.*

He said some things. I said some too. I want to be able to trust him completely, but I can't seem to get out of my own head. And yet . . .

I shake off the thoughts.

"I'm so looking forward to working with you." I paint on my professional smile to allow us to say our goodbyes. And the pair leaves.

Love. I sigh heavily. It feels like such a four-letter word right now. As in *hard*.

But love is also *hope*. It might even be a *cure* for the past. The more I think about what Fin said, the more I begin to doubt my own reaction. Love is a *leap*, I think, consternation rippling across my brow. But it's also the ultimate *peak*—the summit. To love and be loved in return.

Love is the *goal*, for many. *For Fin?* For me.

Love is the *beat* of his heart. It's *warm*, like his body. *Dear*, like him. Love is in his *kiss*. His *hold*. In the *cove* of his arms, my *cave*, it's where I feel most *safe*.

Love is a *gift*. It makes a heart feel *glad*. Love is *kind*.

It's the giving of your *soul* to another and expecting nothing back in return. But having hope. Yes, love is *hope*. And love is . . .

"Mila?"

I pivot, shocked at the sound of Evie's voice. "Hi," I begin, my mind swimming with thoughts, my eyes swimming in tears. "It's so nice to see you."

"You too. Another soon-to-be-happy couple?" she questions, her gaze following the future bride and groom, crossing the marble reception.

"Yes. This is apparently their favorite hotel in London."

"I'll be sure to tell Oliver." She gives a tinkling laugh. "You don't know? Oliver owns the place. We spent the early days of our relationship living here together."

"Oh."

"I know. Living in a hotel. How extravagant! And how ridiculous, with this thing." She glances back, and I notice a dog sitting almost at her heels, its coat curly and eyes intelligent. "What on earth was I thinking?"

"About living in a hotel?"

"And bringing Bo along. Although, at the time, he was part of my diabolically cunning plan to annoy Oliver. But that's another story," she adds, with a mischievous-looking smile. "Have you got time for a coffee?"

I do have time, and while I feel the urge to seek out Fin, to sort this out—to tell him I see what he's doing and that I'm sorry I reacted the way that I did—I also like Evie. She's a woman's woman, if that makes sense. I suppose I want us to be friends.

A reel of images slips through my mind. Dinners, outings, holidays. Fin's friends becoming mine. *Don't put the cart before the horse,* I tell myself as I follow her through the hotel's stylish halls.

The hotel's decor is moody and sort of sexy—vintage chandeliers, parlor palms, and vermilion velvet walls. She leads us out into the orangery, the light suffused by billowing fabric that, along with huge potted palms, makes me think of *One Thousand and One Nights*.

A server is beckoned and our order placed, and we settle into an easy flow of conversation. Evie tells me about the stately home the couple has recently taken on and the charity work she undertakes, as well as regaling me with tales of their wayward rescue dog, who seems to hang on her every word. Until I realize what he's actually *hanging out* for is his share of the petit four. But the way Evie describes it, Bo the doggy seems to live for the sole purpose of making Oliver's life difficult.

"Is that man wearing a velvet jacket?" I find myself saying as a man walks by.

"I think he is."

"It's not yet two in the afternoon. Does he know it's not the 1930s? And this isn't his living room?"

Evie laughs. "You know, I think Fin has one just the same."

"I think I want a divorce," I say, scrunching my nose.

"Did he steal anything? While you were on the resort, I mean."

"Fin?" I shake my head. "I thought he owned the place." Major shareholder, she'd said.

"That never stopped him before. Fin is . . . light fingered, but only from large venues and corporate events. Places he's already paid a fortune to be, now that I think of it. It's not like he needs the things he steals, which is usually something inconsequential—like a bottle of liquor. There was a deck chair once, I seem to recall. I think he enjoys the thrill of being caught."

My brows lift into my hairline. It feels odd that this is something I don't know. *You have a lifetime for discovery,* something whispers inside me. I bite back my smile.

"How are things going between you both, anyway?"

"With our pretend marriage?" I say, lowering my voice.

"You don't expect me to believe that, do you?"

"Well." Yes, because that's how we sold it to them. That's what I expected it to be, but things have changed. Almost without me realizing.

"We see the way you both are. I'm surprised you haven't noticed us grinning like crazy grinning things. When you came to dinner, even Oliver noticed Fin hanging on your every word."

"I don't know . . ." what to say. I need to straighten this out with Fin before I say anything.

"I never bought it, you know. You two pretending that you'd never met."

"Does Oliver grin?" I ask, changing the subject.

"Oliver's face is at its most animated when watching his friend fall in love." Then she cackles uproariously. "He tries, bless him. Or is it *he's trying*?" She laughs again. "But Fin never behaved with women like he does with you. It's not just the loving looks and tiny touches; it's in the things he says too. He treats you like you're one of us, except we don't get adoring looks. The teasing, I mean," she adds as I stare back blankly.

Because he does tease me. And I dish it back. Is that part of his love language? Along with the stuff he says to me, the compliments he pays me. In and out of the bedroom. And the things he does for me—the things he *wants* to do for me. Even when he worries I might be taking advantage of him. *That I might be using him.*

Oh, my. *Fucking hell.*

"Are you okay?" Evie asks as I press my hand to my heart.

"Yes, fine." But I am not fine. And suspect I won't be until I'm with Fin.

"The thing is," she begins again, her tone careful as she holds my gaze. "I wanted to apologize for ragging on him that day. Look, you obviously know about his past, but I shouldn't have brought it up. I suppose I was teasing him, which is what we do. But it was also about you."

"You were testing me, you mean."

"It didn't put you off! Fin is charming and fun, and women just adore him. And he's adored his fair share of women, but he's never loved any of them. Has he . . . told you he loves you yet?"

I shake my head. "Not in so many words."

"But he's shown you."

My gaze drops to my lap.

"I know at first glance it appears he wears his heart on his sleeve, but he's much more guarded than that. And I can't claim to know why that is; I just know if you give him the chance, he'd be the best husband there is. Oliver aside, of course."

Coffee arrives, and the talk turns to lighter topics before I need to catch my train back to East London. *Duty and the flat call.*

"He really did just give you my card?" I ask as I stand and gather my things.

"Fin didn't ask me to employ you as my wedding planner," she replies. "And he really had no idea about our last-minute plans. I did intend on getting married that day, you know. I didn't hire you to marry you off to Fin."

"No, of course. No one could've foreseen—"

Evie puts her hand to my forearm. "That sounds like a two-bottle-of-wine story."

"It is a bit." I scrunch my nose even as my insides flip with delight.

"Check your diary and text me a date, because this is a story I'm *desperate* to hear." Her gaze dips as I realize the dog, Bo, is circling us like a shark. "He heard *wine*," she explains. "He knows it pairs well with cheese. And that doggies get to implement a cheese tax. Right, boy?"

Bo barks, and Evie laughs, sliding her arm through mine. "It's about time there was a little more femininity added to the friendship group."

Friends. Love. Business. Baba. Things just seem to be falling into place. *And all because of Fin?*

"I'm pleased to see business is picking up for you," Evie says as we turn toward the door.

"Me too," I say, pulled from my musing.

"I would've ignored those horrible notes on the message boards even if Fin hadn't given me your card."

"Message boards?"

"The online forums," she prompts as we continue to walk out of the brightly lit orangery.

"Um." I roll my lips inward as a sense of foreboding creeps like a spider along my spine. "I'm not sure I really follow."

"They weren't all horrible. There were people who came to your defense."

I angle my head her way. "Are you talking about the wedding forums?" The places brides hang out *virtually*. They discuss venues and menus and the latest dress styles. Wedding etiquette and honeymoons and where the best alteration service is for when the bride finds herself pregnant before her big day.

"Yes. You saw the posts, right?"

"I tend to see those as conversational spaces purely for those planning their big day." And those paying the bills. "They're not really the kind of space where a service or a vendor should hang out." It's not very professional. I'd looked, of course, in my early days, but I always felt a bit of a creeper. When I established myself, I decided no good could come from looking. I mean, everyone is entitled to their opinion.

"Right, that makes sense. No matter. I didn't put any stock in what was said, and I'm sure most sane people did the same.

Sometimes you can't even believe what you see with your own eyes." Her smile takes on a brittle edge. "I'm sure I don't have to explain why."

Pulse Tok and *A Little Bird Told Us. And people's hurtful opinions.*

But still, I wonder.

◆ ◆ ◆

I leave Evie in the hotel foyer, my mind spinning a hundred different ways as I hurry down the steps and out into the swanky Knightsbridge side street. I'm not far from Fin's place, but that's not where I'm heading as I pull out my phone and call Ronny, who picks up almost immediately.

"Meels, no one calls these days," she says, forgoing a greeting. "Texts are where it's at."

"Ronny, when you were doing your market research, you said you looked at wedding trends. Where did you find your information?"

"Trade publications," she answers. "Online mostly. I also joined a few of the wedding forums to see what people—brides, mainly—were talking about. Those places are weird, FYI—all *DH* this and *MOB* that."

"*Dear husband* and *mother of the bride.*"

"Yeah, those acronyms. How long do you reckon before *DH* changes from *dear husband* to *dickhead*?"

"No idea. Did you see anything about me?" I hurry on.

When she doesn't immediately answer, I know. Did a disgruntled client try to ruin my business? I mentally run through the events around that time as I pull my phone away from my ear to look at the signal strength and battery life. *Not bad.* I need to find a wine bar with a bucket-size glass before I delve into this myself.

"What did you read, Ron? About me?"

"I thought you must've pissed a client off, because there were some comments dishing shit about you. I didn't tell you, because the thread was from months ago. Only . . ."

"Only what?" My heart thumps ominously.

"I registered for an alert on a couple of the threads. Just to keep an eye on them, I suppose. A hunch. And, Meels? The chatter started up again."

"In what way?"

"The same people dissin' you. But others come to your defense. Past clients, I think." A pause. "Where are you?"

"Knightsbridge. Why?"

"I've just finished work. I think we should meet up. Last night, I did a bit of digging. And, well, I have some stuff I think you should see."

"Ronny, quit with the cloak-and-dagger stuff," I say, trying to keep my words light, when my heart feels like it's being squeezed.

"I followed one of the usernames saying shit about you. I looked at other shit she'd posted—other places she'd left a digital footprint, I suppose. And I found her on Bookface and read this weird comment about a forum she's in."

My blood suddenly runs a little cold.

"The forum. What's it called?"

"StarsInHerEyes," Ronny replies.

That's the one I remember coming across on my own internet stalking session while on the resort. The one with the locked thread with Fin's name.

"And fuck me, that place is like being on the dark web."

"You joined the forum?"

"Yeah. There's an initiation—for real. I had to send, like, proper fan stuff. They're all devoted or something."

"Devoted to who? What did you send?"

"Get this. A screenshot of you and Fin. I crossed out your eyes and gave you buckteeth. Pretty mild compared to some of the shit I saw on there."

"What?" He does have a fan club. A fan club of stalkers. *Who all hate me?*

"But the weird thing is—"

"All of this is already very weird!"

"—the weird thing is not that they're all super stans. You know, superfans? Borderline stalkers. Or total fucking weirdos. But that they're *her* stans, not Fin's."

"Whose fans? Stans. Who do you mean?"

"Guess," Ronny demands.

"Charlotte Bancroft." My heart sinks to my boots as I say her name.

"Yep. Her and her minions are to blame for your business almost going tits up."

"But why? I've never even met her."

"You have. You just don't remember."

Chapter 33
FIN

When I'm drinking scotch in my office on a weekday afternoon, you know things are bad.

I turn to the rap of a knuckle on my door, and Josie's face appears around the lump of wood. She looks confused.

"What is it?"

"Your wife is apparently in reception."

"Is she?" My heart beats twice in quick succession, as though I've done something wrong. It's not that I've forgotten, but, fuck, he worked quick.

"I didn't even know you had one of those. A wife."

"That's what happens when you take a vacation." Struggling to keep my outward appearance calm, I turn back to the window. "You miss all the tea."

"I'll ask them to send her up, shall I?"

"I think that would be best." I glance back at her, then my eyes slide over my desk. "Though maybe we should strip the room of sharp implements."

"Do you really mean that?"

I chuckle and give my head a shake, but she comes into the room anyway.

"That's not even yours," she says, swiping an antique silver letter opener from my desk.

"I was just waiting to see how long before Oliver noticed."

"You and your pranking," she mutters, making for the door again.

"Josie?"

She turns on the threshold.

"How about you make yourself scarce when Mrs. DeWitt gets here?"

"You're sure?"

"You wouldn't want to hear a grown man cry, would you?"

"Maybe if it's you," she says, swinging away. "I can see why someone would want to stab you. Sometimes. But try not to allow it until after payday."

"You got it."

My gut twists as she leaves. No going back. But will we be going forward? Together? I roll my shoulders, trying to ease out the tension. Fat chance on that front. Am I an idiot for thinking she might go for this?

Or not go for it, more like. Please.

Fuck. I can't go on like this. I need her. I need to show her how much I . . . esteem? Crave? Love her? How I can't imagine life without her.

I've always been impulsive, but I pray I'm doing the right thing.

I just want to give her everything. I want that everything to include me. I want to be responsible for her smiles, to always be there to dry her tears too.

The way I feel about her . . . there are no words. Love is kind of primal. A part of humanity that's as old as time itself. At first, I desired Mila. I found her curves desirable, her wit and her sharp tongue irresistible—I wanted to suffer its lash.

But the desired, the person, is just an ideal. The perfect person in your mind but not yet real. Then things change, and for me, they've changed fast.

I turn as the door creaks open, then bangs from the opposite wall, held only from bouncing back by my wife's flat palm.

My wife. She is incandescent.

And that's not really a compliment—more an observation.

"Josie, I see you've met Mila."

My assistant's frown appears from behind my much shorter wife.

"I'll just leave you both to it," she says, backing away.

"It was nice to meet you," Mila says, turning her head briefly, ever the professional people pleaser. The only person she doesn't want to please is me. "I'm sorry it wasn't under better circumstances."

It's then I realize she's holding the Jeff Koons balloon dog from the kitchen under her arm. She steps inside, and the door slams. I find myself ducking as twenty grand's worth of whimsy crashes against the original window shutters.

"You bastard!" Her voice is low and vehement. "You careless shithead!" she shouts her next accusation.

"Careless? Me?" I glance from her to the dent in the shutter.

"Yes, okay. I was aiming for your head!"

"There's always next shot." But *careless*? I thought she would've gone with *calculated*. Me? I'd go with *desperate*. "What are you doing here, Mila?"

"You *know*," she hisses.

"Roza is the one with the sight. The rest of us have to wait for explanations."

The look she sends me. It's downright murderous. I wonder if I'll be able to persuade her to fuck me when she finally gets her

367

hands around my neck. What a way to go. I'd enjoy the ride to the very end.

My hand trembles as I set my glass on my desk, but not because I'm afraid of anything but losing her. All the same, maybe I should put the glass in my drawer.

"You *are* careless," she says, swiping up a vase.

Why do I even have a vase in my office? And what the fuck is it with this careless *business.*

"Careless with words," she adds, sort of bouncing the piece in her hands as though weighing it.

"Did you ever work out why I call you *bunny*?"

Her gaze lifts, but not her head.

"Because you bounce like that—just like that vase—when you're in my hands."

"You're careless with people's feelings," she continues, as though I haven't spoken.

"I thought my actions were quite pointed today."

"Bastard!"

The vase flies, and I duck. "You already said that one."

Mila's chest heaves, her hands balled into fists. "You are a bastard, and I can hardly believe it, but you are the one responsible for almost ruining my business."

I feel my brow furrow. This isn't the direction I was expecting. In fact—"Honeybuns, I don't know what you're talking about."

"Don't call me that! And you don't know because you're fucking careless!" This she says on a sob. "The night we met, you were at that wedding with Charlotte bloody Bancroft!"

I shake my head. "Wrong. Matt was my plus-one. I had to bribe the fucker with an expensive single malt to get him to come along." I didn't want to take a date—I didn't want to take him. But I also didn't want to be there alone. "She might've been there, but she wasn't with me. What the fuck is this about?"

"She saw you come out of the closet looking disheveled, and she *heard* you laughing about what we'd done. Laughing about me back at your table!"

"She might've seen me looking less than my usual pristine self," I say edging my way around the desk as Mila follows. *Or stalks.* "But if she did, that's on you. You and your roaming hands, slut muffin."

"Be serious!" she cries. "Try it, just for one minute!"

"I am serious. I'm serious about you. And whatever I've done, I'd rather be sorry for it, sorry for fucking up, than never having tried to keep you."

"You fucked up, all right. You fucked the head of your fan club!"

"My what?"

"Charlotte Bancroft is obsessed! She has a forum all about her career . . . and you. To join, you have to prove your allegiance. Fucking buckteeth and crossed-out eyes!" she says, kind of jerky and angry and all waving hands.

"I don't know what you're talking about." Not only that, but I'm also a little worried. "Are you okay?"

"No, I am not okay. I am very *far* from being okay. Your high priestess tried to ruin me—she set them on me, Fin. Her fans. Her disciples. You laughed, and she painted me as some . . . skank. Someone who didn't deserve to be happy, let alone be paid to arrange other people's happiness—one of the most important days of their lives!"

I straighten, suddenly furious. "I know nothing about that, but I can guarantee you I wasn't laughing. You want to know what I said? To Matt? I remember the moment as clear as day."

"You shouldn't have spoken to anyone. What happened between us was private—I thought it was special!"

369

"It was fucking pivotal," I say, pulling out my phone. Matt answers at the first ring.

"What the fuck is all that noise coming from your office?" he says, forgoing a greeting again. "Are you moving furniture or something?"

"Kind of," I answer, watching as Mila eyes my computer monitor. "Remember the night I met Mila?"

"Yeah," he says suspiciously. "Haven't we already had this conversation?"

"I went to get us a drink and came back without them. You remember what I said, don't you?"

"I told you already, I'm not telling Mila. I'm not your emissary—we're not in fucking high school! And how fucking stupid would we both sound if I told her you had a premonition after a knee-trembling moment in the coat closet with her?"

Mila's brows come down like a shelf as she grasps a heavy-bottomed stapler as an appetizer to my monitor.

"Matt," I demand. "What the fuck did I say?"

"That you'd just met the woman you were going to marry," he mutters. "That you could feel it in your stupid, hollow bones. That match your stupid, hollow head."

"That's all you had to say." I end the call. "Roza was right. Evie too. This is kismet, fate at work, through and through."

"Liar!"

I'm so relieved she's a terrible shot as the stapler thuds against the far wall. That would've knocked me the fuck out.

"That woman hid her identity!" she yells. "She told her followers I shouldn't be allowed near other women's men. That I shouldn't be allowed near you!"

"Maybe it is my fault. Maybe I shouldn't have told Matt, and then Charlotte wouldn't have overheard. But I had to tell someone because I was bursting out of my skin with happiness, Mila."

"That's not true or you would've found me before. You wouldn't have given Evie my card; you would've—"

"I was terrified. My feelings were so fucking big."

"Are you frightened now, Fin?"

I temper my smile—that was a little too *Dirty Harry* for a woman of her stature. "That depends," I say, on the opposite side of the desk now, my gaze flicking behind her. "Can you lift that TV from the wall?"

But then she pulls out my chair, dropping into it quite suddenly. Her hands pressed to the sides of her head, her beautiful hair comes alive between her spread fingers.

"She made people come after me. Told them lies—then made them lie!" Her head comes up. "Why would she do that? She almost ruined me. I lost work, respect, my clients. Money! I was forced back to the place it took me so long to climb from. And for what? What did I ever do to her?"

"Attract the interest of a man who turned her down. A man she probably saw as her meal ticket to more publicity, more opportunities. And then, you married him."

"So, she wanted to be me, basically." Her answer—her thoughts—instantly take the wind from her angry sails. "It's what you said, that I wanted your notoriety. That I was using your body."

"I was hurt, that's all. When the plane landed in London, things changed. I worried all I would ever be to you was a crutch. A name. Not someone who loves you."

"Love," she repeats. *Hopefully?*

"Yeah. I love you. I loved you the day we wed. But you've been on my mind and my heart for longer than that. I'm sorry. So sorry." For what I've done and for what's to come.

"But when the plane landed, how did the press know about us? How did they know to be there? I know how they got the photos on the island, but how did they know we'd married or even who I was before we landed?"

"Because I called ahead. I called them, Mila. I gave them the scoop."

"You . . ."

"Bastard?"

"You deceitful, conniving, fraudulent fuckboy!" she yells, jumping up again.

I just couldn't see any other way, though Matt would die laughing if he knew his part in this.

On the flight back from the resort, I'd googled *Bridgerton*, which he'd mentioned during our phone call. I didn't have time or the bandwidth to watch the show, but I was curious. And grasping at straws. So I downloaded the Kindle app on my phone, along with a couple of books in the series. *Romance books.*

Come to think of it, maybe Matt would die of embarrassment that he'd inadvertently outed himself as a closet romance reader. *Though it kind of makes sense.*

As Mila slept, I found myself absorbed. And I'd learned that, according to the romantic novel dictate, what's needed at the point of a romantic fuckup is a romantic gesture like no other. Failing that, some dastardly underhanded dealing.

And I've got both bases covered.

"If I am, I'm your fuckboy. Yours alone. For the rest of my life, if you'll have me. You were right to be wary—I am almost forty, and I've never lived with a woman. Never committed myself. But I want to. I want to commit myself to you."

"You don't even know the meaning of the word!"

"I've thought about you constantly since we met. In fact, from that night, I didn't fuck another woman."

"Are you expecting a medal? A bloody prize?"

"I'm trying to tell you I didn't want anyone else but you. And that I was too chickenshit to do anything about it. I gave your card to Evie when I really should've found you myself."

"Why should I trust you after what you've done?"

"Just listen to me for a minute, please. You said that love means betrayal and lies to me. Before you, yeah. It did. When I was just a kid in college, I fell in love. Or I thought I did, but my family—they weren't on board. I thought we'd get married, but my grandfather offered her money to leave the state. She took it, and I was devastated, not just about her leaving, but that the man who raised me did that to me. I guess I just made sure never to put my heart in that position again. Because maybe I just wasn't worth it."

She begins to move again, rounding the desk. "It sounds as though you're saying you only love me because I *don't* want your money? That's not trust."

"That's not what I'm saying. I love you in spite of the fact you won't fucking take it. I love you despite the fact you're being pig-headed and proud."

"Don't think I don't know what you're trying to do here. You can't distract me—you called those tabloid . . . Little Bird . . . fuckers!"

"I did." I back away as she advances, but it's just for show. I'm going nowhere. *Ever, if I can help it.* "I did the wrong thing for the right reason. Twice."

Her eyes narrow. "You'd better not have called them again."

"I think you should read your emails."

Chapter 34
MILA

"Why would you do this?" I whisper as I stare at the phone in my hand.

"If you don't love me, if you can't trust me, then I need to let you go. But it doesn't change how I feel. I love you, and I want to make sure you're taken care of."

"I don't want your money," I almost sob. "Why can't you get it through that thick skull of yours?"

"Too bad," he says, ignoring the insult. "You don't want me to help you with Roza? Fine. With that," he says with a vague lift of his hand, "you give her the best life. You don't want to give up Roza's flat? Then buy the building—the whole fucking lot! There's more than enough money for you to do that."

In the divorce settlement, he means. The preliminary documents from his lawyer, sent to me by email.

"I should hate you," I whisper, stepping closer. This time, he doesn't step back. "I should run—run in the opposite direction—because this is just another form of manipulation. Another way to try to control me."

"I thought it was setting you free. How can I control you by making you as wealthy as me? I'm giving you a lifetime of safety and choices, Mila. The means for you to be well."

"Well, that part is at least true." My hands grip his suspenders, my head resting in the middle of his chest. Maybe I should try to hate him, but I can't, and I don't want to. Because this is nothing like before. *What Adam did.* He took—my trust, my dignity, my home, and my mental well-being. But Fin, he gives. And I don't mean his money—his ridiculous divorce settlement—because *that* I see right through.

He's given me his friends, shared them with me. And he's given me space to work out my insecurities. He's given me support, his name, and his body, even when he was fearful himself. And he's given me love.

"I don't have to take the money," I whisper as tears leak from my eyes.

"That's not up to you." He rubs my back like I'm a child in need of comfort. "Not in a divorce."

"I can donate it."

"You could. If you hate me that badly."

I tilt my head and stare up into those stormy eyes. "I can't believe you would do this."

"I can't believe you'd fight me so hard. Do you know how much I'm worth?"

"Well, yes. It's in the letter from your lawyer, idiot."

"Of course, you'll be vilified in the press," he adds with a sigh.

"Oh, again? Great. I suppose they'll call me a gold digger."

"I expect so."

I sigh. "Never mind. I'll just dry my tears with a wad of filthy fifties."

"There's always the alternative," he says as I allow him to unfurl my hand. To press his lips to my wedding ring. "You could keep this on. Stay married to me. Just for, say, forever."

"That sounds like a life sentence. I ought to take the money and run. People will be calling me a gold digger, anyway."

"Can't be a gold digger if you stay blissfully married to me. And I will make you happy my whole damned life."

"There's a gulf between charisma and manipulation, you know." I shake my head. I'm a sucker for the tension in his jaw and that passionate glare of his. He has mad rizz, as the kids would say. Magnetism, charm and appeal. But he also has the capacity for maneuvering and machination. But for good, not to lie or cheat or steal.

What would my life become with him?

"I just want you to be happy, Mila. Whatever it takes."

"Even if I take the money and walk away?"

"If that's what makes you happy. If it means you'll never have to worry again, then yeah. I can cope with that. I'll be crushed, of course. And you'll be entirely responsible. You'd need to learn to live with that. If you could. You know, ruining my whole life. But before you decide, there's one more thing." He slides his hand into his pocket and pulls out his phone.

"No," I say on a groan. "Not something else."

"Watch it. Please."

Chapter 35
MILA

Fin hands me his phone, open to a Pulse Tok account. There's just one video available, saved to the drafts folder. Not yet posted or available for all to see.

"Why have you got one of these? A Pulse Tok account?"

"Just watch it, Mila."

"If this is a smutty video," I begin as my heart beats like hooves, somehow intuiting what this is.

I'm in that dress, veil rippling in the breeze.

Fin is in his light suit, so handsome, the linen barely creased.

I take a seat as I'm handed a pen, our wedding certificate placed in front of me as I bend my head. Then come up laughing.

"Oops!" My eyes dance as I look to Fin. "I signed my own name," I whisper hiss his way.

He's smiling too. Indulgently. Lovingly. But it can't be love. Not that soon.

"What shall I do?" I whisper theatrically, leaning in.

"What do you want to do?" Fin's tone is soft, intimate.

My expression turns pensive. "I was supposed to get married today. For real."

"To your ex? Today was your wedding date?"

I nod. "Yes." Then I frown, more like *Eurgh, no*. "According to my grandmother, my Prince Charming is called Alexander. I'm supposed to marry him today. She has *the sight*, you know." Even as I say it, I'm rolling my eyes.

"Well, in that case . . ."

Fin takes the pen from my hand, and twisting the certificate around, he signs it with a flourish.

"What did you do that for?" My words sound gleeful as I reach for him, kissing his cheek like this is the best game ever.

"Read it."

I lean over the certificate and squint. "You must be a doctor."

"Nope." Using his finger, he spins the certificate again, and I watch as he touches each word with the tip of his pen. "Phineas Alexander Gunning Colton DeWitt. Do you know what that means?" he asks, looking up again.

I shake my head.

"This was preordained. This is real. You and me were meant to be."

The recording stops, loops back.

"Alexander." My hand falls away, my gaze rising to his. "You told me the morning after. It was on our wedding certificate." My words are soft and halting as I process what this means.

"I guess you just weren't ready to hear it." He slides a lock of hair behind my ear, his expression tender. "That wasn't shrooms, Mila. That was all me."

"Really?"

"As God is my witness, I was as sober as a judge."

"And you'd still do this for me? You'd marry me. Love me. And let me walk away with all that money?"

"I mean, you could stay, be rich *and* be deliriously happy. Or you could walk away and earn yourself a stalker." He shrugs, like this is out of his control.

"A stan."

"Weren't you listening? No stan. Your stalker would be called Phineas Alexander Gunning Colton DeWitt."

"I bet he was a really ugly baby," I whisper in a repeat of that conversation. Would it have made a difference if I'd woken the morning following our wedding and remembered? If nothing else, I would've remembered his look of wonder, of determination. I would've known how he made me feel like I was shining from within.

Love is supposed to be a journey, I think as I press up onto my toes. And some journeys are just a little more meandering than others. Some have sharp turns and slopes. Others have nasty bumps in the road.

I slide my arms around Fin's neck and slide my lips over his, our resultant kiss neither delicate nor uncertain. However we got here, I'm so happy we did.

"Good thing that baby is a real looker now," Fin whispers as our kiss breaks. His eyes shine; mine, too, his handsomeness turning hazy.

"Sadly, he's not very modest. In fact, he has a great big—"

"Yeah, he has." His tone turns to pure smut.

I shake my head. I'm in for some ride with Fin. I mean, not *that* way. But also, yes, that way. *Soon, I think.*

"Rich, good looking, and devoted. I guess that means, in the husband stakes, you lucked out."

"You're determined to make me crazy, aren't you?"

"No, smut muffin. I'm determined to always love you."

Epilogue

"We could've gotten a minister in. Or a celebrant, if you wanted."

"What are you talking about?" I turn to Evie, so chic in her teal cocktail dress.

"You." As she points a finger my way, the pleats in the skirt swish. "Didn't you realize you were humming 'Going to the Chapel'?"

"Was I really?" I ask, suddenly feeling as pleased as punch. "Well, no need. Been there, done that."

"Now it's just time for the party," she says, sliding her arm through mine.

My smile feels the size of half a cut watermelon as I pat her arm. "Thanks to you and Oliver."

The pair had insisted on holding a celebration dinner for us, once it became apparent to them that we'd stopped fighting. *And stopped making up.* But what started as a wedding dinner quickly became a party for hundreds after our very own Pulse Tok video went viral. Not the video of our wedding mishap, or *wedding wonder* as I prefer, where a besotted Fin signed his name on the dotted line after mine.

The best mistake of our lives.

That video we chose to keep private, though we brought our friends in on the secret. *Our friends, yes.* What a change that's been.

They're such good people, and Evie has very quickly become like a sister to me.

The Pulse Tok that went viral was a home movie, sort of. A carefully curated montage of holiday-wedding love, courtesy of Sarai. *Complete with the* Dirty Dancing *lift, featuring a very enthusiastic me.*

Fin is convinced she'll be making a fortune from the video, but just as before, she's inadvertently done us a huge favor. Once it hit the internet, the world was into us—rather than onto us—and anyone who had anything to do with Maven Inc. was suddenly so very charmed.

We've been showered with gifts by the world's wealthy, and let me tell you, billionaires know how to gift! From his-and-hers matching Cartier watches to his-and-hers matching Mercedes. *Yes—someone bought us cars!*

Fin, ever the professional, suggested we extend the invitation to include clients, past and present. And I agreed. Especially as we'll be auctioning off goodies and donating the proceeds to charity. *Dementia research—I want to eradicate this thief of a disease.*

"You know what we should've done," Evie says as her feet slow to a stop.

"Dazzle me." I'm not sure how she could top this party at all.

"We should've persuaded Oliver to complete one of those online wedding-officiant courses."

"What for?"

"Just for shits and giggles. Could you imagine his face?"

"Doing funerals maybe, not weddings."

Evie begins to laugh and almost falls over Mr. Bojangles as he contorts himself in an attempt to chew on his bow tie. *The dapper doggy is dressed for the occasion.*

"Damn dog!" she exclaims before ruffling his floofy body.

"Well, I'm going to get back to my checklist," I say, pulling my iPad back in place.

"You should've let us get a company in," she chastises playfully.

"I did let you. My company!" Because, of course, I'll be sending Maven Inc. my bill.

"What time is Baba Roza due?"

These people. They've been so welcoming. Evie even put on a frightfully posh afternoon tea for Baba and me last month.

"She'll be here within the hour." Along with three of the nursing staff. *I hope she's having one of her good days.* She so wanted to be here, to see me in my pretty dress, she said. I have a bouquet of flowers waiting for her; she'll eat a little and drink a small champagne (with permission of her doctor); and Fin has already secured her first dance.

She'll be safe in his arms, I know.

Evie's phone begins to ring, and she excuses herself, leaving me to my checklist and the stunningly dressed ballroom. In truth, I feel a bit strange as I traverse the tables laden with white linens, crystal, and china. I'm usually dressed to blend, not to stun. And this gown, boy, she is a stunner. Jade silk that moves like water across my body as I move. Shoestring straps, a low-cut back, and all the internal support I need for the girls.

I still opt for demure when I'm running an event, but my clothing choices have become a little more . . . daring outside of that. It's hard to not to be comfortable in your own skin when someone else adores you. He doesn't mind that I occasionally bite my nails or that I still say ridiculous stuff when I'm feeling under pressure. He treats me with love. And with grace. And that's had an effect on the way I treat myself, I suppose.

God, I love him.

Now, where was I? *Ah, yes.*

Tables ✓ Too many to count. China, crystal, and flower arrangements all placed with such precision, thanks to Oliver's hotel staff.

Dais and backdrop ✓ Looking like something from a high-end florist.

I move the pen down my list and find myself smiling as I notice my wedding ring. Fin wants to exchange it for something a little more opulent. Too bad I'm quite attached to what I have.

Back to my iPad and list.

Carpet aisle of rose petals ✓ Way over the top, but insisted on by Fin. But if he thinks I'm going to repeat that *Dirty Dancing* lift, he's going to be sorely disappointed. The world almost seeing my knickers once was enough.

I move through the ballroom, just taking in the decoration and appreciating the heck out of my life when—"Hey!" A door opens, and I'm pulled in. "You . . . ," I say, narrowing my eyes. And biting back my smile. My heart pounds, initially from shock but now thanks to the look in my husband's eyes. He's so bloody handsome in his evening suit, his hair a little longer now and sort of messy and dissolute.

"We have to stop meeting like this," he purrs. "Especially when you look so fucking edible."

"You look pretty nice yourself."

"Nice?"

"I knew you'd like that. Being called *nice* is so nice, right?"

He says nothing, but, oh, he looks. And I know that cocky glint. *I'm about to relieve you of your panties,* it says.

"Tell me the truth," his low voice rumbles. "You guessed, didn't you?"

"That you were planning on dragging me in here?" I smooth the silk over my thighs. I can't let him muss me up before the start of the night. *Can I?*

383

Later in the night, however . . .

"I thought for sure you saw one of the waiters clearing the closet out. It was full of chairs and tables. I thought you'd rumbled my plans."

"You have plans?" I shake my head, more in exasperation than denial. "And I thought my surprise was going to be a three-way with a gay pastry chef at the end of tonight."

My surprise for him is a courtesy of my wedding-day boudoir shoot. *A book of sensual prints for his special alone times . . . and a request to be his audience.*

"Nothing says love and devotion like a three-way, huh?"

"What happened to *'happy wife, happy life*'?" I say with a pout.

"I'm saving that experience for our thirtieth anniversary, remember?"

"That's one reason to stick around, I suppose." I give a theatrical sigh.

"I can give you a million others," he purrs.

But he's already given me more than enough reasons to stay. He's given me his love and his support. His devotion and his care. It was Fin who suggested we auction our elaborate wedding gifts, and he's promised a portion of his wealth and his attention to social causes that he knows mean a lot to me.

The site near Baba's old nursing home is to be demolished, and while it will be replaced by a commercial site, Fin has made sure there's funding in place for so much more for the community. There's to be affordable housing—no more dilapidated tower blocks—a community center, health services, and youth projects that are more than just empty promises. I even found him talking to the insult-wielding kids during my very last visit to Baba's flat. Saying goodbye to the place was bittersweet, but to find him outside asking those kids what they'd like to see in the area? It was everything.

"I'm sure I can get you to kiss a man before then," I whisper, fighting a flood of happy tears.

"The only lips I'm interested in kissing are these," he says as he reaches for me.

His fingers thread through my hair, and our lips, mouths, and tongues work in perfect harmony. Breaths mingle, sighs becoming heavier, kisses becoming deeper and dirtier, because we just can't help ourselves. Until . . .

"Wait," I whisper as Fin begins to slide down my body. I know what he's about—we've been in this position once or twice before. And I want, I crave—but unlike some people, namely Fin, I have a sense of propriety. "Not in your friend's hotel, surely? Not when they're holding this party."

"How scandalous!" he exclaims like an elderly aunt as he teasingly ruffles the bias-cut hem of my dress. "Wait, didn't we already fuck in one of his rooms last night?"

"You're incorrigible."

"And that was . . . encouraging."

It's then I realize he isn't on his knees but his knee. He slides his hand into his inside jacket pocket and pulls out a tiny velvet box.

"You won't let me buy you a new wedding ring, so I got you this," he says, pulling out a ring with a trio of diamonds. He takes my hand and slides the ring onto my finger until it meets my wedding band. "Three stones. Yesterday, today, tomorrow," he says, pressing his lips to my knuckles. "I'm yours. With everything I am and everything I have, I'm yours now and forever."

Emotion wells inside as I stare at the ring. "Fin, it's so perfect."

"Just like you."

I shake my head. "Not even close."

"You are perfect for me," he says, his voice teeming with emotion. "Now, let me show you the only other lips in the world I'm interested in."

"Fin!" I fill his name with warning.

"Craving, more like," he says, slipping his hands under my dress. "And you wouldn't like to deprive me, would you, slut muffin."

"That's a horrible name."

"That's why you love it."

The minute his fingers touch my skin, I'm done for, and the scrap of my underwear is sliding down my legs.

"Just a taste," he whispers. "Just . . . let me."

"God, yes." I let out a stuttering breath at the first brush of his tongue, my fingers curling in his hair. I no longer care about silk creasing or propriety. I just need him.

"Fuck," he growls as his tongue swipes through the already-wet ribbon of my flesh again. "Better than anything."

"We really shouldn't—oh, my days," I whisper as he licks long and lushly. "Do that again."

"Again and again and for the rest of my life. Morning, noon, and night, my love, because I fucking love you. And I love fucking you."

"Less talking," I rasp, tightening my fingers in his hair as his lips engulf my clit. As he sucks and kisses, as he makes out with my pussy until my body thrashes against the wall.

"Fuck yes! Get there for me, darlin'. Come for me. Come on my tongue."

His words, his mouth, tip me over the edge, my body flooding with heat and light and joy as my body rises to where his tongue meets my climax.

When I eventually sink back into my body, Fin smiles up at me so sweetly.

"Oh, my," I whisper, my brain cells still rattling loose. So much for *sweet*, as he just lowers his head and licks at me again, working me with the full flat of his tongue. "Too much," I say, twisting away.

"Not even. My wife is defeated by nothing."

My heart hammers, my body pulses. And a crash sounds from beyond the door, followed by a shrill voice. *One I recognize?*

"Evie?" Fin's brow flickers.

I push at his shoulders because I hear her voice too. "Quickly," I say, pulling my dress straight.

"You stay here," he orders, on his feet now.

"As if!" I retort, following him out the storeroom door.

"Mr. . . . whatever your name was. You need to leave." Evie seems to be embodying her husband, chin held high, tone icily frightening.

There's glass on the floor, a plate or two. And Mr. *Whatever* is right. Though I know his name well enough.

"I'm not leaving until you give me my deposit back," he says gruffly.

Adam. God, he looks rough. Dark-circled eyes and unkempt hair. He looks like he's slept in his clothes too.

"As the gentleman on the front desk explained to you, your fiancée . . . sorry"—Evie holds up her hand—"your *ex-fiancée* already claimed the refund when she canceled the wedding booking."

No way. This is too trippy.

"You had no right to give it to that cheating whore!" he yells. "I paid the fucking deposit."

"That, you will need to take up with her," Evie retorts. "And speaking of rights, you have no right to be here. I don't appreciate your tone, and if you don't leave, I'll be forced to—"

"—call me," Fin growls, coming to Evie's side.

"I was thinking more along the lines of *Bo*," Evie murmurs. "Where is the fluffy monster when you need him?"

"That's an expensive-looking suit for security," Adam retorts, his eyes flicking over my husband's muscled frame. He does a double take as his gaze reaches Fin's top pocket, but it doesn't hold, as I come to a stop by Fin's side. "Mila?"

"Hello, Adam," I answer happily.

"Adam?" Fin's gaze flicks down to me, half-disbelieving.

I give a short shrug, because the man does look rough.

"Fin, this is Adam," I begin, as though Fin's hair isn't standing on end and those aren't my knickers hanging out of his top pocket. "Adam, this is my husband, Fin DeWitt."

"What?"

"Oh, this is so perfect!" I exclaim, practically shimmering with pleasure at the look on his face.

"Is it?" Fin asks, waiting for the punch line.

"Adam, you waste of space, I'm so happy to hear you've had a taste of your own medicine."

"You don't know what you're talking about," he begins, though he shrinks back as Fin jerks forward.

I press my hand over my husband's arm. "I've got this," I murmur, then turn back to the waste of space I once knew as *my fiancé*. "I've imagined this, you know? Bumping into you. But I couldn't have dreamed up this perfection. See this room? This is to hold the celebration of our love, right?" I look to my husband.

"You got it, honeybuns."

Honeybuns is good, but I would've settled for *slut muffin* too. *His* slut muffin.

"And look at you," I say scrunching my nose as I give him a once-over. "All sad sack and dumped. Then look at me," I demand happily, all game show hands as I indicate my luck, my friend, and my man. "This beats sesame chicken any day of the week!"

"Are you on drugs?" Adam frowns.

"Nature's own! Excellent sex and horny hormones."

Fin barks out a laugh, and Evie murmurs, "Go, Mila."

"Anyway, it was nice to see you. Under the circumstances." I grin again. I am loving this shit for me! "I'd leave if I were you, before Fin happily punches your lights out. Or Evie's killer dog bites off your testicles."

"I'm pleased I dumped you," he mutters.

"Ditto!" I pucker my lips and press them to Fin's cheek as I pull out my underwear from his pocket. "Because Fin is such a catch. And he loves me for me."

"You're off your fucking trolley." Adam shakes his head.

"I tend to get a bit over the top when I'm coming down from an orgasm. Not that you'd know. See ya!" I say, giving my knickers a wave. They're white, but this is no surrender as I slide my arm through Fin's and hug him close.

There really isn't anything for Adam to do but . . . piss off.

"Buh-bye!" I call after him as my new friend cackles. "And thanks for the upgrade. He's hung like a flippin' horse!"

The door to the ballroom swings after his exit.

"Oh, man. That was the funniest thing I've ever seen." Evie runs her fingers under her eyes as she turns to me. "But, Mila, honey, I think you should go put your panties back on."

"Who made you the fun police?" With a smile Evie's way, Fin takes me in his arms. "Feel better?"

"I feel amazing."

"Then tell me, do I beat sesame chicken?"

"You, Phineas Alexander Gunning Colton DeWitt, are the best thing in the world."

ACKNOWLEDGEMENTS

My eternal thanks to each and every person who picks up this book. It's because of you I get to pursue my dream job. Thanks for letting me entertain you for a little while.

My thanks to Sammia and Montlake for the amazing opportunity and to Lindsey for her insight, advice, and very deft hand. Also to Anna B. and Jenna J. for their astute observations and eagle eyes. Thanks to Nick for letting me borrow elements of Baba Olga and to Layla for picking out those thoughts.

As always, I'm super grateful to my little crew. To Lisa for her support, not limited to flying from the other side of the world to hold my hand. To Elizabeth, Michelle, Susan, and Annette for their support. And to the Lambs. Love you, girls!

Thanks also to Tee. Superstar and all-around good human. Love your face!

Finally, thanks to my family for putting up with my vague answers and spaced-out looks. Thanks to my children, the authors of all my best lines, and to Mike for putting up with the writing monster at all times.

Also, my thanks to the universe for Ned. I wrote Mr. Bojangles into *No Romeo*—My Kind of Hero #1—and apparently manifested the same demon dog into my life. Next time, I'd settle for a million quid . . .

EXCERPT: *THE INTERVIEW*

Hello, Whit. It's been a while.

I give my head a tiny shake and frown at myself in the mirrored walls of the elevator.

Hi, Whit! Remember me?

My frown deepens, because that's even worse. I doubt he'll remember me, given I had braces and pigtails the last time we met.

Hi, Whit. I heard you literally own your own bank these days, so I thought . . .

. . . I'd turn up on your doorstep with my begging bowl. Fine, my résumé.

My thoughts are interrupted as the elevator comes to a smooth stop. The doors glide open, but I find I can't move as I press my hand to my chest, my poor heart flapping like a landed fish. *This is the chance you wanted,* I remind myself. *Spreading your wings. Doing all the things.* The doors begin to close, and I spring forward, turning sideways as I slide between the two.

It looks like I'm doing this.

No big deal.

I haven't seen him in a zillion years, but that's okay.

I slide my phone into my one good purse and hike it higher on my shoulder. No need to check I have the right door, because there's only one on this floor. Plus, the guy at the fancy concierge downstairs called up to let Whit know I was on my way. There can be no mistake. I'm in the right place.

And what a place it is—the lobby downstairs was decked out like a fancy six-star hotel. The low tasteful hum of music overlaid by the sound of my heels on the onyx marble floors; the sofas and a concierge desk; light fittings that look more like art installations. I guess some important people must live here, given the muscle-bound security detail who insisted on going through my purse with a fine-tooth comb. They even made me take off my cute beret, and I don't think they were expecting to find a marmalade sandwich, even if my new coat makes me look like that cute teddy bear the queen of England, God rest her soul, had tea with last year.

Paddington, I think he was called.

I pull off said beret, suddenly conscious of looking like an overgrown toddler. But London is so much colder than I expected. I thought March was supposed to be the start of spring, but it's been gray and gloomy since I arrived. I've seen the sun twice, but I swear it had no heat.

The decorator sure liked mirrors, I think as I stare at my reflection in a passageway that is basically a hall of mirrors, though without the maze connotations and crazy shapes. Their surfaces are mottled with age, or at least made to look that way, the copper and verdigris making a sepia picture of me as I throw my coat over my arm and slide a lock of my summer-blond hair back into place.

At the shiny front door, I straighten my white shirt and give my pencil skirt one last tug. When I raise my fist to knock, the first rap of my knuckles pushes the door open. No one stands behind it with a *Hello* or a *Hi, Mimi, I haven't seen you in over a decade.* I pause, hoping for some sign of life before I press my fingers to the wood and push a little more, remembering every CSI episode that started this way.

"Hello?" My voice echoes as I take a tentative step inside the darkened apartment.

"Come in," replies a voice deeper than I would've recognized. My stomach tightens, in anticipation maybe. It's hard to tell. Is that truly Whit? He sounds so . . . grown up, his tone low and kind of velvety.

Stop being an idiot. He was a grown-up back then. Of course it's him—his mom gave me the address; plus, the snooty concierge called up.

I fold my coat and place it on a console, then make my way deeper into the room. A wall of windows overlooks the shadowy treetops of Hyde Park, the hum of the busy Knightsbridge streets inaudible from below. Recessed lighting falls in distant corners, casting shadows against the walls and rendering the stylish space with an intimate glow. I don't have time to process why the main lights aren't on, because all I can think is he's here.

Whit is seated just a few feet away in a pale-toned armchair, his shiny black oxfords planted wide. His pants are dark, and his shirt, folded to his forearms and open at his neck, is pale. My eyes follow the row of buttons up his torso to his face, but I can't see his expression—I can't tell if he's happy or not to see me—thanks to the fall of the light.

"Whit?"

"Stop where you are."

My feet halt, my heart rattling in my chest at the softly spoken words so heavy with command. His face might be wreathed in shadow, but that's him, all right. Dark-haired and tan, my brother's best friend always stood out like some exotic animal around my much fairer, blander family. And when he opened his mouth to speak, he sounded like a fairy-tale prince.

"Turn around."

"Excuse me?" My words hit the air a little higher than I'd like.

"Turn around. Let me look at you."

Something delicious yet uncertain flutters through me, but it's just a little déjà vu, right? It's been so long. And it's not like I haven't heard something similar from him before.

"Turn around. Let me see you. Look at how tall you've grown since I was last here."

I'm lying to myself, because that request was not the same, even if the sound of his voice always filled my stomach with butterflies before I even knew what it meant. So many nights I've lain awake wondering what it would be like to see this side of him. To hear him say my name in a sinfully sultry tone. To feel those eyes watching me. Experience the brush of his fingertips.

"Lovely." His voice reminds me of bourbon, deep and smooth. "All the way around now."

My heart pounds uncertainly. What am I doing? What is *he* doing? I'm not fourteen anymore. I know what these feelings are, and I recognize that tone. He's never been anything but courteous, never shown any interest in me beyond a kind of distant, brotherly thing. He knows it's me—the concierge called up with my name. So does that mean he . . .

I terminate the thought, unwilling to examine it, and whatever part of my brain is in charge of impulse control short-circuits as he purrs, "Come closer, darling."

My heels tap against the marble floor before my brain registers the motion. "*'Step into my parlor,' said the spider to the fly?*"

His dark chuckle weaves its spell around me, when I should feel embarrassed for my ridiculousness.

"I won't flatter you like the spider," he murmurs, "but I might let you come when I eat you later."

My footsteps almost falter as a throb of sweet percussion strikes up inside. Never in a million years could I have expected anything like this. I couldn't have conjured those words up in my darkest fantasies, despite spending many nights in my head with him. But maybe I lack imagination, because this Whit is neither tender nor sweet. I find I'm more than all right with that.

I notice the lowball glass resting against his thick thigh as he lounges back in the chair. My heart dances an erratic beat as he slowly uncoils to deposit the glass on a side table.

I stop in front of him, locking my knees to keep them from trembling, and startle a little as his hand lifts. His white button-down pulls tight over the swell of his bicep as his finger hooks under the strap of my purse, slipping it from my shoulder. Something almost erotic in the motion evokes the sense of being undressed.

"You're trembling." He curls his hands around my waist, but it does nothing to help. In fact, I'm pretty sure amazement has me immobilized.

"I know." I roll my lips together, but the words fall anyway. "I've locked my knees to stop them from rattling like maracas."

His laughter is a shocking puff of air against my midriff. I glance down and realize he's slipped his thumb under the hem of my shirt to expose a patch of skin above the waistband.

"It's just your wings fluttering." His tone is sort of velvety, and I inhale sharply when his thumbs skim lightly across my skin. "Excitement mixed with trepidation."

"You think I'm nervous?"

"You should be. It'll make the night more pleasurable for us both."

The night? What comes after he eats me to orgasm? Not that I've ever had that pleasure, but if you're going to take risks, it's not the kiddie pool you dip your toes into.

"Lift your skirt."

"I—what?" Have I bumped my head? Am I lying out in the street in a coma?

"Show me." His words are a honey-dipped temptation. As though to sweeten the instruction a little more, he leans closer, pressing his lips to the skin above my waistband.

Warmth floods between my legs, and I'm pretty sure I whimper.

"Such a pretty sound." I feel the loss of his heat immediately as he leans away again. "Hurry now. Show Daddy what he wants."

If *show* me made me warm, *daddy* feels like a burst of wildfire across my skin. Why that flutters my button, I don't know, but I do know Daddy Whit is so freakin' hot.

You're not a deviant, whispers a little voice of dissent.

Shows what you know.

"You look like that might've broken your brain a little bit." His tone is amused. "If you don't like *daddy*, we can always go with something else."

"No," I say quickly. "I've just never—"

"A *daddy* virgin?"

That is so nasty, yet my insides throb.

"I don't like to be kept waiting."

I get the sudden sense that the balance of the moment is slipping. I glance down, everything inside me drawing tight at his disapproval. Weird. He's barely moved a muscle, yet I feel the weight of his disappointment like a spiky woolen jacket I want to throw off. Before my brain registers what I'm doing, my fingers are at the button on the back of my skirt.

"Not that way." He makes an indolent motion with his finger that I take to mean I'm supposed to . . . lift it? My fingers move hesitantly to my thighs. "Yes, sweetheart. That's right."

He settles back as I begin to gather the fabric. His eyes burn through the shadows as I pull it higher and higher until—I can't quite believe—it's gathered at my waist. It feels dirty but somehow on the right side of wrong. And, oh my goodness, he called me *sweetheart*, and I really, really liked it.

I count the beats that pass between us in the throbbing between my legs, before he moves forward, the light catching the blades of his cheekbones as his face comes into the light. He doesn't glance up, seeming to examine my panties, before he hooks a thumb into the elastic at my hip. Pleasure pulses through me. I'm pretty sure I'm going to melt before the navy-colored lace slides down my legs. But neither of those things happens, as his thumb slides away. Not that my pleasure abates, his expression so serious as he trails a slow finger up between my legs.

His head lifts, his gaze catching mine as though daring me to stop him. I won't, of course. All I can think about is how I've never been this close to him and how his eyes are so much more striking than I remember. Flecks of gold shine in the ambient light, amber striations around his dark pupils making his eyes seem tigerlike. A knife-straight nose and broad slashes for cheekbones. His mouth is full, and the divot above his finely carved brow makes me wonder what noise he'd make if I kissed it.

I stifle a sigh, my body jolting, suddenly chasing his touch, as his index finger lightly brushes between my legs in one curling *come hither* motion. It's barely a brush, but, God, how it makes me tremble. One brush becomes another, his touch so slow and methodical. So . . . "Oh, God." My eyes flutter closed as a familiar sensation begins to build.

"Open them, little fly," he instructs softly. Something must flicker in my expression as he adds, "I'm following your lead."

"Flies are—"

"—gossamer winged." My body convulses as he increases the pressure, working the fabric of my panties, where I'm suddenly wet. "'*Will you come into my parlor,' said the spider to the fly. ''Tis the prettiest little parlor that ever you did spy.*'"

"'*The way into . . . my parlor is . . . up a winding stair.*'" He smiles as I join in, my words halting and breathless.

"*I have many curious things to show when you are there.*" He delivers the line with such wicked intent.

"Oh, I just bet you have." My feathery laughter halts as he introduces his thumb. As he presses it to my clit, a mewl escapes my mouth.

"*Will you rest upon my bed?' said the spider to the fly. 'There are pretty curtains drawn around. The sheets are fine and thin. If you like to rest awhile, I'll snugly tuck you in.'*"

His thumb and finger come together to pinch my clit, and I make the strangest noise, my body reacting as though struck by a live wire.

"I'm not sure we need a bed right now," he asserts softly as his arm slides around me, banding my thighs. "Not when you're doing so well."

"No, don't stop. I've never—" But I have no more words as he deepens the damp crease of my panties. Blood rushes to my cheeks, and I'm so pleased for the lack of light. My feminist membership card will absolutely be revoked once they discover that Daddy and the patriarchy own my ass.

"Oh, I've no intention of stopping," he whispers. "Yes, that's it. Such pretty fluttering."

"Oh, God!"

"Not quite, little fly." His assertion is full of dark amusement. I must pull a face again. "Something more generic?" he purrs, his face half in shadow, half washed in the light. "Shall we stick with *sweetheart*, or how about *baby girl*?"

I'd like to assert I don't like either of those options, but that would require at least basic verbal skills. He could call me Genghis Khan, and I wouldn't protest as the mostly unused muscles in my thighs begin to flex and tense. I've never orgasmed standing before—or from a hand over my underwear rather than in. I'm beginning to think I might need stronger quads. Better coordination. Something to hold on to.

"That's it," Whit encourages, and oh, my God, I know I shouldn't be turned on by his praise, but I am. "You're such a good little slut for me."

That. I'm *not* into that.

No way.

Except for right now as pleasure begins to spiral through me from the tips of my toes to my freakin' hair follicles. My body bows, and I fall forward, my hands grabbing his bicep. Somehow, I also seem to grab the remaining threads of my dignity.

"Oh, God, Whit," I whimper, locking my knees against this wave of pleasure. "Me-me. Call me Mimi."

My fingers tighten on his arm as I throw my head back and do the only thing I can. I let go. I'm a little too preoccupied to notice anything else. So I don't see his shoulders tense, and I don't see the color leach from his face, and I wouldn't have anyway, thanks to the dim lighting. I see nothing, hear nothing, and care for nothing but those bliss-filled moments of my release.

KEEP IN CONTACT HERE

Donna's Lambs

Donna's VIP newsletter

mail@donnaalam.com

https://donnaalam.com

Did you enjoy this book and would you like to get informed when Donna Alam publishes her next work? Just follow the author on Amazon!

1. Search for the book you were just reading on Amazon or in the Amazon App.
2. Go to the author page by clicking on the author's name.
3. Click the Follow button.

If you enjoyed this book on a Kindle eReader or in the Kindle App, you will be automatically invited to follow the author when arriving at the last page.

ABOUT THE AUTHOR

Donna Alam is a #7 Amazon Kindle Store and *USA Today* best-seller. A writer of love stories with heart, humor, and heat, she aspires to sprinkle a little joy into the lives of her readers. When not bashing away at her keyboard, Alam can often be found hiding from her responsibilities with a book in her hand and a mop of a dog at her feet.

Follow the Author on Amazon

If you enjoyed this book, follow Donna Alam on Amazon to be notified when the author releases a new book!

To do this, please follow these instructions:

Desktop:

1) Search for the author's name on Amazon or in the Amazon App.
2) Click on the author's name to arrive on their Amazon page.
3) Click the 'Follow' button.

Mobile and Tablet:

1) Search for the author's name on Amazon or in the Amazon App.
2) Click on one of the author's books.
3) Click on the author's name to arrive on the their Amazon page.

Kindle eReader und Kindle App:

If you enjoyed this book on a Kindle eReader or in the Kindle App, you will find the author 'Follow' button after the last page.